D0860042

WITHDRAWN-DOVER

B+T   4/87   18.55

MEMOIRS OF AN INVISIBLE MAN

MEMOIRS OF AN

INVISIBLE MAN

H. F. SAINT

New York ATHENEUM 1987

This novel is a work of fiction. Names, characters, places, and incidents are either the product of the author's imagination or are used fictitiously. Any resemblance to actual events or persons, living or dead, is entirely coincidental.

Library of Congress Cataloging in Publication Data
Saint, H. F. (Harry F.)
    Memoirs of an invisible man.

    I. Title.
PS 3569.A38M4   1987   813'.54   85-48144
ISBN 0-689-11735-3

Copyright © 1987 by H. F. Saint
All rights reserved
Published simultaneously in Canada by Collier Macmillan Canada, Inc.
Composition by Heritage Printers, Charlotte, North Carolina
Manufactured by Haddon Craftsmen, Scranton, Pennsylvania
Designed by Harry Ford
First Edition

TO J

MEMOIRS OF AN INVISIBLE MAN

IF ONLY YOU COULD SEE ME NOW. YOU CAN'T AND COULDN'T, BUT I'M here. And although the explanation is banal, the effect is altogether magical. If you were to walk into this room now, you would find it quite empty—an empty chair before a desk empty save for a pad of un-lined paper. But above the paper you would see the pen, unheld, dancing over the surface, forming these words, pausing now and then in midair reflectively. You would be entranced, or terrified.

Unfortunately, *I* am holding the pen, and if you were quick enough and I were not, you could get a perfectly solid grip on me and satisfy yourself by sense of touch that an unseeable but otherwise unexceptional human being was in the room. Or you could pick up a chair and beat me senseless with it. I am sorry to say that this would not be an unusual course of action under the circumstances, for my condition, although per-fectly anonymous, is undeniably bizarre. It provokes curiosity, and curi-osity, I find, is a fairly vicious instinct. This is a trying existence. It is generally best to keep on the move.

In fact, this should probably be described as the "adventures" rather than the "memoirs" of an invisible man. Certainly I have no intention of going on about my childhood or the particular agonies of my particular adolescence, which was doubtless no more nor less interesting than your own. Nor will we need to discuss the specifics of my entirely ordinary intellectual and moral development. Nothing of this sort would con-tribute to my quite genuinely exciting and superficial story. Nor would it shed much light on the human condition, I am afraid. I understand that you only love me for my disease, so to speak, so that everything before its onset is irrelevant. For the first thirty-four years of my life I was exactly like everyone else, and while those years seemed compelling enough to me at the time, you would presumably not be reading a nar-rative entitled "Memoirs of a Securities Analyst." Anyway, right in the middle of my rather ordinary way through life, a minor but altogether extraordinary scientific mishap rendered a small spherical chunk of New Jersey utterly invisible. As chance would have it, I was at the critical moment included in that spherical chunk. I, together with my immediate surroundings, was instantly transformed: just as in a petrified fossil the structure of the original organism is exactly reduplicated as an arrangement of mineral particles, so my body was exactly reduplicated as a living structure of minute units of energy. It functions very much as before—with, as far as I have been able to determine, only minor differences. But you cannot see it at all.

The point is that it could have been absolutely anyone. I know that each of us is utterly unique and so forth—like snowflakes or leaves. Although, as the wind scatters the proverbial generations of leaves to the ground, it can sometimes be hard to find much metaphysical comfort in one's own peculiarity. Anyway, no peculiarity of mine made it more likely that I should wind up in this condition than you. An improbable and very poor roll of the cosmic dice. God's eye was doubtless on the sparrow at the time.

Whereas I had my eye mainly on Anne Epstein and on her lovely breasts, over which her silk blouse slid wonderfully when she moved. I could see the nipples through the blue-green print, and when she turned to look out the window of the railway car, I could see the delicious white flesh where the shirt front opened between the buttons. We were on our way from New York to Princeton on what you might call the fateful morning. Looking back on it, that morning did have an appropriately ominous quality, with dark storm clouds and bright April sunshine in continual and dramatic alternation, but at the time I noticed mainly the sunshine. I had drunk too much and slept too little the night before, so that it all had a euphoric, dreamlike vividness, and although I knew from experience that this feeling would soon mature into a piercing headache and an uncontrollable desire for sleep, at that moment my mind and body felt nothing but intoxicated, aching delight in the brilliant spring morning and Anne's smooth white skin.

Because we were traveling against the tide of commuters into the city, we found ourselves alone in the decrepit railway car. It had the old seats that you could swing to face either way, and I had pushed one of them around so that we sat facing one another without enough room for our legs. I hadn't sat like this since I was a boy on one of those wonderful long train rides home that began every school vacation, and that association, together with the exhilarating knowledge that I was playing hookey from work on a wonderfully inane pretext, added an additional note of childish, illicit pleasure to the day. She had folded her left arm up over her head, pulling the silk taut over her breasts and ribs. I reached carelessly across and ran the fingers of my right hand down her side, from beside her breast to her hip. She continued to talk but there was a flicker of annoyance and pleasure.

What was she talking about? I remember that she had the *Times* open on her lap—she worked for the *Times*—and she was explaining to me something that was of great interest and importance to her. It seems to me that it had to do with an attempt to redraw local election districts somewhere in the Midwest. There were the two usual parties, but one of the parties—or perhaps both—had factions, and one faction was offering extra patronage to one ethnic group if that ethnic group would support redrawing the district lines to defraud some other ethnic group in order to take something away from another faction even though it would help the other party. It was all meant to be particularly significant because the particular combinations of ethnic groups and parties and factions were not the usual combinations, and the whole thing might therefore portend a major shift in our nation's affairs.

To me it sounded more like a pack of thieves making a deal, but then to me no human activity is so reliably boring and shabby as politics. For Anne, on the other hand, politics seemed to be the only dimension in which human thoughts and acts could attain true meaning, and so I furrowed my brow to indicate concentration and interest; from time to time I nodded at the sound of her voice, which went skidding past me with the same dreamlike and incomprehensible vividness as the dark clouds floating across the window. When it seemed appropriate, I asked small meaningless questions in an earnest voice. As she talked she became more animated. She had extremely fine features and although they became sharper, even harder, when she talked about politics, it only made her more exquisite. Her shoulder-length brown hair and her crisp clothing always seemed to fall casually but perfectly into place: she looked more like an anchorwoman on the evening news than a newspaper reporter. She leaned forward; she unfolded one long, nearly naked leg from the cramped space beneath the newspaper on her lap and braced it against the seat next to me; as she spoke, she gestured with the index and middle fingers of her right hand held together, and when she made a particularly telling point the strong slender fingers tapped the newspaper, her mouth formed into a knowing, ironic smile, and she looked into my eyes for corroboration. And even if I could not quite manage to maintain my interest in what she was saying, my heart and mind were absolutely flooded with interest in Anne herself. She was altogether beautiful.

She also had a sense of humor—extending at times even to herself— and I had found that if I could get through to it, I could sometimes dispel these moods of political intensity. But that could be a delicate and risky operation, and I decided in this instance to try to shift the topic gradually. I asked her the most complicated question I could contrive about the way stories were assigned in the business section. I knew that the answer would have to be more interesting to me than the day's political news and I knew also that Anne would enjoy giving it, because the only thing that was as important to her as politics was her career, and she had just recently been assigned to the business section. Before that she had worked for the sports section, where her main responsibility had been reporting on professional basketball, and before that she had spent four years at Yale, where, as far as I could determine, she had never attended a basketball game or acquired any single piece of information related in any way to business or economics.

But really, it was because of the gaps in her education and the inscrutable personnel policies of the *Times* that we were now together. Less than two weeks before, I had found myself seated next to her at dinner. We had been introduced once or twice before over the past couple of years, but she still found it necessary to ask me what I did, and—despite her striking appearance—my initial interest in her must have been unexceptional, since I remember answering her question straightforwardly. Normally you do not tell people you are a securities analyst unless you want to see their eyes begin to shift about the room in search of someone or somewhere to escape to. For social purposes it is pretty much the same thing as being a chemical engineer. But Anne had startled me with a conflagration of interest. It was probably because of her new assignment at the *Times*. Confronted with a source of useful information, and perhaps also to annoy her fiancé—the origins of love are complex and mysterious— she had put her hand on my arm, looked straight into my eyes with a stunning smile, and begun to ask questions about business and economics, one after the other. The topic of the questions may make it sound quite unromantic to you, but I remember very clearly her wonderfully attentive gaze: she had the reporter's trick of asking questions you wanted to answer and giving you the feeling that she was fascinated by your reply. And she really was altogether beautiful.

I was, of course, immediately possessed by the usual feelings and desires, and I do not recall thinking seriously of much else for the next week. I devoted myself to getting her to lunch with me, to drinks, to dinner, wherever I could get her. She was agonizingly elusive, somehow never able or willing to get free for more than a few hours, whether because of her work, about which she was relentlessly diligent and ambitious, or because of her personal life, in which I tried to show an earnest but not intrusive interest. There was a friend or a fiancé or "just someone I'm terribly close to"—his role seemed to shift continuously—with whom she had some sort of troubled understanding or misunderstanding, but then there was also the fact that she was simply a very difficult person—a quality which set off her extraordinary beauty nicely. It seemed that she was always standing up at the critical moment and saying goodbye—looking straight into my eyes

(6)

and leaving me crushed beneath her overwhelming smile. (No one now can look into my eyes. In an unusual moment of safety and intimacy, someone might smile uncertainly in my general direction.) On the other hand, when she was there she always gave me her full, dazzling attention. She loved to interrogate me, and the longer my answers were the better she seemed to like them. Just as she had earlier made herself terrifyingly knowledgeable about basketball, Anne was now setting out to accumulate as much fact, theory, and opinion about economics and business as she could lay her hands on.

I enjoyed her greedy questioning: everyone enjoys being asked a question to which he knows the answer. It is true that it sometimes annoyed me that the usual priorities seemed to have been somehow inverted in Anne's mind—with opinion in highest demand, theory a distant second, and fact possessing only a sort of decorative charm—but her employer would surely not have wanted it any other way. And as she was very clever and unrelievedly ambitious, she was quickly acquiring an imposing store of information. I told her so repeatedly, and the compliment always pleased her. As for me, I was enchanted by her quick acquisitive mind, her difficulty, her long limbs, her hand on my arm. I posed some questions of my own and listened to her answers with patient, aching interest. I asked about her job, her ambitions, her friends. I asked her to make love to me. From time to time I ran my fingers along her bare arm, and asked her whatever came into my mind. I watched her fine mouth and full hips move.

Now, with my right thumb and fingers I encircled the slender ankle braced against the front of the seat next to me. I ran my hand up the long calf and let it spread my thumb apart from my fingertips. I slid the hand around and over her knee and up along the outside of her thigh. The thumb was still spread so that it ran up the front of the thigh, under the newspaper, and under the linen skirt until it reached the crease of her hip.

She twisted herself in her seat away from my hand and withdrew her leg, crossing it over the other leg at an angle to me. Her mouth set itself in an exquisitely prim expression.

"About last night," she said. "It's not right."

Last night, which despite several hours sleep had not so much ended as spilled over into the morning, had been the first—and, as it would turn out, the last—night we spent together. Our week of lunches, drinks, dinners, flattery, pleading, caresses, smiles, and assurances had culminated finally in her bed overlooking the East River. But now she seemed to be saying that the delicious battle would be resumed and the same ground would have to be retaken. I contemplated this with a mixture of frustration and pleasure.

"What's not right?" I tried.

"It's not fair to Peter."

Peter was her fiancé, or friend, or whatever. I had known him slightly for years, and he had always seemed likable enough, although a bit boring. But then, probably most people found *me* a bit boring. (I believe that as things turned out she married Peter in the end.)

"To be perfectly honest, I haven't had a chance yet to work fairness to Peter into my moral calculations."

This remark seemed to anger her. She stiffened.

"Well, I have, and if you were capable of taking me or anyone else seriously—"

"You're absolutely right," I interrupted. "I don't know why I say these things. Embarrassment, probably. Shyness. It's to conceal from myself and others the feelings and passions swelling up uncontrollably in the old breast." Here I tapped my chest mildly with my forefinger. Anne looked at me oddly. "And moral scruples too. Almost ungovernable moral scruples. All hiding beneath the amiable exterior of a clown." I gave her what I thought was a winning smile.

"The exterior," she said a little nastily, "is entirely that of a banker. Which is what you are."

"Not really—" I protested.

"Securities analyst. Whatever. The point is that you wear those nerdy pinstriped suits and old-fashioned shoes, and you're always stammering and acting so earnest and pretending to strangers that you don't ever quite know what's going on. One look at you and anyone can tell you'll turn out to be wearing boxer shorts. On the outside you're fine. You seem like a perfectly pleasant, mild-mannered, ineffectual, nice person. It's on the inside that you turn out not to be so nice at all. More the *interior* of a clown." She turned and looked aggressively out the window at the dreariest landscape even New Jersey can offer.

"I wear these clothes in the hope that I'll be mistaken for an investment banker, in fact. It's considered a rather glamorous look in some sets. Actually, I've always worn these clothes. They're comfortable, last forever, and no one but you has ever taken exception."

"You should widen your circle of acquaintances. Anyway, you look more like the other kind of banker." She pursed her lips, annoyed at having forgotten. "What you were telling me yesterday . . . *commercial.* . . . You look like a commercial banker. . . . Glass-Steagall Act . . ."

"That's very good," I said, in commendation. "And the year?"

"Nineteen thirty-three. Yes, you have more the aura of a commercial banker. Or maybe of someone from a savings and loan, giving out the toasters and electric blankets to old ladies to trick them into accepting unconscionably low interest—"

"Well, to me, you, on the other hand, look unspeakably beautiful." She turned away again disdainfully, but no one has ever minded such a compliment. "Seriously," I continued in an earnest tone, "you've got to be fair to yourself as well as to Peter." This suggestion seemed to please her, although I had no idea what it might mean.

"The real issue is not just Peter," she began discursively. "It's building a relationship on trust—"

"Absolutely," I agreed, pressing my advantage perhaps a bit too quickly. "What's Peter up to these days, anyway? Isn't he spending a lot of time with Betsy Austin or someone like that?"

"Probably. That would be just like Peter." She paused sullenly and then added, "I've known Peter half my life. I've only known you for two weeks. I don't really know you at all."

More like one week, I thought. I said: "We've known each other for two years—"

"We never had so much as a conversation until—"

"And anyway," I cut her off, "I've thought of nothing but you the entire time. I'm absolutely obsessed. Despite the fact that you are so unremittingly difficult and unreasonable."

"Besides," she said, apropos of nothing—unless in illustration of my last observation—"you're not Jewish."

"This is true," I said slowly, having been caught off balance. Anne loved to attack suddenly from unexpected directions. "But not being Jewish," I went on, "isn't such a big handicap anymore. Naturally, you have trouble getting into the best schools, but nearly all the professions are open to genuinely qualified non-Jews now. And anyway, there *is* always commercial banking, which you seem to feel I—"

"You can make a joke of it if you like, but it's important to me."

"I absolutely don't want to make a joke of it. I only want to understand why it's important. I mean, you're not a Baptist."

"Are you a Baptist?" she asked with what appeared to be genuine distress. Presumably, if she was to consort with Gentiles she wanted them to be Episcopalians.

"No, but if I were, I wouldn't care whether you were."

"Well," she said in a tone of cold moral superiority, "as it happens, I do care."

A thought struck me.

"Peter's not Jewish, is he?" I asked.

"That's not the point," she replied. The question had annoyed her. "And I don't know why you keep harping on Peter. You seem to have some sort of fixation on him."

She twisted in her seat so that her blouse pulled taut over her breasts, and she looked across at me disdainfully. I looked at her with admiration. Her versatility and total lack of principle in these discussions always dazzled me.

"I do have a fixation, but I can assure you that it's entirely on you and—"

"And another thing. It's rude to stare like that at people's breasts."

"Is it? I mean, is it that obvious that I'm staring? . . . Isn't it flattering anyway?"

"One might like to be stared at for something a little more meaningful than one's breasts. And anyhow it makes people uncomfortable." As she said this, she half yawned and stretched languidly, lifting her arms and arching her shoulders back so that her breasts were thrust forward and flattened under her blouse; the nipples stood out in agonizing relief.

"Well, it's hard to stare at your spiritual qualities, marvelous though they are. Your breasts, as a matter of fact, represent to me the exquisite visible manifestation of those qualities which—"

"Do shove it, Nick," she said more amiably. Her eyes became more alert, and she added, "Tell me about today."

"Yes, today," I said cheerfully, misunderstanding her question. "I thought today we might rent a car in Princeton, put in a quick, token appearance at MicroMagnetics, and then drive up to Basking Ridge. Some friends of mine have gone off to Europe for the year and left me the use of a beautiful place there. If the weather holds, we might hope to put together a virtually perfect spring day for ourselves. And even if it doesn't—"

"I'm looking forward to this MicroMagnetics thing. It should be more interesting than the usual."

MicroMagnetics, Inc., as far as I had been able to determine in my rather perfunctory investigations, was a small corporation outside Princeton which performed research on the magnetic containment of nuclear fusion. Its principal asset consisted in the services of its founder and president, one Professor Bernard Wachs, whose imposing reputation for original work in particle physics had enabled him to obtain many millions of dollars of government grants. The only apparent activity of Micro-Magnetics to date had been the spending of this money in rather short order, and from my point of view, its first real contribution to humanity was to provide me with an occasion to entice Anne out into the countryside. For MicroMagnetics, Inc., had the week before distributed to a largely indifferent world, press releases proclaiming the discovery or invention of the "EMF," a new type of magnetic field which was to normal everyday magnetic fields as the laser was to normal everyday light waves. It was—depending on the ultimate value of the EMF—either a failing or a virtue of the press release that it lacked any information more concrete than this loose analogy or any indication of whether the EMF would be of use for fusion containment or for anything else. It was, "Scientists in Princeton, New Jersey, announced today a revolutionary advance. . . ." It was also characterized as a "major discovery" and a "watershed." Now, many if not all scientists think of their work in these terms, and I was entirely unmoved. But there was to be a press conference and a demonstration of some sort, so I convinced Anne that it was a story she really had to cover and told my office I would be out of town the entire day.

It occurs to me that I should explain what I do. Or did. A securities analyst looks at a business and what it owns and does and what the competition does and at any peculiarities of the stocks or bonds which the business sells to raise money; from all this he tries to determine at what price people ought to buy or sell those stocks or bonds. The abstract argument in favor of this occupation is that it helps allocate resources more efficiently to produce whatever it is that individual people most want. The argument against it, as best I can make it out—Anne would be able to present it more compellingly—is that capitalism is boring and evil, and anyone who makes it function better is himself boring and evil. As a matter of fact, I often found my work a bit boring—although I never found any sign of its being evil. I won't impose upon you further by explaining the different types of jobs a securities analyst can do, but I should explain that my particular job was very slightly above average in pay and below average in glamour, had relatively reasonable hours, and required no selling. As long as I satisfied my partners, I remained virtually independent, and as much as 20 percent of the time I enjoyed my work quite a lot—which is a good average for any type of work I have ever heard of.

As it happened, I had a particular responsibility for covering the energy industry, which at the time was a good thing because there had been several years of real turmoil in energy, with great quantities of money to be made and lost, so that my work and opinion were in constant demand. As a sort of frivolous sideline I also followed what was known as "alternative energy," which was even more trendy. This used up very little time, since there was very little in the way of actual securities worth analyzing. Every few weeks someone would announce a scheme to turn water into hydrogen or float icebergs to Kansas with dirigibles or use sunlight to make water run uphill. On the rare occasions when one of these things made scientific sense, you could usually, using even the most optimistic assumptions, easily run the numbers and determine that it didn't make economic sense. As the whole thing was so fashionable at the time, I would get a lot of attention and phone calls soliciting my expert opinion. And then there was always the remote but tantalizing hope that one of these things would figure, in which case you might do very well for yourself.

Certainly I entertained no particular hopes for MicroMagnetics that day. My hopes revolved around getting Anne off as quickly as possible to some pleasant lunch with the best wine my partners could afford and after that making love to her in Basking Ridge in a room looking out on pastures and streams. When I had first formulated this plan I was not certain that I would ever make love to Anne, but now, after last night, I thought that I might reasonably expect to enjoy the best day of this—or perhaps any—spring.

"What," I asked, genuinely puzzled, "makes you think Micro-Magnetics will be so interesting?"

"Well, for one thing, you told me it would be."

"Yes, I suppose I did. And I'm sure it will be. But mainly I said that to entice you out into the countryside." She turned impassively and looked out the window, past which flowed the panorama of decaying industrial buildings that line the railroad tracks from one end of New Jersey to the other, relieved only by occasional clusters of refining equipment painted in cheerful colors. "The main thing really was to get you outdoors, to smell the spring earth, taste the Arcadian delights of New Jersey. To ravish you."

As if I had not spoken, she continued, "And anyway, it has a political dimension for once."

I was genuinely pleased for Anne that the MicroMagnetics dog and pony show might have a political dimension, but puzzled as to what it might be.

"You mean as an alternative source of energy," I tried. "Liberation from dependence on fossil fuels and so on. When you come to think about it, it probably does have political ramifications. . . . Ecological benefits and so forth . . ." I added as a vague afterthought.

"It's not alternate energy at all," she said with irritation. "It's nuclear."

"Nuclear"—as opposed to "alternate"—was bad. I knew that much about politics.

"Actually, I don't think it is 'nuclear' in the sense you mean: it wouldn't have anything to do with nuclear *fission* anyway. All the research these people have done is related to magnetic containment of *fusion*, which has none of the pollution or other nasty properties your environmental friends object to. In fact it's the ideal energy source from your point of view: for one thing, no one seems to be able to make it work. . . . Although now that you raise the issue, I don't think there was any actual mention of fusion in the press release. . . . Anyway, I assume it is just another little twist in the magnetic bottle, and you surely wouldn't have any objection to—"

"It's all nuclear," she said very definitely. "It is a crime against the earth and against future generations. If we had a government concerned with meeting the real needs of the people instead of just helping the rich grow richer, we would be generating power directly from sunlight, instead of poisoning ourselves. The technology exists today."

Her eyes narrowed, and her exquisite mouth set firmly, conveying moral rectitude. I seemed to have annoyed her. Best to keep the discussion on a technical level.

"Although," I said, "with the technology that exists today, you would be paying somewhere between fifty cents and a dollar per kilowatt hour as opposed to six to twelve cents for conventionally generated power. Unless you're counting amorphous silicon as 'technology that exists today,' in which case you would want to see cells with a conversion efficiency of at least seven percent in actual production—"

"If these things aren't 'in actual production' with a 'conversion efficiency' that suits you," she interrupted sarcastically, "it's small wonder, with a government that does nothing but sit by and let big corporations make these decisions by default."

"Yes, I absolutely see the force of what you say," I responded agreeably, since, except for whatever immediate fun you may get out of it, it is always a waste of time to argue with anyone about politics—or about anything else, when you come right down to it. You rarely ever learn anything and you absolutely never convince the other person. "You're probably right," I went on. "Of course, the real question is whether they can get the cost of any of these things down to a competitive level. It's really just a matter of supply and demand—"

"The *real* question is whether we intend to leave ourselves at the mercy of the marketplace or whether we will take our fate in our own hands like rational, moral beings."

I was concerned that she might be getting not only deplorably rhetorical but genuinely angry. The mood, like the weather, seemed uncertain. "By the way," I said, "I meant to ask you about something in the *Journal* today. Evidently, a band of *Times* reporters has been captured with a Cuban adviser. Apparently, the *Times* has these training camps in Ethiopia, and I thought you might be able to tell me—"

"Fuck you." She said this in a matter-of-fact tone and with a pleasant smile. I have noticed—although it is important not to let them get too wound up in it—that people often actually feel better when they can rant on about politics a bit. Perhaps this is the real value of politics. "Actually," she went on, "I *do* want to know about the cost of alternate energy sources. That would be really useful to me. It really is amazing, the numbers you have." She paused momentarily as another thought struck her. "No. Show me the thing about supply and demand curves again. That's what I want."

I was delighted at the opportunity to explain anything whatever to Anne. And then it is always good to feel that one is serving humanity and one's own selfish interests at the same time: perhaps I would be responsible for giving someone at the *Times* a rudimentary notion of the concepts of supply and demand. I took a pad of unlined paper from my briefcase and moved over to the seat beside her. Resting the pad first on my thigh and then on hers, I drew the familiar coordinates.

"Now, this axis represents the price of some good, and this represents the quantity of the good produced. Now for each—"

"Is what you're drawing here for all goods or for some particular good?"

"Well, it's an example . . . that is, it's some particular good. For any particular good, at any particular time, there would be a particular supply curve and a particular demand curve—if that's what you're asking."

"What sort of good? What exactly is a good, anyway? It would be better if you could be concrete."

"It could be any good. Or any service. It could be anything at all, anything that at least one person wants. And that someone can provide, I suppose. Automobiles, wheat, newspapers. Ballet lessons. Handguns. Sonnets. The point is that at any given price there will be some associated level of supply—the amount of the product or service that people are motivated to provide at that price."

"What happens at the ends?"

What does happen at the ends? I tried to reason it out quickly. "Different things, none of them important." I ran my hand along the upper surface of her thigh, feeling it move under the blue linen skirt. She ignored my hand and peered intently at the drawing lying next to it on her lap.

"Try to pay attention and not ask difficult questions," I went on. I drew a pair of coordinates and another curve under the first. "The demand curve—I'm drawing it separately to begin with—is the same idea, but it slopes the other way."

"Always?"

I seemed to recall that you could contrive cases where it sloped the wrong way, but I couldn't remember whether you could always explain them away or whether you just ignored them. I should, I thought, quickly read through some elementary economics text and review some of these things.

"For all practical purposes, always. I don't want to make this explanation unnecessarily complicated."

I slid my left hand under her skirt, and ran my fingers several inches along the inside of her thigh. Her legs spread apart a fraction of an inch to welcome my hand. Then she reached out with her hand and held it firmly to keep it from straying further.

"Actually," I said, "with the demand curve this axis represents the amount that will be purchased at a given price."

Still holding the pencil, I reached up with my right hand and brushed the hair away from her neck. I leaned over and kissed her behind her ear. She continued to study the paper on her lap, but she shuddered.

"What I want to understand," she said—a little absently, I thought, "is how you combine the curves. And why."

I reached over and redrew the second curve, superimposing it on the first. I kissed her again on the back of her neck. Her shoulder pulled up and her head twisted back in a slow little writhing movement. Her grip on my hand relaxed. I leaned over and kissed her on the mouth. She opened her mouth, and our tongues twisted over each other. She took my head in her hands, pulling it toward her. We both twisted sideways on the seat so that we faced each other, our knees jammed together. With my fingers spread, I ran my hands up and down her sides. My thumbs pressed into her breasts. I held her rib cage and felt it swell and contract heavily with her breathing, her heart banging against my hand. I drew my left hand over her breast. As I kissed her mouth, her neck, and her eyes, I slid my hand into her blouse, pulling open a button. I could feel the swollen nipple under my fingers and then my palm. I flattened her breast under my hand. I undid the rest of the buttons on her blouse and ran both hands all over her torso. I leaned forward and kissed the hard nipples. She arched her back, pushing her breasts forward to me.

The space in which we were trying to maneuver was impossibly awkward, the seats too short, and the gap between them too narrow. I twisted around further until I was half standing with one leg on the floor and with the other kneeling on the seat next to Anne. I kissed her on the mouth again, while I ran my hands down her smooth back. I can remember perfectly how beautiful her naked breasts were in that railway car. She started to pull at the knot of my necktie and then, impatiently changing her mind, left it and began pulling open each button down the front of my shirt except the top, collar button. She slipped her hands under my shirt and pulled the shirttails free of my trousers. Her fingers were traveling over my chest and sides and around the small of my back. She leaned over and kissed me on the chest and on the side. I ran one hand across the smooth flesh of her belly and then slid it under the waistband. She sucked in her breath to let it pass. My fingertips ran onto the delicate pubic hairs. I pushed my fingers gently down and felt her hips tilt forward. She slid down a little in the seat, turning further sideways so that her head rested against the window, thereby twisting my hand backwards under her waistband. We were not having an easy time arranging ourselves on the seat. With some difficulty I extracted my hand and pulled her up until we were both more or less standing in the narrow space between the facing seats. As I pulled her toward me, she spread my shirt open to expose my chest and wrapped her arms around my torso and I felt her naked breasts against my skin. We kissed. I pushed my thigh hard between her legs and twisted my pelvis against hers.

Half releasing her, I reached down under the hem of her skirt and slid my hand slowly up the inside of her thighs. She was leaning against the window now. I pushed the palm and fingers of my open hand back and forth between her legs, feeling her perfectly through the thin, moist material of her pants. Her legs opened and her pelvis twisted slowly under my hand. Reaching down with the other hand, I hooked both thumbs over the waist of her pants and pulled them down to her knees. She lifted one long naked leg out of the pants and, snagging them with her toes, pulled them down into a little heap on the other foot. I gently slid my fingers over the soft pubic hair and into the crevice. She began yanking open my trousers, and when she encountered the expected boxer shorts, she yanked them open too and, seizing me with both hands, pulled me erect out into the open.

Writing this now, I see that I owe you, the reader, an apology—or rather a warning—since, knowing that every pornographic novel has a scene in a railway car, you may be misled by my adventures in that railway car about what is to follow. What does not follow—and I confess to some regrets in the matter—is a succession of sexual encounters of ever increasing frequency and acrobatic complexity between ever increasing numbers of participants. In fact, one of the rather melancholy aspects of my present situation—and far more melancholy for me as protagonist than for you as reader—is the relative difficulty of encounters of any kind. Nor do I want to mislead you about the quality of my life prior to that day. This was not a typical scene from my daily routine. I did not often— did not ever, except on this one day—find myself in a sexual frenzy, half-naked, with a beautiful half-naked woman in a public place. If nothing else out of the ordinary had happened that day, it would still have been one of the most extraordinary days of my life.

Or, on the other hand, you may feel that I owe an explanation or even an apology—although I am not sure to whom—for relating this incident at all. Or for the incident itself. And, to be honest, I am not altogether comfortable as I write these things down, since although on most days and in most moods I do not have particularly strong moral feelings about the behavior of eagerly consenting adults like Anne and myself, I understand that there are a great many other points of view on the subject, and I generally disapprove of offending any of them unnecessarily with public displays of sexuality or emotion. I am not at all an exhibitionist—although this may seem a rather empty boast given my present condition. I have no idea what possessed us that day. Rather, I know exactly what possessed us, but not what happened to the usual inhibitions and moral scruples. I am not sure why, that day, we were standing half-undressed in that railway car, in a sexual delirium, gripping each other's private parts and shoving our tongues into each other's mouths. But we were quite alone in the railway car: we had not seen anyone since New York but the conductor, and him only once. And the various feelings we had for each other were probably quite strong. There was the fact that we had been up most of the night. And we were still, I think, quite drunk.

I pushed Anne back down onto the seat. It was not wide enough for her to stretch out, and she was slouched down in a semisitting position with her shoulders and head leaning back against the window. Her skirt was up around her waist, and her legs were spread open, one of them extended along and over the edge of the seat onto the floor and the other drawn up, with her foot braced against the armrest by the aisle. I stood poised over her. She had her hands on my hips. I thought briefly of getting her to the washroom, where we would have enjoyed a greater sense of privacy—at some cost, however, in comfort and convenience. Anne probably made the same half-hearted calculation. The thing was, there was no one in the car and no one likely to enter it. And if someone did, how important would it be in the larger scheme of things? The main thing—the only thing in that agonizingly delicious moment—was to push ahead to certain bliss. *Carpe diem.*

But as I began to lower myself onto Anne, the train abruptly began to brake, and I paused uncertainly to look out the window. My first thought was that we had arrived at Princeton Junction. Damn. But it was not Princeton Junction. It was not really anywhere—or not anywhere this train should be stopping. This was not in itself particularly disturbing: if you have ever ridden on one of these trains you will know that, although they operate on the most important and most traveled rail route in the country, their movements are as random as the physical limitations of steel rails will permit. That is, they are always mysteriously speeding up, slowing down, or stopping altogether at unpredictable intervals bearing no relation to published schedules or the location of stations. And when they come to a full stop, they will pause for entirely random periods of time—sometimes a few seconds, sometimes many hours. The employees of the railroad, if they have any idea themselves what is happening or why, never ever communicate it to the passengers. Then, mysteriously, forward progress resumes.

Under the circumstances, I might have welcomed an unscheduled stop. The difficulty on this occasion was that we were slowing abruptly to a full halt right in the middle of some unfamiliar station. We were on the outside track right next to the platform, and there were people—thankfully only a few—waiting on the platform for the next local. Perhaps they were to be allowed to board our train instead. I certainly hoped not. But at the very least they would be wonderfully positioned to look in through the windows; and as it happened, our particular window of our particular car came to a violent and full halt directly opposite three well-to-do ladies of late middle age. This afforded them a commanding view of Anne sprawled bare-breasted and spread-eagled across the seat and of me poised erect and quivering above her. Were it not for the pane of glass separating us, they could have reached out and touched us. Not, I suppose, that they would have wanted to.

Of course, I had an excellent view of them too, although that was not proving to be of much comfort to me. They possessed portly dimensions and staid clothing befitting their age and station. Their demeanor was forbidding. From the fact that they were standing on the southbound platform, we can conclude that, living midway between the two cities, they had decided to spend their day in Philadelphia rather than New York. They stood side by side facing us. The one in the middle had some sort of needlework in her hands, and from their position it appeared that the three of them had been leaning over it and discussing it earnestly. However, when our little *tableau vivant* was hauled so abruptly before them and deposited there, their eyes turned to us and widened; each of their mouths formed instantly into a little, voiceless O of astonishment and censure. I felt extremely uncomfortable. I suppose they did too, although their discomfort had presumably a very different quality. I suppose my mouth must have formed into its own little O of astonishment, or into some other equally ridiculous expression, because Anne looked up at me and then, letting go of my hips, pushed herself up into a sitting position and turned her head to look out the window and see what was going on. She stared at those three stern countenances for a moment and then tilted her head and shook it so that her hair fell across the side of her face, partly obscuring it. Then she turned back towards me.

I was motionless with confusion and mortification. I thought of bundling myself into my trousers and buttoning myself up right there before them, but that seemed somehow even more silly and humiliating than the existing state of affairs. I wondered if I would feel even more foolish and shamed during the coming moments as my lust collapsed into limp embarrassment. Perhaps I should immediately grab Anne by the hand and drag her to another seat on the other side of the car, where we could collect our wits and clothing. Anne, however, had a different response. With a smile so utterly and mischievously wicked that you would think only a little girl could have produced it, she licked her lips slowly, leaned forward in her seat, and delicately kissed me. The little O's formed by the ladies' mouths grew wider as they watched. Anne drew back an inch and licked her lips once more. She kissed me again. Then *she* deliberately formed *her* mouth into a little O and moved it over me.

Mercifully, there was a metallic clank and a violent lurch, and the train began to haul us out of sight of those three grim ladies. As we drifted out of each other's lives, the one in the center fixed me with her furious gaze. She set her features in an ominous frown, expertly twisted around one finger a thread from her needlework, and snapped it fiercely off. I felt as if my doom had been decreed by stern, suburban fates. I have no idea what punishment they would have wished for me, but if they could have foreseen the rest of my day, they would surely have been satisfied. I remember wondering if it was possible that one of them knew me. Or perhaps, several weeks or months later, I would turn and find one of them seated next to me at a dinner. I felt a bit sick. Somehow, unwittingly, incredibly, I had become part of a live sex act performed before a hostile, disapproving audience. I felt exposed, anxious, and ashamed.

But I also felt Anne's mouth and hands all over my body, her lips and tongue caressing me, and a new swell of bliss mingled easily with my anxiety and shame. I leaned over her again, pushing her back into the seat. I ran my hands over her body, from her hips up over her breasts. I kissed her and as I pushed my tongue into her mouth, I pushed my thumb into her. She writhed on the seat and seized me with her hand.

This time the interruption was the door at the end of the car sliding open with a crash and flooding us with the metallic noise of wheels and rails. I raised myself and peered over the back of the seat. The conductor, a ponderous 250-pound man in a vast black uniform, was working his way down the aisle in a dignified ambling gait. This was even more unsettling than the last interruption: for one thing there was no pane of glass to make us seem like an official exhibit in a terrarium; for another, we had some warning, some time to hide. Frantically we pulled ourselves together as best we could. No time to fasten our clothing, but we pulled it as much as possible across the naked limbs and members and mounds of flesh. Then I pulled the *New York Times* up and spread it out over our bodies from our knees to our shoulders, like a gigantic child's bib. I reached over, retrieved my pad of paper from the floor, and balanced it on my lap. As the conductor arrived, I resumed my lecture on supply and demand.

"When you superimpose the two curves, the intersection defines the point at which the market clears."

The conductor looked down at us. Then he reached up and removed two ticket stubs from a slot in the luggage rack above us.

"That is," I said uneasily, "supply and demand are in equilibrium."

The conductor lowered his gaze again and stared at us. He seemed to feel that something was not quite right.

"Movements in price will tend toward that point . . ." Anne pinched me underneath the newspaper. I must have made some inarticulate grunt, since the conductor gave me a suspicious look. "Although a given short-term movement may not—"

The conductor, leaning over us, proclaimed as loudly as if to a car full of passengers, "Princeton Junction!"

Both Anne and I started. The conductor continued to stare at us. We silently and intently studied our pad of paper with its intersecting curves.

Evidently unable to think of anything more to say or do, the conductor finally turned ponderously and shuffled back toward the end of the car.

The newspaper slid from our laps. The train was already beginning to slow again to a halt. Anne was laughing. I gave her a last, rather violent caress. We both frantically pulled clothing together, fastened buttons, shoved papers into briefcases. Agonizing, aching frustration. We were still tucking in clothing and smoothing hair back into place with our hands as we stumbled awkwardly down the carriage steps onto the platform.

"Damn!" said Anne, laughing.

E STOOD ON THE PLATFORM IN A MOMENTARY DAZE AND WATCHED the train pull away. The sky was completely dark now; it seemed about to rain. Sudden contact with the cool, moist, threatening air made me feel as if I were just now being awakened after a night of insufficient sleep. The handful of other passengers who had descended here hurried off across the platform to the parking lot or to the little train that would shuttle them to Princeton. I announced to Anne that I was going to find a taxi. We had plenty of time—not that I would have cared if we were late—and I meant to go into Princeton and rent a car so that I could escape with Anne from MicroMagnetics at the earliest possible moment.

I was disappointed when my companion replied that she had arranged to have us met. At first I imagined that the *Times* in its magnificence provided its employees with drivers wherever the quest for truth took them. In fact, I was informed, we were being met by a representative of Students for a Fair World.

"Why Students for a Fair World? Princeton Yellow Cabs has better drivers," I protested. Maybe the *Times* really did have training camps in Ethiopia. "Besides," I asked, "why do the Students for a Fair World want to go to all this trouble for us? I know we've all got to pitch in and help each other in the struggle for a better world and everything, but I really feel this isn't the best use of their talents, providing drivers for us. Really, we're doing a disservice to the revolution."

"Shut up," she said affably. "This is probably him now."

Indeed, a member of the revolutionary vanguard had appeared farther down the platform. He was really quite striking—handsome with the small, fine features of a model, longish blond hair swept straight back, and dressed entirely in overlaundered, faded denim. He was young enough so that he might still have been an undergraduate.

"Yes, indeed," I said. "From the autumn line of revolutionaries by Ralph Lauren." He was observing us uncertainly. We were evidently not what he was expecting, but we were the only people left at the station.

"How about letting me do my job?" she said to me and then strode down the platform with a greeting smile. As she approached, he swept one hand through his hair and extended the other in greeting. My heart full of sullenness, I followed as slowly as I could manage to where they stood. If nearly grown men want to put on costumes and play cowboys and Indians or make-believe revolution, it is fine with me; but I didn't want them intruding on my morning. As I came up to them, Anne was thanking him for meeting us.

"Not at all. If you hadn't called and told us this was taking place, we'd have missed it completely. None of us had ever even heard of Micro-Magnetics, and this is just the kind of opportunity we're always looking for. Nuclear poisoning of the environment is an issue with a really broad appeal. And once you get people—"

He stopped as I joined them, and they both looked up at me with slightly startled expressions, as if my arrival had been somehow unanticipated, or inappropriate. I felt a childish but considerable annoyance—annoyance that my day was taking a different turn than I had planned, annoyance at the young person's make-believe work clothes, at his good looks, and at his way of staring at me as if I were an unusual and somewhat suspect form of life.

"Nick Halloway, Robert Carillon," Anne said rather quickly, indicating first one of us and then the other with perfunctory waves of the hand. She didn't seem to want to linger over the introduction. She turned back to Carillon, leaving me with a view of the back of her head, and started to speak to him. But he spoke first.

"Are you with the *Times* too, Nick?" He was studying me with an expression of deliberate and skeptical appraisal.

"Gosh, no." I spoke with the most boyishly ingenuous air I could contrive. "Unfortunately. I mean, I wish I were. Great paper. Tremendous challenge, working there—lot of fun too, I'll bet. And a tremendous responsibility." I cast a glance at Anne, who had been looking at me in amazement and who now turned away again, stonily. "Actually, I'm with Shipway & Whitman. Great firm. Nice people." I grinned a large, friendly, foolish grin.

Carillon seemed uncertain whether I was serious or not, but I suppose he found me offensive either way. As I spoke, he studied my necktie as if he had never seen one before and found the idea vaguely amusing. He moved his head and squinted slightly to make it clear that he was examining first the initials monogrammed on my shirt front and then my suspenders. His eyes traveled up and down my suit, which was grey with pinstripes, as it happened, and came to rest on my shoes, which seemed to be particularly troubling to him. They were very good English shoes made to fit my particular feet, and as things would turn out it was good luck that I wore them that day.

"Who are you with?" I asked enthusiastically.

"I'm with Students for a Fair World."

"Oh, right. Of course you are. I've been hearing all about you. You're the head of the whole shooting match, aren't you?"

"I don't think I'd call it a shooting match," he said a little stiffly. "Shooting is exactly what we're trying to put an end to. And we don't have a 'head.' We organize ourselves by democratic principles with a collective consensus. You may be unfamiliar with the idea."

"But you *are* the head man?"

"I am sometimes chosen to be a spokesperson," he said demurely.

"Gee, that's great. Probably like being president of a fraternity, or a secret society or whatever, in my day. Or an eating club—it *is* eating clubs you have down here, isn't it? Your family must be proud as punch."

He reddened and his eyes narrowed.

"I don't think they see it quite the same way you do. And for once I'm in agreement with them. You're here, I take it, to see whether someone can make a profit on some new variety of nuclear energy."

"That's it," I said cheerfully. "Always looking for the highest rate of return, wherever it may be. That's what makes the world go round, as the poet says. The invisible hand and all. The ruthlessly efficient market."

"Well, I suppose it can only be as ruthless and efficient as the people who operate it," he replied with a sardonic smile. "Perhaps that's why it sometimes seems more the former than the latter."

Really, we were hitting it off splendidly. Anne, who usually had an appetite for ideological conflict, seemed on this occasion irritated, however. She was probably embarrassed by me—a thought which added to my own annoyance. She moved to take control.

"This thing is scheduled for ten-thirty—" she began.

But a thought struck me, and I interrupted. "Say, you don't have a brother or a cousin named Bradford Carillon, do you? Works at Morgan?"

"Half-brother," he replied coldly.

"Great guy," I said, totally inaccurately. "I'll let him know I ran into you."

"Do."

"We've got to get along," Anne said firmly. She had definitely had enough. "How far is it to MicroMagnetics, exactly?"

Carillon seemed to welcome the interruption. It was ten minutes to MicroMagnetics, but the two of them began a discussion, as if it were a complex and engrossing problem, of distances and driving times and alternative routes. They both carefully avoided looking at me or acknowledging my presence. I considered taking a taxi on my own but decided that would seem childishly petulant. Carillon was excusing himself to get the car.

"Why don't we just come with you to the parking lot?" asked Anne.

"No, just wait here a moment, and I'll get everything organized."

The hero of the revolution hurried off up the platform, and as soon as he was out of earshot, Anne shared with me her view of my behavior.

"Jesus Christ. Can't you be civil?"

"I thought I was being civil. I practically had to carry the whole conversation, although I'm not sure why we're wasting our time talking to this guy. We should get into Princeton and rent a car for—"

"It's my job to talk to him. I enjoy talking to him."

"I was enjoying talking to him too."

"Well, you've had enough enjoyment for today. Leave him alone."

"Exactly what I'd like to do. But by the way, what in God's name possessed you to call these people and put them up to harassing Micro-Magnetics?"

This question subdued her instantly; she was visibly uncomfortable with it.

"I didn't put anyone up to anything. Because I take the trouble to follow what happens in the world I live in, I was aware of the active concern of Students for a Fair World with certain issues, and it was part of my job to find out whether they were planning any action in response to a highly publicized event organized by the nuclear industry. And also I wish you wouldn't mention this to anyone else. Especially at the *Times*."

"Anne, my love, this is not a 'highly publicized event.' We shall probably be the only people who bother to come—and if the weather forecast hadn't been completely inaccurate, even that turnout would have been cut at least in half. Furthermore, MicroMagnetics, whoever they may be, would surely be amazed and thrilled to know that someone had included them in 'the nuclear industry.' But I absolutely adore you, and I couldn't care less if you want to organize an armed rebellion in central New Jersey while on salary at the *Times*. I won't tell a soul. As a matter of fact, I'm making an effort to keep on your good side; I'm counting on you to put in a good word for me with these people, assure them that I was really a secret sympathizer all along—I mean in case the question should come up at some point after the revolution."

I smiled my most engaging smile. (I no longer have an engaging smile—or any other smile—at my disposal. It is as if I could only talk to other human beings over the telephone.)

She laughed. "Does he really have a brother who works at Morgan?" she asked.

"Yes. Also a prig."

Standing on the platform with the spring breeze pushing her hair and clothing around, Anne looked splendid. We agreed on a truce. I would be civil to everyone I encountered. Anne would try to acquire in the shortest possible time whatever information she felt she needed from the Students for a Fair World and from MicroMagnetics, Inc., and we would not linger unnecessarily in their vicinity.

As we spoke, we could see Carillon at the end of the platform, where a road ended in a small circle. There was a dirty grey van parked there and behind it two other vehicles. One, I remember, was an elegant old Mercedes; the other, I think, was an American sedan, badly rusted. Carillon was talking to someone in the van through an open window. Abruptly, doors opened on both sides of the van and four or five people climbed out. Revolutionaries travel in bands, never alone. Several other people got out of the cars. I think probably two or three of them were girls, or women. I was not paying much attention to them—not nearly as much as I ought to have. I remember thinking that most of them looked like undergraduates and that all of them were dressed as something else—workers or peasants from other, more exotic cultures. They conferred in the parking lot for several minutes, and at one point I remember they all looked over at us. Then all of them except Chairman Carillon climbed into the sedans. He stood by the van and watched them drive away and then turned and waved to us to come over. The whole thing made me a little uneasy somehow. My instincts were good. I should have paid attention to them.

The van had only two seats, and I graciously assured Anne and Carillon that I was delighted to ride in back on the floor, but it was clear that no one had considered any other arrangement anyway. The body of the van was filled with a jumble of cardboard boxes and what appeared to be building supplies and tools. I clambered awkwardly through the mess and found several loose cushions, which I tried to arrange into a seat for myself. When I sat down on it, I found that I could see nothing out the windows except patches of sky, and as soon as we started off, I felt myself being heaved from side to side with each turn. There seemed, moreover, to be an odd chemical smell in the van.

In the front I could hear Anne and Carillon having an impenetrable discussion about the interrelations of various left-wing political groups, all of which seemed to be identified by initials, like government agencies. I could not have been less interested. I passed the time trying to figure out what the equipment next to me on the floor was for. I could see several coils of electrical wire and at least two large dry cells. Then with an unpleasant shock I realized that the smell all around me was of gunpowder. I was evidently about to take part in a bombing. This would put me in solid with the investment community. It would certainly be the breakthrough Anne was looking for. Put her right onto the front page. INVESTMENT FIRM LINKED TO LEFT-WING TERRORIST GROUP. My hands were trembling as I pulled open the top of one of the boxes and peered inside. More boxes.

Carillon heard me and craned his head around to see what I was up to.

"Everything all right back there?" he asked.

Anne turned her head too and looked back at me.

"Quite a lot of equipment you've got back here," I ventured, as conversationally as possible. "Some sort of hobby, I guess."

"You might call it that. More an avocation. It would be better if you didn't touch anything."

I was quite genuinely frightened. These people seem harmless enough when they mill around in public places haranguing each other about imposing a better world on the rest of us, but properly equipped they can be a genuine menace to themselves and others. I had a vision of Micro-Magnetics being blown to smithereens. This was quickly followed by what seemed a far more plausible vision of our van being blown to smithereens before it could get us to MicroMagnetics. I hoped my voice was not quavering.

"Looks like you're getting a head start on Independence Day this year."

There was a little pause. Then he replied, "You might put it that way. As a matter of fact, we *are* going to have a little explosion today."

Anne, whose head was still half turned in my direction, seemed excited but not at all dismayed by this news. She had her pen and her little journalist's notebook poised for the details.

"That's great," I said. "That's the way to do it. Show them you mean business. Poof. No more MicroMagnetics. That'll make those jokers think twice about what line of work they get into next. Opens up my day too. No point in my checking out MicroMagnetics now. In fact you might just drop me off—"

"We'll just be blowing up a guinea pig today."

"That's the idea. These MicroMagnetics clowns are just guinea pigs. If the thing works here, you can blow up anyone who gets out of line."

"A guinea pig," he insisted coldly. "The little animal in the cage back there with you. We're blowing it up in a small simulation of a nuclear explosion, to make vivid the unacceptable horror of nuclear war."

I couldn't see a cage anywhere, but I felt a great sense of relief upon discovering that no major destruction was being undertaken and that, moreover, there was probably nothing more dangerous than fireworks bouncing along with us in the van. I felt, in fact, a bit foolish about having been so easily frightened. However, Anne, who, as far as I could tell, had just been contemplating the bombing of the entire physical plant of MicroMagnetics with something approaching enthusiasm, had the opposite reaction. She was suddenly aghast.

"You're murdering an animal?"

"Exactly!" said the terrorist, with restrained but unmistakable triumph in his voice. "That's exactly the way everyone reacts. It's one of the contradictions of bourgeois sensibility that people are more upset about one small laboratory animal dying painlessly before their eyes than by all humanity being steadily poisoned with radioactivity. It's by exacerbating that contradiction that we can force people to a higher dialectical level of political consciousness."

"You mean by killing an animal?" Anne asked again, more calmly this time. I could not tell if she was getting the thing into a proper revolutionary perspective or if she was just doing what she thought of as her job.

"That's right. Do you see? Right now all of us are already being made the guinea pigs of a capitalist nuclear industry that values profits above human beings. If by destroying this one animal we can make even one more person understand that, its suffering will have been worthwhile."

Carillon seemed to enjoy speaking this way; he was becoming quite cheerful and animated, and his voice was beginning to resonate as if he were addressing a crowd. In my experience, when one of these people uses the word "dialectic," you are in for it. I was sure that if anyone offered another objection to detonating the animal, he would be off again and there would be no stopping the dialectical process, so I hastened to agree with him.

"That's a very telling point, you know." I tried to sound sincere and deliberative. "Yes, I think that's right on the money." The phrase was ill chosen, and he looked back at me suspiciously. I wished he would keep his eyes on the road. There was a pause in the conversation, and Anne, after a sharp glance in my direction, turned back and uneasily resumed her interview of Carillon, keeping her voice as low as she could in the hope that I would be unable to participate.

I located the cage on the other side of the van. It was not much larger than the animal inside. I opened the hinged door and dumped the guinea pig out onto the floor of the van. It lay where it landed, a fat, passive creature. I crawled back to my cushions, feeling suddenly a bit queasy from the motion of the van. I found that I was now concentrating entirely on the way I was being wrenched back and forth. The turns seemed to be increasing in violence and frequency, and I decided we must be on a back road. I was definitely quite carsick. I wished I were not down on the floor and that I had drunk less the night before. I wished I could see something more out a window than a patch of cloudy sky or the occasional tree branch sweeping sickeningly by. I closed my eyes. Worse. Reopen them. Drive taking too long.

When the van at last came to a halt, I hurriedly pushed open the rear doors and stumbled to my feet with as much dignity as I could manage. No sign of the guinea pig, but I left the doors open to give him as much of a chance as possible. Where do guinea pigs occur in a state of nature? Not in central New Jersey. I did not think much of its chances of survival in the wild, but at least its destiny was in its own hands now.

Anne and Carillon were standing by the front of the van, still in conversation. When I came around to them, Anne looked up at me and said, "I'm not quite finished, Nick."

"Take all the time you want, Anne. There's no hurry. I'll be over in front of the building, getting some air. Bob," I continued, holding out my hand to Carillon, "thanks for the ride. It was great chatting with you and in case we don't run into each other again, I want to wish you every success today and in all your future endeavors."

He nodded curtly, ignoring my outstretched hand, and turned back to Anne. On the other side of the parking lot I could see some of his confederates watching us silently—waiting, I supposed, until Carillon was done with us.

I turned and followed a footpath out of the parking lot through a break in a hedge which screened the parking lot from the building. I found myself on the edge of a large lawn with enormous shade trees, which must have been there for generations. To one side, a drive lined with oaks ran from the edge of the parking lot out to the road a hundred yards away. Beyond the lawn in every direction were fields bordered by trees. It was a beautiful place. The incongruous thing was that in the middle of it all was a brand-new, long, white, rectangular wood frame building of the type that you would expect to find surrounded by asphalt in what is for some reason called an "industrial park." A paved walk led from the parking lot along the front of this structure to the main entrance in its center, where there were two steps up to a threshold flanked by two massive white wooden columns which supported a sort of vestigial porch roof extending no more than a couple of feet out from the rest of the façade. The effect had no doubt been described by the builder as "colonial." Above this oddly foreshortened structure the name MicroMagnetics was spelled out in twelve-inch-high red letters affixed to the building. And above that was a sort of circular shield six feet in diameter on which were painted two huge red letter Ms joined by the pattern of arcs used to represent magnetic fields. It looked like a gigantic M&M candy. This odd new structure must have replaced a much older farmhouse. If you could have somehow got back the farmhouse, it would have been a very beautiful place indeed.

I stepped off the path onto the grass and walked towards an ancient and massive copper beech, sucking in deep breaths of heavy, humid air in the hope that it would make me feel better. A single large raindrop fell out of the dark sky onto my head. Soon it would really begin to rain. I wondered if that might not be an improvement. Perhaps I should stay out in the rain for a while. Why had I come here?

Dully, I tried to survey the situation. MicroMagnetics was an even smaller enterprise than I had imagined. The entire building could not be even ten thousand square feet. Off to one side there was another, much smaller, concrete structure, into which ran enough power lines to supply a small city. They must be doing something here that required a lot of electricity. Could be anything. Who cares? I took several more deep breaths and tried to decide whether or not I felt any better. I decided to tell myself that I did, although two little points of pain were beginning to define themselves in my eyes. Soon those points would extend back and join in the middle of my head to form a piercing headache.

Although it was still early, a few people had already arrived and were straggling unenthusiastically into the building. They all looked like academics to me. There certainly weren't going to be any other securities analysts. I wondered if there would even be any press coverage. Of course, if the *Times* ran something by Anne, the event would have to be counted a smashing public relations success. But I wondered again why Micro-Magnetics wanted a public relations success in the first place. Their press release was useless. What were they after?

Fame and vast wealth, I supposed. The usual.

The revolutionaries were hauling their cartons out onto the lawn and setting up their own little scientific demonstration right in front of the entrance. They did not seem at all concerned that someone might object to their presence, which seemed odd. But evidently they were right: no one seemed in the least interested in them. Academic setting. You always have young people milling around on lawns doing whatever they like. Perhaps someone would have some aspirin inside. Coffee. Some of Carillon's people were crouched in front of the door of the little concrete hut. Not a good place for them.

Carillon and Anne appeared through the hedge and joined the group on the lawn. I watched as Anne wished them all well, then turned and walked out to join me.

"Thanks for waiting." She seemed to be in a benign mood again.

"My pleasure. I wanted the air anyway."

"You all right? You look a bit green."

"I'll be fine," I said. "Dialectical materialism always affects me this way. It's the relentless pitch and yaw of the historical process. How's the revolution coming? Do I have time to get my money out of the bank?"

"The guinea pig is gone. Did you let it out?"

"Why would I try to stem the irresistible tide of revolution?"

"Well, you were the chief suspect. You and the girl with the long blond hair, who apparently has a history of bourgeois sentimentality." Anne was definitely in a better mood. "Anyway, it's gone."

"Pity. What will they do?"

"They're searching for a stand-in. They would probably welcome the opportunity to use you, if you're interested. Shouldn't we go in? It's starting to rain."

"By all means, let's go in. . . . Tell me, do you have any idea what Carillon's people are doing in that electrical shed or whatever it is?" The door of the concrete hut with all the electric lines was open now, and one of the students was standing in the doorway holding what appeared to be a toolbox.

"I think," said Anne, without bothering to look, "they're going to shut off power to the building as part of their demonstration or something. So everyone will have to come out and watch. Have you seen anyone else from the press?"

"No, I haven't. You mean they're going to just shut off all power to a laboratory with God only knows what kind of equipment running in it? Don't you think that's a bit irresponsible?"

"You think anyone is irresponsible who thinks about anything more than making a profit," Anne said good-naturedly.

"Not at all. They're welcome to think about absolutely anything they—"

"And as usual you're more concerned with private property than with people."

"This particular private property is about to contain people. Us, to be precise. They're going to blow us up after all. Look, I'm completely new to terrorism. Isn't the warning phone call before the explosion one of the conventions? Maybe we should let the police or the folks at Micro-Magnetics know what—"

"We're journalists, not police informers," Anne said, beginning to heat up again. "It's not our job to tell anyone anything. It's a question of First Amendment rights—"

"It's kind of you to include me in the 'we' of journalists, but I'm actually only a plain citizen without special rank or privilege. I'm just concerned—"

"You know perfectly well they aren't going to harm anyone. But you do have a point about the police," she said, abruptly becoming pensive. "They ought to have police here. I've never seen one of these nuclear demonstrations come off properly without police." She frowned, genuinely troubled.

"Look, Anne, rather than having to choose between the ignominy of being police informers and the inconvenience of being innocent victims of a brutal act of terrorism, why don't we just cut short our stay here? We'll go in right now, pick up whatever printed material they have, and call a cab. We can rent a car in Princeton and drive—"

"Nick, I'm absolutely going to stay through the press conference and the demonstration. And then we both have appointments with Wachs afterward. After that, I should really get back to New York for—"

"I'll tell you what. We'll go in and see Wachs together now. Then we won't have to hang around afterwards."

"The press conference is going to begin in twenty minutes. We'll never get at him before—"

"I'll get at him."

I took her decisively by the arm and started across the lawn toward the building to find Wachs. At that moment I believed I was going to get my way with everyone and have the day I wanted, and although my stomach seemed to be having a difficult crossing, and the light, of which there was very little, hurt my eyes, a final wave of euphoria swept over me. It may have been the last benign effect of the alcohol I had consumed the night before, but I felt that I had taken control of the situation.

"We'll be gone by noon," I said.

(I would be gone by noon all right.)

As we strode across the lawn, the sky turned almost black, and my jacket was mottled with raindrops. Anne waved cheerfully at the revolutionaries as we passed. They had set up a little metal table on the grass, and behind it they had strung between two poles a hand-lettered banner which read:

THE DESTRUCTION BY NUCLEAR HOLOCAUST OF A GUINEA PIG
REPRESENTING ALL INNOCENT VICTIMS OF
CAPITALIST OPPRESSION AND NUCLEAR DEATH TECHNOLOGY.
WE ARE ALL GUINEA PIGS!

"Good slogan," I muttered to Anne. "Catchy."

Other people were arriving, and as they walked past to the entrance, they glanced without concern or even much interest at the demonstrators. Perhaps people expect a few demonstrators everywhere nowadays.

Carillon, sweeping his hand through his long blond hair, called out, "Anne, have you seen any other media here?"

The familiarity annoyed me, and before she could reply, I called back, "I *think* I saw someone from the *Washington Post*. And maybe someone from *Newsweek*. But I haven't seen any sign of the network crews yet."

He looked at me blankly at first, unsure of how to take my reply. "Well, let's hope," he said coldly.

"I suppose you really shouldn't begin until the network crews are here—"

Anne had a ferocious grip on my arm and was dragging me in through the entrance door. We found ourselves standing in a small reception room with a couch and a table and, facing us, a large desk with a typing stand to one side. Behind the desk sat a woman in her forties whose natural expression of truculent dissatisfaction had been highlighted with the careful application of great quantities of make-up. She took a brief, disapproving look at Anne, and then fixed her gaze on me.

"Take one press kit and go through the door to your left, then straight down the corridor to the conference room at the end. We'll be beginning in a few minutes." Her voice had no warmth in it.

I picked up a press kit. "Thank you. That's extremely kind. I wonder if you could let Dr. Wachs know that Mr. Halloway of Shipway & Whitman is here."

"Professor Wachs can't be disturbed now. You'll have to go through the door to your left and down to the conference room."

"And this is Miss Epstein, from the *Times*," I continued. I was sure that a mention of the *Times* would bring her around.

"If you'll both go down to the conference room, Professor Wachs will be right along." Her brow furrowed momentarily, and she looked suspiciously at Anne. "I believe we already have you down for an appointment"—she peered at a book on her desk—"at two o'clock. And we have *you* down too, for—"

"Actually," I said, "I was hoping we could get a few words privately with Professor Wachs now, before the press conference—in a preliminary sort of way. . . ." My voice trailed off. I had been gazing at the press kit as if it were some entirely baffling artifact which had unexpectedly come into my possession, and now I turned it over and examined the back. It was a glossy white and red folder which—just like the one in my briefcase—would contain Xerox copies of a press release, an uninformative fact sheet, and a curriculum vitae of Bernard Wachs, Ph.D. Staring at it studiously but still not opening it, I twisted the folder slowly around so that it was upside down and squinted at it, as if hoping that from this new angle its significance might be revealed.

"I'm sorry," she said, "but you'll both have to go to the conference room with everyone else." I remained where I was, studying the folder intently. "The door to your left," she said severely.

I carefully opened the folder and peered inside. My brow furrowed as I studied the top sheet, which, being upside down, was indecipherable. I pulled it out, carefully turned it around, and returned it to the folder. The woman watched me in a state of mounting agony until she could no longer contain herself. "You've got it upside down." Her voice had an edge of hysteria.

I looked up at her and blinked. "Got what upside down?"

"The folder."

"Oh, the folder," I said, looking down at it in amazement. "You're quite right. I do." I turned it back around and looked at it. "I think it's possible that he would want to see us . . ."

"He's far too busy now."

"Yes, of course he is. All the same he might want to see us. I don't know, I think he *would* want to see us probably . . ." I opened the folder again carefully and furrowed my brow in puzzlement when I encountered the top sheet, which I had reversed before. "You know, I'm not sure this *was* upside down."

Her eyes widened with outrage and contempt. She made an abortive movement with her right hand as if to snatch the press kit from me, but thought better of it. I began pulling the sheets from the folder one at a time and, after careful consideration, reinserting them in what she clearly felt to be the wrong order or the wrong orientation. The whole process seemed to upset her quite a lot.

"Do you think he might still be in his office?" I asked.

Her eyes darted momentarily to a closed door in the wall to my right.

"*You'll have to go in with everyone else now.*" She was almost shouting.

"Yes, of course." I carefully put the press kit back on top of the pile on her desk, where she regarded it as if it were a live explosive. "The door to my left, you said?" I pointed to the door on my right.

"No . . . yes . . . no!"

I walked distractedly over to the door on my right and pushed it open.

"You can't go in there!"

I found myself looking into an enormous, carpeted, corner office. The furnishings were undistinguished, but through the many windows there were wonderfully pleasant views of the lawn, the trees, and the fields beyond. In the center of the room was a large desk, in front of which stood a short, plump, rodentlike man. His suit had evidently been purchased thirty pounds earlier, and his belt creased deeply into a large paunch. He seemed startled to see us in the doorway, but then, in the brief time I knew him, he seemed continuously startled, always looking about with nervous little inquisitive movements of his head, as if he were some giant squirrel searching for a place to store nuts. His jumpy gaze darted back and forth between us, but he seemed understandably to be particularly taken with Anne, and his eyes kept returning to her breasts.

"You wouldn't be Dr. Wachs, would you?" I asked.

"Yes, yes, I am. How do you do?" He spoke with extraordinary rapidity, shifting his weight constantly from one foot to the other.

"I'm Nick Halloway, with Shipway and Whitman. The investment firm."

"Oh, you're just the person I want to see. I'm very interested right now in money. Capitalization—"

"Professor Wachs," called out the receptionist ominously, "these people—"

"And this," I went on, "is Anne Epstein from the *Times*."

"Oh, that's wonderful that you were able to be here. The *Times*. Come in, come in. I think you're going to be very excited by the work we're doing here." He gazed intently at Anne's breasts. "Is there anything I can tell you—"

"Professor Wachs," insisted the receptionist, "it's very late. You have to—"

"Yes, yes, that's right. We can't spend more than a moment now. Come in for just a moment. You say you're with an investment bank?

Raising capital is our first priority. While I've got you here, maybe I can get you to recommend a good book on that."

"Perhaps it would be more useful to sit down and talk about your capital needs sometime when—"

"Professor Wachs." The receptionist was still glowering in the doorway behind us. "It's almost time. You have to—"

"Amazing facility you have here," I said to Wachs as I shut the door behind me in the face of the receptionist. "Really very impressive—far more extensive than I ever would have imagined."

He seemed pleased. "Yes, you know I designed the whole thing myself. There was nothing here but an old farmhouse. I mean with the builder—Fucini Brothers, Builders. They're very good—if you're ever thinking of doing anything. Very good. It's extraordinary how complex a structure even the simplest building is. Fascinating. They built all of Kirby Park," he added by way of explanation.

"Did they really?" I responded. I had no idea what or where Kirby Park might be, but I thought I should try to gain some sort of tenuous handhold on the conversation. "Did you design the logo yourself too?"

"Yes. What do you think of it?" he asked earnestly.

"Extremely compelling. My compliments," I replied.

"You don't think it looks like an M&M?" There was a troubled expression on his face.

"An M&M?" I asked blankly.

"Yes. You know—the little round candies."

"Oh, of course: M&M's. . . . Does it remind me of M&M's? . . . No. Is it meant to?" I asked earnestly

"No, no, no. I only wondered if it looked like that to you. Something someone said." He seemed reassured by my response.

"The whole effect is really quite striking," I assured him. "The corporate name in red letters, the logo, the columned façade. And the trees," I added as an afterthought.

"The trees. Extraordinary, the trees. We were able to save most of the trees. No need at this stage to get rid of the trees. Wait. I want you to see . . . If you come over here, I can show you the view I have from my desk. You see that beech tree?" He was hopping around the desk excitedly. I did as I was told and went to his desk to stare out the window at the vast copper beech, but he was already chattering on to other topics.

"Here's something that would interest you, Nick. I designed this telephone myself. Far beyond anything on the market. It automatically stores the last five numbers you've dialed. Up to twenty digits—"

"I know you're terribly busy today," I said, "but I just wondered if we could get some information before you get completely tied up with this press conference—"

"Yes, yes. Absolutely—"

"I wonder," Anne interrupted to my irritation, "if you could tell us how you feel about the conflicting needs of society for expanded energy sources and for protection of the environment, as they bear on the issue of nuclear power?"

That stopped him. But before he could waste much effort trying to figure it out, I intervened.

"Exactly," I said. "Specifically, we were wondering why in your press release there was no real mention of magnetic containment. So much of the work you're known for has, of course, been related to the problem of containment—"

"Yes, yes. You're right. This has nothing to do with containment. . . . Actually, you could apply it to containment, if that were . . ." He was looking out the window again. Something outside had caught his nervous glance. "There seem to be some people out front constructing something." A puzzled look came over his face.

"That's precisely what we want to discuss—" Anne began.

"Those are students, demonstrators," I interrupted. "They seem, unaccountably, to have some moral or political objection to whatever it is you're doing here. Which raises the question of just what you *are*—"

"Oh, students," he said, as if that would be a satisfactory explanation for anything whatever. "You're sure they're just students? They don't like it when you take government grants. Protest all the time. But the money is indispensable. All the more reason to raise capital privately. I have to remember to get the name of that book from you. We have to have a strategy for approaching the banks—"

"I believe they plan to shut off power to the building," I went on.

"Shut off power? Why would banks shut off power? You mean the electric company. I thought we had an understanding for the time being. The trouble is, it's literally hundreds of thousands of dollars a year. That's our biggest single problem: the incredible quantities of electricity this work requires. The potential is unbelievable. It's all a question of capital."

I wasn't quite sure whether the potential he was talking about was electrical, scientific, or financial.

"I myself don't know anything at all about raising money," he went on, "and the work we're doing is extremely important—revolutionary—so I'm particularly glad to have this chance to talk to you."

"Well, we're extremely interested in the work you're doing down here," I said. I hoped the "we" would convey vast financial interests. "By the way, you don't happen to have a set of financial statements here that I could have a look at, do you?" I thought as a matter of principle I should ask, as long as we were having this inane conversation. I wasn't getting anywhere in the interview, so I might as well try for something written.

He bustled over to his desk and began burrowing through a stack of papers.

"It's extraordinary," he said. He pulled out a battered manila envelope, peered inside, and handed it over to me. "It's amazing no one has seen it before. The mathematics of it is deceptively straightforward."

Was he talking about the financials?

"It follows inevitably once you set up the proper mathematical representation of magnetism. Beautifully simple, but when you follow it through, it stands everything on its head. Incredible that no one has seen it before."

The folder contained unaudited statements from a local accountant. As a show of politeness, I stared at them earnestly for several moments. The most impressive thing which emerged, aside from the quantity of money obtained from the government—was the fact that this man had somehow talked a bank into financing the building we were in.

"The potential is limitless," he was saying, apparently to Anne's breasts.

The intercom on his desk buzzed. He picked up the phone.

"Yes, yes. Absolutely. We're just heading down there now. I know. No time." He looked up at us as he replaced the receiver. "We have to be getting down to the conference room. It's time to begin. We should talk afterwards. Money is the whole key," he said, looking at Anne.

He led us across his office and out through a door into an interior corridor. Next to that door was another, slightly ajar, and I saw that it opened into a lavatory. I wanted rather badly to use it, but decided not to give up on my interview now. I would hate to have to begin again with this man several hours later.

As we marched down the corridor he continued excitedly, "Now, we really don't have any time to look at this, but I just want to show you the laboratory. Unfortunately, in the format of a press conference I can't really explain in a meaningful way what we're doing here, but I just want you to see this. In this kind of thing you have to gear your remarks to a lay audience and it's difficult to go into some things. Fortunately, I've done a certain amount of lecturing to students with no real scientific grounding at all—'History and Philosophy of Science' and that kind of thing—and I flatter myself that I manage to convey at least a sense of the underlying conceptual substance, but—"

"That reminds me," I said. "I meant to ask you if you might have your current work written up so that—"

"Well, that's the problem," he said quickly, and a troubled expression crossed his face. We had stopped halfway down the corridor, in front of a heavy metal door, and he was pulling out a large key ring. "I had expected by now to have this in publishable—not to say published—form. I shouldn't, strictly speaking, be making a public announcement at this point—before publication, I mean. But," and his eyes darted about, "we need funding. That's the key." He had paused thoughtfully with his hand on the door, and now he observed with apparent surprise the key that he had inserted in the lock.

"A rough draft would be fine," I persisted. "We're all extremely interested in what you're accomplishing here. I don't think most people appreciate the significance of what you're trying to do." I wondered whether I would ever find out, even in general terms, what in fact he was trying to do.

"No one understands what I'm trying to do," he echoed enthusiastically. "Not even the people I work with. It's amazing."

He pushed open the heavy door, and we stepped into the laboratory. The laboratory was certainly amazing. It was a large warehouselike area with a double-height ceiling which must have represented more than half the building's volume, and although it had evidently been extensively cleaned up for the day's events, it retained an appearance of thorough chaos. There were tables everywhere. Tables with desk-top computers; tables with machine tools, with circuit boards, with plumbing. The center of the room was filled with a massive metal ring ten feet across. Through it and around it were coiled further tubes and wires, and around them yet other wires and tubes, which finally spilled out into the rest of the room, connecting to a dozen inexplicable projects on various tables.

When I was a child, computers were referred to as "electronic brains." This would be the intestines.

"Jesus," I said.

"I wanted to show you this," Wachs said, oblivious in his enthusiasm. He led us over to a table where an extraordinarily thin, ascetic-looking man wearing a jacket and tie and running shoes was staring at a computer display filled with a grid of continually changing numbers. He did not acknowledge our presence.

"I don't know if it's obvious to you what's going on here," said Wachs jubilantly, "but right now, at this moment, a magnetic field is being generated—an enhanced magnetic field, EMF, we call it. You could say that an EMF is to a normal magnetic field as a laser is to normal light waves. Of course, that's only a metaphor," he added in a tone indicating that he did not hold metaphors in much esteem.

"Wait," he said, turning to the man at the computer. "Put up the primary matrix so they can see exactly what's happening." The man gave Wachs a brief skeptical look and punched a key. All the numbers changed at once. "You see? To put it in the crudest possible layman's terms, the momenta of the particle spins and orbits are constituting a field which is continuously altering the internal structure of those very particles and yielding a net gain in energy sufficient to maintain the field itself. Of course that's quite misleading," he added glumly. "It's probably simpler, really, not to think of it as matter or energy at all, but just as equations." Wachs waved his hand expansively to indicate that he was talking about the mass of equipment in the middle of the room.

The man at the computer punched a key, and the screen filled with percent signs.

"Fuck," said the man.

"Wait a minute," said Anne. There was a glint in her eye. "Do you mean to say that you're generating atomic energy right here in this room—fission or fusion, or whatever you call it?"

The man at the computer pushed more keys, and the screen went blank.

"Well, you wouldn't really want to characterize it as fission or fusion—although you could describe it as subatomic decay—or even generation, I suppose. Continous change would—"

"But whatever it is is actually going on right there," she insisted, "in that . . . device?" She pointed sternly at the intestinal mass of tubes and wires.

"Yes. That's it. It's extraordinary, isn't it? Right there. Well, actually, a lot of what you're looking at isn't really involved. Some of that equipment is related to work we were doing on magnetic containment. Quite a lot of it could be removed, actually."

As a practical matter, it was hard to imagine how anything could be removed.

"That's fascinating," Anne said, smiling. Wachs in his innocence probably imagined it was a friendly smile, but Anne thought she was on to something. "Could you tell me what safeguards you have against radiation leakage or a nuclear mishap?"

She had a point, in a way: there didn't seem to be any kind of shielding around the equipment. People like Wachs are apt to get caught up in the intellectual delights of whatever problem they are working on and lose track of things like not enough heat in the room, or lethal radiation.

"There's no more radiation here than you would encounter around an average radio transmitter," he reassured her.

I wondered briefly what an "average" radio transmitter might be like, and whether it would meet my standards for personal hygiene, but I doubted that there was really anything to worry about. Wachs and his employees all seemed healthy enough. I was more interested in finding out what they were doing and whether it might be of some value.

"What I want to understand," I said, "is about the quantity of heat or light or whatever it is being emitted by this process, relative to—"

"Electricity," he said. "It's generating electricity directly." He was almost dancing up and down with excitement. "No one will believe this." For some reason, that thought seemed to please him enormously. "Even with this equipment here, we can bring the process to a stable level where it generates as much energy as it consumes. It's actually driving itself now. The only exogenous energy is what powers the control system. Except for that, it could run itself virtually forever."

Right there. I should have paid more attention. I knew that someone was about to shut off power to the building, or at least to give it what used to be called the old college try. And this man was telling me that he had some loopy subatomic process roaring away, which sustained itself but whose control system used outside power. It is important to listen to exactly what people are saying. Just out of good will or good citizenship I might have made Wachs focus on what was about to happen. Think it through. Thoughtless of me. Easy to see these things with hindsight, easy in retrospect to point to the flaw when you have already watched it shear open into a gaping crevasse. I couldn't know what the consequences were. Still, if I had been a little more interested in doing Wachs a favor. Well, it doesn't matter. Too late now. But I am sorry. For him as much as for myself. Although, really, the man was a lunatic. When they tried, with the help of his utterly uninformed colleagues and suppliers, to reconstruct what he had actually done in that laboratory, it seemed incredible that he had not long ago electrocuted himself and the entire staff of Micro-Magnetics. You can't just pile together equipment like that, one idea on top of another.

"It's an absolutely structured process," he was explaining to Anne, who had begun to grill him about licenses and federal safety standards. "Not like an explosion at all. If I took you through the mathematics, you'd be amazed. It's absolutely beautiful. And really so simple, the whole thing. It's amazing that no one has seen it before, although in a way it's all right there in Maxwell—"

"What I'm trying to understand," I interrupted, "is whether this process, whatever it is, can generate more energy than just what it needs to maintain itself? Can you get more electricity out than you put in? Or is that some sort of theoretical limit?"

"No, no, no. That's not a theoretical limit at all. That's the whole point. It wouldn't be even a practical limit, if we just had the money for a full-scale generator."

People go about saying this sort of thing all the time. Usually the theory turns out to be all wrong, or the machine too expensive to build, or both; but you never know. Anyway, there is nothing to be gained by contradicting people.

"Well, if what you say is true—or even arguable," I assured him, "money shouldn't be much of a problem for you from here on in. At the very least, you'll have endless grants—if not fabulous wealth. Tell me, what sort of fuel does this thing use?"

"Fuel?"

"What sort of matter is it that is having its structure continuously altered or whatever—"

"Dr. Wachs!" The receptionist had tracked us down. Her voice was like doom. "We're going to be nearly fifteen minutes late getting started." She glared.

"Yes, yes," he replied excitedly. "We should get in there right away."

He scurried out of the laboratory with me, Anne, and the receptionist chasing behind. We entered a long, narrow room at the end of the building. A large oval table had been pushed down to one end, and the remaining space had been filled with rows of folding chairs. In the back a slide projector had been set up. Anne insisted on sitting in the front row, which disappointed me since I was half hoping to sneak in a short nap, but she, I suppose, wanted to keep a close watch on the nuclear criminal.

There were roughly two dozen people in the room. A few of them might conceivably have been journalists. More likely, however, all of them were academics. Probably they were all friends or colleagues of Wachs's. Nevertheless, Wachs began by introducing himself and assuring us that he was not going to subject a nonacademic audience to a technical account of his work. A scholarly paper was in preparation and would in the course of time appear in an appropriate journal. And although normally publication of such an article would predate the sort of public announcement he was making today, the significance of his results and the need for support of ongoing research had induced him to present preliminary results informally.

With no warning the lights went out and we found ourselves in total darkness. For an instant I thought that the Students for a Fair World had already struck, but from the startled silence emerged the excited, rapid-fire voice of Wachs, intoning: "Accustomed as we are today to think of magnetism as the vector of spins and orbits of subatomic particles, it is often with considerable astonishment that we discover how entirely differently men at other times in history have viewed the set of phenomena that we tend to group together under the term 'magnetism.' As early as the sixth century B.C., the Greek philosopher Thales observed the extraordinary ability of lodestone to attract other pieces of lodestone, as well as iron."

From the back of the room came a sudden commotion of clicking and whirring, and a picture of a large stone appeared unexpectedly and incongruously at the front of the room.

What in the world was going on? This must be Wachs's idea of how one explains things to people outside one's own field. We were getting part of the lecture course in the History and Philosophy of Science for humanities majors.

I was going to have difficulty sitting through much of this. My hangover was rapidly being intensified to an insupportable level. The contrast between the piercing brightness of the images on the screen and the darkness of the room was aggravating an already evil headache, and every time the slide machine would click and grind, violently wrenching yet another image onto the screen, I would feel a little wave of nausea, a sort of motion sickness. I began to cringe at the advent of each new slide.

"In the year 1785 the Frenchman Charles Coulomb . . ."

Whirr. Clack. An incomprehensible instrument appeared which could have been used as an illustration in the history of anything. Gunnery. Contraception.

After ten or fifteen minutes of this, we were still not out of the eighteenth century. I was sure a lot of important work had been done in the nineteenth century. If I could slip out of the room for a while, I might find a lavatory or go outside and clear my head. I could still be back in plenty of time for the twentieth century. I clambered out of my seat and felt my way to the door. When I pulled it open, the light in the corridor illuminated me, and I felt the gaze of everyone in the room on me. I leaned over to the person sitting nearest the door and apologized in a loud half-whisper.

"Excuse me. Feeling a little bit off. Be right back."

I pushed the door shut behind me and hurried back down the corridor toward the entrance. Just moving around would make me feel better, I thought. I was wrong. There was no one in the reception room now: everyone must be attending the lecture. Perhaps some fresh air, a walk on the lawn. I pushed open the door and stepped out onto the porch. There was a steady, uninviting drizzle. The students, undeterred by the weather, were right there on the lawn in front of me, erecting some part of their fair world. One of them looked at me and waved; he started toward me as if he wanted to ask me something. I waved vaguely back at him and retreated quickly into the building again, locking the door to be safe. I didn't want to talk to anyone. An insupportable wave of nausea flooded over me. Really what I wanted was a lavatory. After that I might come back and curl up on the couch in the reception room. Just for a few minutes. I tried the door to Wachs's office. Locked. I went back into the corridor and pulled open the first door to the right. Janitor's closet. The next door, however, opened into an enormous and quite splendidly equipped bathroom, which had, in addition to all the usual plumbing, an open shower stall and a sauna. There was a stack of freshly laundered towels and along one wall a row of hooks from which hung running suits and other random pieces of clothing. The employees of Micro-Magnetics must have used this as a sort of locker room.

I went to the W.C. and tried to precipitate whatever purgative convulsions my body was capable of. When I was done I felt much better. But my headache was, if anything, worse. I leaned my head into the wash basin and turned on the cold water. Try to clear my mind. The water was too cold and the position extremely uncomfortable. There was a medicine cabinet over the washbasin. In it I located a bottle of aspirin and took three. I noticed that there seemed to be a sort of continuous, high-pitched whining sound just inside the auditory range, but I could not decide whether there was really such a sound or whether it was a sort of overtone incorporated in the pain of my headache. The lights seemed to be swelling and dimming with the throbbing in my temples. The pain in my head was really quite extraordinary. Making it hard to think. I decided there *was* a whining sound, but I couldn't make up my mind whether or not the pitch was actually shifting up and down rhythmically.

I straightened my clothing and looked dully at my own image in the mirror. I realized that my entire body was sweating. I turned and looked at the shower. A quick shower and then back to the press conference. Plenty of time. A bit presumptuous of me to come in and use their bathroom like this. Embarrassing if someone walked in. But they would all be watching the slide show. And it would make me feel much better. I took off my clothes and hung them carefully on one of the hooks. It annoyed me that there were no hangers. Weedy people, scientists, I thought crankily. Soon everyone will be an engineer or a computer programmer and there will be absolutely zero demand for dry cleaning. I should find out who makes dry cleaning equipment and go short. I folded my socks and underwear and set them carefully on my shoes. I stepped into the shower and ran it first warm, then cold, then very hot, then cold again, then off. I felt very much better. I stepped out of the shower and, taking a towel off the stack, began slowly to dry myself.

Somewhere within the building an electric bell went off. It was the kind of harsh, overwhelming bell that announces the end of class at school— everyone closes notebooks, gathers up books, retracts ballpoints, shuffles out into the corridor—and for an instant I thought inanely that Wachs's lecture must have ended. No, it was some sort of alarm bell. It went on ringing, like one of those burglar alarms that go off in the middle of the night and ring continuously, sometimes for hours, until the shop owner or the police come. It is always a marvelous relief when one of those alarms suddenly stops. I wished this one would stop. I really did feel much better, I told myself, but my head was still not at all clear. Above the sound of the bell there was still that painful throbbing whine. Someone ran by in the corridor, shouting something.

All the commotion would have something to do with the Students for a Fair World. Probably they had shut off power to the building. No, the lights were still on. Perhaps just the power to the laboratory. Or perhaps they had simply set off a fire alarm. That would make sense. What they mainly wanted was to get everyone outside so they would have an audience for their demonstration. As I thought about it, I was more and more disinclined to give them that satisfaction. I could hear a lot of shouting and slamming of doors throughout the building; people were trooping down the corridor. Really, all this was nothing more than a school fire drill. If I stayed out of sight, I might spend the entire time comfortably inside while everyone else was herded out into the cold drizzle. I went over and locked the door by which I had entered the bathroom. To make sure, I hid my clothing under one of the sweatsuits. The thought of coming out so well compared to my fellows made me feel better.

I pulled open the door to the sauna and peered inside. It was warm; someone must have used it that morning. I turned the heat all the way up and went out and got four towels from the stack. I laid out two of them as a sort of mat on the cedar bench which ran around the inside of the sauna and folded up the other two to serve as a pillow. I unscrewed the light bulb inside the sauna and lay down in the darkness to let the heat soak through me.

I must have lain there for ten or fifteen minutes, floating between consciousness and sleep. With the door closed the sound of the alarm bell was pleasantly muffled, and the commotion in the rest of the building seemed remote. I was therefore startled when the door I had locked clattered open and a man burst into the center of the lavatory. I raised myself on my bench inside the sauna and peered out at him through the window of the sauna door. He held what must have been a passkey in his hand and wore on his head a white helmet with some sort of insignia. It was presumably prescribed dress for running up and down corridors during fire drills—or perhaps he had it in case of aerial attack. He shouted officiously, "Anybody here? Anybody here!" The real unpleasantness of emergencies is often not the emergencies themselves but the occasion they provide for normally tolerable people to dress up in uniforms and bustle about issuing arbitrary commands. I remained silent. The man, from his position in the center of the room, peered intently around and found nothing out of order. Evidently he could not see me in the unlit sauna. He turned, walked partway across the room, and for some reason peered down into the bowl of the W.C. Fortunately, I never forget to flush. A good traditional upbringing always stands you in good stead. He continued across the room and pulled open another door, which seemed to open directly into Wachs's office.

"Anybody here? Anybody here!" Apparently not. He returned back through the lavatory, closing each door behind him.

During this intrusion, it came to me for the first time just how unpleasantly embarrassing it would be if I were discovered now. It is normal enough when visiting someone's home or place of business to use the W.C.—and to use the washbasin as well, in a limited way, to wash up—but people do not generally expect you to barricade yourself in the bathroom and take extended showers or naps in the sauna, should there be one. It would seem a bit arrogant, I supposed, no matter how diffident and vague my explanation. And by now I had probably broken some set of fire regulations which someone or other was sure to take very seriously. Worse than that, the fellow in the official helmet would want to force me, for my own safety, to vacate the building. I had a vision of myself standing naked on the lawn, clutching my clothing ridiculously in my hands, while overprivileged children lectured me on my political failings. It was a press conference of sorts: there might even be a photographer to capture the moment. On the other hand, the man with the helmet had come and gone. It now seemed pretty certain that I would get away with it, entirely unnoticed, and I felt particularly smug at the thought that, unlike everyone else, I would not have to stand foolishly in the rain.

The only unpleasant thing was the incessant sound of the alarm bell and the pulsating whine above it.

When I no longer heard any movement in the corridor, I climbed out of the sauna and turned on the shower again, starting it very cold and gradually adjusting the temperature upward. I hoped that by the time I was finished, all the revolutionary confusion would be concluded. Surely everyone else was out of the building by now. I wondered if I would be able to hear the simulated atomic blast. I turned off the shower and began drying myself.

With no warning the lights went out and the alarm bell mercifully stopped. Evidently the revolutionary vanguard had managed after all to cut off power to the building. Undismayed, but inconvenienced by the darkness, I groped my way to the door into Wachs's office and pulled it open. That admitted enough sunlight so that I could dress. With the alarm bell extinguished I noticed more clearly that unpleasant, piercing, whining sound. Some piece of equipment must still be operating. I got my clothes on and used the mirror over the washbasin to comb my hair as well as I could in the semidarkness.

Then I was startled by a series of short, powerful horn blasts of the type you hear in submarine movies—and conceivably even in real submarines. As I recovered from my surprise, I think I laughed out loud. How and why had they ever assembled all these improbable noisemakers? And what were they meant to communicate?

As I think back on it, I wish they had found one which could have communicated to me a sense of blind unreasoning terror—something to drive me in panic from the building.

Taking what would turn out to be a last casual look at myself in the mirror, I went into Wachs's office, where I would be able to see what was going on through the windows. Staying in the center of the room to avoid being noticed by anyone outside, I surveyed the pageant unfolding before me. I felt again pleased with myself. If it weren't for that excruciating whining sound. There was a fire truck on the lawn just beyond where the drive turned toward the parking lot, although as far as I could tell there was no sign whatever of any fire. Well, if there was in fact a fire, it would be an easy matter for me to get out: I was on the ground floor. There were two state police cars: Anne and the Students for a Fair World must have been relieved to see them. There were several people with white helmets. Everyone with any kind of uniform appeared to be gesticulating or shouting instructions, but none of them seemed to have succeeded in establishing any authority or order. The people who had been driven out of the building milled forlornly about on the lawn, glumly looking at the Students for a Fair World or at the fire engine. A steady drizzle descended on them all.

Evidently, the atomic blast had not yet taken place. A few yards from the building the demonstrators had laid out a sort of metal tabletop which was apparently to be the site of the explosion. In the middle of it there was some sort of device nearly two feet high, covered with plastic, perhaps to keep it dry. From under the plastic, electric wires ran approximately ten yards to a spot on the lawn where most of the demonstrators had clustered around an assortment of cartons and random equipment. Several of them were hunched over and seemed to be attaching something—presumably some sort of detonating device—to the wires.

Two of the young people in the group were attempting to stuff a cat into the cage that had been in the van. The cage, in my opinion, had been too small even for the guinea pig, and the cat seemed quite a lot larger. You would have wanted its full cooperation to get it through the door of that cage; but whereas guinea pigs are apparently rather tractable creatures, cats are not. This cat in particular seemed entirely disinclined to function as a guinea pig—much less as a symbol of all victims of capitalist oppression and nuclear death technology. It writhed, clawed, and snarled. Gradually it captured the full attention of the bedraggled crowd on the lawn, who seemed both dismayed by the treatment of the beast and confused by its description on the banner as a guinea pig.

Eventually they had the cat rammed more or less inside with the door shut, although it quite filled the cage and its legs protruded angrily out in all directions. Then they removed the cover from the mechanism on the metal table, revealing an elaborate sculpture of pipes and tin cans and wiring, and placed the cage on top.

Carillon now stepped out from the group of revolutionaries and raised a megaphone to his lips. For the benefit, presumably, of those who did not know how to read, he intoned the words prominently displayed on the banner: "The destruction by nuclear holocaust of a guinea pig representing all innocent victims of capitalist oppression and nuclear death technology. We are all guinea pigs!" Through the closed window it was difficult for me to hear even his amplified voice, and I stepped closer to a window, although I kept discreetly to one side of the frame. To be perfectly honest, I wanted to see the explosion. For that matter, everyone on the lawn was watching just as intently. When you come right down to it, people of all political persuasions love an explosion. Although I, for one, found the inclusion of the cat distasteful.

"We live in a society," Carillon continued, "driven by greed." Apparently the sogan on the banner was only the text: we would have to listen to the entire sermon now before we could see the fireworks. I prayed that he would hurry: the whining noise was becoming insupportable. Perhaps I should leave the building after all. "A world in which people are valued less than profits and property."

At this point Wachs appeared, charging ludicrously across the lawn as fast as his plump legs would carry him. He seemed very angry, frenzied even. He had, I suppose, reason enough. He was headed straight for Carillon, whom he evidently held personally responsible for whatever disruption and damage was taking place. Carillon, noting in time the approach of the capitalist oppressor, cut short his address and shouted, "ZERO!"

The people on the lawn instinctively turned their heads away from the anticipated blast, raised arms, or stepped back. The demonstrators clustered around the detonator contracted inward as the igniting switch was thrown.

There came the wonderfully satisfying sound of a very large firecracker—an order of magnitude better than a cherry bomb—resounding through the trees.

But the startling thing was that the complicated device surmounted by the caged cat, on which all our gazes had been riveted, remained absolutely as it had been. It turned out to be a perfectly safe place to keep a cat. Instead, one of the cartons next to the detonator exploded dramatically. Perhaps they had mistakenly wired up some spare bomb which they were holding in reserve—I never understood precisely what their error was. But this is one of the problems with liberal arts education. These people were probably all English majors and should never be allowed to handle explosives, or do close work of any kind.

Everyone's gaze shifted to where the explosion had actually occurred. From the blasted carton a splendid column of black smoke rose straight up almost eight feet into the air and began to spread out in the familiar mushroom form. The proportions did not seem quite right—the column was too long and slender—but on the whole, the effect really was quite impressive. Someone had put some effort into the thing, and in conception it was a definite success, even if the execution had been a bit sloppy.

All around the explosion, whether from the actual force of the blast or more likely from the surprise of having bombed themselves, the demonstrators shot out like jack-in-the-boxes in every direction. Although I couldn't be sure, given the general confusion and prevailing dress standards, it seemed to me that one of them looked a bit ragged down one side. There was blood, and his clothing and perhaps his arm seemed to be chewed up in an ugly way.

Wachs, who had stopped in his tracks for the duration of the explosion, shrieked something I could not make out at Carillon and raged over to the device under the banner. He seized the cage containing the cat and slammed it angrily against the bomb mechanism, breaking off parts of it. Carillon, outraged in turn by this destructive attack on his unused bomb, charged over and began shouting at Wachs. Everyone on the lawn watched them in fascinated silence.

That horrible whining noise, which I thought had begun to subside, now suddenly swelled to a new level of intensity, and it seemed to me that from the direction of the building there was an eerie glow illuminating the figures on the lawn. Wachs looked up at the building and an expression of horror filled his face. It may be that in that instant he became the one person who understood—perhaps the only person who would ever understand—what was about to happen. He drew the cage back over his shoulder and, screaming at the top of his lungs, "You *asshole!*" he slammed it as hard as he could against Carillon's head. The cage flew free of Wachs's hand and went banging along the ground, breaking open. The cat exploded from it and set off in a frantic run toward the building. Carillon staggered back from the force of the blow. He held his hand to his face, which had been torn open by the cage and was bleeding freely. He was staring at Wachs with an expression of amazed horror. I could see his mouth forming the words: "You must be out of your fucking mind!"

The two of them were momentarily motionless as they stared at each other with aggrieved rage. The unbearable piercing noise in the background—I knew now I should have to flee the building, it was becoming so painful—subsided again slightly and then swelled once more to a new, overwhelming, mind-splitting intensity. At the same time the quality of the light shifted again, illuminating everything in an unearthly brilliant glow.

As the noise and the light incredibly elevated themselves once more, Carillon's face and Wachs's face suddenly contorted into final, unspeakable agony and, as if in echo, expressions of horror appeared on the faces of Anne and all the others watching in safety in the background. Then I saw—it was the last thing I saw or remember—the banner, the bomb, and the flesh of Wachs and Carillon bubble brilliantly into electric flame.

THE MORNING ARRIVED AS USUAL. UNPLEASANT. JESUS, THE SUN IS BRIGHT. Like being poked in the eye. Both eyes. Must have left the damn curtains open. Roll over and try to find a pillow to cover my head. Sound of sirens outside. Whole body aches. Head and eyes most of all. No pillow. Not even in my bed. I was lying on the carpet, and I realized with distaste that I had slept in my clothes. I must have passed out on the floor the night before. Have to stop drinking so much. Not worth it. These mornings. What had I done the night before? My mind was not working. Excruciating headache. Brutal sun. Not a siren: a cat howling somewhere. I tried to form in my mind a floor plan of my apartment and locate my position in it. Must be on the living room floor. Except the sun rises in the east. Who was I with last night?

Suddenly my mind filled with the final, pulsing vision of Wachs, Carillon, and the bright red banner of the Students for a Fair World all transfigured horribly into flame.

Jesus.

I was wide awake now. I cannot possibly communicate the incomprehensible horror of that moment. I could make no sense of what I saw. I was lying on my belly looking more than twenty feet straight down into a large empty pit. It was like waking up to find yourself dangling from the ledge of a third-story window. But I couldn't see what sort of ledge I was resting on or what was preventing me from plunging to my death. Evidently not much, because even when I turned my head—ever so carefully—I couldn't see anything supporting me at all. This heightened my terror to the point of panic. My heart was pumping like a trapped rabbit's. I had somehow to keep control of myself, hold down the terror. I had to think out exactly what my situation was, what I should do.

First of all, I had to keep absolutely as still as possible to keep from slipping off and plummeting to the bottom. I would systematically inventory my surroundings, not letting the fear flood me. Twisting my head very slowly and only a few degrees, I surveyed the cavity over which I was somehow suspended. It seemed to have been excavated with incredible care to create a perfectly smooth round basin nearly a hundred feet across and, at the deepest point in the center, about forty feet in depth. The surface of the basin seemed to be lined with charred dirt and rocks, but it was difficult to be certain because of its extraordinary smoothness. In a band ten feet wide all around the rim of the pit, the earth had been burnt and all vegetation incinerated. But immediately behind this charred perimeter the grass grew green and the trees bloomed, untouched by whatever had happened. I was suspended—I still could not determine how—at a level slightly higher than that of the surrounding lawn and roughly halfway between the rim and the center of the pit.

Barely holding down the nausea and terror, I tried to put everything together. I knew roughly where I was. I recognized the lawn, the trees, and the drive. This had been the site of MicroMagnetics, Inc. Where the building had stood there was now nothing but a vast hole in the ground. I concluded that there had been an explosion which had left an enormous—and somehow utterly smooth—crater. The heat or radiation from the blast had evidently incinerated everything for another ten feet beyond the perimeter of the crater, to form an absolutely perfect circular band around it. As for me, I had somehow been thrown free of the blast and had landed on something. What? A tree perhaps. Like someone in a bad film who hurtles off the edge of a hopeless cliff and lands fortuitously on a lone shrub several feet below, to dangle over the abyss.

It didn't quite make sense. Everything within the spherical range of the blast seemed to have been absolutely obliterated: there was not the slightest trace of the building or its contents. But hadn't I been in the building? And do explosions in the real world leave perfectly round craters smooth as glass? And above all, what had I landed on, and how could I get down? Why was no one here to rescue me?

Everything seemed eerily still and deserted. There was only the unearthly, incessant wailing of a cat somewhere. But Anne and the others had been standing safely beyond the range of the explosion. There had been dozens of people. Firemen, policemen. Fire engines. Where was everyone? Why had they left me here?

I tried a cry of "Help!" But even in my state of near panic, I knew that it was a poor effort. What did it matter? If anyone were there, they would see me suspended out in the open over this vast cavity.

I would have to figure out how I was suspended, what I was perched on. I tried, without moving the rest of my body, to tuck my head down to get a look at my body and whatever it was perched on. But no matter how far down I forced my head, I couldn't seem to get a view of myself—or anything else. Strange, because I could feel something like a carpeted floor against my face. I slid my hands carefully around until they were under my chest, as if I were about to do a push-up. Very cautiously I raised my upper body and slid my knees forward until I was on all fours. I paused to make sure my position was stable and then tilted my head down to see what I was kneeling on. I saw nothing whatever except the opposite side of the crater, and this incomprehensible visual result produced an instantaneous, dizzying wave of nausea: I felt that I was tumbling forward in a somersault through space. I think I must have shrieked and thrown my arms out in an instinctive attempt to grab hold of something. This left me grotesquely sprawled, but I saw at once that I had exactly the same view, the same position relative to the crater, as before. And I still had the tactile sensation of lying on a carpeted floor. I had in these few seconds become horribly seasick. I thought that whatever I was kneeling on was rocking unsteadily back and forth, but I couldn't be sure, and I fixed my gaze on the edge of the crater while I tried to pick myself up. Less carefully now, but with even greater terror, I pushed myself up again onto all fours and then to a kneeling position. I kept my hands on the floor—it absolutely felt like a carpet—for extra balance.

I repeated the experiment with as much deliberate calm as I could muster: I shifted my gaze in a gradual arc from the crater rim in front of me down to my legs and whatever floor supported them. Again my gaze encountered nothing but the crater bottom far below. Again this created a sensation that I was tumbling head over heels. But this time I held myself steady until I knew I must be looking directly at my legs. No legs! Jesus! I shrieked again. It came to me instantly that both my legs must have been blown off. Jesus. I must be dying. "Help here! Jesus!"

On the other hand it also came to me that I was kneeling, or anyway it felt as if I was kneeling. I remembered reading somewhere that people who lose limbs go on having or imagining sensations in the missing limbs. But it didn't make any sense. My mind was inundated with panic: my thoughts were colliding in total chaos. I had to get myself under control and think out my situation. I shut my eyes to gather my wits. This produced no change whatever. I could still see everything with perfect clarity, no matter how tightly I squeezed my eyelids shut. It was horrible, but nothing could have added to my sense of horror at that moment, and it produced in me a sort of grotesque amusement. People are forever having arms and legs blown off in sensational accidents, but I couldn't recall a case of eyelids being blown off. Keeping my left hand on the ground for balance, I brought my right hand tentatively up to my face. With my fingertips I felt the area around the eyes. Eyebrows all right, not burnt away. Gently I touched the right eye with my forefinger. Definitely an eyelid. I could feel it move. I could feel the eyelashes.

There was another odd thing: I couldn't see the finger. Or the hand. I covered both eyes with the hand. There was absolutely no change in my field of vision. The sun was higher now and I could see everything around me—trees, lawn, bright blue sky—just as clearly as ever before in my life.

More clearly, perhaps. Trembling, I reached down and felt my missing legs. It seemed that they were intact and in the appropriate place. I straightened up so that my weight was on my knees, and ran my hands over my entire body. It was all there—clothed, furthermore, in the usual business suit. Still, no matter how I turned my head or focused my eyes, I could see nothing of myself. In fact, there was nothing whatever to be seen anywhere within the spherical area of the crater. I could feel myself to be materially intact, and I was conscious and thinking after a fashion. And I was dimly aware of hearing myself whimper inarticulately. But then, I could plainly see that I was no longer material at all. I simply could not make my mind work; the situation was too terrifying and illogical. Trying to think clearly was like trying to run in waist-high water. But finally, in a flash of dreadful insight, I arrived at an explanation which covered all the facts. Evidently, I was dead.

I had, for one reason or another, not given much serious thought to the afterlife anytime recently. Probably not since childhood. Random images of winged angels on clouds, demons tending fires, collided in my mind. Abandon all hope! Done! Because all these vulgar images of haloed saints and pearly gates were like shooting stars lighting up momentarily against an infinite black universe of despair. Despair at a life not so well lived, including doing those things which I ought not to have done. And not those which I ought to have done. A shallow life, filled with wasted afternoons and evenings. And days, weeks, and years. There was a sort of celestial judge, I recalled, consigning souls to their final abodes. If there were two choices, I reasoned dimly, the outlook was poor. The headache, nausea, and plain terror I felt were inconsistent with the basic idea of paradise. You couldn't have headaches in heaven. The Catholics, it seemed to me, had some other possibility—Purgatory, or Limbo. But for some reason I pictured that as a vast version of one of those rooms filled with sleeping babies in maternity wards.

But I could not have reached any sort of final destination. I was still at MicroMagnetics. The former site of MicroMagnetics. It flitted through my mind that MicroMagnetics, Inc., no longer had any financial prospects worth calculating. I was right here where my life had been brought to an end. It must be, I reasoned, that I was whatever it is that people call a ghost. I knew even less about ghosts than about heaven and hell. An image of the Flying Dutchman floating off the Jersey coast formed and dissolved in my mind. Ruddigore. As far as I can remember there has never been a time, even in my earliest childhood, when I believed in ghosts. I could never abide people who believed, or pretended to believe, in ghosts. I have never understood the appeal of ghost stories. In fact, I have never understood the point of ghosts. Usually they seem to be doomed to wander the earth restlessly for ages—which, when you stop to think about it, is exactly the existence that most people choose for themselves insofar as

longevity and wealth permit. Or else they are condemned to remain for
centuries at the scene of some terrible event in their own lives. The latter
fate seemed to fit my own immediate situation quite well, actually. Although to haunt New Jersey through the ages seemed an odd doom.
Still, it was an improvement over the possibilities that had been running
through my mind moments before. An extraordinary improvement. A
world of difference.

My mood picked up a bit. My heart was still whirring like a wind-up toy
and I was still trembling, but I felt as if I had struggled to the surface of
the uncontrollable terror in which I had been drowning. The ghost hypothesis gave me some frame of reference, however distasteful. If I had
to be an entity in which I had not previously believed, "angel" would
have been more satisfactory. "Ghost" lacked theological dignity. But the
status of angel was clearly beyond hope now. And, in any case, the whole
question was surely far too complex to be described with words like "angel" and "ghost," which represented only the crude notions of uncomprehending mortals. Apparently I would have time to consider these
sublime issues. There was even the possibility—I hardly dared formulate
it in my mind—of some sort of immortality in my present form. Or at least
of some existence of a duration incomparably greater than I could have
expected in my previous form.

Come to think of it, how *would* I seek answers to these questions?
Looking around me, the world seemed as opaque as ever, its ultimate
meaning, if any, obscured by the trees and sky and other random things
blocking my view—and by my own shifting moods and fragmentary
thoughts. How would I learn of the conditions and responsibilities of my
new existence? Would I be coming into contact with other immaterial
beings? Also, how would I slake my awful thirst? With a pang of horror
I thought that the thirst might be the beginning of some eternal punishment—for overindulgence, no doubt. I should try to find some water and
see if I could drink. Could I move about? How? And if I could float in
midair forty feet above the bottom of this crater, why not a hundred feet
or ten feet?

My mood plummeted again. I was kneeling on a carpeted floor, and
the rules for moving about on it were exactly the same as they had always
been. Putting this hypothesis to the test, I leaned forward and explored
the floor around me with my hands. Without any particular destination,
I began to inch forward on all fours. Nothing to look at but the dizzying
sight of the crater surface far below. I stopped and, bracing myself with
my hands, carefully, slowly, raised myself to a standing position. I stood
in place for several seconds, keeping my gaze fixed on the surface of the
crater, since there was nothing closer to look at, trying to get my balance
but feeling the whole time as if I were about to pitch over in one direction
or another. Sickening. Then, because there was nothing else to do, I slid

my feet forward over the carpet in one, two, three, four tiny, cautious, shuffling steps, groping in front of myself with extended arms. The feeling was indescribably eerie. I was moving my body just as always: I could feel myself shuffling across the floor. But I could not see anything happening. I could not see anything at all but the edge of the crater yards away. My left hand encountered a desk. I slid my hands along the edges to get a sense of exactly where it was. I ran my fingers over its surface: it was covered with papers and books, all perfectly intact but utterly invisible. I was in Wachs's office. Everything was intact; everything was exactly as before: the carpet, the desk, me. The only difference was that everything was absolutely invisible.

Now, people may become ghosts, or angels. They may go to an eternal reward. They may, for all I know, play harps and float above the clouds arrayed in radiant vestments. On that morning, in that incomprehensible and terrifying situation, I entertained all sorts of extravagant and unlikely ideas. But even then I knew there could not be an afterlife for desks or broadloom. No theological purpose, however mysterious, would be served. Some altogether extraordinary but drably logical catastrophe had transformed me and my immediate surroundings, leaving us absolutely invisible but otherwise unimproved.

However fantastic this conclusion might seem in the abstract, I saw at once that it was the least fantastic explanation of my situation that fit all the facts. After all the ridiculous and terrifying things I had been imagining, it was a relief to have solved the problem and to have arrived at what by comparison seemed like a straightforward, common-sense understanding of what had happened. Beyond that, I was not sure whether I should feel joy or despair—or what I should do next. I was not sure of very much at all. I was trembling. I had to stop and think this out.

Keeping my left hand on the desk, I carefully inched my way around it, located the chair with my right hand, and sat down. It was a leather swivel chair, and from it I could survey my entire surroundings—insofar as they were visible. I had to fight down the panic and make myself take a long, careful, rational look all around. The sun was up well over the horizon now. It was a beautiful, bright, cloudless morning, and I could see everything with extraordinary clarity. Even beyond the range of the explosion—it hadn't been an explosion, really—something seemed quite different. For one thing my vision seemed subtly altered, sharper than . . . How long had I been lying here unconscious? Probably since the morning before. Perhaps twenty hours. Look at everything and think it through.

The main thing was that what I had perceived as a crater was not a crater at all: it was evidently a spherical area in which everything had been rendered invisible but remained perfectly solid. The sphere included all of the MicroMagnetics building together with a good deal of shrubbery, lawn, and earth around it. In fact, as I and others would learn several hours later, this was not quite correct. The sphere had a hollow core: at its center, where Wachs's equipment had stood, everything within a radius of fifteen feet had been absolutely obliterated. But then, sitting trembling at Wachs's desk, I still assumed that everything within the sphere had suffered the same fate as I and the desk and the chair—that is, it was exactly as before, but unseeable.

Unseeable by me, at least. I considered the possibility that the only change had been to my vision, so that I could not see objects near myself, but everyone else would be able to see them perfectly. No, that seemed the least logical of all the improbable explanations I could contrive. You could not alter someone's vision in such a way that he could see *through* other objects. Furthermore, the boundary of the sphere within which everything was invisible to me remained fixed no matter how I moved. No, it must be the objects that were altered, not my vision. Or perhaps the objects and my vision both. It was hard to think straight about these possibilities, but that seemed like a logically consistent alternative: an unaffected human being might be able to see everything; only I, or another altered person in the sphere, would be unable to see the altered matter.

Could there be another human being here?

My mind filled again with the vision of Wachs and Carillon bursting into flame. I knew with horrible certainty that neither of them had survived in any form. Looking out ahead of me I judged that they had been standing somewhere on what was now the charred perimeter encircling the apparent crater rim. In that band there was nothing but ash and cinder, not even the form of a tree; everything had been incinerated. All the other people had been standing farther out, where everything was untouched and exactly as before. Not quite as before: there was something different. Perhaps the fence in the background—I didn't remember a fence. But someone else might have remained in the building, like me. Like that damned cat. If only that cat would stop howling, I might be able to think more clearly. No, there would not be anyone else left in the building. They had been quite thorough about clearing everyone out. Why, I began to ask myself, had I insisted on remaining? I alone. Never mind. No point in going over these things.

I experimented with the objects on the desk before me. I flipped through the pages of a book. I rapped a pen sharply on the desk top and listened to the clear tapping sound. I found a stapler and stapled together some papers. It all worked perfectly. I cannot tell you how uncanny it felt touching, holding, manipulating those objects without being able to see them, or myself, or anything else within twenty feet. The sounds and tactile sensations floated in front of me somewhere in thin air as if in another dimension. I didn't know where to focus my eyes; I felt again a mounting nausea. I wished I could close my eyes.

My head ached excruciatingly. My entire body ached. With another dreadful shock of understanding, I realized that I must, almost certainly, be dying. God, I hoped that when they rescued me, they could see me somehow. How otherwise would they be able to give me medical help? I must be dying. I hoped not. Even in this horrible form I hoped that I could survive somehow. I had no idea what might have happened to my body. Leaning forward in the chair, and beginning with my feet, I ran my hands methodically over my entire body, trying to detect any tangible injury. Nothing, thank God, although how could you feel the effects of radiation with your hands? Even my clothing seemed to be absolutely intact. I loosened my necktie. As I ran my hands across my belly I realized that my bladder was painfully full and that it had been making me horribly uncomfortable for some time. I had to urinate at once. Twenty hours. Thirsty too. Weren't headache, dizziness, and nausea symptoms of radiation poisoning? Probably I had only a few hours. Stop, and think through all the symptoms. But the most urgent thing was that I urinate.

Such is the power of civilization that it never occurred to me that I could do anything other than use the toilet. I knew there was one only a few yards away, but I had to figure out just where it was and then get myself there. I tried to reconstruct in my mind an image of the building from what I could remember of the day before. In the walls in front of me and to my left—I turned my head although there was nothing to see— were windows looking out over the lawn. Along the wall behind me were bookshelves, a blackboard, and the door into the corridor which ran the length of the building. In the wall to my right were two doors: one leading into the reception room and the other, near the rear corner, opening into the bathroom.

It was there that I would have to make my way now. Even if I was dying rapidly, I had to relieve my bladder one last time. Then I could go for help, for whatever that might be worth. With both hands resting on the desk top for balance, I carefully raised myself to my feet and saw to my complete astonishment that I was not alone after all.

Standing upright and looking back toward the other end of the building, my line of vision now extended over the screen of shrubbery and across the parking lot to a large field, which had been incongruously bisected by a chain link fence at least ten feet high with strands of barbed wire coiled along its top. I was certain it had not been there the day before. Protruding above the bushes I could see the roofs of two large vans and a sedan which had been left in the parking lot, but everything else had apparently been cleared away, and the entire area on my side of the fence was deserted and motionless. However, the far side of the fence swarmed with people. At that distance, and with my field of vision interrupted by trees, shrubs, and the fencing, it was difficult to make out exactly what was going on, but I could see that the people were wearing military or police uniforms and that the uniforms were not all the same. There was every imaginable sort of vehicle: jeeps, trucks, tractors, vans, sedans, all in drab, solid colors—grey, white, or khaki—which proclaimed them as government property. I could see people erecting temporary buildings, standing in line to use portable toilets, assembling what looked like radio equipment, walking about with clipboards, but I had no sense of what the purpose of all this activity might be.

They had for some reason built an entirely new access road from the field directly to the far side of the parking lot. At the point where the road intersected the fence, there was a large gate, also made of chain link. As I watched, men were hanging opaque green fabric over the inside of the fence, so that my view of the field full of people and equipment was rapidly being closed off. I turned slowly in place and with a vague apprehension saw that the entire area around me—comprising several acres and including the lawn, the parking lot, and part of the adjoining fields—was encircled with the same metal fencing shrouded with fabric.

I could see that it was all being fenced in, that someone was taking extraordinary pains to ensure that no one could get at or even see from a distance the remains of MicroMagnetics. For some reason it was all going to be a secret. But I did not try to think it through. It felt to me then rather that I was being shut out. The sight of all those people purposively bustling about on the other side of the fence filled me with longing for other human beings. I needed their help. I was mortally ill, probably beyond help—I hardly dared hope that there might be some chance of survival—but I desperately wanted them to come rescue me. I needed their comfort. I was dying.

"Help!" I cried. My voice was thin with fear and strangely closed in. "Over here! Help!"

Nothing. No one turned. No one had heard. No one would come. Soon the last section of fabric would be hung over the fence and I wouldn't even be able to see them. Why were they all way over in that field building roads and fences anyway? Why weren't they here, where there was a genuine disaster, a tragedy, a need, instead of pitching their bloody boy scout camp?

Of course they couldn't hear me. I had to be rational. I was a hundred yards away; my shout was feeble; if they heard anything it would be the howling of that damned cat. Where was that cat? Probably in the next room. With a terrified start I remembered that I was inside a closed building. No one would ever hear me. Or see me. They would never know I was here. Radiation. They must be sealing off the area because of radiation. For months. Years.

I would have to get to them for help. If I could manage it. I was trembling and I felt hopelessly debilitated. I was probably too weak with radiation poisoning to walk that far. Hopeless. Be calm. I would have to try. Calm. I had to urinate first. The pressure on my bladder was unbearable. Once I had urinated, I could try to get out of the building and make my way to human help.

I ran my hands along the edge of the desk to determine the axis of the building, and then, keeping one hand on the desk for balance, I set out across the void, with little shuffling steps, for the bathroom. When I had inched forward several feet, I had to let go of the desk. Horrible. Resist the impulse to drop down on all fours again. Nothing to see for thirty yards. I held my hands out in front of me like someone walking through a dark house and forced myself to watch the nearest rim, which was on my left. That seemed to help my equilibrium a little. I felt as if I were on a tightrope: the more I thought about what I was doing, the more difficult the process of walking became. It came as a startling relief when, after a few more sickening steps, my invisible hands encountered the invisible wall. The cat—I was certain now that it was in the next room—intensified its howling. With more confidence now, I felt my way along the wall until I came to the bathroom door.

Searching with my right hand, I located the doorknob, twisted it, and swung the door open into the bathroom. Keeping hold of the doorknob, I took several steps into the room and groped with my outstretched left hand until I located the washbasin. Then, hanging on to the washbasin with one hand, I reached out and found the toilet. It was difficult to contain myself. Twenty hours. I pulled off my jacket, letting it fall to the floor, yanked my suspenders over my shoulders, pulled open my trousers and undershorts, frantically pushed them down my legs as I twisted around—there was no question of accomplishing this from a standing position—and lowered myself onto the toilet seat. With an exquisite sensation of relief, I released my bladder. Listening to the extraordinary sound of the invisible stream of urine cascading into the invisible toilet bowl, I felt much, much better.

When I was done, I twisted around, found the handle, and pushed it down. The toilet exploded with the familiar flushing sound, but its occurrence in thin air was so eerily ridiculous that I emitted something between a laugh and a sob. All this noise stirred the cat up to a new frenzy of howling. However horrible my situation was, I could see that it was at the same time ludicrous. Really, I was feeling very much better.

I stood up—this time without bothering to hold on to anything—and pulled up my trousers. Remembering the existence of a bottle of aspirin from the day before, I found the door of the medicine cabinet, swung it open, and began poking my right hand along the shelves. I encountered many small objects, some identifiable (shaving brush, tube of toothpaste, toothbrush) and some not. A number of them were sent clattering noisily into the washbasin or onto the floor through blind clumsiness. But I found the aspirin bottle. Or at least I hoped it was the aspirin bottle: it had the right shape. But even assuming it was aspirin, would it be of any help in my oddly altered circumstances? Worth a try. I had a very bad headache. Bad pain of various kinds. The childproof bottle top gave me some trouble, but by the time a little wave of rage had swept over me, I had defeated it. I tilted some tablets into my left palm, carefully counted off three with my right forefinger, and pushed them into my mouth. I always take three, because the directions say to take one or two.

I turned on the cold water and, bending over and pressing my mouth to the tap, washed down the pills. I went on drinking greedily. The water was wonderful. I was, I realized, horribly thirsty. But after about a dozen swallows, the tap ran dry. Why would that happen if the building was intact? Because the water line would have been cut off at the perimeter where everything was incinerated. But there would be a hot water tank. I turned the hot water tap and tepid water came streaming out. I used it to brush my teeth and splash water on my face, and then I drank again, for a long time. I definitely felt better. I even thought about attempting to shave but rejected the idea as unrealistic.

I would go now and get help. But I wanted my jacket, and to my annoyance I had to get down on all fours again and search for it on the floor. I would have to remember not to set anything down casually that I would be wanting again.

When I stood up again, I saw a black sedan moving slowly out of the parking lot and down the access road, away from me. There had been people here! And now they were leaving again! The fencing was now completely covered, and when the car had passed through the only remaining opening and the gate had swung shut behind it, the entire area was completely closed off. Except for the two vans left behind in the parking lot, everything within the fencing had been withdrawn, and everything outside it was screened off from view. There was no movement, no indication of humanity anywhere. Watching the car disappear, I was overcome with desolation, like a man overboard, hopelessly watching a ship sail away toward the horizon.

Then, mysteriously, first one van and then the other began moving behind the shrubbery, turning out of the parking lot and proceeding ever so slowly across the lawn parallel to the front of the building. Both vans were dark grey and had inscrutable, tinted windows, so that it was impossible to make out the occupants. The first was the size of a normal delivery van. The second was more than twice as large; from an opening in its roof an elaborate antenna protruded, and from its rear end strands of heavy cable were unrolling onto the ground behind, like a trail deposited behind some enormous snail. The smaller van halted almost exactly opposite me and thirty yards back from the rim. The second van halted behind it. For several long minutes there was no movement. The effect was somehow sinister, and, rather than feeling jubilant at not having been abandoned after all, I stood there motionless, watching with uneasy fascination.

The front door of the smaller van opened. A muscular black-skinned man with an unsmiling, expressionless face climbed out of the driver's seat and walked back to the other van with an erect military gait. His garish red Hawaiian shirt only heightened the impression that he customarily wore a uniform. A large, almost fat man climbed out of the bigger van and began to talk to him. The second man, too, although he wore elaborately tooled leather boots and a fancy western shirt with little pearl buttons glistening across the front, nevertheless contrived to look like a soldier or a policeman. As he talked, he repeatedly broke into hearty laughter, but his small, squinting eyes remained wary. The black man stood there silent, listening impassively.

After several minutes a third man appeared from around the other side of the van. He was older than the others, in his mid-forties, and wore a dark grey business suit which, having been made for no one in particular, hung loosely over his frame. His hair was cropped extremely short, almost shaved, and the scalp, which despite his athletic bearing was unwholesomely pallid, creased into folds, making his head appear repellently naked. He walked with a precise, almost rigid gait to a door in the middle of the van and stopped. The door abruptly swung open, revealing a short Hispanic man, who said several words and then disappeared back inside, leaving the door open.

The man in the business suit then walked over to where the black man and the cowboy stood, uttered several sentences to which they listened attentively, and then turned away from them. He seemed to be in command: the moment he finished speaking, the other two walked briskly to the back of the smaller van. He remained where he was, ignoring the others once he had set them in motion and staring coldly straight ahead— directly at me, I thought. No, his eyes were moving carefully over the whole site. I still did not know whether he could see the building or whether it was as invisible to him as to me. But I would find out soon, when they rescued me. I would find out exactly what had happened to me. They could not yet know that there was a human being alive here. I should let them know.

"Help!" I called out. No one turned.

The black man and the cowboy had pulled open the back door of the smaller van and were helping a man encased in a large, bulky white suit climb laboriously out. It was the sort of suit that deep-sea divers used to wear. Or astronauts. Or, it struck me unpleasantly, the sort of suit that you see on the evening news when a damaged nuclear reactor is being inspected. It was just as I had feared: there was radioactivity. I was dying, and as that thought filled my mind, I felt myself becoming weaker.

"Over here!" I cried. No sign that anyone had heard. Too many walls in the way. It was pointless to use my remaining strength to shout. In a moment the man in the protective suit would be in the building. I lowered the toilet cover and sat down on it feebly to await my rescue.

My prospective rescuer was unused to his suit. He was moving his arms experimentally and taking small, careful steps forward and backward. At that distance I could see nothing of his face behind his tinted face mask. In one hand he held a sort of metal wand several feet long that was connected by a cable to the bulky midriff of his suit. He waved it experimentally across the ground. It must be a Geiger counter or whatever they use to measure radioactivity. The Hispanic man had appeared again at the door of the larger van, and the other three men were each putting on the sort of earphone and microphone device that television newsmen and football coaches wear. Everyone became very still. They were evidently testing the equipment. Then the man in the business suit nodded, and the astronaut set out.

He proceeded ponderously across the lawn, directly towards me, one slow, deliberate step after another, as if he were on the surface of the moon, sweeping his Geiger counter back and forth in front of his path like some space-age vacuum cleaner.

I awaited his arrival with a mixture of eagerness and despair. I wanted to be rescued. But what difference did it make? I was surely dying. On the other hand, my situation was so extraordinary that it was impossible to be sure of anything, and whatever hope there was would be offered by these people. I wished the man would hurry.

The other three men were clustered on the lawn, unfurling a large roll of papers. They would point at the papers, then look up and point toward me and then point at the papers again. Building plans. They had a set of building plans, and they were going to use them to direct the man in the white suit through the building by radio. Once he was inside the building, where he could hear me, I would shout again.

He reached the edge of the charred band around the rim. He stopped and turned to face the three men on the lawn behind. One of them—the fat one—left the others and disappeared into the van. Several minutes later he reappeared. Why was this taking so long? Then the astronaut nodded awkwardly, like a robot, lifted his arm slightly in a sort of rudimentary salute, and proceeded away from me, following the boundary of the charred band. He waved his Geiger counter over the ashes as he went.

"In here!" I shouted. Why was he going away from me? "Help!"

He continued along the rim. When he had moved a little more than twenty yards away from the point on the circumference nearest me, he stopped and turned toward the others again. A discussion seemed to be taking place. The man in the business suit had a pencil in his hand, with which he was making marks on the plans. Something had been decided upon. The astronaut turned back to face the crater and then, cautiously, he stepped into the charred band and up to the edge. He looked down into the crater for a few moments. He swung the detector slowly out over the edge.

I now knew that everything was invisible to them too, and I was so intent on witnessing the imminent, extraordinary moment of discovery that I nearly forgot my own situation.

The man lowered the detector carefully until the end of it hit the invisible surface of the ground. He pushed on it a little. He tapped all around in a little circle. He pushed again, leaning his weight onto it. He paused and half turned toward the others. They were absolutely still. He turned back to face the edge again.

Then, like a boy testing thin ice, he tentatively swung one foot out over the edge and lowered it onto the invisible surface. He pushed down several times as if expecting to plunge through, and then, with the other foot still poised in the air over visible ground, he shifted his entire weight onto the first foot. Balanced incongruously on one foot in midair, he looked like an acrobat in a clown suit performing an improbably difficult but ultimately silly trick. With his head bent as far forward as his suit would permit, he watched himself carefully bring the second foot down. He paused again, staring down at his own feet. Then, to give the ice a final test, he made a sort of awkward jumping movement, which, because of the suit, did not come to much. Still gazing down intently, he took several more steps out over the crater and stopped. He slowly turned and faced the men on the lawn.

No one moved. He looked truly miraculous standing there in midair. Even I was amazed by the spectacle. For although my own situation was far more extraordinary, it had inherently very little visual impact.

Then I saw that the man in the business suit had begun to speak into his microphone. He made a little gesture toward the crater and looked down at his plans. The astronaut made a clumsy nodding movement and turned around again. He took several more steps toward the center of the crater, waving the detector before him, until it abruptly banged up against the invisible front wall of the building. He moved in closer and slid the detector over the surface as high as he could reach and as far out to each side. Then he bent laboriously at the waist and laid the detector on the invisible ground. He watched it for a moment, as if expecting it to fall after all to the bottom of the crater. He pushed against the wall, testing it, and then began exploring it with his massively gloved hands. Soon he seemed to have located something: he delineated its rectangular contour by moving his hand around it several times. It was obviously a window.

There was a long delay, and I could see that the three men on the lawn were not satisfied with the discovery. They were having an animated discussion in which they referred frequently to the plans. Then, presumably in response to some command, the astronaut pushed himself up flat against the building, facing into it, and extended his arms straight out to the sides along the wall, like a human signpost. This seemed to solve their problem. The man in the business suit indicated with his pencil two invisible points over the crater and drew an imaginary line between them. Evidently they had misjudged the orientation of the building. Perhaps the plans were incorrect, or perhaps they had been misled by the angled path from the parking lot. All three men, enlightened by this information, shifted their positions several degrees, to face the invisible building at the appropriate ninety-degree angle.

The astronaut now picked up his detector again and began to move along the front wall back in my direction. He kept his left hand in contact with the wall, and when he encountered the next window, he again delineated it for the others—to their apparent satisfaction this time. Only a few more steps would put him at the entrance to the building, but at the excruciating rate at which he was progressing, it was impossible to say how long that might take. And then he would have to work his way through the building to me. I felt myself becoming frantic with impatience, and finally I could wait no longer. I stood up and set out to meet him.

I meant to walk, to work my way carefully toward the entrance, but probably I started to run. I had my hands out in front of me to check for walls and doors, but my foot caught on something—a towel or a piece of clothing left on the floor—and I went lurching forward onto the bathroom tiles. I felt a stupefying impact through my entire body and an excruciating pain in the elbow on which I had come down. Damn! Have to take it slowly. I raised myself to my knees, banging my head on the door frame in the process. Damn! Staying on all fours, I crawled pathetically into Wachs's office and along the wall to the door into the reception room.

Still kneeling, I reached up and found the doorknob. I turned it and pulled. No movement. Keeping it turned, I pushed. Nothing. The door was locked. Stay calm. It doesn't matter. They'll get it open.

The man in the protective suit had reached the entrance and was less than ten feet away, so that although two doors separated us, I could see his face now through the tinted face mask. Half leaning forward and half crouching, he located the two steps before the threshold and laid down his Geiger counter again. He began moving his hands over the door. His right hand found what he was looking for, and he made a sort of waving gesture with the other arm. It would be the doorknob. He was having trouble turning it with his bulky, badly articulated gloves. The cat was howling insupportably now. It suddenly occurred to me that the cat must have been watching the man as well, although what it made of the spectacle I could not imagine. Abruptly the man's hand swung forward several inches. He had the door open!

It could not have been open more than a crack, but I found that suddenly I could hear him quite clearly.

"A fucking cat! I swear to God, it's a fucking cat! Can you hear it? It's a fucking cat! There's nothing else it could be! Jesus! A fucking invisible cat!"

He paused, evidently listening to whatever they were saying to him through his earphones. I couldn't hear any of it. "Yes, sir," he was saying. "Sorry, sir. . . . No, sir. This cat is going absolutely *nowhere*. . . . I'm pretty sure it's right at the door. . . . No, sir. No problem. In no way is this cat going *anywhere*."

I was looking straight at the man, right into his eyes. I cannot say why I did not call out to him at that moment. I had been screaming uselessly for help off and on all morning. Now help was here. I had only to speak. But I didn't yet. Perhaps the knowledge that people were at hand whenever I wanted them reassured me enough that I felt I could do without them a little longer. Then, too, I was caught up in the drama of the explorer's progress, and I wanted to see how he would do with the cat. There was no need to interrupt just then. And perhaps—looking back on it, I am not sure—perhaps I was feeling the first pathetic, childish pleasure in my invisibility. I was right there, but they couldn't see me. Why give up the secret just yet?

The man still seemed to be holding the door open just an inch or two. He had retrieved the detector and was pushing it through the crack and twisting it around inside the reception room. For some reason this made the cat abruptly cease howling. I heard the evil hissing sound that cats make when they are angry or desperate.

"Any reading? . . . Still nothing? This whole place is as clean as my elbow. I ought to take this suit off. . . . Yes, sir."

My heart leapt. He seemed to be saying that there was no radioactivity. I almost spoke out to him.

He withdrew the detector and laid it aside. He had one hand on the doorknob and one hand down at the threshold in what must have been the opening between the door and the frame.

"Kitty kitty kitty," he chanted. "Come on, kitty kitty kitty." The cat was emitting a steady hiss. The man's arm slid slowly forward. "Kitty kitty kitty." Suddenly the hand that had been holding the doorknob shot out and down, and the man lunged forward a step. He held his two hands in front of him, the palms facing each other and separated by the thickness of a compressed cat. There was a nasty snarl.

"Got it! I got it! *Easy*, kitty! Easy! Hold it!" The man was inside the building now, precariously stooped over. He clutched his hands violently to his chest in an apparent attempt to pin the struggling cat. He straightened himself with a jerk. He swung his right hand suddenly down onto his stomach where it seemed to writhe for a moment. "Hold it, you fucker!" Then his left hand slapped down to his thigh. He was trying to lift his right leg. Then he swung his entire body violently around to the left and lunged back toward the door. It was difficult to say whether he collided with the door or the frame or both, but he collapsed in an ungainly heap.

"Shit! Oh, Christ, that hurts. . . . The fucker is gone. Shit. . . . Through the door. Sorry. Jesus. . . . It must be headed straight toward you. Try and stop it!"

The men on the lawn, to whom these remarks were presumably addressed, seemed to know that this was not a promising course of action. The large man in the western shirt took a step forward and without much conviction started to chant just loudly enough so that I could make it out, "*Here*, kitty kitty. *Here*, kitty kitty." The other two men stood glumly in place, staring straight ahead at the moaning figure writhing in midair. "*Here*, kitty kitty." I knew nothing about how Kitty was generally with strangers or about the quality of Kitty's previous life, but the last twenty-four hours had certainly been trying for her. It seemed unlikely that Kitty would be seeking human companionship anytime soon. The cowboy tried one more, "Here, kitty," and then, without looking at the others, stepped uncomfortably back into the group.

The man in the spacesuit was continuing to apologize as he slowly picked himself up. "Yes, sir. . . . I understand that, sir. . . . No, sir. You're right. There's no way I can be absolutely sure the cat is out of the building, sir. . . . Yes, sir. I am closing it up, sir. I'm coming right away, sir."

It took me a moment to comprehend that the man was about to leave the building, and when I did, I was instantly overcome with unreasoning panic again. "*Wait!*" I shrieked, more loudly than I had screamed since childhood. "*Help!*" I banged on the door with my fists. "I need help over here!"

The man in white was absolutely motionless. Through the tinted visor I watched his eyes staring past me—through me—blankly mistrustful and afraid. Trying, probably, to collect his wits. He pushed the door open again, stepped warily back inside, and very carefully shut the door behind himself, as if afraid that I might hear him. Then he shouted out in my direction.

"Where are you, buddy? I can't hear you very well."

"Over here," I shouted back. "On the other side of this door." I banged again with both fists by way of illustration. Of course, he couldn't hear me sealed up in his damned spacesuit and with them jabbering at him the whole time through his headset as well. He had stopped moving again and was staring stupidly in my general direction. "For Christ's sake, man, get me out of here! You've got to get this door open! The door is locked!"

Without moving, and still staring warily, he began to speak very softly—but not to me. He seemed to think that, because he could barely hear me, I could not hear him.

"Can you guys hold it for a minute? There's something you should know about here. Jesus! There's a fucking human being in here! Jesus. . . . No, I can't see him! Can you see him?" This last was uttered with a sarcasm tinged with fear. "He seems to be in another room. Says he's locked in. Jesus, this is crazy. I can't hear him very well. He says he wants to get out."

There was a little pause. Then he shouted out to me again. "Can you hear me, buddy?"

"Just barely," I answered, not quite so loudly this time—and not quite so forthrightly. I liked being able to hear half of his conversation without his knowing. Still, it was troubling that my rescuer and I were not establishing a relationship of trust. He was of course on unfamiliar and unsettling terrain. As was I. And my disembodied voice must have been uncanny. And then, the escape of the cat was on their minds. But the fact was that none of them were doing anything to help me. Instead of rushing to my rescue, they were standing back with uncharitable wariness. The astronaut had his back to me now and was facing the three men on the lawn, who were in animated discussion. Abruptly they stopped and looked over in our direction. Evidently something had been decided on. The astronaut turned back toward me and shouted.

"Can you see me, buddy?"

Good question. Someone had come up with a very good question indeed. They had no way of knowing the laws of this little invisible universe. Perhaps the invisible man saw all the invisible objects perfectly, just as before. Perhaps the invisible wall was opaque to him, as a wall should be. Or perhaps not. Or for that matter, perhaps he could see nothing at all: perhaps invisible men are blind.

"Can you see me?"

"No," I answered. "I'm in here." I suppose the escape of the cat was on my mind as well as theirs. Soon, of course, I would have to explain my situation to them accurately. So that they could give me the medical help I needed. But there was no need to get ahead of myself; they didn't need that information now. We would all be cautious.

There was another pause. The men on the lawn were talking to my rescuer in white. Then he shouted to me again.

"Listen, buddy, I can't get the door open by myself. Can you hang on while I get some help? We're going to get you out of there real soon."

Clearly, he couldn't get the door open unless he tried. Without thinking much about how I should proceed, I started to run my hands over the surface of the door, searching again for some way to unlock it myself. Several inches above the doorknob I found a lock cylinder with an empty key slot.

"Are you O.K.?" he added, almost as an afterthought. The question overwhelmed me: I tried to think what an adequate and accurate answer might be, and I felt my eyes filling with tears.

Not receiving an immediate reply, he continued. "Tell me, buddy, how does everything look in there?"

I had no wish to discuss that melancholy topic. "I just want to get out of here," I answered.

"You'll be out real soon," he shouted.

"Get me out of here now! Please!"

"I've got to leave for a minute and get help. You're going to be all right. I'll be right back. You hang on, buddy."

For some reason he slowly backed out of the building, as if I were an animal that might attack him. He closed the door, turned, and walked back onto the visible charred rim of the crater, where he stopped and remained patiently standing.

For nearly ten minutes none of us moved. The men on the lawn stood gazing in my direction; occasionally one would speak to the others and then settle again into silence. Why were they standing immobile, when their only thought should have been to rescue me? They seemed to be waiting for something. I was afraid and angry. But I waited passively. There must be some reason for not breaking open the door at once and getting me out, something I didn't know. Something terrible perhaps. Probably something to do with the radiation—something they had to guard against, or something they had to do to help me.

Then, in the background, I saw the fence gate swing open. A white van with a flashing light on its roof drove through and moved slowly towards the parking lot. The black man walked over to meet it and motioned it up to the other two vans. I had difficulty reading what was written across the front until I realized that the word AMBULANCE had been lettered in mirror reflection. Of course! They had only been waiting for proper medical support, before they tried to move me. My situation was horrible, but I had to stop myself from becoming suspicious and angry and afraid of the people who were trying to help me. Stop myself from becoming insane. Perhaps I already was. I hadn't thought of that. Perhaps that was the explanation.

Whatever the problem was, they would soon have it in hand, thank God. As the van made a final turn on the lawn and stopped, I read on its side MOBILE MEDICAL UNIT, followed by an assortment of random numbers and letters. Only a matter of minutes now. It would be good to talk to another human being, after what I had been through.

The black man walked up to the front door of the van, and the white-jacketed driver got out and began talking to him. Two more men in white medical uniforms climbed out of the rear of the van and joined them. It looked as if they might be arguing. The black man was shaking his head. Then one of the men went back into the van and returned carrying an empty stretcher. The black man took it from his hands and leaned it against the side of the communications van. The conversation seemed to become desultory; the medical personnel peered nervously at the crater and at the man in the bulky suit standing motionless at its edge. Everyone was once again inexplicably immobile. The elation I had felt a few moments before was showing cracks of anxiety. The men on the lawn threw occasional expectant looks at the gate. They were waiting for something else.

At least another five minutes must have passed this way. Then the gate swung open again, and a black sedan pulled through and drove directly up to the other vehicles. The driver climbed out of the sedan, taking an uneasy look at the crater. He went around and opened the trunk, from which he pulled out two large green canvas sacks. At a sign from the black man, he dumped these on the lawn next to the car and returned to the driver's seat. The three medical men, with apparent reluctance, climbed into the sedan. Why were *they* leaving? I needed them. One of them paused halfway into the car, pointed at the medical van, and said something. The black man nodded curtly in reply and turned away. The sedan turned on the lawn and drove off toward the gate. The men on the lawn all watched as the gate opened, admitted the car, and closed again behind it.

The moment the gate was closed, they all turned back toward the crater. The man in the driver's suit immediately stepped back onto the invisible surface and began to make his way back up the invisible steps and through the invisible door of the building. They were keeping everything a secret from the outside world. But how could they keep it a secret once they had to take care of me? I hated the sight of those medical men disappearing behind the gate.

The three men on the lawn were pulling at the sacks. Out of one of them they produced another spacesuit, which the black man began to put on, somewhat uncertainly. Meanwhile the man in the western shirt was opening the other sack. From it he pulled out and carefully unfolded what appeared to be a large net.

A *net*? Goddamn it! They had sent away the only vaguely medical-looking people I had seen and were coming to get me with a stretcher and a *net*!

The original astronaut had made his way back into the next room again. He was shouting at me.

"I'm back, buddy. Can you hear me? We've got medical help here. We'll have you out real quick now. You O.K.?"

"I'm great." I was feeling my way along the wall between the two rooms. I reached the corner formed with the front wall of the building and turned along it. I remembered that there were two, perhaps three, windows. I reached the first of them and lifted. It slid open. I swung first one and then the other leg up over the sill so that I was sitting on it. Then, twisting around so that I was lying with my belly on the sill, I carefully lowered myself out the window until my feet settled on the soft invisible lawn below.

I WALKED OVER TO THE EDGE OF THE CRATER AND STEPPED ONTO THE VISIBLE rim. The surface was charred black and hard like cinder, and I thought I could see it smudge slightly under my steps. It was immediately easier to walk: even though I could not see my own feet, I could now at least see the ground beneath them. As I continued past the charred rim out onto the soft green lawn, I found that I could distinctly see the grass crush each time I placed a foot down and then spring up again as I raised it. This annoyed and disappointed me; I was already beginning to understand that if I was not going to be entirely visible, it was better not to be visible at all. Anything in between was unsatisfactory, combining all the disadvantages of both conditions. But I was encouraged to see that no grass stain seemed to be adhering to the soles of my shoes.

I had not really made any reasoned decision to escape rescue; I was simply acting out of instinct—out of anger and fear, I think. It was the net mainly. The sight of the net had sent me charging through the window and across the lawn, pushing aside the paralyzing terror of sickness and death. I did not yet quite realize that I was a sort of fugitive, but I knew that for the time being I would stay clear of these people, see what they wanted, not let them know exactly where I stood. I would leave myself a choice for now.

I took a wide circle around the man in the business suit and his cowboy companion and stepped up carefully behind them. As I had thought, they were studying architectural plans of the building. I joined them in their study, keeping a good eighteen inches back for fear one of them might make some abrupt movement and collide with me. I suddenly became quite conscious of my own breathing; it seemed extraordinary that they did not notice it. I conceived a strong desire to clear my throat, and when I swallowed, the noise sounded to me like an explosion. But they remained oblivious to me.

They had the roll of papers open to the floor plan of the ground floor, and I set about systematically memorizing it. I would have liked a look at the second floor as well, but I never got more than a glimpse at it.

The man in the western shirt, who was actually holding the plans, was maintaining a continuous conversation with the two men in diving suits. "All right, Tyler, you're right in front of the entrance now. Remember, you've got two steps up and you're on a kind of little landing in front of the door. Morrissey, you leave that door open for Tyler?" He had the kind of southern accent and gregarious manner you associate with the army, commercial airline pilots, and CB radios. His extra bulk stuffed his elaborate shirt and gave his face a porcine expression, and, despite his continual joviality, made his little eyes seem wary, almost mean.

The other man, although he was plainly in charge, rarely spoke, and when he did it was to issue a brief command in a quiet, emotionless tone. Although his features were perfectly regular—many people would no doubt describe him as handsome—there was something reptilian about the creasing, hairless flesh of his face and head. I disliked him from the first. He turned away from his subordinate to look at the horizon, and I could see in his left cheek an almost imperceptible twitching movement; he was probably angry, I thought. Removing his headset with deliberate precision and placing it in the side pocket of his jacket, he turned slowly back to the other man and spoke in a soft but unpleasantly intense tone.

"Clellan, you know Morrissey and Tyler better than I do. I want you to find the most appropriate method of impressing upon each of them the critical importance of locating the man in the building. It is of very great importance to me; it is of very great importance to the government of the United States; it is of very great importance to the person in the building; it is of very great importance to Morrissey and Tyler. I am relying upon you, Clellan." He turned and walked over to the communications van, which he entered through the side door.

"You men hear that? You hear what the Colonel says?" asked Clellan a little uneasily. "We're not screwing this one up. You forget about the cat, Morrissey. But don't forget about the cat, if you get me. Is he still not answering? . . . Well, keep talking to him. He has to be in there. Can you hear him moving or anything? . . . Listen, the guy may be in pretty bad shape. Hell, he *must* be in bad shape—or we'd be looking at him. *Jeeeesus!* . . . He might have passed out. Tyler, when you get the door open, you wait this side of it until Morrissey finds the guy. Then you move right up with the net. Even if he's not moving, you get that net over him right away, hear? . . . You don't know what's in this guy's head. It's not good for him or anybody else if he gets crazy and wanders off. I hope to tell you it won't be good for you guys."

By this time they were in the reception room, and Tyler was bent over the door to Wachs's office. He had a large ring with keys on it, and he was evidently searching for an invisible keyhole in the invisible door. A difficult task—and with those enormous gloves, perhaps an impossible one.

"Don't forget to try the doorknob," Clellan was saying. "Oftentimes, you'll find the keyhole right in the doorknob. . . . You got it? . . . Above the doorknob? . . . How many inches? There may be other locked doors. . . . You've got to try both keys. One opens just the front door; the other opens everything else in the building except the laboratory. The laboratory should be the only one we don't have. Only the guy who ran the place had that key—that was for security." This seemed to strike Clellan as hilarious for some reason, and he exploded into loud laughter. The Colonel, who had returned from the van and stood beside him again, turned and looked at him impassively. Clellan became silent.

"You got it? . . . O.K., ease that door open real slow. He could be lying there on the floor right behind it. We don't want to hurt him. Tyler, make sure you keep that net folded up and out of sight. The main thing is, don't upset him."

Tyler seemed to be holding the door open just enough for Morrissey to squeeze through. They were taking no chances of my slipping away like the cat. When Morrissey was inside, Tyler pulled the door shut, keeping hold of the invisible doorknob, so that his arm remained oddly extended as if he were waiting to shake hands with someone. With his detector Morrissey was poking gingerly at the floor all around the door.

"Jesus, Morrissey, he has to be in there somewhere," Clellan was saying. "Keep looking. And be careful. Don't step on the poor bastard. Any contamination? . . . Nothing. Keep sweeping it, though. The guy himself could be contaminated from somewhere else, even if the room is clean. All right, Tyler, you better get in there too. Go in easy and lock the door behind you."

This took Tyler several minutes. Morrissey was meanwhile moving along the front wall of the room, waving his detector back and forth, colliding awkwardly with the furniture. At one point his detector encountered something soft near the floor, and he thought he might have me. "Move in easy! Come up with that net, Tyler!" Clellan began to yell. It turned out to be a small couch.

Clellan was growing unhappier by the minute. "Jesus. Where is the fucker. You sure you heard someone before, Morrissey? . . . Tyler, I want you to move north along the west wall. About ten feet and you come to another door. Then right around the corner another door in the north wall. I want you to get to those doors and tell me if they're locked, hear?"

Tyler began to retrace his steps to the west wall. Morrissey was moving systematically with his detector back and forth across the room, as if he were mowing a lawn. When he came to the desk, he laid down his detector and patted the entire surface with his hands; then he climbed laboriously down onto his hands and knees and reached under it. As he worked his way through the office he encountered many things, some of which he had trouble identifying. ("Maybe it's a wastebasket," Clellan would say. "See if it has a bottom.") But nowhere did he encounter a human form. When he had completed his search of the room, he laid down his detector and looked at Tyler, who had by then located the doors and determined that both were unlocked and one was ajar. Then both men turned and looked at us expectantly. Standing in midair in their white spacesuits, they seemed like supplicants from another planet.

"Damn!" barked Clellan.

"Disappointing," said the Colonel, at almost the same instant, in an eerily flat tone.

Transmitted over the radio, this had the effect of causing both men to twitch in midair in unison.

The Colonel and Clellan looked at each other, and then each of them made some adjustment to his headset, which apparently shut off transmission.

Clellan spoke first: "We don't know for sure that there was ever anyone in there, sir. In fact, it's pretty unlikely, when you think about it. We've only got Morrissey's word on it. It's pretty strange in there. Maybe Morrissey's head doesn't work so well in there."

The Colonel was silent for a long moment; he seemed to be considering this.

"That's a possibility, of course," he said at last. "But I am inclined to accept Morrissey's report. . . . Of course, you know him, and you're in a better position to assess his reliability. He's your man."

The Colonel spoke slowly in a detached tone as if he were giving most of his mind to thought rather than speech.

"I would, by the way," he went on, "like to see everything we have on both Morrissey and Tyler. And on the man in the communications van— 'Gomez,' isn't it?"

He became silent again, narrowing his eyes and wrinkling up his pallid face, and then continued. "No, there certainly seems to have been a cat; and a human being—no matter how much more extraordinary it seems— is logically no more unlikely than a cat. In any case, Clellan, we lose nothing by assuming that there *is* a man in there. And if there is, the potential benefits are incalculable."

He paused again as if trying nonetheless to calculate them.

"Incalculable. The scientific implications alone . . . Standing here now, we can hardly begin to conceive of the scientific and medical uses of a totally invisible, complete, living human body. Even the most obvious experiments would yield information never before obtainable. Devising ways to take advantage of the opportunities would become almost a discipline in itself."

A moment before, having looked at the building plans more than long enough, I had been about to leave my new friends, but the conversation had suddenly taken a turn that held my interest totally, and I remained standing there with them, absolutely still, trying to hold my breath during the pauses.

"Of course, we have to assume that he won't survive long in this condition. Still, even in a very short period of time, he could be of incalculable value."

"He'd make a hell of a field agent too," offered Clellan. "Think what it would be like running *him*. He could go *anywhere! Anywhere!* You could have any information in the world. Or at least a whole hell of a lot more than anyone else. Jesus! You could about write your own budget—whatever damn thing you wanted. Wouldn't anybody say 'boo.' Jesus! We'd be running half the damn government."

Clellan seemed to be having trouble getting a firm grasp on the opportunities my existence suddenly presented. As he tried to articulate them, they kept expanding faster than his imagination could accommodate them.

"Jesus. There's just no limit—"

"That's enough, Clellan," said the Colonel very quietly. He was looking pensively at the horizon. "At this point our only concern is to locate the man as quickly as possible."

"But, Jesus," continued Clellan, his enthusiasm uncheckable, "think of what this guy could *do!*"

"The question is what he *would* do, what we could persuade him to do. The same question as always. You would have all the usual problems in enlisting his cooperation, together with some altogether unusual difficulties. . . . Although you might have some advantages as well."

"Would we really have to turn him over to the scientists?" asked Clellan.

There was a pause before the Colonel answered. "Probably. But we might be able to keep control of him ultimately. The question is whether we can keep this whole thing secret. So far no one really knows with certainty that there is anything more interesting here than a hole in the ground . . ."

"You mean we might get him back when the scientists were done?" asked Clellan hopefully. "Not that there would be much left after they were through with him," he added.

"In any case," the Colonel said, "we have no idea about either his physical condition or his state of mind. He may be lying unconscious a few feet away from Morrissey and Tyler. He may equally well be physically sound but mentally incapacitated. He may be thoroughly deranged, incapable of making a rational judgment or taking a responsible decision. That would be almost likely, under the circumstances."

"Well, the scientists would still get plenty out of him, I suppose," said Clellan glumly.

"Or he may be simply hostile," the Colonel continued. "It is probable that he was one of the demonstrators. He did choose to enter or remain in the building without authorization after it had been evacuated. The people who organized the demonstration like to call themselves Marxists, at least when they are talking to each other. It might be worth considering what it would be like having him working against us."

Clellan's little eyes widened, and his mouth opened and then closed again. This thought seemed genuinely to distress him. The Colonel was pursing his lips again and staring through narrowed eyes into the distance. I waited quietly. All of us waited—Tyler, Morrissey, Clellan, and I—while he thought out what direction he would give to the day's events.

And while I waited to see what he would do, I tried feverishly to decide what direction my own efforts should take. I was by now thoroughly terrified at the prospect of finding myself in the care of these people. The thought of the awesome contribution I might make to science had quite overwhelmed me. I tried to imagine some of the very useful experiments that might be performed on "a totally invisible, complete, living human body." Several things came to mind, such as brightly colored fluids being forced through vital organs, but nothing I wanted to make a firm commitment to right then.

On the other hand, I was just as terrified by my grotesque physical condition. I desperately wanted to be cared for. By qualified people, with my interest at heart. And I had the sense that the longer I delayed in turning myself over, the worse things would be ultimately. The Colonel was probably right, I thought: I was not able to take a responsible decision. I needed a little more time to think things through. But it seemed that my choices were about to be radically narrowed. If these people got hold of me now, it was likely that I would not be making very many decisions at all. More qualified people, better able to assess my value to humanity, would be helping me out with the decisions. I had no doubt that they would have my best interests and those of all humankind constantly before them. They would know what was important and what not.

What was important to me was to get away.

"Have those men work their way through the rest of the building, as fast as they can," the Colonel said suddenly.

"We could make better time with more men," Clellan suggested.

"We'll work with the men we already have. I don't want anyone else to know what's happening in here. We've got to try to keep control of this situation. We want first of all to find that man and secondly to make a complete inventory of whatever it is we have here."

Clellan put his headset back on and began giving instructions to Morrissey and Tyler. The Colonel turned abruptly in place and stepped directly towards me. I jumped awkwardly out of his way, stumbled, and fell to the ground, crushing and denting the lawn. My heart pounded with terror, but if he noticed anything at all, it must have seemed the slightest flicker of shadow in the corner of his eye. His gaze was still focused on the horizon as he strode past me to the large van. I thought of heading straight for the gate to see whether and how I could get through it, but first I wanted to find out what he planned to do.

A few minutes later he reemerged from the van holding a cordless telephone set. As he spoke he looked appraisingly at the fencing.

"... That's exactly right. I want the guards at ten-yard intervals around the entire perimeter. ... Immediately. You can start on the alarms and the rest of it once they're deployed. ... Bring in as many men as you need. ... That's right. Tell them that literally nothing—not so much as a squirrel—is to get over that fence in either direction. ... Yes, that's right. Tell them that there may be contaminated animals here. If they see *any* movement whatever in the fence, they are to fire, even though they can't see what is causing it. ... No, I do not want to take down the screening to give them a better view. You might remind them that we are inside: they should try to angle their fire, but they should shoot at any movement. ... Yes, I am aware of the risk. ... The gate is not to be opened under any circumstances except on my orders. We'll be following new procedures. ..."

As he spoke, there was an ear-shattering explosion of amplified static behind us. I turned and saw that a turret composed of loudspeakers pointing in four directions had appeared magically through the roof of the van. It emitted three echoing reports like gunshots—someone tapping a microphone to test the system.

"*Attention all personnel.*" The words came booming out in a lightly Hispanic monotone at extraordinary volume. "*Attention all personnel. Do not approach the perimeter fence. The perimeter is under continuous surveillance by armed guards who have been ordered to fire upon any movement or breach of the perimeter. This is for your protection. Any unauthorized persons in the area are instructed to make their location known to us immediately so that we can come to their assistance. Repeat. Any unauthorized persons in the area are instructed to make their location known to us immediately so that we can come to their assistance.*"

This message was repeated. The Colonel continued to dial his telephone and issue instructions, although I could not understand anything he said over the din. When the loudspeaker had completed the message for the third time and had ceased transmission with a final, shattering pop of static, the Colonel, holding the receiver to his ear, looked up at Clellan.

"Clellan, who has a copy of the list of the people in the building yesterday?"

"We have one in the van, sir."

"No, I want one outside the perimeter."

"Simmons has one."

The Colonel spoke into the phone again.

"You can get the list of known names from Simmons down here. Start with the demonstrators. We may not have all their names. The ones we've talked to are terrified out of their wits: two people are dead and a building has been destroyed, and they aren't used to taking responsibility for things like this. Get to all of them before they calm down and find out if anyone is missing besides the one called Carillon. Then go to work on the employees—and any colleagues, students, friends, or family who might have been familiar enough with the place to be comfortable about staying in the building when everyone else had been evacuated. Then go through the rest of the list. We know that someone remained inside the building, and we have to determine as soon as possible who it was. . . . No, no description. Probably an adult male, but we don't have adequate confirmation of that."

Clellan, meanwhile, was watching Tyler and Morrissey crawl through the air, exploring an invisible bathroom. With his finger on the plan, he traced a path for Morrissey from the toilet to the shower and monotonously discussed each step of it with him over the radio.

I turned and walked away, across the thick, soft lawn. I think I owe my freedom in large part to the absolutely splendid weather that day. The sun shone brilliantly, and the spring foliage was a vivid green against the clear blue sky. It may have been the most beautiful day of the year, although I never quite took it in at the time, since I was sweating with fear from morning to night. I was like a mountain climber scaling a sheer rock wall: my mind was absolutely concentrated on each minute contour of the problem I faced, on each potential handhold, on each potential error, so that it never would have occurred to me to turn my head to take pleasure in the beauty of the view—even though the view was a large part of what had set me off on the climb and kept me going. A cloudy, oppressive sky might have tipped the balance the other way: I might have waited passively to be rescued. But as it was, beneath the clammy trembling fear I felt something approaching exhilaration as I walked across the lawn. It would be, after all, a good game. The risk was unpleasant to contemplate. On the other hand, if I was careful, if I survived, I would have not only my freedom but the additional pleasure of outwitting these people. Even then that childish thought was part of the calculation. And although the terms might get worse the longer the game went on, presumably I could always surrender on some terms. The important thing was to stay alive and stay free, to keep the choice for myself. The important thing was to get away.

I set out across the grass toward the gate, hoping that I would see some way to slip through it. When that proved hopeless—as I knew in my heart it would—I intended to make my way along the fence looking for some opening or some unguarded stretch. Very likely that would yield nothing either; still, the thing would only grow more difficult the longer I put it off. Whatever the odds, I might as well make my assault on the fence now. But as I watched my footprints appear magically on the lawn like the diagram of a dance step, I began to comprehend my situation with a new clarity. My understanding of it opened up like a wound. If you have ever as a child had daydreams of invisibility, you will surely have imagined it as a state of extraordinary, almost limitless freedom. You never left a trace. You could go anywhere, take anything. You could listen to forbidden conversations, find out anything. No one could stop you, because no one knew you were there. No one could set rules or limits for you.

Well, surveying the visible record of my fox trot across the lawn, I could already see some limits. And I had just spent nearly half an hour with two other human beings, watching them every moment for any indication of a movement that could result in a collision with me. The entire time some part of my mind had been thinking how pleasant it would be to clear my throat, and I had found it necessary to take continuous and excruciating care not to sneeze or sniff. Invisibility would be difficult. Rather than a magical state of extraordinary freedom, it would be a series of tedious practical problems. Like life under any other set of conditions, come to think of it. Still, if I hoped to maintain my freedom, I could never make a noise, I could never carry or wear anything in the presence of other people.

Except that I could, of course, carry the things I already had on my person—because they were invisible too. And anything else I might salvage from the building. That was it. The remains of the MicroMagnetics building were the only store of invisible objects in existence, and anything I might ever in my life want to carry or wear or use without betraying myself would have to come from here. And almost surely, I would have to get it right now. I should assume that I would never have another chance. If, indeed, I really had a chance even now. I turned back across the lawn toward the building. It was, as they say, a unique opportunity, a once-in-a-lifetime offer, for one day only. I would provision myself for the rest of my life. It might not turn out to be a very long life, but for once it seemed prudent to base my plans on the most optimistic assumption.

As I approached the building entrance, I came directly into Clellan's line of vision, and I watched him and the Colonel carefully as I walked, so that I would know immediately if they noticed my footprints. That they never did that day was, I suppose, because they had not yet thought through what sorts of signs they should be looking for. When I stepped onto the charred rim, I dragged my feet a bit to make sure I didn't leave a recognizable track there. I noted again with relief that neither grass stains nor ashes were adhering to the soles of my shoes. Tyler and Morrissey, in contrast, seemed to carry a great deal of dirt and ashes on their soles: they had left enough smudges at the entrance to the building so that I could now see where the steps and the threshold were.

The two of them were in the reception room again. Morrissey had a large red felt-tipped marking pen, with which he was trying to make a line on the wall. He was having difficulty holding the pen in his bulky glove, and the ink was not adhering well. It was as if he were trying to write on a pane of glass: each stroke of the pen left only intermittent streaks glistening mysteriously in the air where the wall was, and when he swept his hand back over the streaks, all the ink came off on his glove. Tyler was down on his hands and knees trying the same procedure on the carpet with much the same results. I wondered what in the world they could be trying to accomplish. They looked like children in a nursery school.

I stepped right into the room with them. I was careful to feel my way and avoid any collisions with walls or furniture, but I was confident that, encased in their suits with the continuous hearty drawl of Clellan in their headphones, they would not hear me pass by. I found the door to Wachs's office, opened it, stepped through, and carefully closed it again behind me. When the latch snapped into place, Tyler looked up suddenly. We both remained motionless for a moment; then he went back to his attempt at defacing the invisible carpet. I waited a bit longer and then walked to the bathroom.

I was moving around more confidently now. I knew roughly where the walls and furniture were in these rooms, and I was developing a sense of when my unseeable foot would strike the unseeable floor as I walked. But it was still a laborious process. I was always groping with my hands in front of me, and with each step I still waited until my foot was securely placed before I shifted my weight onto it.

I found the medicine cabinet and got the aspirin bottle again. I felt much better now, but I extracted a few more pills anyway and swallowed them without water, before dropping the bottle in the side pocket of my jacket. Then I felt along each shelf of the cabinet, pulling out objects and dumping them into my pockets. A razor, dental floss, shaving soap, two plastic combs, razor blade cartridges, a hairbrush, an electric razor, nail clippers, a shaving brush, a small pair of scissors, a pair of tweezers, a small metal box full of bandages, a roll of adhesive tape. I also encountered half a dozen bottles of various shapes which emitted an assortment of perfumes. These I left where they were. On the edge of the washbasin I found a bar of soap, and on a ledge above it two toothbrushes and a plastic cup, all of which I jammed into my jacket pockets with the other things.

(78)

I needed some better way of transporting everything. I had not even gone through one room, and my pockets were already so heavy that I was afraid of tearing what was to be my only real suit for the rest of my life. I felt my way across the room to the shower and, with some difficulty, unfastened the shower curtain from its hooks and laid it out flat on the floor. Onto it I threw first all the towels I could find in the room and then the running suits hanging on hooks by the sauna. Then I emptied my pockets onto the heap. On a shelf above the hooks I got a woolen cap and a scarf and a metal box, which, because it was heavy, I opened to see if it was worth taking. Gauze, cotton, wool, adhesive tape—a first-aid kit. Onto the heap. I worked my way around the walls of the room, looking for any other shelves. I was sure I remembered having seen running shoes, and I went down on all fours and searched the floor until I found them: two pairs of running shoes and a pair of rubber sandals. I didn't stop to see if anything fit. No time. I had to pack my things and go.

In the reception room Tyler and Morrissey had abandoned their marking pens and were now playing with brightly colored electrical tape. Even working together they were having a great deal of trouble cutting off pieces of the tape, and, once cut, it refused to adhere to the wall. It did, however, seem to adhere well enough to the fingers of Morrissey's gloves. Tyler tried, with only partial success, to pull the tape off Morrissey, and soon there were bits of it fastening together the fingers of his gloves as well. Through the wall I could half hear them talking unhappily to Clellan about their difficulties. They seemed benign enough for the moment, but I knew that soon they would begin working their way through the building, and as I went through myself, looting, they were bound to become aware of me.

Having studied the building plan I was able to locate the janitor's closet adjoining the bathroom without much difficulty, and there I found two shirts, a pair of trousers, and a pair of tennis shoes in very poor condition. I also found another, larger metal box. It took me a little while to figure out how to open it. Running my hands all around it I found two latches, which I was eventually able to snap open. These things can be difficult when you cannot see what you are doing. The top swung back, pulling up with it several interior shelves, on which I was immediately able to identify a pair of pliers, several screwdrivers, and a set of socket wrenches. A toolbox! I was elated by this discovery. But because in my examination of the tools I had somehow disarranged them, the box would not close again, and when I tried to straighten the tools out quickly, things only became worse. In the end I had to unpack half the box, laying everything out and systematically repacking it, before I could get the thing shut and latched again. Through all of this I was kneeling uncomfortably on the floor of the closet, becoming more and more unhappy about the time I was losing. I noticed that my shirt was wet with sweat, and I pulled off my jacket and laid it on top of the toolbox. My necktie as well. What use was a necktie now?

I could hear the voices of Tyler and Morrissey only very faintly here, not well enough to make out anything they were saying. I looked over at them. Morrissey was still holding a roll of tape. Tyler had opened a toolbox of his own, which floated waist-high in midair; he must have set it on a desk.

Returning hurriedly to my search of the closet, I pulled out a bucket, some rags, a box of plastic trash bags. I unscrewed the wooden handle from a push broom. I could think of no particular use for these things: I seemed to be choosing them almost at random, and I wondered anxiously if I was taking the right ones. But I had no experience to help me judge what I would need and no time to try to reason it out. I did know that I should take absolutely every bit of clothing I could find and any fabric that might eventually be used as clothing. Beyond that, I took everything portable that might conceivably be useful as a weapon or a tool—or that struck my terrified fancy.

In the back of the closet I found a stepladder about five feet high. Not nearly enough for the fence. I decided to leave it where it was. I carried everything I had picked out of the closet back into the bathroom and heaped it on top of the shower curtain. The toolbox, which was too heavy, and the broomstick, which was too long, I laid down on the floor next to the other things. I had to keep everything together. When you cannot see things, it can take forever to find them. This existence can be like searching for contact lenses all day long.

Tyler and Morrissey had now given up on the tape and were working with a large roll of cable. They would lay it out on the floor along the junctures with the walls. When they came to a door, they would cut the cable with an enormous pair of wire cutters and leave an interruption. In this way they methodically outlined the reception room and two small adjacent rooms—closets or storage rooms. They were superimposing a visible floor plan on the invisible building. It struck me that Wachs's office would almost surely be next, and I wanted to go through it before they did. Really, I should have started there. I would have to hurry now. Stay calm and work as efficiently as possible.

I got hold of all four corners of the shower curtain and dragged the bundle back into the middle of Wachs's office. I sat down at his desk and explored the desk top, coming up with a letter opener, a ruler, a stapler. Ignoring the now useless stacks of papers, I went on to the drawers, in which I found paper clips, rubber bands, scissors, a Swiss army knife, three key rings heavy with keys of every sort, a microcassette recorder, plastic credit cards, Scotch tape.

And, all the way at the back of the right bottom drawer, a gun.

I have never had much feeling about guns one way or the other. But the discovery of this one was exciting. It must surely, I thought, improve my situation—perhaps a great deal. I felt as if I had grown more powerful, and I found myself glancing over at Clellan and the Colonel standing out on the lawn. It was a pistol, a very small pistol. Right then, in spite of my hurry, I thought it worthwhile to take some time examining the gun: I wanted to be sure I knew what I had and how to use it. It took me several minutes to get the magazine open, since I was starting without the vaguest idea of how the thing worked. I emptied it, counting the bullets, one two three four five six, and then practiced pulling the trigger and setting and releasing the safety. I carefully refilled the magazine, counting the bullets again to be sure I had them all, and slipped the gun in my jacket pocket.

There should be more bullets somewhere. Not in these drawers. The trouble was that an invisible gun was pointless without invisible bullets, and I had only six. They would be in this room somewhere; I would have to take the time to search. Perhaps twenty minutes later—it was difficult to judge the passage of time—I had gone through the rest of the room and added to my store, among other things, a ball of twine, two extension cords, a telephone, an umbrella, a raincoat, and a pair of rubbers—but no more ammunition. I had become almost frantically obsessed with the need to find more bullets, and it was only with difficulty that I was able to make myself abandon the search before I jeopardized everything I had already accomplished.

My heap of objects had become very large by now and would be diffi- cult to move about. Furthermore, Tyler and Morrissey might walk in at any moment and literally stumble onto it, and I would lose control of the whole lot forever. I had to get everything out of the building, away from their search. Stepping over to the wall at the end of the building and groping along it, I located a window and slid up the lower sash. The noise seemed to me cataclysmic, and I looked back over my shoulder—or, for all I knew, through it—to see whether Morrissey and Tyler had heard. They seemed quite caught up in their work. They were doing a wonderfully thorough job with the reception area. They had laid little lengths of cable along the window ledges, and now they were wrapping electrical wire around the legs of desks, tables, and chairs so that you could see quite clearly how the entire room was laid out and furnished.

Returning to my pile of invisible objects, I knelt down and located the four corners of the shower curtain and gathered them into one hand. Then I picked up the whole thing and half carried, half dragged it over to the window. I could hear things dropping out of the bundle as I went. I had filled it too full; I had to be more careful. No room for mistakes now. I hoisted the bundle up over the window sill, with what seemed to me an insupportable clatter, and lowered it to the ground below. Then I went down on my hands and knees to search the floor for whatever I had dropped in transit. All I could find was a bunch of keys and an athletic sock. As I knelt on the floor pocketing those items, Tyler and Morrissey pushed open the door and joined me in the office.

They were getting to be very good at their work, and they went right to it—cutting and laying their cable around the edge of the room and wrapping up the furniture with neat little twists of wire. Unfortunately, they started along the wall that separated the office from the reception room room and the bathroom. Perhaps I should have waited—or simply climbed out the window and abandoned the field—but the broomstick and the toolbox were still on the bathroom floor, and I definitely did not want to risk having them get possession of that toolbox. Anyway, they seemed so absorbed in their work; and they hadn't noticed me when I had walked right past them in the reception room before.

I got to my feet and walked ever so slowly, one step at a time, right between them to the bathroom door. For some reason the door was not open wide enough for me to slip through, and when I gently pushed it, there was an awful creaking noise. Tyler stiffened. When I put my foot down on the tiled bathroom floor, the leather sole made a noise. I heard Tyler speaking into his microphone in a low monotone.

"He's in here with us now. He's moving around in here right now. . . . Yes, sir, I'm absolutely certain."

Morrissey had stopped moving too. Bending down and patting the floor carefully, I located both the toolbox and the broomstick and then slowly lifted first the one and then the other. The broomstick made a little scraping noise as I got my hand around it. All three of us remained still for several long minutes. Then I began moving across the floor toward them, with each step bringing the edge of my heel into careful contact with the floor and then slowly rolling my weight onto the sole of my foot.

I should have left the bathroom by the other door and followed the corridor down to the other end of the building. But I hadn't been there yet, and I was afraid of stumbling or, even worse, of finding myself trapped behind locked doors. I knew my way through the office quite well by now, and I thought that once I got onto the carpeted floor I could walk noiselessly. But just as I stepped alongside Morrissey, I heard him say, "You're right. He's right here. I can feel the fucker moving. I can feel the floor move."

He lunged right at me. It might have been only a guess, but it was a very good one. I shoved the end of the broomstick as hard as I could into his belly. I had no idea how much it would take to have some effect through his protective suit, but what I had done was evidently sufficient. He doubled up and collapsed onto the floor with a sort of gurgling moan. Tyler seemed uncertain at first about whether to pursue me or to go to Morrissey's aid, but as he looked about helplessly and saw nothing much to pursue, he bent over Morrissey. Morrissey and I did not seem fated to be friends.

I continued right on into the reception room, out the front door, and around the corner of the building until I stepped into my pile of things. I found that more objects had spilled out the sides. I would have to secure the bundle somehow if I hoped to take it with me. I set about tying first one pair of diagonally opposed corners and then the other. I was getting used to not being able to see either my hands or what they were manipulating, but it was still like stumbling around in a dark house, and tying the knots was for some reason particularly hard. When I had finally completed the task, I slipped the broomstick through the knot and levered it—somewhat painfully—over my shoulder. Then, picking up the toolbox with my other hand, I set out across the lawn.

I could think of no reason for them to search the lawn, but I wanted to leave the things where there was no risk of anyone's stumbling into them by accident, so I deposited everything at the base of the enormous beech tree, where low, spreading branches made it impossible for anyone to walk by without crouching. I kept the gun with me.

I walked back and continued foraging through the offices, beginning with the reception room and working my way down the building. I went as quickly as possible, rummaging through desk drawers and closets, pulling out anything that might conceivably be of value to me, and throwing it into a heap in the center of the room, to be lugged away when I was done. In the reception room I found a couch—really, Morrissey had found the couch—from which I was able to remove six covers from cushions and pillows to serve as sacks for the rest of the booty. My hoard under the tree was growing large. Too large—how could I hope to carry it all? I tried to be more selective, concentrating especially on clothing and cloth. Several of the rooms had curtains, which I pulled down. I came up with another pair of running shoes, and as the sound of my leather-soled footsteps in the uncarpeted corridor had become agonizing to me, I tried them on. They were a half size too small, but with the thin socks I was wearing they seemed quite bearable, so I laced them and threw my shoes on the pile.

I found two more raincoats. Good luck that it had been raining yesterday. Perhaps not. I might not have stayed inside. Pointless to think about these things. I had to keep moving. Soon I would have to face the problem of getting past the fence with all these things. Or even without them. I had no idea. I would keep on going through the rooms and work on the problem of the fence when the time came. Although it was perhaps better thought of as the problem of the guns. The problem of the colonel who had ordered the people to shoot the guns.

Twice Gomez got into the smaller van, drove out through the gate, and returned again several minutes later. Each time he passed in or out, I stopped and watched. The gate would slide open just enough to allow the vehicle to pass, almost scraping on both sides. The area beyond the gate seemed to be enclosed by more fencing and a second gate. Hopeless. Think about it later.

The first time, Gomez had come back with more wire and twine for Tyler and Morrissey. But the second time, he emerged from the rear door of the van holding two leashes in his hand. Attached to the leashes were two dogs. They were the sort of dogs you see in films, pursuing escaped convicts through marshes or across moors. He tied the end of the leashes to the rear bumper and then disappeared again into the other van.

I cannot begin to say how the sight of those dogs discouraged and terrified me. What chance would I have once they set after me? I was in a relatively small, entirely enclosed area. It might turn out to be impossible to get past the fence in any event, but it would certainly be impossible with dogs in pursuit. I would have to make my assault on the fence immediately, and I would probably have to abandon the idea of taking anything much with me.

On reflection, I might have more time after all.

Clellan and the Colonel were over in front of the large van, their attention fixed on Tyler and Morrissey in the building. Gomez was out of sight entirely. I walked out toward the dogs, and as I walked I reached into my pocket, took out the revolver, and slid off the safety.

The dogs lay panting slowly on the lawn. As I came up to within several yards of them, one of them started and clambered awkwardly to his feet. I raised my arm, pointing the gun toward the animal's head. I realized that my aim was fairly hypothetical, as I could see neither the revolver nor my own arm and, for that matter, did not even know precisely where I was standing. I decided that, if I was to avoid making a horrible mess of an already unpleasant business, I would have to get closer. I took three careful, absolutely noiseless steps toward the creature and tried to move the gun right next to its head. I misjudged the distance and poked him in the nose. Emitting a single pained bark, he snapped and then began a long, low growling sound. I recoiled. Someone more familiar with handguns would doubtless have shot instantly. But I only stood and watched as the other dog climbed to its feet and began barking.

There was, over the course of the next few minutes, a good deal of growling, barking, and sniffing about. However, my initial terror turned suddenly to relief, as I realized that none of this activity was particularly directed at me. They had no idea where I was! They seemed to hear even the slightest noise, but evidently they could not smell me at all. In better spirits again, I turned back to the building to get on with my work.

Morrissey and Tyler were moving along very quickly now. When they had finished delineating Wachs's office and the bathroom with cable and wire, they outlined the corridor that ran the length of the building and then began on the other offices, working down the building behind me. After a while they ran out of cable and they began outlining the walls with white twine, which showed up beautifully against the black surface of the apparent crater below us. Over the next several hours the building took form all around us like some enormous model constructed of pipe cleaners. Tyler would go first into each new room, waving his detector in front of him, officially to check for radiation but in practice to locate desks, chairs, and walls. Then he and Morrissey would climb awkwardly down on their knees—something their suits were clearly not designed for— and lay out the string, Morrissey doing the perimeter of the room and Tyler marking off the furniture. All the while they would be talking to Clellan: "Large desk here, in the middle of the room. Swivel chair." Or, "I've got two doors here in the west wall. Can you tell me whether one goes into the next room? Do you show a closet on the plan?" Or, "The fucker's in the next room. He's moving through ahead of us. I can hear him. I swear to God. He dropped something in the next room. . . . He's moving through the building ahead of us."

For a while I was indeed moving through the building just ahead of them, but they were always about to overtake me, and I decided to circle back and follow them, staying a room or two behind. That also let me take advantage of the string and wire they had already laid out, so that I could move around without worrying about crashing into furniture and walls. On the other hand, I had to be careful not to give myself away by moving furniture that had already been marked, and I no longer dared sit in the chairs as I went through the desks.

Morrissey and Tyler were working hard: you could see that what they were doing was exhausting and difficult, especially because of the suits and gloves they had to wear. The mood was poor: everyone remembered the loss of the cat—not to mention the loss of the human being—and Morrissey surely remembered the broomstick shoved into his stomach. They were conscious of my presence, and it made them nervous and irritable; perhaps it made them afraid. It certainly made me nervous and afraid, all of us working together in the same space. I could not help making noise as I moved about pulling open drawers, carrying things from room to room. Once I pulled a drawer too far out and had to listen to it crash to the floor. Tyler and Morrissey came running—or as close to running as their suits would permit. Long before they actually found the right desk and the drawer lying on the carpet beneath it, I was well out of the way, watching from the next room.

"He's going through the desks," Morrissey reported. "Like he's looking for something. You want us to do something about it? . . . I don't know what. But it's creepy. I'd like to get my hands on the fucker. If we could get out of these suits. . . . Yes, sir."

When several minutes later I knocked over a chair, they did not even bother to get up. They looked up and listened for a few moments and then turned sullenly back to their work.

I should have begun the actual escape sooner. I should have faced the problem of the fence. But I told myself that I was waiting for Morrissey and Tyler to open up the laboratory. I am not sure exactly what I hoped to find there, but I think my reasoning to myself was that there would be useful tools there. And I think I felt that there, at the source of the disaster, I might find some enlightenment, some explanation of my ludicrous condition—why it had happened, or what I might do about it.

By early afternoon we had all finished with the rooms in the front half of the building. I had looted them, and Tyler and Morrissey had outlined them in string. As I was returning from the tree, where I had deposited my last load, I saw that Tyler and Morrissey had come out of the building and were making their way as best they could in their suits to the edge of the crater. Clellan had come right up to the rim to meet them, bringing with him the dogs. The manhunt was about to begin. The dogs no longer frightened me much, now that I knew they could not smell me, but I was still wary of getting close enough so that they could hear me, and I decided to watch the pursuit from the lawn with Clellan. I walked over and waited about ten feet away from him while he turned the dogs over to Morrissey and Tyler.

The dogs were from the outset unenthusiastic about Morrissey and Tyler, perhaps finding their attire unreassuring. I sympathized really. It developed that the lack of enthusiasm was reciprocated: there was a good deal of discussion about which of the men would actually handle the dogs. In the end Tyler was designated—probably because he accepts misfortune with better grace, or at least with a stolid stoicism.

With Clellan's help, Tyler managed to wrap the two leads around his massively gloved hand, and after some tugging and a few smart jerks he got them to what even a dog must have perceived as the edge of a rather large and deep pit. Tyler proceeded ahead of them onto the invisible surface, but they were apparently not in the least heartened by his ability to float in midair. With a little more pulling and yanking, Tyler managed to get both dogs to place their front paws past the visible rim, but there they stopped decisively. They were evidently willing to be dragged over the edge and down into the void, but they were not at all willing to levitate. They braced their legs and froze. There was not even any barking now. Tyler turned back to face the dogs and pulled on the leashes with both hands. Morrissey came up behind them and bending over with great difficulty tried to coax them and push them with his hands. One of them began to emit a long, low-pitched growl which concluded abruptly with a savage bite into Morrissey's unfortunately well-protected arm.

Clellan uttered words of encouragement. "That's it. Just ease 'em on out. They'll be all right."

But there was no sign so far that they would be all right. Tyler had managed by now to drag them several feet onto the invisible surface, but they both continued to resist, growling evilly. He was standing in the doorway, unable to haul them up over the steps.

"That's good," said Clellan. "Hold it for a minute. Let 'em get used to it."

Tyler stood there for quite a while waiting for them to get used to it. The dogs, now that they were not being pulled forward, ceased pulling back, and the leashes went slack. The two creatures remained cowering there over the void. I was in a position to sympathize with them. On the other hand they, at least, could close their eyes.

Suddenly one of the dogs sprang up and bolted for the rim. Tyler, standing in a posture of sullen resignation, was unprepared for this and was pulled off the doorstep into a heap on top of the other dog. Tyler's only comment was "Shit!" but the dogs made a great deal of noise, especially the one underneath Tyler. Clellan spoke continuously, saying things like, "Take it easy. Easy there. Let's get those dogs inside and calm 'em down." Despite the reassuring words, there was an overtone of impatience in his voice.

Morrissey took this opportunity to suggest in his whining tone that without the protective suits which he and Tyler were being forced to wear, they could be more effective as well as less uncomfortable. He specifically suggested that "if we could get these fucking suits off, we could get our hands on that fucker in there."

Clellan was of another mind. "Morrissey, you are going to keep that fucking suit on until you're told to take it off. And if you say one more word about that fucking suit, you'll live in that fucking suit until you can't remember what it was like to be out of it. You'll eat in it, sleep in it, piss in it, shit in it until next summer. You understand, Morrissey?"

Morrissey, although his reply was inaudible, seemed to understand. He stood there quietly. Tempers were fraying. Clellan turned back to Tyler. "Get those dogs in there and take 'em through the building. Hear?"

Tyler responded by giving the leashes several savage pulls. The dogs, feeling the slip collars contract violently about their necks, let out startled yelps. Although Tyler was managing to maintain his stony composure, he was clearly angry.

"These dogs are going for a *walk*," he announced. He wrapped the leads around his glove several more times until his hand was almost under the dogs' chins, and he began to march up the stairs and into the building.

(87)

The reluctant, half-strangled animals had their noses pointed desperately up in the air and their legs braced resolutely against any forward movement, but Tyler dragged them determinedly along.

"That's right, dogs. We are going for a walk, you and me." Tyler hauled them into the reception room and made a small circle around the invisible desk. There was an almost manic tone to his controlled rage, as he towed the frantic creatures along the floor. "You don't smell nothing here? That's fine. We're gonna try the next room." He marched into Wachs's office, pulling the dogs behind him, and made another angry circle.

"O.K.," said Clellan uneasily. "Take it easy, Tyler. O.K." Tyler was dragging the wriggling dogs down the corridor. "O.K., Tyler. *Hold it!*" Tyler stopped and turned slowly to face us. "Tyler, you can tie those dogs up somewhere in there. Maybe they're gonna get used to it after a while. Maybe not. We'll let 'em be. Right now we're gonna open up the laboratory." Tyler pulled the animals into an office and looped the ends of the leashes around the leg of a desk. The dogs were understandably unhappy. They could not see the desk leg and in trying to work out their situation I think one or both must have collided painfully with it. They did not seem to adjust very quickly to their new surroundings—or lack of them.

Suddenly, without any warning, an unspeakable, unearthly wail arose, and in the terrible moment before I comprehended that it came from one of the dogs, the thought swept through my mind that I had died after all and been consigned to the inferno and that this terrible sound was an indication of the eternal torment to come. The other dog joined in. For several long minutes we all stood there, incapacitated by the sound, until finally the Colonel made a sign and Tyler removed the dogs to the lawn.

Ten minutes later Gomez arrived at the edge of the rim, unrolling what looked like electrical cable from a heavy metal spool as he went. Morrissey and Tyler then took over the spool and threaded the cable through an invisible window, across one of the offices, and into the central corridor. There they attached a power drill to it, and Morrissey began laboriously drilling holes in thin air. He was cutting open the door to the laboratory. I walked carefully down the corridor and stood almost next to him, waiting for him to admit me.

I could see that Morrissey was having trouble. The drill was heavy and difficult to hold in place with the massive gloves. Intermittently he would stop drilling and push a small power saw against the door. I was unable to understand exactly what he was doing, but I remembered that it was a metal door and I could see that it must be thick. He worked for over half an hour at it, sweating inside his diving suit and unable to manipulate the tools properly or even to feel exactly what he had accomplished. He had stopped speaking, and when Clellan would ask him for a progress report, his answers were curt.

I waited patiently beside Morrissey the entire time. I would have liked to offer some suggestions on how to attack the door, but despite our shared interest I did not think that he and I would be able to work together successfully. He pulled a large screwdriver from his toolbox and twisted it violently about in front of himself. He was using his entire weight to prize something—presumably the lock mechanism—free, but as only he and the screwdriver were visible, it made a particularly odd pantomime. Then the screwdriver twisted abruptly in his hand, he gave a little push with his shoulder and another push with his hands, and announced, "I got it. It's open."

He paused, listening to whatever Clellan was telling him over the radio, and then bent down to pick up the radiation detector. As he straightened himself again, he turned back and looked straight through me. It disconcerted me for an instant. I turned too and saw that he was looking at Tyler, who was coming down the corridor to join us now that the laboratory was open.

Morrissey did not wait for him. Holding the detector in his right hand, he used the left hand to push back the door. The long wait had heightened my irrational eagerness to get into the laboratory, and I decided to follow Morrissey straight in, ahead of Tyler. As Morrissey stepped past the door and let the hand that had pushed it open drop down to his side, something slammed violently against the entire length of my body. I was aware of taking the impact particularly against my forehead, nose, left cheek, and the toes of my left foot, but I was stunned as much by the surprise as by the actual force of the blow. Even though I had begun, over the course of the day, to be accustomed to the invisibility of my surroundings, that impact with no warning and no visual explanation overwhelmed me, and I stood there in a daze for many seconds before I comprehended that the heavy metal door had been pushed into me automatically by a closing spring. I reached dully up to feel my nose and cheek, which were throbbing with pain. Tender, but nothing broken. No sign of blood.

Although I was looking straight at Morrissey the entire time and saw him abruptly freeze at the sound of the door hitting me, I stopped thinking about him entirely until I heard him speaking sharply into his radio in a near whisper.

"He's right behind me. The doorway!"

Tyler, for the few steps that remained, charged up the corridor and through the doorway toward Morrissey. It was hard going for him in his suit, but he managed a ponderous run with his arms extended to seize me. At the same instant Morrissey wheeled about, dropping his detector, and lunged at me. They both had their hands on me, and if they had not been wearing those suits and those clumsy gloves, they would have held me easily. In total panic I pulled loose from them, shoving and hitting them at random to get free. At some point I took a blow to the head. I staggered away from them along the wall inside the laboratory. I felt my heart pounding as if I were a rabbit in a trap. When I tried to check my face again for damage, I found that my hands were trembling. I stood and watched to see what they would do next. Once they lost contact with me, they straightened themselves. Tyler stepped a little to one side, and I heard the door swing shut next to him. He took a step back and stood there barring the exit.

"We got him," Tyler said into his headset. "We got him in the lab. . . . No, he's loose in here, but I'm blocking the door. It's the only one, right? He won't get out of here. . . . I'm not moving. Look, what kind of readings you getting in here? . . . Nothing? Morrissey has a point, sir. We'd be better off without these suits. . . . Yes, sir. . . . Yes, sir."

Then Tyler looked up at the middle of the room and spoke in a loud self-conscious voice. I did not realize at first that he was addressing me.

"Listen, fella, we know you're there. We want to help you."

There was a pause. I said nothing.

"Listen, you got to let us know where you are."

There was another long pause. None of us had anything to say.

Tyler remained with his back pressed against the closed door, watching apprehensively for some sign of me. But Morrissey bent down, picked up his detector again, and set out toward the center of the room, waving the detector slowly back and forth in front of himself. I watched with great interest: he would be heading straight for Wachs's extraordinary device—whatever it was that had created this grotesque situation. The way seemed to be clear: he was not encountering any furniture or equipment; and he had become quite skillful at walking on the invisible surface, so that it was with considerable confidence that he stepped forward and plunged into the void. Or at least it must have felt to Morrissey as if he had plunged into the void. In fact, he pitched quite abruptly into a nasty heap about ten feet below me and Tyler, and then slid gently down and forward another five feet as if he were on a playground slide. The detector, which he had lost hold of in the fall, slid down beside him.

For what may have been half a minute, he lay there motionless. Then he began moving his limbs, slowly unfolding himself until he lay sprawled on his back, suspended a little less than halfway between where Tyler and I stood and the bottom of the apparent crater. He began speaking.

"Yeah, I'm all right. I don't know. . . . There's a hole here," he explained—rather superfluously, I thought.

He tried to stand. He seemed to be having trouble with one leg.

"Ankle. Goddamn, it hurts!"

Favoring one foot, he began to step carefully forward toward us. After the first few steps he found himself on a steep incline. His feet slid out from under him, and he fell forward, sliding back down on his face, feet first, to where he had started.

"Shit!"

He slowly picked himself up, turned around to face the opposite way, and set out again, with the same result. He got up again. This time he limped around the bottom in a little circle. He bent over and felt the surface. He straightened and looked up.

"I'm in a hole," he explained again. His voice had an aggrieved, almost whining overtone. "It seems to be round. It feels smooth. I'm slipping on it. There's no way I can get out of here alone. Someone's gonna have to get me out."

I concluded at first that there had been an explosion or fire at the center of the laboratory which had opened up a hole in the floor and that Morrissey had fallen into some sort of cellar. But I could not remember a cellar on the plans. I went down on all fours and crawled toward the edge, feeling my way carefully with my hands so that I would be sure not to join Morrissey. When I reached the edge, I ran my hand down along the surface of the cavity. It was perfectly smooth. I ran my fingertips over it and scratched at it with my fingernails. It seemed to me to be a perfectly smooth cross section of floorboard, followed by concrete, followed by hard-packed dirt. In shape it seemed to be as flawlessly spherical as the apparent crater surface that surrounded us. I crawled about a third of the way around the edge of the cavity to verify this hypothesis. The rim seemed indeed to be perfectly circular. Apparently the invisible sphere in which we found ourselves had a hollow core, perhaps thirty feet in diameter. Whatever piece of equipment had caused all this must have somehow exploded or imploded or otherwise disintegrated itself, leaving nothing but the cavity into which Morrissey had fallen.

I decided to stand up and walk. I had lost interest in the laboratory. I wanted to get out.

Tyler, I noted, was not moving from the door. He was doing nothing whatever to help Morrissey or to make it any easier for me to leave the room. For some reason he had raised his arms and was holding them bent in front of himself, as if he were being attacked. I realized with a little surge of pleasure that I was the attacker against whom he was defending himself: with Morrissey trapped in the hole he had no one to help him if I went after him. It was not at all clear that he could hold the door against an invisible adversary. Still, I was reluctant to assault him. I might find a chair or some other sort of club, but even then he would be hard to hurt in his heavy suit, and I was above all afraid of any struggle that might end with me being dragged into the cavity.

Clellan, I saw with dismay, was walking across the lawn towards us. There had been no indication of any radioactivity, and he might be about to walk right into the building to support Tyler. I felt my chances contracting rapidly around me. There was no time for deliberation. I would have to make my decision and act. I reached into my pocket and fit my hand around the gun.

"Tyler?"

At the sound of my voice, Tyler stiffened. Although he knew well enough that I was there, the disembodied voice must have seemed uncanny. He didn't answer.

"Tyler? Do you hear me?"

"I hear you, fella. What can we do for you?"

"Tyler, I want you to move away from that door."

"I can't do that, fella. Listen, we—"

"Tyler, I have a gun in my hand. Now I know you can't see it, so I'm going to fire it once, just so you can hear how it sounds." I fired it at the wall beside him. Tyler flinched instinctively at the noise and began to speak.

"Listen—"

"Now, Tyler, if you don't move away from that door right now I'm going to kill you."

At the report of my gun, Morrissey had immediately begun to tear off his suit, and Clellan had started running into the building. Clellan was holding a gun in his right hand. This was his first attempt at moving on the invisible surface and he couldn't run at full speed, but he was coming quickly all the same, holding his left hand out in front to avoid running into closed doors and watching the pieces of string and wire that marked the walls and furniture. He was through the building entrance and into the reception room: he would be down the corridor in a moment. My choices were running out.

I pointed the gun at Tyler's legs, or tried to—it was difficult to be sure exactly where it was pointing—and pulled the trigger. There was an instant's delay after the shot and then blood began to ooze out of a little hole in Tyler's suit at about the level of his waist. Horrible. I had wanted to shoot him in the thigh. The other horrible thing was that he remained standing against the door, staring blankly ahead.

"Move!" I shouted.

Perhaps he was stunned by the shot. Perhaps he didn't even understand that he had been hit. Clellan was into the corridor. I found myself lowering the gun and pulling the trigger again. This time Tyler let out a little shriek and hunched forward, clutching at his left knee. I dropped the gun back into my pocket and stepped quickly up to him. Before he could straighten up again, I pushed in behind him so that my back was against the door, put my hands against his back, and pushed him as hard as I could. He pitched forward onto his face. I got my arms around his lower legs and lifted them, still pushing him forward, until he toppled head first into the cavity and shot down to the bottom, knocking over Morrissey. Behind him he left a little arc of blood in the air.

I turned to face Clellan just as he reached the entrance to the laboratory. I reached out, got hold of the door by the hole that Morrissey had made in it, and pulled it open just as Clellan reached out with his left hand to feel whether it was closed. In his right hand he still held a gun. Finding no door, he stepped uncertainly forward, looking down at Tyler and Morrissey below and then looking hopelessly around for some sign of me. He took another apprehensive step forward past the door I was holding open for him. Tyler, struggling painfully below, managed to raise himself to his feet momentarily, before his leg gave way and he collapsed to the floor of the pit again. He tilted his head up and looked at Clellan.

"Get back!" Tyler shouted hoarsely.

Too late. I had slid my left leg in front of Clellan, and now I clamped my right hand hard onto the back of his neck and shoved him forward, so that he tripped over my leg and plunged into the cavity with the others. His gun discharged as he went in. When he reached the bottom, he capsized Morrissey and slammed into Tyler, and the three of them tumbled into a heap.

As I turned to leave the building, I realized that I was trembling with horror and relief. I had never shot anyone before, never harmed anyone physically. No time to think about that now. I looked across the lawn and saw the Colonel, immobile and expressionless, staring toward me.

I would, I decided, have to speak to him. He was the one person who could arrange to let me through the gate. The only alternative was to assault the fence somehow, and I had a brief vision of my bullet-shredded remains hanging from the barbed wire. "Vision," is of course the wrong word, and it occurred to me then that they would experience my remains only by sense of touch. Unpleasant for everyone. Much better to try to talk to the Colonel. I had, I reasoned, some momentum and some credibility, having just shot Tyler and trapped all three men in that hole. I felt a wave of revulsion at the thought of the blood appearing at Tyler's midriff; I had not wanted to shoot him that way. No choice. Can't think about it now. And now I had only three bullets left. Anyway, if I could not find any other way to persuade the Colonel to let me out, I could make a very convincing threat to shoot him.

When I came up to him, the Colonel was speaking by radio to the men in the building. I looked back and saw that they had formed themselves into a human ladder, Clellan standing on Tyler's shoulders and Morrissey on Clellan's. Morrissey was grappling above his head, trying to pull himself up onto the edge, while Tyler at the bottom tried to brace himself so that the weight of the men above him would not push him around and up the opposite side. There was a little pool of blood floating between Tyler's feet at what must be the bottom of the cavity; all around there were translucent red smears in the air; and the clothing and faces of all three men had become blotched with stains as they crawled over the surface of the cavity. The three of them, extended in sequence, belly out, formed a dramatic human arc in midair, as if they had been frozen in flight as they swung out suspended from a trapeze.

"Have you got it?" the Colonel was saying. "Good. Can you get Tyler out yourselves? . . . I'll come over if you need me, but I prefer that we stay spread out if possible. . . . How is he?"

I hesitated uncomfortably. I knew I should get on with this—the longer I delayed, the worse my chances became. But even under the best of circumstances it is awkward striking up a conversation with a stranger, and the circumstances here were grotesquely poor in every respect. Anyway, I wanted to know how Tyler was. I couldn't hear the answer. I hoped he was not dying. Looking back, I saw that Morrissey had managed to struggle out of the pit and that Tyler had slumped back down to the bottom of the cavity, where Clellan was bending over him.

"All right," the Colonel continued. "I've alerted the medical people. Get him into the ambulance and out to the gate as fast as you can and come straight back. Until something further happens, we're going to try to keep working here. Gomez will keep himself locked inside the van. If anything happens to me or the van, stay spread out and try to get to the gate as best you can. We'd like to get him alive, but if you're attacked, you'll do whatever is necessary. And Morrissey? . . . When you're taking Tyler out through the gate, be careful. Our first priority is to make sure this person doesn't leave the area unless he's under our control."

The Colonel unhooked his headset and pushed it into his side jacket pocket. He lifted a portable telephone as if to dial a number, then paused to watch as Morrissey unrolled a spool of black electrical cable into the pit.

This seemed like a good moment to speak. Or rather it was not a good moment—there was no possibility of a good moment now—but it was as good a moment as I was likely to see.

"Hello," I ventured.

He gave a start, more a massive twitch. That one time I did startle him.

"How are you?" He spoke slowly, still trying to take in the situation. Then he offered his hand.

"How are you," I returned. The extended hand was an embarrassment. There could be no question of letting him take my hand.

"Very well, thank you. My name is David Jenkins." When I did not respond, he went on. "Is there anything you need immediately? We're here to help you." His soft, insinuating, always earnest voice was composed now. He withdrew his hand slowly. As he spoke, his eyes were carefully searching all around for some visible sign of me. The grass was thoroughly trampled where we stood, but I nevertheless kept myself absolutely still. I was five feet away from him and a little to one side.

"There's nothing, really. Thank you. I just wanted to talk to you for a few minutes—to try to work something out. By the way, I'm sorry for whatever trouble I've caused."

He waved his hand as if to dismiss whatever insignificant inconvenience I might have created.

"Particularly shooting Tyler," I went on. "I didn't—"

"It was our fault as much as yours. I'm afraid we've handled the situation badly. The important thing now is to get you the attention you need immediately." He raised his telephone as if to dial.

"Just a moment!" I said hurriedly. "I really don't need any attention. That's what I want to talk to you about. I think it would be much better not to involve anyone else in this."

His finger paused in midair and did not dial. His eyes continued scanning the area for some clue to my exact location.

"I just want to get some medical personnel in here," he said. "We owe you an apology: we should have had them here right along. Sometimes I think we place too high a priority on security. But now that we have you here, the important thing is to get you looked at right away."

"That's really the problem, isn't it? I mean getting me looked at. It doesn't seem likely to come to anything. Anyway, I'm feeling remarkably well, everything considered, and I absolutely don't want—"

"We have to have you examined immediately by qualified physicians." His voice was silken. His hand remained poised over the telephone.

"I'm not sure a physicist wouldn't be more useful than a physician. Probably no one would be very useful when you come right down to it. But if any health problems arise, I have a very good man in the city—"

"We would want specialists for your condition."

"I don't suppose they've had time to develop specialists for my condition, have they? Although, once I went to my doctor *he* would be the specialist for my condition, wouldn't he?" I knew that this conversation was taking a wrong turn, but I did not seem able to stop it.

"There's no reason why you shouldn't have your own doctor on the medical team. Why don't you give me his name, and we'll get him out here right away. You know, I sense that you're apprehensive. After what you must have been through, it would be surprising if you weren't. But I just want you to understand that we're here to help you. We're going to do everything for you that's humanly possible."

He formed his features into what was surely meant to be a warm and reassuring smile. It was a smile which—with no human visage available to which it could be directed or from which a response could be elicited—seemed to perish quickly from exposure.

"I appreciate that very much," I said in a firmer tone, "but I want you to understand that I've already decided I don't want any help. All I want—"

"By the way, I don't know your name. What *is* your name? Mine is David Jenkins."

There was something compelling about his voice, so that, caught off guard by the question, I felt trapped into answering and said the first thing that came to mind.

"You can call me Harvey."

I had in my mind the image of a gigantic, invisible rabbit standing next to Jimmy Stewart, and the moment the name was out of my mouth, I regretted it. No point in antagonizing him and making him more mistrustful. But Jenkins, however intelligent he may be, is always absolutely literal.

"Well, Harvey, I know that the last twenty-four hours must have been incredibly painful and disorienting for you, and no one in the world could blame you for any uncertainty or misgivings you might feel, no matter how irrational. But beyond that, Harvey, I sense that you're in some way particularly apprehensive about us, which is also understandable, and it might be useful if I told you a little bit about who we are and what our responsibilities here are. We're concerned with coordinating the collection, analysis, and synthesis of information—and beyond that, and more importantly perhaps, with the distribution of information throughout the various strata of governmental and quasi-governmental entities."

"You mean intelligence?" I offered helpfully.

There was a pause before he continued.

"I hesitate to use the word 'intelligence,' Harvey, because for so many people it conjures up an image of double agents and microfilms and assassinations, and while there is unquestionably a place for field work in intelligence gathering, it is important to understand that ninety-nine percent of the results come from the laborious analysis of newspapers and periodicals."

I said nothing, but as I watched Clellan expertly knotting the cable around Tyler, I tried to visualize Clellan, Tyler, and Morrissey sitting at desks, poring over Russian scientific journals.

"Every society, even a free society—*especially* a free society—has to make provisions to gather and protect the information necessary for its own survival, and that's really all we're concerned with. Now, as it happens, my own background is primarily scientific, and, probably as a result of that, most of my career has been devoted to scientific intelligence and security. But the thing I want you to understand is that there is nothing whatever political about our work.

"We know, of course, that you probably came here to participate in a political demonstration, and I just want you to know that we're not uncomfortable with that, and there is certainly no reason for you to be uncomfortable. We're here to help you, and we don't care what your political beliefs are. Although I'll tell you, Harvey, I think it might turn out that you and I have a great deal more in common than you might at first imagine. For one thing, the people who go into government service—whether it's intelligence or anything else—have every sort of political belief you can imagine, but there's one thing they all have in common: they aren't motivated by financial gain or private personal greed, or they wouldn't be there. Whether you agree or disagree about any particular point of policy, these are people who are working for their country, for the good of society as a whole; they are people who have made a commitment to serve something beyond their own personal interest.

"Just so," I said agreeably, although uppermost in my mind at the moment was my own personal interest in getting past the fence. "I absolutely agree with you—in a general sort of way, at least. By the way, my political views are quite a lot more moderate than you probably think." It seemed a good idea to offer some reassurance on this point. "Extraordinarily moderate, in fact—"

"But you did come here with the Students for a Fair World?"

"Well, yes, of course." I did not want to throw him off that false track, because, although he might be less inclined to trust me if he thought I was one of the demonstrators, it would slow down the search for me if I ever got out. "All power to the people, is my feeling." What exactly did these people believe? "From each according to his abilities; to each according to his needs," I tried. I rejected "property is theft" as too strident and "I like Ike" as inappropriate. "But within that context, I believe in working responsibly within the system for gradual change. . . . As a matter of fact, I was very much interested in what you were saying about government service representing one kind of commitment to something beyond personal interest."

"Exactly," he returned, clearly pleased at having evoked a positive response and eager to build on it. "I would have to say that the real reward of working in the public sector is the opportunity to get beyond the petty greed and selfishness that seem to permeate so much of our society. And I suspect that's something you can respect, Harvey, just as I can respect the fact that when you came out here you were acting out of a commitment to do something to bring about a better world, rather than just benefit yourself. And you've paid a terrible price for your commitment. A terrible price."

I had the impression that he would normally have liked to be looking earnestly into my eyes when he delivered these sentiments. As it was, he could not even be sure exactly which way to face, much less how I was responding, and if I failed to answer him promptly, he had to wonder whether I was still there. It must have made the dialogue difficult for him.

"It's as you say," I offered. "Whatever happens to me, I want to be sure that I do the right thing here. I'm trying to think this through. It seems to me that I suddenly have a unique opportunity to be of service to the world."

"Well, that's right, Harvey. However horrible this may be for you, it puts you in a position to make an extraordinary scientific contribution to humanity, and frankly, I admire—"

"Well, yes, of course there is science and so forth. But I want to make sure I don't spread myself too thin, so to speak. Actually, I was more interested in what you were saying about the importance of intelligence for the preservation of a free society. You and I have to be sure that we make the most of the circumstances we find ourselves in, that we take advantage of each other's particular abilities and qualifications. It seems to me that you and I should be figuring out how we could most usefully work together. I should be working with you as some sort of intelligence agent, don't you think?"

His brow furrowed and his lips pursed, but he said nothing.

"The more I think about it, the more obvious the whole thing becomes," I went on. "You've maintained extraordinary secrecy here, given the spectacular nature of what's taken place. No one but your men here knows I exist, and even they wouldn't have to know anything about our future relationship. Of course, I would have to rely totally on you for guidance. Without you I wouldn't have a clue what to do or for whom. I probably couldn't even survive. But with your direction we could have access to virtually any information, anywhere. I don't know anything about intelligence, but the possibilities seem almost unlimited. What you said about serving something beyond our own personal interest really struck home. I can see that this is my opportunity to be of service, and I mustn't let it pass me by."

"It is," he said very slowly, "one possible way we could proceed."

"I'm really very lucky that someone like you happened to be in charge here, David, someone I can work with, because the key to the whole thing is that you will be the only person who knows of my existence. Otherwise, they could probably guard against me fairly easily. But this way you will simply be someone with extraordinary access to information. I imagine that in your line of work it's not altogether unusual to refuse to disclose your sources. Of course, the situation would entail quite a burden of responsibility for you. You would be put in a unique—in an awesome—position in the intelligence community . . ." (I seemed to remember that it was referred to as "the intelligence community" in newspaper articles, although I doubted that it had many of the usual attributes of a community.) "With you functioning as my control—isn't 'control' the term you people use?—we would be virtually omniscient. As I think about it, the whole thing seems very exciting. And, as you say, rewarding."

His lips separated as if he were about to speak and then came together again. His eyes narrowed and he stared off reflectively in the direction of the other men. Morrissey was hauling Tyler up out of the pit, while Clellan was pushing from below. They got him up over the edge. He rolled over on his side and drew up his legs. I would have liked to know how he was.

When Jenkins began again, he spoke softly and with a new intensity, I thought. Although I always find it difficult to know what, if anything, is in his heart.

"Harvey, I think you are right. I agree with you. And I want to tell you that if someone had to be caught in that building, I'm glad it turned out to be someone like you. I admire you, Harvey, and I think we're going to work well together. Now, the first step," he said briskly, as if he were casually mentioning an incidental detail, "is to get you properly looked at so we can see how we can best proceed—"

"David, I think that would be a terrible mistake. If we're going to work together, my whole value lies in no one's knowing about me. Otherwise, they can defend against me, or at least they'll know where they stand. The main thing is to make sure that no one knows but you—not even the people you work with. If you start calling in doctors and scientists, we'll lose this whole opportunity. *Everyone* will know about me. And on top of that, you and I will lose control of the situation. Someone else will be deciding where I go and what I do. It seems to me that what we have to do now is to arrange for me to slip out through the fence without anyone at all knowing."

"Harvey, I think you'll be surprised at the extent to which we can keep this situation secret—and by the amount of control we can maintain over it too—"

"David, we couldn't possibly maintain enough security for *our* purposes. And as for keeping control over the situation, I'm concerned that I would have none whatever, and while I don't have any doubts about being able to count on you, David, I think it would help us establish a relationship of mutual trust if I were able to leave freely, entirely on my own. I'm ready to put myself in your hands: you can work out the details of how I get out unnoticed. Perhaps you could have a section of the fence removed for repairs. But when you make it possible for me to get out, that will be a kind of a seal on our bargain, a show of good faith. Which we'll need if we're to work together."

"Harvey, I want you to try to understand. You need medical help very, very urgently, and even if, for the moment, you don't realize that you need that help, I still have an obligation to see that you get it. You've been through quite a lot, Harvey, and you have to understand that you may not be in any condition to make these judgments for yourself, so that I have a responsibility to decide what is best for you, even if you don't see that it's for the best. Furthermore, Harvey, you have to understand that I don't have the right to let you leave here on your own. If something should go wrong, if something should happen to you or you should have a change of heart, I would be responsible. You've suddenly become very important, not just to yourself but to all your fellow citizens—to all humanity. Some very important decisions have to be made about what is best for you and who should have access to you and what you should be doing, and those decisions have to be made by qualified people with your interest and everyone else's interest at heart. We have to keep control of this situation, for your sake, and for everyone's sake, and I think you can understand that."

"Well, I'll tell you," I said, trying to keep the edge from my voice, "I'm afraid I'm going to have to go on making these decisions for myself—for the time being, anyway. It's just force of habit, really: I'm used to doing it. And one thing I've already decided pretty definitely is that I have no interest whatever in becoming a laboratory animal. I've thought about it quite a lot, and I've come to the conclusion that it doesn't lead anywhere. No real future in it at all. It's just not right for me. Some people would probably love it, but I'd get tired of it right away. Also I'm uninterested in being a side show freak. I wouldn't exhibit well."

"Harvey, I sympathize with the way you feel." He shook his head earnestly. "You just have to understand that our main concern here is to help you."

"Well, if you really wanted to help me, you might begin by helping with the security at the gate. It all seems a little excessive, really—I mean the barbed wire and the automatic weapons and so forth. Unfriendly, if you want to know."

"Harvey, that's not directed against you, or anyone else. It's just standard procedure."

"You mean you have a standard procedure for this situation already?"

"It's really for your protection," he went on.

"If you're concerned with protecting me," I insisted, "you have only to say a restraining word to the guards, and I'll be on my way. I really want to work with you in the future, and, as I see it, you and my fellow citizens and my fellow man and so on will all benefit enormously. All I ask is your help with the barbed wire and the guards and all the other provisions that you've laid on here for my protection."

"This has been an extraordinary ordeal for you, Harvey, but I think you can understand that you can't just walk away from here unsupervised."

"I really don't see why not. It seems like a perfectly reasonable and natural thing to do. Furthermore, it's something I'm legally entitled to do. Wouldn't you say?"

"Well, not necessarily, Harvey." His tone became even more carefully patient and reasonable as the words became more threatening. "You have to understand that, entirely aside from the very substantial issue of national security, there has been extensive damage to private, and probably public, property here. And much more seriously, at least two people have lost their lives. These occurrences apparently resulted from the illegal possession and use of explosive substances in connection with a violent demonstration by a radical political group. Another man has been shot today, and we don't know yet how serious his condition is.

"At the very least, both local and federal authorities would be under a clear obligation to detain and question you. I think you can appreciate that, Harvey. Now, whether beyond that there would be criminal charges, I can't say. I think I could be of real help to you there. Whatever has transpired yesterday and today—and we may never be able to determine with complete certainty what actually has transpired—I think that, given what you've gone through already and the positive attitude you've shown in your conversation with me, even if there are some problems arising out of your actions, things could be worked out reasonably, with some understanding on all sides. But it is crucial that we handle this well from the outset, so that the whole affair presents itself in the right light. I think I'm in a position to reassure you—"

At the mention of my shooting Tyler, I had turned to see what was happening to him. All three men were out of the pit now. Clellan and Morrissey had loaded Tyler onto a stretcher and were carrying him across the lawn toward the medical van.

"Do you know how Tyler is?" I asked.

The Colonel without hesitation pulled his headset from his jacket pocket and put it on.

"Clellan, can you give me a report on Tyler's condition? I'm talking to the man who shot him now. . . . That's right. He's here with me now. . . . No. He's extremely concerned about Tyler's condition."

The two men halted in the middle of the lawn, turning their heads toward us. Then Tyler, lying on the stretcher between them, turned his head too. The three of them stared at us without moving. Then Clellan spoke several sentences into his microphone, and the Colonel pulled off his headset and addressed me again.

"They can't say at this point. As far as they can tell, you shot him once in the thigh just above the knee and once in the abdomen. The bullet exited without touching the spine, but they have no way of knowing whether the bowel or any vital organ has been punctured. Would you like to speak to Tyler yourself?" He extended the headset toward me.

I made no reply. After a moment the Colonel held the headset in front of his mouth and spoke. "Morrissey, you drive Tyler to the gate. Then get back and help Clellan in the building." He pocketed the headset again.

"Are you still there?" he asked.

"I'm here. But I'm leaving now, with or without your help. It's up to you. But I have a gun pointed, as best I can tell, directly at your head. If you don't arrange to have the fence opened up, I'm going to shoot you. Just as I shot Tyler."

Jenkins did not flinch or show any fear or emotion.

"You can do that," he said calmly. "I don't think you will, but you may. But you should understand that it won't help you get past the fence. In fact, it will probably make it more difficult. And it will make things more difficult for you subsequently, no matter what happens."

Pointless. This was all pointless.

"David, of course I'm not going to shoot you. I only hoped that I might be able to get you to do what I think you really ought to be doing anyway. But if you really don't want to work with me on the basis I proposed, then I'll have to leave on my own. As soon as possible, I should think, before you do any more work on that fence."

"Well, Harvey, I can't stop you from doing that if you want to," he said very patiently. "But I'm horrified at the thought of your trying to get past that fence. You couldn't possibly succeed; it would be tragic. I hope you won't try it."

"That's a risk we'll both have to take, apparently. But I should think it would be a pretty big black mark against you to have destroyed me pointlessly. I am a unique specimen."

"It would not be counted as a success, it's true. On the other hand, it wouldn't be thought of as worse than permitting you to go off on your own. And although I don't like to think of it in these terms, I suppose that your body would have some value to mankind. Whereas, if you went off on your own, you might die a hundred yards from here and never be found."

"That would be a pity."

"Well, as a matter of fact, I think it would. But anyway, what would you do if you did get past the fence? Where would you go? How could you hope to survive on your own in this condition? Where would you live? What would you eat? You don't even know what you require to survive. And if you did know, what could you do about it? Could you take a bus or a train? I'm not sure you could even walk down a street safely. Before you attempt anything foolish, I'd like you to give some real thought to these things."

"If I encounter any insoluble problems, I'll be back in touch with you."

"Harvey, I just want you to understand that I'm not threatening you.

I'm only explaining to you what we're under an obligation to accomplish here. By the end of the day we will have completed an initial survey of the building and its contents, and we'll have it sealed off. By then we'll be ready to blanket the entire area with a gas that will render you and anyone else without a gas mask unconscious. We will sweep the entire area within the perimeter fencing, inch by inch. I want to stress that we're doing this above all for your sake, Harvey. At that point, I'm afraid, you will either have given yourself up or you will have been apprehended. But if you somehow did manage to get past the fence, we would of course come after you."

"How could you hope to track me down once I was out of here? I'm standing right in front of you talking to you, and yet even now you wouldn't be able to get hold of me."

"Well, Harvey, I suppose in the worst case we could make a public announcement. We would then have every man, woman, and child in the country—in the world—watching for you. But I don't think that would be necessary. I think you are right that we are ultimately far better off if no one knows about you. We do have some experience in locating people. And in this case we would be in a position to devote very substantial resources to the task."

"No amount would be enough. And anyway, who would believe in my existence? You and I have become almost offhand about invisibility, but your average, sensible, well-informed person will not want to provide money or moral support or even the time of day for a search for invisible men."

"Harvey, I want you to look at that building," he said softly. "It's remarkable, isn't it?"

I looked at it. Clellan had found the stairs to the second story and was mounting them, as if he were climbing magically up to the sky. It was indeed remarkable.

"Whoever administers this building administers an unlimited budget. If I walked the right three people from Washington through this building tomorrow, I could have enough funding to locate a hundred of you. And that would be only the beginning of what we could accomplish."

What he said seemed credible. The building was altogether miraculous. I watched as Clellan seated himself at an invisible desk on the second floor. He glared down at us like some overweight, truculent angel. He knew I was there. His malevolent stare reminded me that I was in increasing danger. I had a great deal to do, and I was wasting my time. Our conversation was at a hopeless impasse: there was no possibility that either of us would persuade the other of anything.

"Look here, David. Everything you say makes sense, and I think we're really in basic agreement. It would probably be madness to try to get past the fence alone, and I suppose I'll have to do things your way. But I'd just like to take an hour or two by myself to think things through first. It's been a difficult day for me. You'll be around, I suppose?"

"I'll be right here when you want me, Harvey. You take your time and arrive at your decision freely. But Harvey?"

"Yes?"

"Before you go, I just wanted to ask you what it was like."

"What what was like?"

"Turning invisible. It must have been horrible for you. Were you conscious the whole time?"

"Unconscious mostly. Until just before you arrived."

"What in the world did you think when you came to?" He seemed genuinely interested.

"A great many things, most of them quite silly. Although no sillier, I suppose, than what turns out to be the actual state of affairs. I thought I was dead, gone to my reward or whatever."

This was the first person to whom I had been able to tell what had happened to me. Perhaps it would turn out to be the only person.

"And what did you do while you thought that?"

"What did I do?" I returned blankly.

"Yes. Did you pray? Or were you waiting for some sign, some revelation? . . . You must, at least at that moment, have seen everything differently."

"I suppose so. Look, David, I know we should all think about these things more, but I'm theologically kind of a bumbler. All thumbs. Anyway, right at the moment my main concern is to get off by myself for a bit. I'll get back to you soon and we can chat then."

"Of course," he responded reasonably.

As he spoke, I took one careful step backwards. His eyes were scanning the ground again, and it seemed to me that he was looking straight at the point where I had placed my foot. I brought back the other foot beside it. I could see blades of grass slowly straightening up where the foot had been and others being crushed as I put it down. Jenkins's eyes were fixed on the spot.

He stepped casually forward. I crouched down as low as I could get. Both his hands shot out suddenly toward me, the right hand open as if to shake mine, and the left hand reaching out around where my torso had just been, as if to give me a friendly clap on the shoulder. Encountering nothing, he looked a bit foolish, but he left his arms extended for a moment, in what looked like a gesture of supplication. From my crouching position I extended one leg as far back and to one side as I could. I shifted my weight carefully onto it, and then took another giant step. After his initial disappointment and confusion, Jenkins had begun to search the ground again for some sign of my new position.

"Just remember, we're here to help you," he said earnestly.

I took several more careful steps back away from him. As I turned to walk away, he was still studying the ground before him.

I would have to confront the problem of the fence now. Somehow I would have to get over it or under it or through it. I realized that, although I had had the fence in the back of my mind all day, I still had no real plan, no real idea how I might accomplish this—nothing but a vague vision of myself slipping through the gate unnoticed or crawling through a depression under the fence like an animal. Now that I actually had to do something, the whole enterprise seemed quite implausible. The area was sealed off and guarded more thoroughly and ruthlessly than a prison camp. Looking around me, I had no idea of what to do, where to begin. I was going to be shot. And if I wasn't, I would be caught and caged. I had to keep moving.

The first thing was to look at the entire fence systematically, then decide what to try. Whether to try. Perhaps something would suggest itself. I walked back to the building. Clellan and Morrissey were finishing up the floor plan of the second story. Working now without any protective clothing, they were moving extremely quickly and they seemed particularly miraculous, adroitly stretching out their pieces of string like magicians, ten feet up in the air. I went straight through the reception room and around to the janitor's closet for the stepladder, which I brought out onto the lawn. Opened up, it was about five feet high, wonderful for changing light bulbs but not of much use for climbing over ten-foot cyclone fencing.

I folded up the ladder again, hooked it over my shoulder, and walked out to the gate. I set it up to one side of the gate itself and about six inches from the fencing. I climbed the steps carefully, rocking forward and back a little so that the legs would dig into the earth. In my experience, stepladders are never adequately steady. In order to see over the top of the fence, I had to climb right up onto the top of the ladder, so that I had nothing to brace myself against. I felt myself teeter sickeningly. More for balance than support, I held a strand of the coiled barbed wire between the thumb and index finger of my right hand, being careful not to move it and attract the attention of the men below.

Directly behind the gate, an area thirty feet long and ten feet wide had been fenced in and covered with sand. The sand was wet and there were men raking it smooth. As they drew their rakes across it, each tine left a perfectly clear fine line. Each step left a beautiful footprint. On either side were low platforms on which men in uniforms stood holding what I assumed to be automatic weapons of some sort. Very unpromising. Sickening.

I could not see very far because of the way the perimeter curved, but in both directions the ground had been cleared in a ten-foot band along the fence, and sand was being spread. I wondered how far they had gotten and how much longer it would take to get all the way around. Not far off, I could hear chain saws. Closing in. Chances contracting. Along the fence, each on his little platform, stood one guard after another, holding his gun. My sense of balance seemed to evaporate, and I felt myself teetering. I had a vision of myself tilting out over the lawn, my feet pushing the ladder into the fence to draw the gunfire onto me.

I kept hold of the strand of barbed wire and slowly, unsteadily, bent myself at the knees until I could slide one foot off the top of the ladder and lower it to the next step. Much better. Another step down, and then I bent over and got the top of the ladder with my hands. I clambered down to the ground. The relief was wonderful. I could have laughed out loud. Except that I still had to find a way out.

I folded up the ladder and started along the fence, looking for any flaw that might offer an opportunity worth the risk. I watched especially for any depression in the ground that might leave an opening I could use to work my way under the fence. I looked in vain for a stream crossing the perimeter. The fencing seemed to be everywhere set well into the ground. They had been very thorough in screening the view through the fence, and nowhere could I find so much as a crack to peer through. About fifty yards along from the gate I could hear that I was opposite the chain saws and mowers. I risked mounting the ladder once more to survey their progress; at the top I raised myself up on one foot for only an instant and immediately lowered the other foot back onto the penultimate step. A momentary glimpse was enough. It would not take them long. The fence ran for most of its length through fields, so that there was very little for them to cut. They would be slowed down, however, on the east side where the fence bordered a wood. It was there that I would have my best chance, and I worked my way around to that side, inspecting the fence carefully the entire way.

Twenty minutes later I had found what I wanted. I made one more brief, precarious ascent of the ladder to get a full view of the area. I didn't like my prospects particularly, but I decided it was worth the risk. Worth a shot, as the unfortunate expression goes. Keep moving.

I placed the stepladder directly in front of the nearest fence post so that I would be able to find it again. It is extraordinary—maddening— the way even the largest objects can be impossible to find when they cannot be seen. Ask Colonel Jenkins.

I returned to the building, where Clellan, Morrissey, and the Colonel were all hard at work. Each of them sat in a different room, diligently writing at an invisible desk, Clellan and Morrissey upstairs and the Colonel downstairs—a troupe of levitating pantomimists representing office workers in an imaginary building. They were making lists, cataloguing all the objects in all of the rooms. I wondered why, of all the tasks they might have undertaken in this extraordinary situation, this particular one had been chosen. But they were, as the Colonel had pointed out, all in government service: it must spring from some primal bureaucratic drive.

I went into the building to look for tables. They had made my task as easy as it could be under the circumstances. Each chair, table, and desk had been marked off by a neat little loop of wire around the bottom of each leg, and with the help of those outlines I could immediately locate everything worth inspecting in each room, and I could carry out what I wanted now without stumbling into walls and furniture. I moved around with confidence, making very little noise and never entering an occupied room.

Most of what I found was useless. The desks were too heavy to move alone, and the typewriter stands would be too insecure. I might have done better in the laboratory, but I was unwilling to risk being cornered either there or on the second floor. In the ground floor offices I knew I could always escape through a window if they heard me and blocked off a door. In three of the offices I found small tables, one of which was more than four feet long and two feet wide. The other two were smaller, but at least all three seemed to be the same height. In the reception room in front of the couch I found a splendid low, narrow coffee table six feet long. From the tops of these tables I removed magazines, computer terminals, coffee cups, papers, and telephones, all of which I carefully set on the floor underneath them. I then slid the pieces of wire off the ends of the legs, leaving the outlines on the floor as neat and rectilinear as possible. Then I lowered each table out the nearest window and carried it to the fence where I had left the stepladder.

Unable to find any more usable tables, I went to the conference room and carried off two wooden folding chairs. Finally, I returned to Wachs's office, where I got down on my knees and, with the help of my penknife, prized up the edge of the carpeting and pulled it back so that I could inspect the undermat. It was rubber, about an eighth of an inch thick. Exactly what I wanted. With the penknife I carved off several large pieces of it and then pushed the carpet back in place as well as I could, although I didn't much care if they noticed my work. I couldn't imagine what they would make of it. On my way back with the matting, I stopped at my hiding place and searched through my sacks until I located a ball of twine. I would have preferred some real rope.

Back at the fence I set about experimenting with different arrangements of the furniture I had assembled, but when I placed the first two tables together, they made a sound that seemed to me as loud and vivid as an auction gavel. I listened several minutes for any indication that I had agitated the guard. I could not afford to take unnecessary risks: I had to take the trouble to do things right. Disheartened, I laboriously carried all four tables twenty yards away from the fence to where I could experiment in relative safety.

Fifteen minutes later I was ready to carry them back again. I positioned two of the tables end to end, parallel to the fence and about nine inches out from it, so that they formed a platform seven feet long beside it. I cut off pieces of twine and tied together the two pairs of adjacent legs, wrapping each pair half a dozen times. Then I opened up one of the folding chairs and used it to climb up on top of the tables. I stood with my feet over the joint of the two tabletops and bounced gingerly up and down to drive the legs into the ground. Then I shifted my feet to first one and then the other pair of outer corners and did the same thing. I could see clearly each of the holes made by the table legs. They were the only visible sign of my work. I spread the largest piece of rubber mat over this platform as a tablecloth to make the next layer of my structure less likely to slip. Then I lifted the larger table and set it up at one end of the platform. On the part of the surface that remained free I placed one of the chairs, to create a step between the two levels of tabletops. Then I set the remaining chair on the ground at the end of the entire structure so that I had a sort of stairway composed of chair, table, chair-on-table, table-on-table.

I got the twine and began tying everything together as best I could without being able to see the twine or the furniture or even my own fingers. I had no idea whether I was accomplishing anything, whether the whole thing would work, but I felt much better now that I was working feverishly at a concrete task. Although I had a crude picture of the whole structure in my mind, there was of course nothing to see and no way to determine what could most usefully be fastened to what, but I lashed tables and chairs together wherever I could, hoping that it would prevent the whole structure from sliding disastrously apart. When I checked over what I had done, I found that much of the twine was already slack. Ominous. I retied everything.

I took another piece of rubber mat and, climbing up onto the first level of tables, laid it over the upper table. I decided to climb up the rest of the way, both to test the security of the whole structure and to get a look at the other side of the fence. The surface of the top table was less than six feet above the ground, but standing on it I felt as if it were sixty. I suppose the structure was still reasonably stable, but I could feel the soft ground yield under it. And I could see nothing, neither myself nor what I was standing on. My sense of balance faded, and I was not sure whether I was standing or falling. I got down on all fours. I mustn't lose control of myself. I had to keep working along. Stand up. Look at the guards. Chain saws still not in sight. Get down. Never think about falling or the sick feeling in the belly. Keep moving.

I climbed all the way down and brought the stepladder over. The whole thing seemed implausible, but I wasn't going to think about it. I got up onto the first level of tables, lifted up the stepladder, and centered it on the surface of the highest table. I got out the twine and lashed the ladder legs to the table legs. I cut off a small piece of rubber mat and draped it over the top of the stepladder. My stairway had reached its full height. When I climbed up onto the top table again to check it, I was relieved to find that the top of the ladder was several inches higher than the barbed wire coiled along the top of the fence.

I clambered down once more and dragged the coffee table over. Holding onto it I climbed up until I was crouched on the top table again. I hauled the coffee table up carefully and balanced it on one end next to the stepladder. The whole structure was at its most unstable, and the next few minutes were hateful. I had to climb up to the second stair of the ladder and slowly lift the coffee table up to chest height, twist it around over the fence, and try to hook it over the branch of the maple tree on the other side. As I extended the table out over the fence, I could only guess where the legs were, and I was terrified of catching the top of the fence with them. Unsure even of whether the table would be long enough to reach the branch, I lowered it slowly. Held out at that angle, the weight of the table became almost unsupportable, and I was afraid that if it did not catch the branch, I would be unable to lift it again and would have to let it fall onto the fence.

I felt the far end come to rest on the branch. I paused for a moment to enjoy the wonderful feeling of relief, and then began to lower the near end slowly onto the ladder top. The branch appeared to be higher than the ladder: there should be enough clearance, but I watched the barbed wire carefully. The table came to rest on the ladder. I reached out and verified that there were several inches between table and fence. I paused again. I twisted and pulled at the table until I was sure that both legs were hooked over the limb, and then, tilting the table on one edge, I slid it further out and hooked one leg through a fork in the branch. I reached out and checked the clearance again. At least six inches.

The table was barely long enough. The near end overlapped the top of the ladder by just four inches, and I was afraid that when the branch was weighted down, it might pull the table off the ladder. I spent another ten minutes lashing the table and the ladder together with twine. I particularly wanted to get that right. In my mind I had a picture of myself being dumped onto the loops of barbed wire along the top of the fence, creating a sudden and dramatic deformation in them. The guards would find the effect curious, but they would not lack for a course of action. Presumably they would shoot until the wires sprang back to their proper shape again.

I set about making a final test of the structure. Climbing up the ladder to the penultimate step, I twisted around and gripped the edges of the table. Very carefully, I climbed up onto the unseeable tabletop and inched my way on all fours out to the middle of it. It was not a pleasant vantage point. I was crouched in midair, looking straight down on a barbed wire fence and, a few yards off in either direction, at two men with guns whose job it was to shoot me if I made a mistake. The structure, now that it was hooked into the tree, was more stable, but it still swayed and heaved with every movement of the branch. I was supported by something that I was absolutely unable to see and that therefore had for me a sort of hypothetical quality.

It is often better to move than to think. I slid my hands back down beneath the table just above the fence and then rocked up and down to make sure that there was still some clearance even with my full weight directly on top. Several inches. The guard to the right must have heard the leaves rustling. He looked up, but not particularly in my direction. I waited a moment and then crawled the rest of the way over to the branch and climbed out onto it. Home free.

I was tempted to keep going. I could see my way down through the branches to the ground. Not carrying anything, I would make no noise. I would be gone. I could see the men with their chain saws now only fifty yards away. They would not be long. And this was a tree they would certainly be cutting down. But I had done all that work, assembled all my equipment and supplies. I would need them. Without them I was finished anyway.

Returning over my bridge, I had to crawl backwards, feet first, so that I could get back onto the stepladder. When I was on the ground again, I checked the position of everything in the pyramid to make sure that nothing was about to slide out of the pile. Then, ridiculously, I stood back, as if to admire my work, in which I felt an anxious satisfaction. It was by now late afternoon. I had completed a difficult task, built something which, if it had been visible, I would have enjoyed surveying with pride. As it was, it remained more a private conceit than a public monument to my determination and ingenuity. And anyway there was no time. I had been working on my construction for two hours. I was tired, sweating, anxious, afraid. The chain saws were getting nearer. The Colonel might at any time figure out what I was doing. I had to keep moving.

I made three or four trips back to the beech tree, hauling back all seven sacks full of random objects, the tool chest, and the broomstick, and heaping them together under my pyramid. I kept an eye on the men in the building all the while, so that if one of them suddenly decided to check along the fence, I would be ready to leave everything behind and run for it.

When I had everything assembled, I took the smallest sack and, mounting the ladder, lifted it up onto the coffee table. I climbed up after it, pushed it carefully across ahead of me to the other side, and then climbed down through the tree to a branch from which I could lower first the sack and then myself to the ground. I carried the sack about twenty yards back into the woods and left it on the ground next to a particularly misshapen pine tree, which I was confident I would recognize. No time for a more distant or cleverer hiding place. I watched the ground in front of me as I walked, trying to avoid making any noise that might alert one of the guards, but by now the noise of the chain saws was probably too loud for that anyway.

I repeated the entire trip seven times, until I had everything safe in a large heap in the woods. It had taken nearly a full hour, and the nearest chain saw was now barely twenty yards away. I was sweating and trembling with the tension, but elated. I was nearly done here.

I climbed back over the fence and hurried to the building. There was not much time, and I had one important task left. The Colonel and his men were as I had left them, miraculously sitting in midair, working at invisible desks, walking about through the void, picking up and setting down objects which one could only try to imagine. Each of them had a clipboard full of information about their little, magic domain. The Colonel was right, I thought. It would be a sort of empire. The spectacle before me was irresistible. It would convince anyone that vast amounts of money should be budgeted, vast numbers of people assigned to the study of these extraordinary phenomena. And to the capture of the invisible man.

I went into Wachs's office first and closed the doors. I was making noise, but I no longer cared. I grabbed all the loose sheets of paper I could find, crumpled them two or three at a time, and tossed them under the desk. Then I pulled all the books off the shelves, spread open the pages, and tossed them on top of the paper. Crouching down, I took the cigarette lighter from my pocket and held it lit to the edge of the pile until I felt the heat of the flame spreading through the paper. I moved around and lit the pile on the other side. I could smell the fire now. I waited until I felt the heat swell up and push at me and saw the air grow turbulent and distort my view.

I hurried out of Wachs's office, closing the door behind me, and ran down the corridor, past the room in which the Colonel was sitting and past the laboratory, to an office at the other end of the building. This time I dragged the desk over against the wall before setting the fire, to make sure it would spread to the building. I was making a lot of noise, and all three men were looking in my direction now. On my way out, I set another fire in the reception room. I left the building with as much paper as I could carry.

When I got back to the fence I could hear that the chain saws were right there now. I spent another five or ten minutes crumpling paper and filling my structure with it, and as I mounted my exit stair for the last time, I set it alight. Bringing one of the folding chairs with me, I climbed up and over to the tree. There were men cutting underbrush right beneath me. I got the chair down and then crawled back out onto the table, cut loose the twine that tied it to the stepladder, and pulled it over into the tree. I could feel the heat from my burning tower of ladder and tables.

I took a last look at the building. The three men were running through the building now, and you could see from the way they moved that they were in a state of agitation near panic, although, floating in thin air, their gestures seemed exaggerated, almost ridiculous. Morrissey was still up-stairs, and I wondered if he was trapped. The air above the building was visibly turbulent. When I descended the tree, there were two men with chain saws standing a little apart from it and looking at it appraisingly. I went to my hoard and set about lugging it further into the woods, where there would be less chance of discovery. When I had moved everything to a new point fifty feet away, I paused and rested for several minutes. I was quite confident now that I had escaped. The odds had swung around in my favor—for the moment at least.

There were sirens now. They seemed to be entering the enclosed area. Suddenly there was a deep, resonating boom behind the fence, as if some-thing had exploded, and the sky above MicroMagnetics seemed to shud-der. I saw a patch of flame high up where fire had spread into the visible trees beyond the building. I hoped it would continue to spread and oblit-erate any sign of my escape. I returned to my work, moving my things in stages until I had everything neatly stored ten feet in from the road on the other side of the wood.

Behind me the sky filled with the sound of chain saws and sirens and turned a brilliant orange from the burning trees and the sunset. Standing there alone in the woods, my heart pounding and my body shaking from fear and exhaustion, MicroMagnetics and all the extraordinary things I had seen—and not seen—already seemed remote and unreal, a receding dream. There was, nevertheless, the preposterous, terrifying, inescapable fact that I was invisible.

OR PERHAPS HALF AN HOUR I SAT TREMBLING BESIDE MY INVISIBLE possessions and rested. I was on the edge of a road that seemed barely important enough to justify the faded white line painted down its center. It was wooded on both sides. To the right it seemed to run back toward the entrance drive of MicroMagnetics. To the left there was no particular reason to believe that it led anywhere. In the time I sat there, the only vehicle I saw was a state police car. It passed slowly, heading toward MicroMagnetics. Several minutes later it reappeared, heading in the opposite direction at the same deliberate speed. In another ten minutes it cruised past again, and I understood that it was patrolling the road.

I felt, I suppose, like any escaped prisoner: elated at having scaled the prison walls but terrified by the lack of refuge in the world beyond them. It seemed safer, therefore—almost comforting—to sit and contemplate what I had escaped from rather than what I had escaped to.

I had certainly precipitated a great deal of activity. I could hear siren after siren howl up to the other side of the enclosed area and then become abruptly silent. They must be admitting even the fire engines very cautiously through the gate. They had not lost interest in me. The whine of the chain saws persisted as they continued clearing around the outside of the fence, and every now and again I heard an unpleasant burst of automatic gunfire. Perhaps they were shooting animals fleeing over the fence from the fire.

I hoped the fire would be a success. I hoped it would utterly consume the building and every invisible object in it—everything that could make my existence credible. There seemed to have been some sort of explosion, which was promising. Who would believe the Colonel now, without that building? I thought of fires I had seen and of how little had remained, even of those objects which we customarily think of as unburnable. I hoped the fire would spread for miles until they had trouble even locating the site of the building. The more confusion and destruction, the safer I would be. Whenever the chain saws paused, I could hear people shouting and large vehicles moving. Certainly this fire, at its center at least, would present the fire fighters with some peculiar problems. I wondered how the Colonel would deal with it. No doubt he was doing the very best job that could be done, with unimpaired efficiency and self-control—despite what must have been unimaginably intense feelings of disappointment. Not to mention rage.

That was, of course, a problem. I had been telling myself all day that I was keeping all my choices alive. At any time I could change my mind and present myself to the authorities. (*I've been thinking things over, and I've decided to put myself in your care after all. It isn't that there was ever really any doubt in my mind—I just needed to get my thoughts in order, if you know what I mean, and I'm extremely sorry about any inconvenience I may have caused. . . .*) That was the thing. The inconvenience had swelled to rather monstrous proportions in the last few hours. As I watched the flames fill the darkening sky and thought of Tyler on the stretcher and wondered whether the others had all got out of the building, I considered that my range of choices was perhaps not so broad after all. I felt myself shuddering. For a moment I thought I might vomit.

I got quickly to my feet and walked out to the road. Important to keep moving. I wondered what was in Jenkins's heart at the instant when he comprehended that the building was on fire. Forget that for now. Keep moving. I stood on the edge of the road and studied the place where I had left my invisible baggage, memorizing the sequence of trees and shrubs and the angles of the branches. I wanted to be absolutely sure that I could recognize the spot, even in the dark.

What I needed urgently was a car that I could load up with my possessions and drive away. The saws were still going, which meant that they were still working at keeping me inside, but any time now Jenkins might find the remains of my bridge over the fence—or simply decide that it would be prudent to assume that I could have escaped. He would begin to search, or even enclose, a larger area. And if they did determine where I had crossed over the fence, they might find my possessions beside the road quite quickly. It would be safer to get as far away as possible to search for a car, but there was no time. From the look of the road, I might walk for miles without finding anything, whereas I knew that there must be an extraordinary number of vehicles at the MicroMagnetics site, many of them probably unattended.

I set out, walking back towards the entrance to MicroMagnetics, keeping on the left edge of the road in order to be absolutely sure that I would see any vehicle coming toward me. No one was going to swerve to avoid me. A red pickup truck came up from behind and passed me. I was relieved to see that the road had not been closed off to civilian traffic. The two occupants were staring up over the treetops at the glow of the fire in the distance, and the truck slowed until it was barely moving. When the patrol car reappeared, its roof lights began blinking in a threatening pattern, and it pulled up directly behind the truck, twenty yards beyond me.

"*Let's keep it moving.*"

The instruction was spoken in a flat, neutral tone but amplified out of all human proportion, as if it were a divine injunction booming out of the heavens. My entire body twitched in a moment of terror before I realized that the command had come from a megaphone in the police car. The truck started forward with a violent jerk and sped away down the road. I could see that even if I was able to find a car, I was not going to have much time to load in my possessions.

A minute later I came around a bend and saw that ahead of me on the left, another road ran at a right angle into the road I was on. Just beyond the intersection, a roadblock had been created out of state police cars and large yellow plastic barrels. A gap had been left just large enough for a car to pass, and in front of it stood a state trooper. The red pickup truck was just coming up to the intersection, and I saw the trooper wave it away down the side road. There it immediately pulled over and stopped, joining a dozen other cars and trucks parked at random off both sides of the road. Their occupants loitered in little groups by their cars and stared up at the flames in the distance or tried to get information from the policeman, who, however, seemed to be maintaining a posture of aloof reticence toward the public. The patrol car, which had been following the pickup truck, executed a U-turn in the intersection and headed back up the road toward me. I stepped well off to the side to let it pass and continued toward the roadblock.

As I approached the small congregation of human beings, all completely ignorant of my presence, I had a sudden sense of my own strangeness and isolation. I walked warily up the center of the road, watching everyone around me carefully, afraid that someone would without warning walk into me—or worse yet, start up a car and run right over me. Every moment that I spend in proximity to other human beings is shot through with unrelieved anxiety. I have to be constantly vigilant for any sign of a sudden movement or an illogical change of direction that will turn into some ludicrous collision, or some final grotesque mangling of my unnoticeable form. And if the other human beings have large animals or machinery under their capricious control, things are even worse. I was beginning to see what life would be like.

I paused just before the intersection and looked longingly at the vehicles parked outside the road block. Pointless to think of taking one. I had to assume that all of their owners were standing right there. It became clearer to me that I was trying not just to find a car but to steal one. Somewhere on the other side of the roadblock there would be fields full of vehicles, some of them perhaps with ignition keys left in them.

Whether that would be of use to me would depend on whether there was some way to get one around or through the roadblock.

I walked across the intersection and, giving the trooper a wide berth, went up to the barricade to examine the situation. Just beyond the roadblock six or seven more state troopers stood about talking to each other and drinking coffee out of white Styrofoam cups. Beyond them, another hundred yards down the road, I could see the beginning of the drive into MicroMagnetics, and beyond the drive, half-screened by the rows of trees that lined it, was the large field I had seen earlier in the day, over which vast numbers of men and machines seemed to be swarming. What possible purpose could they be serving? It was dusk, almost dark, and I could not really make out what they were doing, but their activity seemed oddly unrelated to the adjacent site—or former site—of MicroMagnetics itself, which was concealed behind the shrouded fence. I could see brilliant orange and white flames rising into view above the fence and spreading through the treetops, and I could smell the delicious smoke. It was quite beautiful: neatly contained in its perimeter and surrounded by all that purposeful movement of men and vehicles, it seemed more like some enormous foundry than an uncontrolled outbreak of destruction.

The local people outside the roadblock seemed to share my enthusiasm and interest. However, the state troopers, in whose midst I now stood, made a point of looking as little as possible at the fire. It was evidently beneath their professional dignity to betray any fascination with the drama of events; they spoke very little and in matter-of-fact tones. Occasionally one of them would have an incomprehensible dialogue through a police car radio. I took a position just to one side of the point at which vehicles would have to stop and waited to see what I could learn about security procedures. But there was very little to learn, since there seemed to be no traffic aside from police cars. After a quarter of an hour, it dawned on me that further up the road, past MicroMagnetics and the field full of military vehicles and personnel, there must be another roadblock through which all the official vehicles entered and left the area. But surely *someone* must pass through this way or they would have closed off the road entirely.

I was almost ready to give up and begin walking again when, in defiance of the state trooper waving it off, an extraordinarily decrepit grey station wagon pulled into the roadblock. At the wheel sat a boy of seventeen or eighteen with a not entirely successful mustache. Through narrowed eyes he watched the policeman and waited with nervous defiance for him to speak first.

"I'm sorry, this road is closed."

"I'm going through," the boy said provocatively.

"This road is closed. You'll have to back it up."

"I live on this road. I go up this road every day."

The trooper responded with absolute evenness. "Take your operator's license and your registration out of your wallet and hand them to me, please."

The boy repeated himself in an aggrieved tone, "I go over this road every day." He was pulling out his license and registration. He handed them to the state trooper. A man in civilian dress, whom I somehow had not noticed before, stepped up beside the trooper, who passed the cards on to him without looking at them. The man examined the cards and then leafed through a stack of papers fastened to a clipboard. He walked around to the rear of the car and looked at the license plate. He walked back and with a brief nod handed the cards to the trooper, who handed them to the boy.

"Thank you," said the trooper, with his own unsmiling nod.

"I've lived here my whole life. I use this road every day."

The trooper made a little motion with his hand indicating that he could proceed and then stepped back. The station wagon continued on through.

Which was fine for the station wagon but not very encouraging for me. What would their reaction be when the driver's license and registration floated out of the window and hovered in midair for their inspection. Still, I wanted to wait and see what happened when a vehicle was leaving the area rather than entering it.

It was another ten minutes before an old pickup truck came rattling up from the direction of MicroMagnetics. I watched closely. No one seemed much interested. It slowed down as it passed between the barrels, and another boy, much like the first, shouted out, "Reilly! Kevin Reilly!" The trooper, who was still on the side of the road from which he could talk to drivers of incoming cars, glanced casually at the passenger window of the cab as he made his waving motion. The pickup, without ever coming to a full stop, continued on through the intersection and sped off down the road.

That was more promising. Definitely worth a try. And suppose they did stop me. They would be a bit mystified if they looked into the stopped car and saw no driver, but I should be able to escape easily enough. I would not be much worse off than I was now.

I turned and set out along the road toward all the activity in the background, to look for some sort of parking lot. There were open fields on both sides of the road now, and on my right I had an unobstructed view of the fence that shielded the MicroMagnetics site. As I walked I watched the fire beginning to subside behind it. When I reached the beginning of the tree-lined drive leading into MicroMagnetics, I stopped. The drive itself was now cut off by the fence and completely deserted, since the Colonel's men had constructed their new access road further on, but strewn about the field on my left, immediately opposite the old drive, were roughly two dozen cars, completely unattended. None of them appeared to be military or police vehicles. They looked somehow familiar.

When I recognized the grey van, I felt a wave of something resembling vertigo. Carillon's van. Less than thirty-six hours ago I had arrived in it, looking pretty much like anyone else. Now I looked like no one at all. Thirty-six hours. It seemed like the proverbial eternity. Or no time at all: just an abrupt, meaningless discontinuity in the chart. It was Carillon's fault, come to think of it. Asshole. Damn him. Although I suppose you could just as well say it was Wachs's fault. Or no one's fault, if you like. As a matter of fact, I would just as soon not give either of them credit for anything as extraordinary as my present condition. Not much satisfaction to be had from anger at them, anyway: they had both done worse out of it all than I.

My mind flooded again with the ghastly image of the two of them on the lawn, bursting into flame.

The important thing was to keep moving. I stepped off the road and walked into the field to look at the cars. They were scattered about the edge of the field chaotically. It looked as if, at some point during yesterday's grotesque events, all the cars in the parking lot had been hurriedly towed out of the lot and dumped here. The owners would already have been evacuated from the scene, and the way things were going now, it might be some time before anyone got around to arranging for them to return and claim their cars. There was quite a varied selection to choose from: sports cars, station wagons, sedans, even an old convertible.

It was Carillon's van that I wanted though. I knew that at once. For one thing, it was more than big enough to hold my entire hoard. It even had a large, convenient sliding door on one side and double swinging doors at the rear to make my task easier. But I was also pleased with the fact that it was Carillon's—or, if not, it would quickly be connected to Carillon. Whether they stopped the van now at the gate or found it later miles away when I was done with it, they would assume that one of Carillon's friends had made off with it. Jenkins, when he found out, would of course think of me at once, and it would confirm his assumption that I was a student for a fair world. I found myself hoping that the Students for a Fair World would turn out to be an immensely successful mass movement, with a vast roster of members, and that it would take years to track them all down. If it was enough trouble, they might never get around to checking up on Nicholas Halloway.

There was one other thing about the van. I had a clear picture in my mind of Carillon standing in the parking lot yesterday morning and casually tossing the keys in through the open back doors.

The van had been left facing the road at an angle. I circled around it to the sliding door, which was on the side away from the road. I took a long careful look around in every direction. It was almost dark now, and as far as I could tell there was no one anywhere near. I took hold of the door handle and gently pulled at it. It did not yield. I gradually increased the force. Suddenly it gave way and slid open with a violent grinding noise, while in the same instant the interior roof light automatically ignited, brilliantly illuminating the van like a signal lantern in the dark field. For one terrified moment I was paralyzed. Then I lunged at the light and switched it off, stumbling onto my hands and knees on the floor of the van, with my heart racing.

I climbed back out of the van and stood on the ground outside for what seemed like a quarter of an hour, waiting to see whether anyone would come. In the distance there was every imaginable sort of noise and activity, but there was not a sound, not a movement, anywhere in the field around me. I climbed back into the open van and searched the grimy metal floor on my hands and knees until I found the keys. I climbed up into the driver's seat and got one of them into the ignition. It turned, and little red indicator lights lit up across the dashboard. I turned the key off again, leaving it in the ignition, while I continued my inspection of the van. I carefully opened both front doors and the back doors to make sure they were all unlocked. It meant putting up with the excruciating noise of pushing them shut again, but I had to know.

No maps in the glove compartment. I would have liked a map of New Jersey. I took a thick plastic windshield scraper around to the rear of the van and jabbed it into the light over the license plate until I felt the bulb smash.

The sound of the chain saws stopped.

I climbed back into the driver's seat and rolled down the window at my side. I sat there for several moments, collecting my wits and my nerve. Don't think about it. Turn the key and start the engine. You have to keep moving. Check the hand brake. Into low gear, let out the clutch. I rolled slowly out onto the road with the headlights still off. I wanted them to have as little warning as possible of my arrival.

When the cluster of cars and policemen came into view, I switched my headlights on and accelerated, driving through them at an aggressive pace and halting abruptly as far forward in the roadblock opening as I plausibly could.

"Reilly," I shouted out the window. This, I hoped, would be the only account I would have to give of myself. But a policeman—not the one who had been there before—walked slowly forward toward my window. He held a large flashlight in one hand. Behind him I could see the same civilian with the clipboard start back around the car to look at the license plate.

In another moment the policeman would surely be gazing in amazement at the empty driver's seat. Should I just wait, hoping against the odds for some other, better outcome? Let out the clutch and run for it? Forget the van and scramble out the other side door? Decide now.

"Thank you!" I shouted amiably through the window, as if the hoped-for permission had actually been granted. I let out the clutch and pulled away at a confident but not excessive speed. I had a glimpse of the police-man's face registering both surprise and indecision. Thirty yards down the road I leaned out the window and took another look: he still stood un-certainly in the same position, his flashlight lighting up a little circle on the road beside him, as he gazed after me.

He might decide to do nothing, to ignore it. Or he might, at any mo-ment, decide to come after me, or more likely to radio other police cars and have them come after me. Especially the car patrolling this road. I should get off this road anyway. Not safe here.

I watched for the place where my things were. On the left, in the illumi-nation of my headlights, I picked out the sequence of trees. I kept going. I didn't dare stop. I was watching the right side of the road now, hoping the patrol car wouldn't appear yet. Both sides of the road were wooded now. In another quarter-mile there was a dirt road off to the right. I pulled up just past it, switched down to my parking lights, and began backing up the dirt road. By the time I saw the lights of the police car appear through the trees to my right, I was a good twenty yards off the main road. I switched off the parking lights and turned off the ignition.

The police car cruised slowly past, heading toward the roadblock. If the police in it were looking anywhere, they would be looking at the opposite side of the road toward MicroMagnetics. The police car's tail-lights disappeared from view. I waited. Several minutes later it reappeared, coming back toward me. I let it pass. When the taillights had disappeared again, I switched on the ignition and started the engine. I made myself count to ten. Mustn't hurry it. Don't take an unnecessary chance. I switched on my headlights, slammed into gear, and drove for all I was worth out the dirt road and left onto the asphalt road. When I got to where my things were I pulled several yards past the spot, made a U-turn, and pulled over to the left side. I wanted to be facing away from the road-block: I was not going to drive past the roadblock again. The van was half off the road at a slight angle with the motor running and the head-lights on so that I could see my footing.

Leaving the door by the driver's seat open, I ran back to the rear of the van and pulled open the double doors. Then I charged over to my cache, grabbed the first sack my hands encountered, lugged it back, and swung it as far into the van as I could reach. I had at least six or seven minutes, maybe more. One at a time, and then two at a time, I hauled the sacks into the van. Seven. I was certain there were seven. Then the toolbox, the table, the broomstick. I had to search awhile for the broomstick. I must have wasted half a minute looking for it. I swung the rear doors shut again. No sign of the patrol car yet. I ran back, went down on my hands and knees, and groped around on the ground for anything that might have slipped out of the sacks. My hand ran against the edge of a large, hard object. The folding chair. I had forgotten about the folding chair.

At that moment the headlights of the patrol car appeared in the distance ahead as an expanding glow over a rise in the road. I lunged for the van with the chair in my hands, and heaved it in through the open door as I clambered up into the driver's seat and pulled the door shut. The glow had turned into two distinct beams of light aimed directly at me. Release the hand brake. Clutch in; shift into low gear; let the clutch out carefully—don't take a chance on stalling now. I pulled away, crossing obliquely over to the right side of the road. They were still more than fifty yards away. No reason for them to think I had been stopped: it should look to them as if I had been driving toward them the whole time.

I accelerated steadily. Looking into my headlights, they would not be able to see the empty driver's seat, and by the time we passed each other I was going forty miles per hour. Not much time for a good look. I saw, or thought I saw, their brake lights go on in my rearview mirror. I was terrified, but I resisted the temptation to accelerate past fifty. I kept watching the rearview mirror. No headlights appeared.

After I had driven what seemed like a very long time and was probably under five minutes, I came to an intersection. There was no road sign. I turned right, onto the other road, simply because it made me feel as if I was getting further away. At the next intersection I turned left onto still another road. I drove along like that, making random turns, for fifteen minutes until I gradually began to calm down. There was no reason to believe that the police had decided to look for the van. And by the law of averages I must be getting further and further away.

Then suddenly I found myself entering a town. When I saw the first streetlight, I felt as if someone had shone a searchlight on me. I slammed on the brakes, wheeled the van around in a violent U-turn, and headed right back out of the town. I imagined the grotesque spectacle I would create. Some aging couple stepping carefully out onto the main street from the bowels of the local "Colonial Inn" would look up and see a driverless van roll by. Or it would be the local teenagers loitering in the center of the village. Or perhaps the local policeman, parked by the side of the road in his unlit patrol car, would watch as an absolutely empty vehicle pulled magically up to the town's only stoplight. There would be shouting and pointing. There would be pursuit.

At the next intersection I made another random turn. Where was this going to get me? How far could I go in any direction without encountering towns or lights or people? It was ludicrously unfair that invisible I created a spectacle, when in my normal state I would have been utterly inconspicuous. What was the point of driving around in circles in the middle of New Jersey until I ran out of gas?

A moment later I found myself stopped at a red light. Across the intersection was an automobile whose headlights stared straight at me. The driver must be looking right at me. Or right at my absence. How would he react? What would he do? It struck me abruptly that I had no idea how he was reacting, because I could not see him: his windshield revealed nothing but the reflected glare of my own headlights. The light turned green, and as we passed each other, I looked at his side window. On the glassy black surface there was a meaningless movement of reflected shadows; behind it, I thought I could just make out the vague form of a driver. Why had I never noticed till now how little one could see through car windows at night? Because I hadn't been paying attention. Fortunately, people are rarely paying attention—which is the only reason I have ever had a chance of remaining at large. I rolled up my side window.

I began to calm down again. No one was going to notice that my van had no visible driver. I could probably drive wherever I liked in complete safety. Except that eventually I would run out of gas or the sun would come up. The gas tank was three-quarters full. Where was I going?

I slowed down. I had to think things through. I had a van full of irreplaceable objects. Ideally, I would like to take them home. The trouble was that I lived on the other side of the Hudson River, and to cross the Hudson River you have to be prepared to drive up to a well-lit tollbooth and hand a toll collector two dollars. I had in my pocket about $150 worth of invisible bills, which I ought to remember to destroy at the first good opportunity. But even if I were somehow to get hold of some visible money, I did not see how I could pay a toll. Or buy more gas. I had to find a temporary storage place for my things on this side of the Hudson. Someplace I could reach on half a tank of gas.

Everything was becoming clearer as I thought it out, and I could see now where I had to go. It occurred to me, however, that I still had no idea where I was.

I began at each intersection to choose the most important-looking road. Like someone lost in the wilderness always following running water downstream: sooner or later you will encounter civilization or the sea. I was rewarded eventually with a route number, although not one I recognized. It was labeled South. I slowed down, making sure that there were no headlights approaching, and made a U-turn. I stayed on that road until I arrived at a well-marked intersection with a sign for Route 202. I was fairly sure I wanted that: I made the turn marked 202 North.

There was much more traffic now, and other vehicles were passing me. I went through an enormous, well-lit traffic circle where there were cars all around me. I drove through towns. No one seemed to notice my apparent absence, and I found that my unreasoning panic had subsided to nothing more than gnawing anxiety. I noticed that I was tensely hunched over the wheel, and I forced myself to sit back in the seat and try to relax.

In less than forty-five minutes I was in Basking Ridge, and in another few minutes I had found Richard and Emily's house. My memory was that there was no other house in sight, but to be sure I switched off my headlights before turning into the drive, and I drove the van up onto the lawn and around behind the house, so that even if someone should come up the drive, they would not see it.

The night air was cool, and I devoted several minutes to locating my jacket in one of the sacks. Then, taking the flashlight from the van, I went over and retrieved the keys to the house and barn from their hiding place under the porch steps. I pocketed them and set out to reconnoiter the grounds. There was the house itself, a small barn, a pump house, and an old icehouse. I settled on the icehouse. It was unlocked and empty, both indications that no one would have any interest in it. Lying on the saw-dust floor were some old, weathered pieces of lumber. I fetched a ladder from the barn and used it to lift several pieces of the lumber up and across the rafters so that they made a sort of platform well out of reach of any caretaker or child who might wander in. They looked as if they might have been up there for fifty years. I drove the van around and backed it right up to the door of the icehouse. In twenty minutes I had stored all my invisible things securely in the rafters and smoothed the sawdust floor again so that there was no sign of my visit. I assumed that I would be back in a few days to retrieve everything. But barring some extraordinary piece of bad luck, everything should be safe there indefinitely. When they were in the United States, Richard and Emily came down here on weekends, but most of the time the house stood empty. As long as no one had seen the van here, there was no reason Jenkins should ever learn of the existence of this place.

I climbed back into the van and drove back out the drive, not turning on the lights again until I was a quarter of a mile down the road.

A S I GOT FURTHER AWAY FROM BASKING RIDGE AND CLOSER TO NEW YORK, I began to feel, for the first time, almost secure. I had successfully escaped; I had hidden all my supplies; and in another hour or two I would be safely back home in my apartment in New York. There I would have everything I needed, and once I had had a few days rest, I would retrieve my invisible things as well. I should be able to live there indefinitely. I would have to work out something with my office. And I would be declining all invitations. Melancholy. But if I was discreet I ought to be able to live quite comfortably on my own, unnoticed, unsupervised, unexamined. Colonel Jenkins would be busy following college students about; there should be no reason for him ever to bother me.

Unless someone reported me missing.

Anne, for instance. Because I had, in fact, been missing for over thirty-six hours now. Why hadn't I thought this through until now? My mind was not working properly. She couldn't have said anything right away, or Jenkins would have suspected my identity from the beginning. That meant she must have thought I had been outside the building and had left on my own. There had probably been a lot of confusion. But by now a day and a half had gone by without her hearing a word from me. At some point she would start to worry. Or at least to wonder what had become of me.

I slammed on the brakes and turned abruptly into a closed gas station, pulling up alongside a telephone booth. I dialed the *Times*, billing the call to my credit card, and asked for Anne Epstein. It must be nearly eleven by now, and I could be reasonably confident that she would not be there.

"Steve Beller," said an impatient and flatly unfriendly male voice.

"Hello. I'm trying to reach Anne Epstein."

"She's not here now."

"Do you have any idea where I can reach her? I've been trying to get her all day."

"We can't give out home numbers. Try in the morning."

"I have her home number. I've been trying to catch her all day. Could you possibly take a message? I realize it's—"

"What is it?" he asked curtly.

"If you could just say *Nicholas Halloway has been trying all day to reach you.*" I said it slowly, with emphasis, in the hope that he would write it down just like that.

I thought of calling her at home and actually speaking to her, but that would have meant deciding what I wanted to say to her.

In a few more minutes I was in Newark. The brightness of the street-lights made me anxious, but the streets were nearly empty, and I tried to make myself stop thinking about it. For twenty minutes I drove in circles, trying to locate the railway station and wishing I could ask someone for directions. When I had finally encountered the overhead tracks and followed them to the station, I drove back away from it again, to find a suitable parking place for the van. I was confident that Newark would offer the kind of parking I wanted.

I pulled up alongside a fire hydrant, several feet out from the curb, and switched off the ignition, leaving the key in it. The street was relatively deserted, but further down the block there was a group of people, probably in their teens and twenties, sitting on a stoop or leaning against the cars parked in front of it. On the roof of one car they had set up a large portable radio—as large, come to think of it, as any stationary radio I have ever seen. They were drinking beer and smoking and intermittently shouting along with the music in Spanish. When I pulled up, several of them glanced over in my direction.

I climbed back through the van, opened the rear doors, and slid out onto the street. I could smell the fragrance of marijuana and hear little shrieks of laughter over the music. I went to work with my penknife unscrewing the license plate, and when it clattered onto the ground, I kicked it along the curb and through a metal grill into the sewer. The young people down the street were all eyeing the carelessly parked van now. Several of them had stood up to get a clearer look. Leaving the rear doors open, I walked across the street to watch. Two of the young men were ambling slowly down the sidewalk. One of them peered in the side window of the van, while the other walked around to the rear.

"Everything all right in there?" said the one at the window. He waited a moment for a reply and then banged the flat of his hand against the side of the van twice.

"Anybody home?"

The other man was peering warily into the body of the van through the open rear door. I turned and walked away. It seemed unlikely that Carillon's van would ever be located. The only question in my mind was whether it would be sold whole or dismembered on the spot. A car in the city streets with anything wrong—a flat tire, an unlocked door, a missing license plate—is like a bleeding animal in shark-infested waters. The predators strike instantly and strip it clean to the skeleton.

I walked back to the railway station and found the platform for the train into New York. I was dreading the next hour of dodging through crowds on public transportation, but it was almost midnight and I had no difficulty avoiding collisions with the few other passengers boarding the train. Once I was sure they were all settled, I even allowed myself the luxury of a seat.

At Pennsylvania Station I waited until all the other passengers had left the train and then hiked up the empty stairways, rather than risk the escalator. As I was trudging up the last flight, a teenager in running shoes came flying four stairs at a time straight down at me, shrieking maniacally. Not a particularly unusual occurrence to a New Yorker, but, cowering along the railing, I barely remembered in time that it was now up to me to scramble out of the way.

When I emerged into the main hall it seemed to me as if I were returning to New York after an absence of years. I felt a relief verging on joy at being back, but at the same time I felt utterly remote and cut off from the human beings scattered through the cavernous room, none of whom could be aware of my existence. They were no longer people I might speak to or know: they were only objects, whose unpredictable movements across my path constituted a mild danger against which I had to maintain my guard.

With an occasional wide detour around a zigzagging drunk, I made my way across to the West Side IRT, climbed over a turnstile, and boarded the last car on a northbound train. Although it was almost empty and I was exhausted, I remained standing. At Forty-second Street I got off and changed to the crosstown shuttle. There were more passengers there, and many of them boarded at the near end of the train and walked through to the other end during the trip, so that I had to keep dodging them as they came by, and I finally climbed up and stood on a seat to let them pass. At the East Side IRT, I waited for the express. Not as much exiting and entering and moving around on the express trains. I got off at Eighty-sixth Street and waited until everyone else had left the platform before beginning the hike up the two flights of stairs to the street. I was very tired. Only a few blocks.

At Eighty-eighth Street my adventure nearly came to a messy end. With the traffic light green for me, I started across the street. At the same moment the driver of a cab that was stopped behind the crosswalk, seeing that the intersection was clear, shot onto Lexington Avenue against the light, catching me with his side mirror and spinning me into a parked car. I shrieked with surprise and pain. I thought at first that his side mirror had ripped off my arm, but as it turned out, my arm had ripped off his side mirror. The cabby slammed his car to a halt and climbed out, leaving it stopped in the middle of the intersection. He was fat enough so that his walk back to the mirror in the crosswalk had a sort of stateliness. Although what had happened must have been utterly inexplicable to him, he had an expression more of belligerence than of puzzlement. Probably he found a lot of things in his daily life inexplicable. He picked up the mirror and looked around truculently. By this time the next wave of traffic had come down Lexington, and cars were blocked behind his cab and using their horns. He ambled back, climbed into his cab, slammed the door, and turned down Lexington.

My arm seemed to be intact. As I stood there clutching it stupidly, I found that I was trembling—more from nerves and exhaustion than from any injury, I decided. I couldn't take any more of these narrow misses. Only a few more blocks. Stepping back up onto the sidewalk, I caught a toe on the curb and stumbled forward. More and more mistakes. I had to pay careful attention to everything. At the next corner I walked around behind the cars stopped for the light. Be careful crossing the street. Stop, look, and listen, as they told me over and over in school. Absolutely exhausted. When I reached my building I was still trembling.

My apartment occupied the entire top floor of a brownstone between Fifth and Madison. The three flights of stairs were sometimes demoralizing, but because of the way the lower floors of the building had been extended into the back lot, my apartment had been left with a large terrace facing south, and I was afforded a pleasant illusion of being surrounded by vegetation and sunlight. You entered the building through two windowed doors, between which there was a tiny vestibule containing the mailboxes, the doorbells, and an intercom.

I looked around to make sure no one was in the street, pushed open the outer door just far enough to get through, and slipped into the vestibule. I pulled out my keys, and, out of habit, set about opening my mailbox, a task which I found had become quite difficult now that the mailbox key was invisible. Looked like all junk mail. I slipped it into my side pocket. It took me another few minutes to single out the house key from among the eight keys on my key ring and then get the inner vestibule door open. I began the long trudge up the stairs.

I was most of the way up the first flight when I glanced down and saw the bizarre spectacle I was creating. The white bundle of mail in my pocket would be clearly visible to anyone who looked in from the street or out from one of the other apartments, and it would seem to be bobbing inexplicably through the air up the stairway. I crouched down and looked through the windowed vestibule doors: no one seemed to be on the street. I had to think more clearly about what I was doing. I was just too tired. Could any of my neighbors in the building have seen me through their little peepholes? I should be walking softly in order not to encourage them to peer out in the first place. Taking the packet of mail in my hand, I bent over and held it next to the baseboard, where it would be less noticeable, and in this awkward position climbed up the remaining stairs.

The stairway ended on a landing in front of my door. I got out my keys again and went to work on the last two locks. My body ached to be inside. I needed to eat and drink, to lie down, to sleep. To be safe. Get the right key—it was a Medeco, with slanting teeth—use a finger to guide it in, and turn. Then the other key—one of the ones next to it, but which one? Hold onto the Medeco and try each of them. The first one wouldn't go. The second slid in and turned. The door swung open. I stepped in, switched on the lights, pulled the keys out of the lock, and pushed the door shut behind me.

Home free.

I nearly swooned from elation and relief. I was safe and secure within my own walls, behind my own doors. Nothing could happen to me now. They couldn't get me here. A momentary fear passed over me like a shadow: could they have tracked me down already? Could they already be here waiting in the apartment? Not yet. They wouldn't be looking for me yet. I would be safe here for a while, perhaps a long while. Perhaps indefinitely. Why should they ever figure out who I was? I was safe, at least for now, in these familiar, altogether private surroundings. I could sit down now and have a drink and think what to do next. I felt myself salivating at the thought. I stumbled deliriously into the kitchen, dropping the mail onto the kitchen table and tossing my keys on top, just as always.

The air was still and stuffy. Careful. Before I opened the kitchen window I would have to switch out the lights. Otherwise some peeping neighbor would see the window sash rising mysteriously of its own accord. Come to think of it, he might see a lot of curious events: the mail sailing magically through the room and landing on the table. New Yorkers, who live over, under, and all around each other, take extraordinary pains to avoid any intimacy with their neighbors, to avoid even meeting or speaking to them; but they are always watching, peering, spying.

I turned off the lights again and worked my way through the entire apartment, systematically drawing each shade and curtain. Then, when I had opened some windows and got the lights on again, I found myself hurrying toward the refrigerator with rapidly mounting anticipation, and, as I pulled open the door, I remembered half-consciously that I had not drunk anything since morning or eaten anything for almost two days. Beer. I pulled out a bottle and with trembling hands twisted off the cap. It was wonderfully cold going down, and the alcohol gave me a feeling of well-being so acute that I thought I would weep. Once again I was aware that I was almost swooning from euphoria and exhaustion. Sit down.

Home now. Safe. Plenty of time now to sort things out. I felt the euphoria spreading through my body.

Soon—impossible to know exactly how long, in my trancelike state—I was back at the refrigerator opening another beer and looking to see what there was to eat. A half-full container of moo shu pork. It would be several days old, but it wouldn't require any preparation. I got some chopsticks from the drawer and frantically pulled open the top. The sight and smell of the food set off an explosion of hunger in me, and I felt the saliva running in my mouth. I was shoveling the food in uncontrollably and swallowing it almost unchewed. When the box was empty, I drank down the second beer and resumed my search of the refrigerator. Still standing in front of it, I tore the top off a quart of coffee ice cream and began greedily spooning it into myself. I noticed peripherally that I seemed to have spilled some food down my front, but for a while I continued eating compulsively. Better to stop and clean my shirt, I thought. Important to keep it invisible. I set the ice cream down on the table, with the idea of going over to the sink and wiping off my clothes.

But when I looked down at myself, I saw that I had not spilled anything at all. What I had done was to pour into my invisible esophagus a hideously visible brown and yellow mixture of moo shu pork, coffee ice cream, and beer. The sludgy concoction was piling up in my stomach, of whose exact location I had never, until this moment, really been quite sure.

I was becoming a sack of vomit and fecal matter. I suppose, on reflection, that that is what I had always been, but nature had not formerly imposed this aspect of the human condition quite so vividly upon me. The nasty facts had been discreetly enveloped in opaque flesh. Now I was to be a transparent sack of vomit and fecal matter. I cannot begin to tell you how distasteful it was.

It was also disheartening. Frightening. I had thus far assumed—even almost grown used to the idea—that if I could not look like everyone else, at least I would be entirely invisible. All my hopes of avoiding capture had been built on that assumption. Now it appeared that not only would I not be safely invisible after all but I would be manifested in the visible world exclusively as a gastrointestinal tract. Ludicrous.

I could not stop myself from looking down. It—"I" was really the appropriate pronoun—was ugly and becoming uglier. Sickening. Perhaps I would have to dedicate myself to serving science after all. Damn! I felt very close to throwing up the whole mess. But I needed the nourishment. Or perhaps not. Perhaps I—my transformed body—could not digest normal food anyway. Perhaps I was dying. Like everyone else. Human condition and so forth. Hideous, the way, as the food churned slowly through the stomach, the color and consistency altered. Foul.

A more hopeful thought came to me. I seemed to remember reading somewhere—perhaps it was in a school biology text—that the human body replaces itself cell by cell many times during its life span. How many times? How quickly? Perhaps, as I ate and drank and breathed, my body would gradually reconstitute itself out of normal, visible particles of matter. Perhaps I should be eating as much as I could force down. Speed up the process. In a few weeks I might look like a human being again. It would be just a matter of holing up in my apartment here until I was back to normal. An exhilarating thought.

An unrealistic thought, I decided, and my mood plummeted precipitously again. Life, and especially its misfortunes, are rarely so neat and clear-cut. The most likely thing was that I would be neither visible nor invisible but rather a blotchy translucent sack of filth. Perhaps the laboratory workers would grow accustomed to looking at me.

I couldn't help looking down at myself. Small amounts of milky brown sludge were being squirted into the small intestine. Invisibility, which a few minutes before had seemed a horrible fate, now seemed infinitely desirable. Damn.

All I could do was wait and see what would happen. In the morning I might be able to tell what I was doomed to look like. Or not look like. I poured myself a tumbler of Scotch and went into the bedroom. Standing in the middle of the room, I took a good swallow and watched it gurgle rhythmically down my esophagus to join the rest of the sewage in my stomach. Disgusting. My condition was unspeakably, hopelessly disgusting. And at the same time ridiculous. Hard, in a way, to take it seriously. I felt, almost, like laughing out loud, but I was afraid the laughter would turn into vomiting. Have another swig of Scotch and calm down. Think things through in the morning. Lie down on the bed for a moment. Hopeless. I should take off my clothes. Rest a few minutes first. Close my eyes for a moment. Doesn't help, see right through the eyelids—grotesque. Feels better anyway with the eyelids down. Not hopeless. Serious but not hopeless. Like the Prussian and the Austrian: the situation serious but not hopeless. Hopeless but not serious. Shit. Ought to get clothes off. Serious but not hopeless . . . but not serious. . . . Shit.

THE MORNING SUN WAS FLOODING IN THROUGH THE UNSHADED WINDOW and soaking into my body. It felt wonderful. Although I seemed to have passed out with all my clothes on. Must have drunk too much. Have to stop doing this. Must have slept forever. Groggy. Didn't even get under the covers.

I could feel the rough bedspread against my cheek and see the empty bed, still made up.

Empty!

The bed was empty!

Invisible! I was invisible! My mind exploded into total, terrible wakefulness, and I knew exactly where and what I was.

Jesus!

I was trembling. How many more days would there be like this, waking up to that horrible shock of realization? If you're lucky, and careful, and get control of yourself, maybe a lot more days. You have to stay calm, if you hope to keep going.

What about the food in my digestive system? Another layer of panic. I looked down at myself. I do not know what I hoped to find. Any outcome would have horrified me, I suppose. What I did in fact find was that I could just make out two short, translucent strands in what must be my colon. Some indigestible fiber or gristle. The moo shu, probably. Except for that, I was utterly invisible again. Somehow, during the night, the food I had eaten had been converted by my body to its own peculiar chemical or physical state. Or structure. Or whatever it was. Whatever I was. The whole thing—my condition—was incomprehensible. Preposterous. I felt like whimpering, and it may be that I did.

I had to fight down the panic, keep control of myself, figure out what to do next. Think things through calmly.

I had almost returned to complete invisibility. I tried to reason out whether that was good or bad, but my mind seemed unable to get hold of the problem. It didn't matter whether it was good or bad: it was the way things were. I had to figure out how to proceed from here. Calmly.

First of all, I would take off my clothes, which were sweaty and uncomfortable. I hung up my suit and pushed the rest of my clothing into an empty laundry bag. I would have to keep track meticulously of every invisible possession. I emptied a dresser drawer and neatly laid out the contents of my pockets in it. What might I have left lying around last night? I walked into the kitchen and ran my hand over the surface of the table, finding the keys on top of the mail and carrying them back to the drawer. Everything in order.

As I sat on the toilet urinating, I tried to decide whether anyone would notice the little transparent bits of undigested food in my lower intestine. How long would it be before I passed them? I went to the sink and drank at least a quart of cold water, watching it cascade down and collect in the stomach. How long would it be visible there? As I began to brush my teeth before the mirror, I was startled to see the toothpaste suddenly whipped into a fierce, foaming, Cheshire Cat grin. Rinse thoroughly. The smile became an outline formed by traces of toothpaste trapped in the crevice between gum and cheek. A regular walk in the fun house, my daily life. Somewhere there was an electric razor. In the cabinet under the sink. I got it working and began to attack the two-day beard, stopping frequently to check my progress by running my hand over my skin. Not being able to see either the beard or my face made the process seem even slower and more tedious than usual. And I had never liked electric razors anyway. I supposed I would never use anything else now. Not much point in shaving at all, really, but I kept at it anyway. At least I wouldn't have to worry about getting the sideburns even.

As I stood in the shower soaping myself under the hot water, I suddenly saw the form of my body outlined by the streams of lather, and I began rubbing the soap over myself furiously. Pointless. I got out of the shower and dried myself. The last traces of the Cheshire Cat grin were nearly gone, and the water in my stomach looked like a faint wisp of mist. I decided that it was very unlikely that anyone would ever notice the tiny threads of food still lodged in my colon.

It felt good to be clean again, and it would have been nice to put on some fresh clothes. But fresh clothes would look odd walking through the apartment without a body in them: all the shades would have to be kept drawn all day. The only invisible clothes I had brought into New York were the sweaty ones I had worn and slept in for two days. Well, that was a practical problem I could deal with right now. Do one thing at a time and keep going. I dumped my invisible clothing out of the laundry into the bathtub, turned on the cold water, and poured in some liquid soap.

I walked disconsolately into the kitchen. I had to eat. Some bacon and eggs would do nicely, and I found that I was salivating at the thought. But if I ate now, I reasoned unhappily, I would be an unsightly sack of half-digested food for the rest of the day. For how long, actually? Under nine hours: it was 10:17 A.M., according to the kitchen clock, and I had eaten last night around one in the morning. To be safe, I should fast during the day and eat at night, when there would be less risk of an encounter with other people. Was that possible? Can people live on one meal a day? I looked down at my belly and wondered again whether I had absorbed any nutrition from the food I had eaten. Perhaps I should eat now and plan to go out at night, when any opacity in my body would be less noticeable anyway. What reason would I have for going out anytime, night or day? What reason or hope would I have of doing anything except cowering in this apartment until they came to get me?

I tried to think what to do next. What did it matter? It was all absolutely pointless. My body surely couldn't survive in this state. And if it could, they would find me soon. They would track down everyone who had been at MicroMagnetics. I couldn't manage this alone; I needed help. I should call Anne. With someone I could trust to help me, I would be all right. Risky. I had to calm down and figure out what to do next.

Just keep moving. One thing at a time. I sat down at the kitchen table and began automatically going through my mail. Invitations to subscribe to the *Kiplinger Letter* and *Newsweek*. I tossed them into a discard pile. Save the whales. Catalogues from L. L. Bean and Talbott. Why do they keep on sending them? I cannot remember ever having bought anything from a catalogue. Certainly not likely to in the future: no use for the blucher moccasins or the Moose River hat now. No, wait—if I was ever going to buy anything again it would be through the mail. Or by telephone. I set the catalogues aside to save. Personal appeals from Ronald Reagan, Edward Kennedy, Jesse Helms, and Coretta King, each of whom had singled me out as a Concerned American and favored me with a computer-generated letter. Bills from New York Telephone, American Express, Manhattan Cable. Any point in paying these? What difference could it make? I was outside the whole economic system now. Outside the human race. No. I absolutely had to pay them. That was my only hope. I would go on paying my bills, meeting my obligations, treating the outside world as if I were still there, occupying my position in the usual way. Everything as usual. Then I might go on indefinitely, living here in safety, just like anyone else. I opened the bills and put them on top of the catalogues. Pay them later. No. Pay them now. Have to keep going. Do each task as it comes up. Otherwise I'll sit here staring at my intestines until they come for me.

I took the bills in to the desk in the bedroom, where I made out the checks and sealed them in the return envelopes. How would I mail them? Wait till the middle of the night and try to sneak them unobtrusively down to the corner mailbox? Stupid. I wouldn't get away with that very many times. Damn. I would think about the problem later. Not now. I left the envelopes in a pile on the desk. I was going to have a lot of problems. A lot of uninteresting, everyday things would prove insolubly difficult.

I needed someone to help me with these things. The question was whether I could count on Anne not to say anything to anyone. I should call her anyway. But what would I say? How much should I tell her? She might know what Jenkins and his men were doing. Ought to think this through before calling. Without having thought anything whatever through, I rang the *Times* and was told Anne was out. I left a message and then tried her home number. No answer. I realized that I wanted very badly to speak to her. I began to imagine her rushing over to take care of me.

I drank another glass of water, watching first the esophagus and then the stomach abruptly take form and then gradually fade from view. It all went so quickly with water. I should try to find out how the body digests food. Perhaps I would find the process less repulsive if I could follow it analytically. I remembered the sickening spectacle created by my meal the night before and decided to defer eating until I was ready to sleep again. Colonel Jenkins would be systematically tracking down everyone who had been at MicroMagnetics, and I knew that above all I could not afford to be full of food just when some government investigator arrived to interview me. Of course, if someone came I could not answer the door anyway: I would pretend I was not home. But what if they knew I was home? They would call before coming. Should I be answering the phone? Anne would be calling soon, and I wanted to talk to her. They would probably try to reach me at my office first. What would they be told there? That was the most urgent question. That, or how I would feed myself when the meager supply of food in the kitchen ran out. The most urgent question was: what should I be doing right now? So far, I was moving about the apartment aimlessly, in a trancelike panic, unable to make myself think clearly. It was like one of those dreams in which it is absolutely vital that you run, but you are somehow unable to make your legs go. I ought to talk to someone. Get a handhold on the human world. Settle myself down.

I dialed my office number.

"Mr. Halloway's office," my secretary answered. I felt comforted by the sound of her voice, and for a moment I thought I would weep.

"Good morning, Cathy."

"*Hi!* Where are you? I was afraid you weren't going to show at all."

(134)

"What do you mean?" I was startled by both the question and the urgency in her voice. I usually came in after ten and often not at all: there was nothing unusual about my not being there now. And as for yesterday, I had told her I might be out of town.

"You've got a Mr. MacDougal in reception."

"MacDougal?"

"Gordon MacDougal. Of Hartford Oil. Your ten o'clock appointment."

"Damn!" I had forgotten all about him. Who exactly was he? I could remember only that he was someone I had not much wanted to see but had not wanted to offend either and that I had made the appointment weeks ago, pushing it as far into the future as I decently could. He would have some kind of story he wanted to sell me. I had probably meant to keep rescheduling this meeting toward the horizon, in the hope that the whole thing would eventually fall off the edge of the world.

"I completely forgot about this one. . . . Actually, I'm not feeling very well. I'm home in bed. Let me see . . . you'd better switch me over to him. . . . No, wait. Do you have me down for anything else today? I don't have my book."

"No, nothing today. But Roger Whitman wanted to arrange a time to get together this afternoon. Said he wants to find out something to do with natural gas, or transporting it or something. Monday—"

"Look, switch me over to MacDougal so I can make my apologies. Tell him I've got a flu. You apologize too. And see if you can figure out who he is or why I made an appointment with him in the first place. Tell him you've never known me to miss an appointment and then make another appointment—as far in the future as you can without pissing him off even more. You can make it at his office. Then, when you're done with him, call me right back. I'm at home."

There was a clicking, and I was on hold. Then a male voice with a very restrained overtone of grievance said hello.

"Hello, Gordon?" He started to answer, but I went on talking. "This is Nick Halloway. I'm really sorry to have stood you up this way." He tried to interrupt with an assurance that it was quite all right, but I kept going. "But I just woke up with a hundred and two fever. To be perfectly frank, I just slept through everything. I must have some sort of flu. I'm perfectly happy to come right in now, although I hate to keep you waiting there any longer. And the way I'm feeling I'm not sure I'd be much use to anyone." He said it sounded as if I should stay in bed. "I'm really sorry to have dragged you there for nothing." He said that was all right and that he had to be in New York anyway. Damn. Where had he come from? I wondered whether there could possibly be an oil company with its headquarters in Hartford. Maybe there is a Hartford, Texas. "Well, I'm sorry for my own sake to have missed you. I'm really interested in what you people are doing—an intriguing situation." I didn't know what they did or what their situation was, but every situation seems interesting to whoever is in it. My own situation, I remembered, was horribly interesting. I had to end this call and get on with it.

"Listen, Gordon, I've asked my secretary to reschedule with you whenever it's convenient for you. I'm supposed to be out of town most of next week—assuming I'm out of bed—but anytime after that." I hoped he would only be in New York for the day. He would want to get back to wherever it was. Hartford, Oklahoma? "In fact, I'd really welcome a chance to get out and look at your operations directly." Get up? Down? Hartford, Alaska? "It's better if you schedule it with Cathy: I don't have my book in front of me. . . . Well, I'm really sorry. . . . Yes, I look forward to it too. . . . Goodbye."

It was true: I didn't have my book. The little black book I always carried with me, containing all my appointments, business and social, and, in the back, fifty pages of names, addresses, and telephone numbers. And, scattered through the calendar, birthdays, annual reminders, tax-deductible expenses, lists of obligations and things to be done. Utterly invisible, unreadable, useless. Not that it mattered. I would have entirely different things to do now, and it was difficult to imagine many future occasions for calling those telephone numbers.

I picked up the phone again, before the first ring had ended.

"Hello?"

"Hi, Nick. It's Cathy."

"How's MacDougal? Give you any trouble?"

"He's fine. You have an appointment with him here at two P.M. on the twenty-third."

"Good. Sorry to stick you with that situation. Can you give me my messages for the last two days?"

"Sure, just a second. Mr. Peters of Badlands Energy, returning your call. A Mr. Riverton—wouldn't leave a number or a business—said it was personal."

"Billy Riverton. That's fine. He just wants to play squash."

"Lester Thurson, of Spintex. And Roger Whitman wanted to get together with you—"

"Right. I'll give him a call. No one else called? No one called and didn't leave a name?"

"That's everything I've got. I told them you were out of town. That's what you wanted, right?"

"That's perfect. Listen, I'm feeling a little off today. I don't think I'll be in unless I'm doing a lot better this afternoon—"

"I'm sorry to hear it. Is it serious?"

"No, no. It's nothing. Just not quite myself. Listen—"

"Have you been to the doctor?" Cathy was someone for whom visits to various doctors were an important feature of daily life. I myself hadn't seen a doctor in years.

"No, I haven't. I don't think a doctor would be . . . Actually, that's an idea. I might go out and see a doctor at some point."

"Shall I say you're out sick?"

"No. No. What I want you to say is that I was in earlier and had to go out again. Say that I'll be in and out of the office all day. Hard to catch. Just take messages, and I'll get back to whoever it is."

"O.K."

"Listen, Cathy. Could you do me an enormous favor? I hate to ask, really, but I just don't feel up to getting in today. Could you possibly bring some things by my apartment so I can work at home?"

"No problem. What do you want?"

"Just dump all my mail and messages into a folder. Wait, I'll tell you what: look in the lower left drawer of my desk. There should be a black pocket-sized agenda from last year. Bring that too. I seem to have lost my agenda with all my appointments and phone numbers. And why don't you Xerox the next few weeks' pages in your appointment book. Do I have anything important in the next few days?"

"Wait a second. No. You were supposed to be in Houston Monday. Don't forget you have the monthly review on Thursday."

That would be the first real problem. The one meeting I really had to attend.

"I'll be fine by then. I'll probably be all right tomorrow. It's just a question of whether I want to travel again. Why don't you cancel Houston. I'll probably come into the office instead. Look, is there any money in petty cash—or do you have a couple hundred dollars in your checking account? I'm completely out of cash and I just don't feel up to going to the bank. Haven't got any food in the house. I'll give you a check when you come by."

"No problem. I'll cash a check on the way. How much do you want?"

"Two hundred would be fine—or make it two fifty, if you can."

"Are you O.K.? Do you want me to pick up some food or anything?"

"No, no. I'm fine. Actually, if you could pick up a *Journal* and a *Times*, that would be great. I really appreciate this. I think I've just got one of these twenty-four-hour things. I'll see you in a little while. You have my address, don't you?"

"Twenty-four East Eighty-ninth. Are you sure you don't want me to pick up anything at a drugstore?"

"I'm fine. Oh, and when you go out, remember to tell whoever's taking calls that I've just gone out and I'll be back in this afternoon. Nothing about being out sick."

"Fine. I should be there in under an hour."

"I'll see you then. Thanks very much, Cathy."

I hung up the phone and sat there for a moment thinking. Better to deal with everything as promptly as possible. I dialed the main office number and asked for Whitman.

"Hello, Roger?"

"Nick. Thanks for getting back to me. I wondered if we could get together sometime today to go over something—just for twenty minutes."

"Absolutely. The only thing is that today is pretty tight for me. In fact I'm out of the office right now and I don't know when I'll be back this afternoon. Is it something we could put off until next week?"

"I promised to get back to someone on this by Monday morning.... Is this a good time for you? Maybe we could go over this thing on the telephone."

"Sure. That might be better for me, actually."

"I'm looking at a situation down in Louisiana. Deltaland Industries, it's called."

"Chemicals and feedlots?"

"That's the one. Fertilizers. Interesting little company. Earnings have been flat for years, and they're selling at around six times, but they have these stockyards, a lot of them closed, actually—"

"That's right," I said. "I've heard something about them recently, or read something. Some sort of asset play."

"That's it. They carry these stockyards on their books at purchase price, but they've also acquired these natural gas reserves...."

As he talked I became aware once again of how odd the telephone receiver seemed, floating magically over my chair. The sight, to which I should already have been accustomed, produced an unexpected wave of nausea. I ought to be paying attention to Roger, who was reading off wellhead prices and contract expiration dates. I could see why he was calling me. He hates numbers and arithmetic. He also hates reading anything with small print and no pictures. I like Roger, but I often wonder why he is in this business. He is in this business because his aunts were inexplicably willing to let him manage vast gobs of money, and with the fees, he can pay people like me who are willing to perform long division and read 10Ks. He was asking a question about natural gas deregulation.

"The whole issue of deregulation as it bears on pricing is extremely complex," I ventured, not sure exactly what the question had been. I took it that this answer had not been adequate, as there was a silence at the other end of the line.

"And what kind of value would you assign to the reserves at this point?" I ventured, hoping to get myself back into the discussion.

"That's what I'm trying to get your help on," he responded. There was a discernible undertone of puzzlement and annoyance in his voice. "Is this a bad moment for you?" he added.

"No, no, not at all. I just have a lot of things on my mind today. Sorry if I seem a little distracted. I just wondered if you'd already made a first pass at the numbers. Actually, I'm a little off today. A bit of flu."

"You all right?" he asked.

"Absolutely. Look, Roger, I just don't want to give you a hasty answer on this. What with the uncertain regulatory picture and the shifting political context, the whole natural gas area can be extremely tricky. Extremely. I'll tell you what. I'm working at home today until I shake this flu, and Cathy's about to bring some stuff over to my apartment. Give her whatever you've got, and I'll give you a call as soon as I've had a chance to look through it.

"Sure, Nick. I appreciate it. But if you're not feeling well, don't—"

"I'm fine. Too much wine, women, and song, probably." Whitman would like that. You just have to jolly him along.

"That's the ticket. If you have to cut back somewhere, I would recommend the song. Say, that reminds me. That girl you were having lunch with at the Palm the other day . . ."

Anne.

"Anne Epstein," I said. "But she's not a girl, which is why your chances with her would be negligible. She's a *person*. In fact she's a reporter for the *Times* business section."

"Jesus, she looked just like a girl to me, Nick. In fact, more like a girl than pretty much anybody I can think of offhand. If at any point you find you're not getting along with her, I wish you'd just mention to her that I would like to leave my wife and family and follow her wherever she wants to go."

"I'll try to remember to tell her, but she wouldn't be interested. She doesn't go for the fascist capitalist pig type. You probably even vote Republican."

"What about you? You voting Farmer-Labor these days? Although, as a matter of fact, she did look a little bored with you. She probably needs—"

"I never vote for anyone. I'm saving my vote for a truly nice candidate. I've got to run now, but I'll probably see you this afternoon. And I'll get back to you right away on"—what was the name of that stock?—"on that natural gas question."

"O.K. Thanks, Nick. I appreciate it. So long."

I should give Anne's number another try. I should eat too. I was starving. Perhaps literally starving. I wondered again if it was possible to live eating only once a day. With Anne's help I could manage. It was just that she was apt to want to help by writing a story about me. Tragic victim of nuclear technology.

First things first. Cathy would be here soon. I had to work out how I would handle that—and be careful not to make a mistake, overlook something. I took a sheet of paper and a pen from my desk drawer and began to write, watching with amazement as the pen danced over the paper.

Cathy,
Had to run out to the doctor. House key and apartment keys enclosed. Sorry to make you hike up all those stairs. There is a check for $250 on the coffee table. Dump the mail and the cash anywhere in the apartment. Talk to you this afternoon.
Thanks,
Nick.
P.S. Please leave both keys locked in the apartment.

I folded the note around my spare keys and slipped everything into an envelope, on which I wrote "Cathy Addonizio." Walking out onto the landing, I became conscious again of how silly the whole thing was: the envelope bobbing and swooping through the air. It was a late weekday morning: the other tenants would all be in their offices, and it was unlikely that my landlords would be peering out their peephole at the deserted entrance hall, but there was no point in taking risks. The secret of survival, not to speak of success, is to take the risks you have to take but never the ones you don't. I held the envelope out over the railing and let it drop: steadied by the weight of the keys inside, it plummeted three stories straight down and landed with a plop on the carpet in the middle of the ground floor hall. Even if someone did hear it, there would be nothing extraordinary to explain away—nothing like the sight of an envelope walking unaided down the stairs.

Taking a quick look at my digestive tract to be sure that all signs of my last drink of water had entirely dissipated, I walked down the three flights of stairs to the entrance, pausing to listen for any sound of people moving behind my landlords' door. Nothing. I waited until a woman walking her dog in the street out front had passed by, and then, pushing the entrance door open, I slid the envelope along the floor and quickly picked it up and wedged it partway into my mailbox, with the name showing.

I was startled by the enormous feeling of relief I experienced on regaining the safety of my apartment, and equally startled to find that my heart was racing: after what I had been through the day before, this simple task, devoid of any real danger, should have seemed inconsequential. But the unrelenting anxiety, the continuous fear of making some small error that would lead to discovery, was grinding me down. One mistake and I would be noticed, and once noticed, I would be done for.

I laid out on the coffee table in the front room a check to Cathy Addonizio for $250 and my payments to Bloomingdale's and American Express. Nothing to do now but wait for her. Rather be doing something. I went over and began rinsing the invisible clothing in the bathtub. Better not do that: I wouldn't hear Cathy come in. What if she used the bathroom and for some reason plunged her hand into the tub? I went and got an old bedspread and threw it into the tub on top of the clothing. Too many things to think about; too many contingencies to guard against. How long could I go without appearing at my office? Have to try to make some arrangement with Whitman to work at home. In the worst case I would quit. How long before the authorities arrived? That was the real question. Not safe here. No point in thinking about it now. Have to find a way to put them off. It was safe for now; I would have some warning.

It would be good to have another drink of water, at least. Better wait until after Cathy's visit. It suddenly occurred to me that all the doors between rooms ought to be open, just in case she inadvertently walked toward me and backed me out of a room. And then what if she heard me moving? Breathing. Yesterday I had moved past people outdoors and in noisy public places—streets, railroad stations, subways—but in an empty apartment you could hear everything. It would be like sensing the presence of another person in the dark. It suddenly seemed to me that by having Cathy come here I had arranged my own destruction. She would enter the apartment and know instantly that I was there, or at least that something was wrong. I felt like someone who has hired his own assassins and sits waiting for the sound of their tread on the stair.

But it came as a relief when I finally did hear Cathy's tread on the stair, followed by the sound of the key sliding into the lock. The door swung open and she stepped into my apartment. I was standing by the door to the kitchen, so that I could observe her and at the same time be ready to escape at once from the room if anything went wrong. I was immediately startled by the forthrightly appraising way in which her gaze moved over the room. It was not the way you would look around if the owner were there greeting you. She walked over to the coffee table and laid out on it the large manila envelope and the two newspapers that she carried under her arm. Then she opened her handbag and took out a letter-sized envelope—that would be the money—which she set on top of the pile. She picked up my check and the envelopes underneath it, inspecting each of them and then placing them in an outside pocket of her handbag. Perfect. Everything had worked perfectly. Now she would be leaving, latching the door behind her.

But for some reason she set down her handbag before walking to the door. And when she got to the door she double-bolted it and fastened the chain lock. I had never once during my tenancy fastened that chain lock. What could she be doing? What was she suddenly afraid of? She turned around and headed straight toward me. I was dumbfounded. It seemed that she knew exactly where I was. The game was up, as the expression goes. I was so nonplused that I nearly spoke aloud to her.

Never give up until you have to.

I stepped back into the kitchen and watched as she walked right past me into the center of the room. She took another long, appraising look around and then ambled into the bedroom. I followed her, standing in the doorway where I could get out of her way again when she decided to come out.

The first thing she did was to open the closet door and peer carefully inside. Evidently, the authorities had already tracked me down and were using my secretary to spy on me. But what, exactly, was she looking for? She came out of the closet and looked at the top of my dresser. She pulled open one of the top drawers and glanced inside. The drawer below contained my invisible objects. What was I going to do, when she got to it? Almost absent-mindedly, she pushed the top drawer shut and turned away from the dresser. This was not a systematic search. If she was a police spy, her training had been sloppy. She turned again and studied a photograph of me with some friends on a porch on Cape Cod five summers before.

I grasped, at last, what was happening. She was simply curious. She was a snoop. I was at the same time relieved and outraged. She was plainly without the slightest scruple or concern for the rules with which civilized people try to protect their own and each other's privacy. I was surprised, because I had known her for several years and had always held a very different opinion of her. But then today I was seeing her in a situation in which it seemed to her that there was absolutely no risk of being found out.

She walked over to the desk and, expertly placing the fingertips of one hand on a small pile of correspondence to hold it in place, she flipped through the pile with the other hand. Nothing interesting there. She opened my checkbook and began leafing through the notations of my expenses and income for the last two years. That infuriated me, and I considered making some sort of noise from the other room to frighten her off, but I thought better of it. Let this intrusion run its course. What difference did it make? Anyway, all of my life up to yesterday was irrelevant now: why protect it from intruders? And probably I was beginning to recognize how little privacy we all have. You think you have secrets, but what the people around you are protecting and respecting is not your privacy but the pretense of it. Everyone knows more than you think, enough to wither you with shame, but if they are civilized they don't let on—and you return the favor.

Cathy flipped to the last page of entries to get the current balance in my account. Then she pulled the main desk drawer all the way out and began poking about cautiously. A handwritten letter caught her attention, and she carefully picked it up and withdrew it from its envelope. It was from a great-aunt, instructing me in my prospective duties with regard to an estate of which I was to be an executor but not a beneficiary. Well, that was one small benefit of my situation—they would have to look for someone else now. Cathy quickly lost interest in the letter and refolded and replaced it.

All the way in the left rear corner of the drawer she found a little stack of Polaroid photographs of a girl I had known. They were all much the same: a woman sprawled naked across the couch in the next room, smiling salaciously. Cathy studied each of the pictures at length. The sight of her doing that I found somehow compelling, and I took a cautious step toward her so that I could watch her more closely. She was quite intent. There was the photograph that had always appealed to me more than the others: Pam with one leg raised and resting on the back of the couch and her head tilted back provocatively, her lips parted. Cathy paused on the next one, which was bordered along one side by a blurred segment of my leg. I watched her moisten her lips with the tip of her tongue. As she shifted her ample weight from one foot to the other, I could hear the rustle of her clothing. I had never felt any sexual interest—no, it is never, or almost never true to say that you have never felt sexual interest in someone with whom you are in continual proximity: on certain days, in certain moods, those thoughts and desires flicker over the situation as naturally as random shadows. But I had hardly been conscious of any such feelings about Cathy, and anyway, it is much easier to find sexual gratification than a good secretary. You have to be careful in these situations: what you hope will be no more than innocent pleasures of the flesh are apt to mushroom uncontrollably into emotions and obligations that can poison a good working relationship.

But now, as I watched Cathy flip back to the photograph that included my leg, I thought with pleasure of what it would be like to seize her by the shoulders and force her onto the bed. It would be quite a surprise for her. She returned the photographs to the back of the drawer and bent over so that she could get a closer look at the remaining contents. Hoping for more photographs, presumably. She gently pushed the drawer back in and took another look around the room. Then she lifted her arm, glanced at her watch, and abruptly strode past me. I never had time to move. I felt her clothing brush against me and smelled her perfume. But she never noticed me as she marched out of the bedroom and into the bathroom, where she matter-of-factly yanked her underpants down to her ankles, hoisted her skirt up to her waist, and sat down on the toilet.

I watched her sitting there and heard the sound of the urine running into the toilet. The sight of someone urinating does not as a general rule hold much appeal for me. There was, of course, the view of her naked legs, but, more than that, I found it fascinating to observe another person who was utterly unaware of being observed—and particularly at such close proximity. The unguarded movements, the adjustments of clothing, the facial expression uncomposed for other people, the betrayal of character. It was, in the end, more fascinating than infuriating to observe Cathy revealing her inquisitiveness, her unqualified lack of concern for my privacy.

I watched with distaste but interest as she lifted the hem of her skirt and, peering down at herself, wiped the excess urine with a fold of toilet paper. She half stood up, pulled up her pants, and flushed the toilet. Then she stepped in front of the mirror and with her hands still under her skirt pulled her blouse down tight over her large breasts. Turning sideways to survey herself from another angle, she adjusted the blouse at the waist and walked out of the bathroom. I stepped out of her way and followed her, two steps behind, to the couch, where she picked up her bag, and then to the front door. She turned and surveyed the room once again, her gaze lingering on the coffee table: in her absolutely reliable way, she would be checking off the items there—newspapers, mail and messages in manila envelope, $250, keys—to be sure that she had done her job perfectly. She opened the door, stepped out into the corridor, and pulled the door shut, twisting the doorknob both ways and then pushing on it, to make sure it had latched properly. From one of the front windows, I watched her come out the entrance and walk toward Madison.

When she had disappeared around the corner, I hurried back into the kitchen. Hunger and thirst were going to be my biggest problem. If they did capture me, at least I would be able to start eating some real food again. Maybe. Probably they would want to give me little measured doses of everything—so that they could keep track of the caloric content and the saturated and unsaturated fats, and the quantity of zinc, and so forth. What exactly are unsaturated fats? That was one of many things I would no doubt be finding out.

I took another glassful of water and watched it gallop unpleasantly down into my stomach. Now it would be another ten or fifteen minutes before I was properly invisible again. The trouble with water was that it did nothing whatever for hunger, no matter how much of it you consumed. Jesus, I was hungry.

I went back to my desk and looked up the number of the supermarket around the corner on Madison Avenue. A voice with the accent and the flat, indifferent rudeness of New York answered.

"FoodRite."

"Hello. I'd like to make an order for delivery."

"Name?"

"Halloway. I'd—"

"Address?"

"Twenty-four East Eighty-ninth. I—"

"Apartment number?"

"Fourth floor."

"I need the apartment number."

I thought of explaining that there was only one apartment on the fourth floor, but you can't let yourself get drawn into these dialogues. "Four," I said.

"Four what?"

I thought briefly of calling another supermarket. "Four A," I said.

"Whatdoyouwant?"

"By the way, I wonder if it would be possible to pay by check."

"Do you have a check authorization on file at this branch only?"

"No, I don't, but I always shop at your store—at your branch only, as it happens—and I'd like—"

"Come into the store in person anytime before five, and you can fill out an application for approval."

"I'm not feeling very well today. Not well enough to go out. I'll pay cash. Although you might stick an application in with the order—"

"Whaddyawant."

"Let's see . . . I think I'd like some of those little bouillon cubes."

"Beef, chicken, or vegetable?"

"Which is clearest?"

"Clearest?"

"Yes, clearest. Which one is most transparent?"

"I don't know anything about transparent. Maybe the chicken. They're all the same."

"Send me one. . . . How do they come?"

"Cardboard container. Twenty-five servings."

"Give me one container of each. Then, a case of Canada Dry club soda. Better send some six-packs of tonic as well—four six-packs. And some limes. And lemons. . . . A little package of each. What about gelatine?" I remembered there was always a box of gelatine in my mother's kitchen, although its actual use was obscure.

"What about it? You want it, we got it."

"It's quite clear, isn't it?"

"What's this clear thing? We have gelatine if you want it. What do you want to do with it, anyway?" he added suspiciously.

"I'm looking for clear foods. No color, and easy to digest. It's my doctor: he's told me to eat only clear foods."

"Look. Why don't you come in to the store. We got a whole section on health foods. No artificial insecticides or preservatives. I'm not saying you don't pay for it, but you know what you're getting. And you got the peace of mind. Whether it's mainly health or religious, it's all natural."

"It's really only the color of the food that I'm supposed to—"

"I told you: there's no artificial coloring or preservatives. You want some granola? We also got unpasteurized milk. It's up to you."

"Send me a package of the gelatine. What about those transparent Chinese noodles? Do you carry those?"

"Sure. One package of shining noodles. What kind of doctor you seeing, anyway? Chiropractor, right?"

"Sort of. If you can think of any other clear foods . . . or even just foods that are especially easy to digest . . . preferably white, I suppose, if they aren't clear."

"Look, I don't digest food; I just sell it. You ought to come in to the store. I can see you got problems, but that way you can take your time, figure out what you want. We only got three phones here and a lot of people want to call in orders."

"Of course. You're absolutely right." FoodRite lost $12 million in the last fiscal year. With any luck, they would soon close this branch and this man would lose his job. "I hate to waste your time. Why don't you send me some fish, a pound of some very clear type of fish, and a small sack of potatoes—"

"That it?"

"Yes. Let me try that for now, and—"

"Someone be in all afternoon?"

"Yes. How much—"

"You'll get a bill with the delivery." Click.

I called the liquor store, where a much more amiable and accommodating man took my order for two cases of white wine and three quarts of gin. The druggist seemed mystified when I questioned him about the transparency of various vitamin pills, but he promised to do his best.

The first to arrive was the delivery boy from the liquor store, and when he rang up on the intercom, I buzzed him in and unlocked my front door, leaving it slightly ajar. I went in and turned on the shower and then stood waiting in the doorway between the bathroom and the living room. When the doorbell rang, I shouted across the room, "Come on in!" The doorknob turned, and the delivery boy appeared sideways, holding two cartons and a paper bag in his arms and pushing the door open with his shoulder. He looked around the room expectantly.

I held a hand over my mouth to create a muffled sound, and shouted, "I'm in the shower. Just leave everything by the door. There's a check on the table. The two dollars are for you."

He set down the cartons and the bag and went over to the table. He pocketed the two dollar bills and then, after studiously comparing the bill with my check, he folded the latter and put it in his shirt pocket. "Thank you!" he shouted. At the same time he picked up from the coffee table an antique silver box and inspected it with interest. He put it down again and took a leisurely look around the room.

"Thank you!" I shouted back. "Goodbye!" I was again startled to see how differently a person will behave when he believes himself to be entirely unobserved.

He walked back toward the entrance and stopped to examine a cluster of photographs on the wall. "Goodbye!" he shouted back. He continued studying the photographs for several seconds and then let himself out.

The next delivery boy was from the pharmacy, and he was small, white, and diffident. He touched nothing except the check I had left out for him, but he glanced furtively about the room the entire time he was there, and he bent over and tried to read the mail that Cathy had brought and that I had left half-opened on the table. I wondered if I behaved in the same sneaky, prying way when I was alone in new surroundings. It struck me suddenly that studying this child from the vantage point of my invisibility was precisely the same sort of sneaky curiosity. And come to think of it, I was a securities analyst: it was my job to be a prying sneak. Holding my hand over my mouth again, I shouted out my explanation that not only was I in the shower but I was ill and would he mind taking down the bag of garbage in the hall.

Finally, a pudgy seventeen- or eighteen-year-old Hispanic boy arrived with the groceries. He wore black trousers that were too tight and an even tighter T-shirt with the word HARVARD lettered improbably across the front. Around his neck was a gold chain, from which several coins and a ring hung, crowning the name of our alma mater. He let the door swing shut behind him and stood there passively, cradling the bag of groceries in one arm. His gaze went directly toward the doorway in which I stood and through which he could hear the shower. He took another two steps forward, still staring through me at the half-open door of the bathroom.

"You can just leave everything in the living room," I shouted. "The money's on the table. Keep two dollars out of the change for yourself."

He continued to gaze at the bathroom door for a long moment and then spoke.

"I can bring it into the kitchen for you." His voice was not yet completely changed.

"Just leave it there," I shouted, but, ignoring my command, he walked straight at me. Unable to think of anything I could do to stop him, I stepped into the living room to be well out of his way. He walked on through to the kitchen, but as he passed the bathroom door, his gait slowed and he peered in. The shower curtain was drawn and it was by now like a steam room in there, but his intrusive gawking made me nervous. He deposited the sack of groceries on the kitchen table and headed back out. This time he came to a stop in front of the bathroom door and stared straight in.

He wanted a look at me in my shower. I was repelled and angered.

"The groceries are on the kitchen table," he said softly. He waited for my reply, but since I was now standing directly behind him, whereas he thought I was standing directly in front of him in the shower, I couldn't very well give a reply. With the fingertips of his right hand he gently pushed the door open a few more inches and craned his neck for a better view of the bath.

"Is there anything else you want me to do?" he asked.

There is nothing so grotesque as the display of sexual wants which one does not share. I see it all the time. People peering, staring, glancing furtively at breasts, at genital bulges in clothing, at underwear, pictures, children, animals, at God knows what. They find little figures of lust hidden everywhere in the carpet.

The boy continued to stand there, peering into the steamy but vacant bathroom. I had to bring this to an end. Reaching carefully around him, I got hold of the doorknob and pulled the bathroom door abruptly shut. He was startled—perhaps by the wordless rebuff itself, perhaps by its slightly eerie quality: he had clearly pictured me as standing in the shower, but he would have to conclude now that I was standing six feet closer, concealed directly behind the suddenly closed door. He remained staring a moment longer and brushed one hand across his trousers.

The boy turned and went into the front room, where he found the money and counted out my change. Before letting himself out, he too studied the photographs. Perhaps I would feel better if I removed all personal photographs from the walls.

As soon as he was out of the apartment and I had the door locked again, I went straight back to the kitchen to unpack the groceries. It was not a particularly splendid shipment of provisions, but I found myself quite interested all the same. I had firmly resolved not to eat anything before evening, because, although I had no plans to go out or to have anyone else in the apartment, it seemed safest not to compromise my invisibility until after dark. You never know what might happen. I put the club soda and the tonic and the little package of fish in the refrigerator and then opened up the bouillon and gelatine packages and set them out on the table where I could take a good look at them. I think I told myself that I was planning the evening meal. I couldn't remember when I had last had bouillon, but I must have had it sometime in my life, because the pathetic sight of the little cubes in their foil wrappers made my mouth water. I had not eaten anything for over two days now except last night's meal of moo shu pork and coffee ice cream. To hell with it. I was starving. I heated up some water for bouillon. I decided to try the beef—it sounded somehow more substantial. Under the circumstances, it tasted exquisite.

I watched with less revulsion now the way in which the dishwater-colored liquid collected in my stomach. You can get used to almost anything. I could see that, although it was going to take longer than water, it was already starting to fade and dissipate. Once I'd gone this far I might as well try the others. I went back to the kitchen and made up a serving of the chicken bouillon. It too was delicious beyond imagining.

I was feeling better now, although I yearned for some solid food. Better not take a chance. If I could live on bouillon and vitamins, I would never be visible for more than fifteen or twenty minutes at a time. That reminded me that I ought to be taking the vitamins, and I opened the package and swallowed two of them, watching as the translucent amber capsules descended jerkily down to my stomach and sat there, slowly dissolving. Eventually a hole was eaten through one of them, and the contents gushed slowly out in a spreading stain. It was really quite fascinating. Too bad, in a way, that no one else could enjoy the spectacle.

I eagerly examined the gelatine, which turned out to be a powder packaged in little paper envelopes. I was still not quite sure what gelatine was and the labels gave me very little help, but there seemed to be protein in it, which I assumed to be a good thing, and research indicated that seven out of ten women reported an improvement in their fingernails, which was of rather less interest. I was invited to send for a free booklet detailing the facts on the restoration of brittle, splitting, breaking fingernails. Another free booklet on gelatine cookery offered recipes for Fabulous Foods that are Fun to Fix. I was half-inclined to go for that one, but the sample recipes for tomato aspic and chicken mousse disheartened me. "3 wonderful ways to freshen up your menus." I made up another cup of bouillon and poured a packet of gelatine into it. If there was a difference, it tasted worse, but perhaps I was just beginning to get tired of bouillon. I got out the package of shining noodles and looked longingly at it. No. I had to make myself stop eating for now.

I went back to my desk and called the office again. Cathy answered.

"Mr. Halloway's office."

"Hi, Cathy. Thanks for dropping off all the stuff."

"You're welcome. How are you? What did the doctor say?"

"I'm fine. I just thought I ought to see a doctor after all . . . just in case, I mean. Sorry I wasn't here. Did you have any trouble with the keys or anything?"

"No trouble at all. I just dumped everything on the table. What did the doctor say?"

"Just a virus. Listen, have there been any calls for me?"

"Simon Cantwell of Bennington Trust—"

"You can throw that out." I would never have to waste my time giving him free advice again: that was one good thing.

"And a David Leary from the U.S. Industrial Research Safety Commission." That would be it. A pulse of fear ran through me. "Sounded like some sort of government agency," she went on.

"When did he call?"

"Twenty minutes ago. Two fifty-five."

"What did he say?"

"Nothing. He wants to arrange an appointment, I think. I've got his number."

"What exactly did he say? As close to word-for-word as you can get."

"I don't know. He asked to speak to you—that's all. I told him you had stepped out of your office, and I asked for his name. He said he was David Leary of the U.S. Industrial Research Safety Commission, and he would like to arrange to meet with you for several minutes and was there some time this afternoon when he could come by and find you in. I said you were extremely busy and you would be in and out of the office this afternoon and out of town most of next week. If he would leave his number, you would get back to him as soon as you possibly could. He said it was very important that he see you and that it would only take a few minutes and he gave me a number. You want me to save it or throw it out?"

Throw it out. Pretend it doesn't exist. Damn!

"Give it to me," I said.

"594-3120."

"Did he say anything else? Anything at all."

"No." Cathy sounded puzzled.

"How did he sound?"

"What do you mean? He sounded . . . Is this something serious?"

"No, no. It's nothing. Just a nuisance. I just . . . There was a sort of fire at the place I visited Wednesday, and I just don't want to get involved with some investigation. . . . Endless questions, giving testimony that—"

"Hey, do you mean that big explosion that was on television? Where the demonstrators blew themselves up? Did you see that?"

"There really wasn't that much to see. It was—"

"You mean it was that place—MicroMagnetics—that was blown up? That's incredible! I saw it on TV! It was on the eleven o'clock news! I never put that together—they never said the name. That's amazing! Did you actually see the people killed?"

"No. Or yes. I saw them from a distance." (I could see them right now, pretty clearly, if I weren't making an effort not to think about their faces melting.) "I was outside the building, pretty far away. I really couldn't see that much."

"Incredible. MicroMagnetics. To think that I talked to them just the day before, to make your appointment. Did you leave the building because you had a premonition?"

"No," I said, a little irritated. "I left because they were evacuating the building. . . . Actually I left a little before that, which is why I really didn't see much of anything." I would have to sit down and work out exactly what my story was. I should already have done that. "I just happened to leave—I wasn't feeling well."

"That's incredible. That's exactly like this very close friend of mine who one time was supposed to be flying on one of those little planes to Nantucket and at the last minute she just decided for no reason at all not to take it, just because she had this feeling about it, and the plane went down with no—"

"Yes, fate is forever playing little tricks on us, I find." I looked at the telephone receiver floating in midair, and I felt sick. "If Leary calls again, tell him I'll be calling him."

"Anything else you want me to tell him?"

"No! Just take messages. Wait. Tell everyone I'll be back later this afternoon. I'll check back with you at the end of the day."

"All right." She sounded aggrieved.

"Cathy?"

"Yes?"

"Thanks again for bringing by all that stuff. I appreciate it."

"You're welcome. I hope you're feeling better. It must have been a terrible experience."

Jesus.

"No, not worth thinking about. Goodbye."

"Goodbye."

Well, they were after me. Of course, there had not for a moment been any doubt that they were after me. The telephone call from Leary, whoever he was, should really have been reassuring: it meant that they did not yet know just whom they were after. If they did know, they would not be calling my office: they would be at the door; they would be surrounding the building. At this point Nicholas Halloway was still just one name—probably a rather unpromising one—on a long list to be systematically checked out. But that call was demoralizing all the same. It was as if someone had fired a shot right through the walls of my would-be haven. The fact that I had been braced for the shot all day only made it worse.

It was a question of time now, of seeing how long I could stall them, keep my name at the bottom of their list. Perhaps, if I handled them skillfully enough over the phone, I could deflect them indefinitely, keep them from ever finding out that I was the one they were looking for. Anyway, the longer I could throw them off the better. I just had to keep creating the impression that everything was going along normally, that I was leading my life as usual. I would just be terribly busy, always going out of town suddenly and canceling my appointments. I would always have just left when people called. How long could I keep that up? Perhaps, if I handled it well, my colleagues, my friends, and the authorities would all gradually lose interest in me.

The first question was whether I could put off calling back Leary until Monday morning. There would be nothing out of the ordinary about that: it was Friday afternoon. Better to delay as much as possible at every stage. No. Better to deal with it head on. Fix a definite appointment right now. I couldn't risk having these people arrive unannounced at my office. Or at the apartment. And anyway, the more responsive I was in my dealings with them, the less interested they should be. But I dreaded making the call.

First I should think it through, work out a detailed account of what I was supposed to have been doing for the last two days. That would be only prudent. I couldn't afford to be at a loss for an answer. I sat there with pencil and paper, writing out a complete sequence of events with times and names. None of it would stand up terribly well under close inspection, but I was careful not to have myself talking to anyone or doing anything that could be conclusively refuted with a simple telephone call.

The papers! Cathy had brought me the newspapers. There might be valuable information in them, something I ought to know before talking to Leary. I went into the other room and searched through the *Journal*, but there was no mention anywhere of the events at MicroMagnetics. Extraordinary. I've always thought their news coverage was thin. Deep in the nether regions of the *Times* was an article entitled LABORATORY MAY HAVE VIOLATED BUILDING CODE. By Anne Epstein.

> The Mercer County District Attorney, who is investigating a fatal fire in a Lamberton, New Jersey, research laboratory yesterday, suggested today that the laboratory may have violated local building and fire ordinances. . . . Two deaths . . . A fire department spokesman declined to speculate on whether such violations might have caused . . . A local official speculated that demonstrators might have damaged electrical lines. . . . A spokesman for federal investigators refused to comment on reports that . . . Officials insisted that no radioactive material was located . . . Meanwhile, in an action considered unusual for an accident of this type, authorities have closed off . . .

No information whatever. Zero.

Why hadn't Anne returned my calls? She might know something useful. I called her number at the *Times* again. Not in. Couldn't be reached. Monday. I could leave a message. I left my name.

Call Leary.

I picked up the phone and dialed the number, clearing my throat and trying to compose myself. It was essential that my voice not quaver. If I got through this, I would be safe at least through the weekend, and maybe much longer.

"594-3120," answered a female voice. Always reassuring when someone answers with a phone number like that. Personal touch.

"Hello, is this the U.S. Industrial Research Safety Commission?"

"To whom would you like to speak?"

"I'd like to speak to Mr. Leary, please."

She didn't ask who I was. There was an immediate warbling sound on the line and then a male voice saying, "Leary."

"Hello. This is Nicholas Halloway returning your call." I thought I sounded all right. Calm, civil, but not solicitous: I should absolutely not sound as if I cared in any way about this call. Indifferent.

"Thank you for calling back, Mr. Halloway. I'm calling from the regional office of the U.S. Industrial Research Safety Commission in connection with an investigation into the incident on Wednesday, April third, at the MicroMagnetics, Incorporated, research facility in Lamberton, New Jersey. I would like to confirm that you were at the Micro-Magnetics facility on that date."

He spoke in such a mechanical monotone—almost as if he were reading a prepared speech with some difficulty—that it took me a moment to realize I had been asked a question. No, I longed to answer, I was not there, not on that date, or any other. I was miles away. This is all a mistake. Goodbye.

"Yes," I said. "Terrible thing. Horrible. Although actually, I'm afraid I can't really be of much help to you. I wasn't paying much attention at the time—I mean after they evacuated the building. I wasn't feeling well, and I didn't actually see the explosion or whatever it was. Probably a waste of time to talk to me at all."

"We need a signed statement from everyone present at the time of the incident, and particularly as no one seems to have gotten any statement from you immediately subsequent to—"

"I was really a bit off that day, and what with the rain and all, I took the first ride I could get—some people from the university, faculty of some sort. Nice of them to take me."

"We don't want to trouble you any more than necessary, Mr. Halloway. If you're going to be in your office, I'd like to stop by right now and get this out of the way. It should take only a few minutes."

"That would be fine except that I'm just on my way out of the office now, and to tell you the truth I'm running a little late—"

"I'm only a few minutes away, Mr. Halloway, if—"

"Really?" I said. "Where are you? Perhaps I could stop by your office at some point."

"That's not necessary, Mr. Halloway. If you could spare—"

"Just let me get out my appointment book here. I understand you want to do this as promptly as possible. . . . Let's see, I'm out of town most of next week. . . . You probably have a lot of people to chase after. . . . How about the week after next? I can set aside as much time as you like, say, a week from Tues—"

"I could meet with you later this afternoon or anytime this evening, as soon as you're free."

"Or—wait a minute—what about the end of next week? Early Friday morning, before—"

"Or I can come to your residence over the weekend."

"That's extraordinarily kind. Unfortunately, I'm getting out of the city for the weekend. I can see that you really want to get this out of the way, and I want to accommodate you. . . . It's just that this is an incredibly busy few weeks for me just now. . . . You know, it occurs to me that we might be able to do this right now over the telephone. I could take a few minutes and answer all your questions right now."

"Mr. Halloway, we don't want to inconvenience you, but I'm going to need a few minutes with you in person. I could see you tonight before you leave, or Sunday evening. Where will you be this weekend?"

"That's extremely kind, but just let me take a look at my schedule here and see if I can't work out something more convenient for both of us. Tell me—I'm looking in my book—when do you absolutely have to have this wound up?"

"No later than Wednesday morning, I—"

"Let me see. . . . I'm going to just move some appointments and make time. . . . You think half an hour would do it?"

"That would be more than—"

"I'm going to leave a full hour clear just to be sure. Two o'clock, Tuesday afternoon, in my office?"

"Two o'clock Tuesday then. I'd like to confirm your address: Three twenty-five Park Avenue, twenty-third floor, Shipway & Whitman."

"That's it. I look forward to meeting you. Very impressive the way you people are getting right on this so quickly. I hope you'll let me know if there's anything else I can do to be of help."

"There is one other thing you could do right now."

"Yes?" I said, feeling apprehensive.

"We'd like the names of all the people you knew at the scene of the incident."

More names for their list. I considered briefly giving him some random names in order to enlarge his task, but decided that was a risky tactic.

"Of course. There was Anne Epstein, from the *Times*: she was the person I came with, actually. And come to think of it, she was the only person there I knew."

"Did you meet anyone or hear anyone addressed by name while you were there?"

No point in lying. They would have talked to Anne.

"As a matter of fact, you're right. I saw the student who was blown up, Carillon. I didn't really talk to him. Anne interviewed him. And there was Wachs, of course. I introduced myself to him in the hall before he went in to hold the press conference."

Wonderful. The only people I had spoken to were the two principal lunatics. And I had talked to them just before they incinerated themselves. If this man were doing his job properly he would insist on seeing me immediately.

"One other thing, Mr. Halloway. Were you aware of anyone remaining in the building after the evacuation, or of anyone being missing afterward?"

"Not that I know of. But I was one of the first people out. They seemed to be doing a great job clearing the building. Of course, you must be concerned that there might have been other victims."

"Thank you, Mr. Halloway. I'll see you on Tuesday."

No, you won't. You won't see me ever. Nor will anyone else.

Goodbye. Goodbye.

I felt in a way relieved. I now had at least until Tuesday afternoon, almost five days. Maybe I did. I wondered if Leary knew what he was really looking for. There must be several Learys dividing up that list. Would they all have been told that they were looking for an invisible man? Unlikely. But if Leary did know, he would call right back to my office. Because if I really was there, in plain view of receptionists and secretaries and colleagues, then his question was answered. I dialed my office again and got Cathy.

"Cathy, I just got off the phone with your friend Leary of the Ministry for Industrial Sabotage or whatever. Highly tedious and difficult to escape. He hasn't called back again, has he?"

"No."

"Well, if he does, tell him I just walked out of the office, and I'm going out of town forever, and if I do come back my schedule will be full. Actually, I gave him an appointment for two o'clock next Tuesday at the office, but I absolutely don't want to take his calls or waste any more time on him until then. If he calls back, make sure you tell him I just stepped out. I'll be here at home the rest of the afternoon. If he or anyone else calls, give me a call here and let me know. Thanks. Have a good weekend if I don't talk to you."

It was four o'clock. When the phone had not rung by five, I knew

I was safe until Tuesday. I don't know why I felt relieved. I had only deferred the problem for four days. But that was something.

I went into the kitchen and mixed myself a gin and tonic to celebrate. They certainly wouldn't be coming for me this evening. Remembering Cathy's report of seeing the fire on the evening news, I switched on the television in the kitchen for the six o'clock local report. It was comforting to sit there passively watching the familiar, amiable faces of the "Metro News Team." I was even beginning to enjoy watching my glass tip the liquid into the air and seeing my esophagus take a brief liquid form before fading again from view. I was hoping for extensive coverage, with dramatic tape footage of the terrible events at MicroMagnetics. The newspapers were too busy with weighty matters like politics, but I knew that the Metro News Team had an unblemished record when it came to coverage of fires. I looked forward to it. It would make me feel almost smug. And it might make the whole thing seem a little more real and less dreamlike if I could listen to other people describing those events.

I watched the mayor visiting a neighborhood shared uneasily by Hasidic Jews and Jamaicans and talking of racial harmony to a small and sullen band of passers-by. Undersecretaries of state continued their endless shuttling in and out of Lebanon. A Ukrainian holiday was given a traditional celebration in a Queens nursing home. The weather was predicted. Baseball and basketball games were played.

Then a brief view of flames against a background of trees and Joan's voice: "Fire broke out for a second time in as many days at a small laboratory near Princeton, New Jersey, when smoldering remnants of the original blaze ignited a fuel tank. A spokesman for local police says that although the laboratory was the site of research related to nuclear fusion, there was *no* nuclear material at the site and *no* risk of contamination. However, authorities are keeping the area cordoned off as a precautionary measure." The flames and trees abruptly vanished, revealing the familiar view of the Metro News Team at their desks. Joan, turning to John, said earnestly, "John, that fire was apparently set off when an explosive device carried by antinuclear demonstrators accidentally detonated, and as we reported yesterday, it claimed the life of at least one demonstrator and one scientist. Authorities say that they are still searching the debris for any sign of further victims, but it may be some time before the final death toll is known. Police are seeking several members of the protest group who are believed to have information about the blast, but at this point no formal charges have been filed. We'll be bringing updates on that story as it develops." Joan frowned solemnly. "Thank you, Joan," said John.

That was it. I continued to watch, sitting through the national news: more undersecretaries piling into Lebanon—soon there would be enough of them so that they could form their own faction there and demand participation in the government; flooding interfering with crops somewhere; something about Bulgaria; the Dow Jones Industrials up nearly twelve points at closing. Who cares now? I couldn't concentrate. I was invisible. Why weren't they covering my disaster? Even without me, it seemed so interesting: radicals, sabotage, fire, death, and some sort of scientific breakthrough—I wish I knew exactly what sort. But then they didn't seem to have gotten any of the really interesting facts, and the uninteresting ones they *had* got were mostly wrong. Perhaps they were right after all: it was just another fire.

After the news was over, I tried to watch some sort of situation comedy, but I found that I was having trouble concentrating, and I switched it off. It was getting cooler, and I remembered that I was naked. It was unpleasant, walking around naked all day. I went through the apartment pulling all the shades and curtains, and then put on my bathrobe, wrapping it tight around me and knotting the belt. It was a full-length robe and it made me feel more substantial. A human shape. I put my hands in the pockets so I wouldn't have to see the empty sleeve openings. Perhaps I should put on slippers as well. As long as you don't look in a mirror, you never notice that you are headless. I mixed another gin and tonic. Amusing the way the ice cubes float across the room and into the glass. Really, I could safely eat the fish and the shining noodles now.

While I prepared the food, I switched on the television again. There was some sort of political discussion on Channel 13. After that I found a basketball game. The food was unspeakably good, even if it did make a rather slimy mess in my stomach. Pale and glistening, like a massive slug. I opened a bottle of the white wine to go with it and drew my bathrobe tighter across my torso to close off the view. Tomorrow I would really try to limit myself to bouillon and vitamins. It was just a matter of getting used to it. This was not so terrible. I was far better off than Wachs or Carillon. Why hadn't Anne called? When the wine bottle was empty, I poured myself another gin and tonic.

I dialed Anne at home. She picked up on the first ring.

"Hello."

"Hi, Anne. How are you?"

"Oh, it's *you*. I'm glad you called, Nick. I wanted to talk to you."

"I was afraid you might have called while I was out," I said. "The reason I've been trying to call you—"

"I'm sorry I've been so difficult to reach. I've been working on this SFW story."

"SFW?"

"Students for a Fair World. You know: Robert Carillon. Micro-Magnetics. It's an incredible story."

"I saw your article in the *Times* today."

"That was terrible. They're trying to kill the story. Stonewalling us on everything. The thing today was just to keep the pressure on. But did you see what I did on it yesterday?"

"I never got to the paper yesterday. I've been so busy—"

"Front page."

"That's great, Anne. I—"

"Do you have any idea how incredible this story really is?"

"I—"

"Nobody knows what really happened down there. It's absolutely unbelievable. They're trying to keep a lid on it, but I'm going to blow it wide open."

"What do you—"

"It's a complete cover-up! Have you seen the official statements? They're saying the whole thing was just a fire. And on top of everything else, they're blaming it on the demonstrators. But they can't cover up a story like this. Once I get some hard evidence of what actually happened down there, I'll blow the whole thing open. The *Times* is behind me a hundred percent. I don't care if this takes a year—"

"What have you found out so far?"

"Do you realize," asked Anne, "that this is the most serious disaster in the history of nuclear power?"

"It is?"

"Two people dead. *Two fatalities!* That's why they have this total news blackout. Do you realize that they've closed off the entire area? You can't get near the place. It's a massive cover-up. They have government investigators interviewing every single person who was there, and at the same time they're saying it was just a fire. Those people down there were completely government funded, and they had no permits of any kind—no safety inspections. Nothing. They were in violation of all kinds of federal, state, and local regulations. This is a fantastic story."

"I can see that," I said.

"It has a human dimension too." I had never known her to be this excited about anything. "You have these two people, complete opposites: one, despite being born with every privilege, chooses an altruistic life working for political justice; the other, from not such a great background, makes the opposite choice, for personal profit, even to the point of working on nuclear energy. And they die together in this nuclear accident, actually almost *physically fighting*—God, I'd give anything for a picture of it. It's really an incredible story."

"Sort of 'parallel lives,' so to speak." I spoke absent-mindedly. I was picturing the two of them again, struggling on the lawn.

"That's it. That could even make a good title. 'Parallel Lives.' The whole thing is perfect for the Sunday magazine. It really holds a mirror up to the American soul in the 1980s: altruism versus greed, morality versus science, nonviolence versus nuclear power, the contrasting social backgrounds, even the different physical appearance of the two of them. You didn't see anyone there with a camera, did you?"

"I didn't, really."

"And I know there's absolutely a book in it."

"Well, I'm glad I got you to go down there. It's really worked out well for you."

"That's true, isn't it? It *was* your idea to go down there. I'd forgotten that. Well, it's an unbelievable opportunity for me. It's going to lead to a lot of things. This is the most important thing that's ever happened to me."

"That's great. Actually, I wanted to talk to you about something related to the . . . accident."

"That reminds me. I have to talk to you. You're very important in all this."

"That's good to hear. I—"

"You were one of the last people to speak to Carillon. I want everything you can remember about his state of mind, about the political statement he hoped to make. Anything he said. It could be very—"

"Anne, I know the story is uppermost in your mind just at the moment, but . . . I wanted to ask you about something else, if you have just a moment."

"Sure," she answered dubiously.

"You and I . . ."

"What is it, Nick?" It was hard to tell whether it was concern or impatience in her voice.

"It's hard to know exactly where to begin. I want to ask you something straight out. As important as this story and your career, or whatever, are to you, suppose I were to ask you, right now, if you were willing to drop everything and go off with me somewhere? For good. Just the two of us. Tonight."

"Is something the matter, Nick?"

"No. I'm just making this proposal. Now or never. We both give up everything else in our lives and go off together."

"Nick, could we talk about this sometime next week? I have to get back down to Princeton tonight. I'm so tied up with this story, I really can't think about anything else right now. I mean, you're extremely important to me. . . . Has something happened to you?"

"No, no. Nothing. Listen, Anne, something that happened the other day . . . seeing those two people die there, or whatever . . . Anyway, it's forced me to take stock and try to figure out exactly where I'm going from here in my life . . . and it's important to me to know exactly where you stand. You're the one person—"

"Nick, have you brought these feelings up in therapy?"

"What?"

"Have you talked to your therapist about these things?"

"I don't have a therapist."

"Well, you should, you know. It's important to have someone to talk to about these things. There are some things a person can't handle alone. Nick, could you describe to me exactly what you saw at the moment the fire broke out? I mean, they're saying it was just an ordinary fire. But what did you actually see happen to Wachs and Carillon when it broke out? This is really important."

"I wasn't looking at that precise moment. Anne, I think you're right, actually: maybe we should put off this discussion for now and talk sometime next week. I could collect my thoughts and give you any useful information then."

"That would be good. I'm sort of in a hurry now anyway."

"I did want to ask you something else, Anne, while I've got you. I got a call today from some sort of government investigator looking into—"

"Don't tell them anything."

"Did they talk to you?"

"Sure. They're talking to everyone who was there."

"Did they ask about me?"

"Of course. They asked about everyone. Why?"

"What did you say?"

"I didn't tell them a thing about anyone. Didn't you talk to them down there after the accident? Were you one of the people who left right away?"

"I left right after I said goodbye to you. Remember?"

"Yes, of course," she said vaguely. "It was such a madhouse there. I was really busy. It's an incredible story."

"It really is," I agreed. "I'd better say good night."

"Good night, Nick. Take care."

When I hung up the telephone, I noticed that the television was still on. Basketball game. Hard to focus on it. Ridiculous to start putting all your hope in other people. Just a way to avoid facing problems you really have to solve by yourself. Tuesday. Don't think about it. Deflect them somehow. This was shaping up as a solitary sort of existence. Fuck you, Anne! Well, what claim did I have on Anne's loyalty? What had I ever done for her that she should suddenly reorganize her life around me? Saturday, Sunday, Monday, Tuesday. Four days. Three and a half. When your need is great, you start assuming other people have to help you. This isn't really the sort of situation in which you can confide in other people. (*Charley? This is Nick—Nick Halloway. You remember. I'm calling because a little something has come up and I wonder if I could ask a small favor. I've just become totally invisible and also I'm being sought by the authorities in connection with some felonies and I was wondering if you could put me up for a few years until I die or get caught or something. Oh, and I'd really appreciate it if you didn't mention this call to anyone.*) Damn you, Anne!

Another gin and tonic would help me sleep. Already lurching a bit. "Drunk" might not be too strong a word. The magic bottle tipping in mid-air over the magic glass. The magic glass spirited into my bedroom, onto the bedside table. Amazing feats of levitation. I could be the greatest magician of all times. Amaze and mystify vast audiences. No. Uninteresting. No performer, only tricks. No one for them to applaud. Nothing to love.

There was a movie, I remember . . . pictures of a head swathed in bandages. One long bandage. I should get one. Are people ever actually bandaged like that for real injuries? A cliché, those head bandages. Might as well wear a sign reading Invisible Man. I remember him—I think I remember him—unwinding the bandage. To start with, there's the surface of a human being. . . . Unravel it, round and round. Winding sheet. What's the point? Winding and winding. Nothing there.

WOKE EARLY AGAIN ON SATURDAY AND LAY THERE FOR A LONG TIME, staring at the wall and brooding miserably. It is difficult to get back to sleep when you can see through your eyelids. That call to Anne. Never try to operate a telephone under the influence of alcohol. I went back and forth over the whole, ludicrous conversation in my mind, trying to remember whether I had said anything that might give me away. How could I ever have thought of confiding in Anne? By now my story would have been in distribution throughout the civilized world on the front page of the *Times*. Anne's career prospects would be in splendid shape, and I would be in a cage. It was perfectly obvious that I could not turn to anyone else for help. It was self-delusion to imagine otherwise. It might even be self-delusion to imagine that there was anything much I could do to help myself. Wait for Tuesday and see whether I would get away with it all.

Maybe I would not be so much worse off if I did get caught. The best I could hope for on my own was to lie here cowering alone in my apartment. It would be almost a relief if they did come and get me. Let them take care of me. It would be like living the rest of my life in a hospital. (*Time for our bath now. And then we're going to have some important visitors.*) I would probably have important visitors all the time, coming to stare through me. (*Can we watch him eat? Is it all right to speak to him?*) And after my performance to date, they would scarcely be willing to allow me even the slightest freedom.

I ought to make myself get up. Not just lie here in my bed brooding until they came to get me. Although it wasn't clear how getting up would make things any better.

Only the agonizing need to urinate finally got me going. I showered for half an hour and then trudged into the kitchen, where I heated up a large pot of water and dumped in a dozen of the bouillon cubes. Why fool around with a cup at a time? If I was going to limit my diet to bouillon, I would at least have to force down enough of it to keep myself alive. I drank a good quart of the stuff there in front of the stove, keeping my bathrobe on so I wouldn't have to watch the activity in my stomach.

I wandered restlessly into the other room and switched on the radio, but the music seemed like so much noise to me and I switched it off again and went back to ladle out another cupful of bouillon. How long could a human being subsist on bouillon? The mind would go before the body. It was unwholesome staying cooped up in this apartment without exercise. I shed the bathrobe and tried running around in little circles out on the balcony, but it was difficult to get my heart into it.

I went back into the kitchen and pulled open the refrigerator door. Bleak. I picked up a shriveled half lemon and sucked at it in desperation. The sourness was almost painful, but it did have a wonderfully un-bouillonlike taste. In the cabinet I found an unopened loaf of sliced, white bread, which had been sitting there since the Sunday before and was going a little stale. I tore off a little piece and began devouring it greedily. It seemed delicious, and I could not stop myself from stuffing the rest of the slice into my mouth. I glanced down to watch its progress in my digestive tract. It seemed to go pretty quickly—much faster than the fish the night before. I really ought to be timing this. I should be using these days of safety to figure out whatever I could about my condition. Telling myself I was performing a valuable experiment, I got out a stop-watch and gobbled up another slice of bread.

Soon I was standing in front of the full-length mirror with pencil and paper, timing the digestion of everything I could find in my kitchen. From bread I moved on to strawberry jam and honey, then sugar, salt, and flour. I cooked and ate a potato, an onion, several frozen string beans, and a dozen peas. I opened cans of tuna fish and sardines. I even tried some canned tomatoes, with visual results worse than anything I could have imagined. I would chew a bite of each new food thoroughly and then wait until it was well down the pipeline and had begun to break up and dissipate, before I started on the next food. I worked my way gradually through everything edible in the apartment, becoming progressively more methodical, until I was measuring out equal, teaspoon-sized portions of each substance and carefully writing down exact results for each. All this was providing me with valuable information, and it was also giving me something useful and absorbing to do. It was preserving, more or less, my sanity and keeping my mind off next Tuesday.

I was not much of a cook in those days, so that my larder was rather limited, and by midday I saw that I would have to do something to broaden the scope of my scientific investigations. I put in another call to FoodRite.

"I remember you," said the same voice. "Clear food, right?"

"Yes, that's right, except that actually I feel I'm ready now to try—"

"I been thinking about your problem, and I got some ideas for you," he persevered.

"That's very kind. Why don't you put whatever you've come up with right into the order along with—"

"You ever try winter melon?"

"I don't know that I have. Send one along by all means. I'd also like one of every other kind."

"Every other kind of what?" he asked.

"Every other kind of melon. Of fruit, actually. And one of each kind of fresh vegetable. We could leave the canned and frozen things for the next order."

"*Every* kind of fruit and vegetable? What about clear foods? What about your health?"

"I'm feeling quite a lot better, thanks. Maybe you could put the smallest portion of each kind of meat into the order as well. You know, a small piece of pork, one of beef, and maybe some ground beef as well, and some chicken, some lamb—say, one chop. And fish. Fish is a good idea. However many kinds of—"

"Do you know how many kinds of fruit we have here?" He sounded upset. "What about the clear foods?"

"I'm still extremely interested in clear foods. In fact, they should form the foundation of my diet. Fish usually comes in little packages, doesn't it? You could just pick out the smallest package of each—"

"You know someone has to bag and weigh each piece of fruit in this order? Have you talked to your doctor about this?"

"I'm changing doctors, actually. The last one seemed rather rigid. If you could also throw in a *Times* and a *Barron's*."

"What does that mean, anyway: one of each fruit? You want one grape? One pea?"

"Well, you choose the portions. I appreciate it. I'd like some baked goods too: bread—white and rye and any other kind—and any pastry, doughnuts, whatever you have. And if you think of anything else that might be good, just add it to the order. I'll rely absolutely on your judgment."

By this time my entire digestive track was filled with extraordinary swirls of color, and I had to lock myself in the bathroom during the delivery, but I immediately set back to work eating my way through my new supplies. I continued without any break for the rest of the afternoon, chewing and digesting and recording times, until my neck was sore from bending over to examine apple seeds in my intestine, and my mind was a blur of numbers.

As I became more accustomed to the extraordinary ugliness of it, I began to experience considerable amazement and interest at the sight of my own interior. It is a disgrace, really, how little people are taught in the schools about their own bodies. I was quite surprised, and quite unhappy as well, to realize that I was particularly ignorant about the process of digestion, having only the most primitive idea of how the body's plumbing is laid out and no idea whatever of the chemical processes by which food is consumed and converted to the body's uses. In fact, it is quite extraordinary how little scientific work is going on in these areas and how much remains unknown. I myself have by now devoted a good deal of study to these questions, although my own research efforts have had more of a practical than a theoretical bias, serving the narrow but important goal of keeping me fed and free.

But even on that day, with my inadequate understanding of the chemistry involved, I was able to arrive at the fundamental scientific conclusions and precepts that would govern my diet. First and foremost, *avoid fiber*. I realize that other people have different ideas about the proper dietary role of fiber, but for me total abstinence from fiber is critical to survival. Seeds and kernels of every kind are also to be avoided at all costs, as are the skins of fruits. An undigested seed can linger in the lower intestine for days, making for an extremely unsightly appearance. Leafy vegetables require extreme caution. Sugar and starches, on the other hand, are the foundation of my diet. It is extraordinary how quickly the body breaks them down. I consume an immense quantity of pastry, although I have to be constantly on the lookout for hidden nuts and raisins. Most of my protein comes from fish rather than meat. I try to avoid coloring and dyes—although the natural ones tend to be, if anything, nastier than the artificial.

Another important rule for life that I have learned is to chew my food carefully. In general I have found that a lot of what I was told as a child turns out to be quite sound. If you could once see, as I have repeatedly seen, what the human digestive system actually does, you would always chew thoroughly. Flossing after every meal is another imperative for me. And, for that matter, questions of grooming—such as cleaning carefully under the fingernails—can hardly be overstressed. Of course in my case, little signs of bad grooming will not so much detract from my appearance as constitute it in its entirety. Fortunately, my invisible body and invisible clothing do not form what engineers refer to as a good mechanical bond with visible substances, which means that, although I often have trouble getting a secure footing, at least dirt and dust do not adhere to me very well, and it is possible to meet the rather high standards of cleanliness I have been forced to adopt.

I discovered another interesting thing that day. At some point in the early afternoon, as I stood in my darkened apartment with the shades drawn, trying to determine the exact dissipation time for white chocolate, I had the idea of opening the door to the terrace and inspecting the process in the sunlight. But for some reason it seemed harder rather than easier to see what was happening. No, it was rather that the sludge was suddenly dissipating much faster. Perhaps it was the sunlight. I tried several more swallows, alternating between darkness and sunlight, and determined that the light did indeed speed up whatever it was that was taking place in my stomach. For another hour I experimented with this effect, recording two sets of times for each food, until the sky clouded over and drove me back into the darkened apartment.

I became so maniacally caught up in my research that I failed to notice that I was glutting myself, and it was late afternoon before I realized that I was on the verge of nausea. It was with a sense of accomplishment, of having put in a solid day's work, that I put away my remaining provisions and mixed myself a gin and tonic. Time to rest from my labors. I felt much better—partly, no doubt, because for the first time in days I was no longer hungry—and the gin enhanced my sense of well-being. I was safe, and I still had most of the weekend ahead of me. I settled down at the kitchen table and got out the newspapers. Why in the world had I bought *Barron's*? What use was that now? I leafed through the *Times*, looking for something about MicroMagnetics. Odd that there was nothing.

I switched on the television, remembering the Metro News Team's promise to bring "updates on the story as it develops." Nothing. I went on watching local news programs for days, but there was never another word about MicroMagnetics. Other fires raged: in Brooklyn tenements, in Bronx social clubs, and even in a Manhattan office tower. Lives were claimed. People were interviewed in bathrobes. That's the thing: they need fresh footage of flames and weeping sisters-in-law. It all made me feel a bit abandoned by the world.

I mixed another gin and tonic and switched the dial around until I found a movie. Pleasant being safe at home. No point in thinking about Leary. Lots of time still. When the movie ended, I felt a bit of panic and I immediately searched out another. It would be hard to say how many of them I watched before I finally staggered into my bed.

I was awakened by the sound of the Sunday *Times* being dropped at my door. I stumbled out and retrieved it. I considered frying some bacon for breakfast, but when I looked down and saw the various indigestible bits of gristle and fiber in my intestine, I thought better of it. Only another two and a half days of safety, and then I would have to be prepared for the worst at all times. I would have to have myself clear by then, just in case. I made some toast and looked through the paper. Deep in Section One I found an article headed FATAL PRINCETON FIRE LEAVES LINGERING QUESTIONS ABOUT NUCLEAR RESEARCH SAFEGUARDS. By Anne Epstein. I read through it twice. There were all sorts of quotes from federal officials and from university spokesmen and from citizens' groups, but about the recent events at MicroMagnetics there was no real information whatever. Which was both a relief and a disappointment.

I put on some Haydn and went through the paper, never quite finishing or taking in anything. More to be doing something than because of any hunger, I put what was left of the peach and the banana in the blender and drank down the mixture. Delicious, although unsightly. I watched the digestion, thinking I ought to do some more timing, but I let the idea drop. Too tedious. Day of rest. I could see that beyond my drawn shades it was a beautiful day, and I knew that I would have felt better if I could have gone outside. With an effort I made myself go and stand in the open doorway to the terrace. There would be thousands of people in the streets and the park today.

In the afternoon I turned on the television and watched a golf tournament and a tape of a tennis tournament and part of a baseball game, and I can't be sure what else. Sometime during the afternoon, earlier than usual, I began drinking beer, and then gin and tonics. The television was irritating, but I kept it on until sometime in the middle of the evening, when I stumbled dully in to bed.

On Monday morning I woke abruptly at dawn, and I realized that I was becoming increasingly frightened as my appointment with Leary grew nearer. I tried to reassure myself that I would be able to put him off for a while longer—I have never heard of an appointment that could not be rescheduled at least once. And anyway, I was presumably contending with some sort of bureaucracy, which could be counted on to move very slowly and probably in the wrong direction. They could spend years chasing after Carillon's friends. But the fact was that Leary had clearly been told he had to meet with everyone in person. If I handled him well, I might stall him for a long time—perhaps even indefinitely—but from the moment tomorrow when I canceled this first appointment, I would have to be constantly prepared for the worst. I would have to assume that they might arrive at any time. Which was apt to become rather a strain.

I got up and began wandering nervously through the apartment, cleaning up some of the mess I had created during the last two days of dietary experimentation. Of course I might simply leave the apartment altogether. The trouble with that was that I had no place to leave it *for*. I needed someplace where I could digest some sort of meal out of sight, and where I could lie down and sleep without worrying that someone would stumble over me. The Colonel had been right: I would have a difficult time on my own.

Probably, though, I should go outside right now—just for a walk, to clear my head. I was going a bit stir-crazy, staying cooped up inside like this for days. No. No reason to leave the safety of my apartment now—especially when it would involve making the entrance doors swing mysteriously open for anyone in the street to see. I would not be able to do anything out there without attracting attention. Stay here and get everything in order.

I looked through the material that Roger Whitman had sent me, and then at half past nine I called and told him what I thought he wanted to hear about natural gas and deregulation, making it complicated enough so that he would lose interest quickly. I also told him that I would be working at home that day.

"I'm a little behind," I told him, "and I can get more done here, where I'm not constantly interrupted by the telephone."

Perhaps I would be able to arrange to do the whole job from my apartment. If I did all my work and answered all my telephone calls, I might go on indefinitely without anyone ever realizing that no one at all was seeing me ever. In the worst case I would acquire a reputation as an eccentric. A sort of financial Nero Wolfe. Might enhance my reputation for brilliant against-the-herd insights. The key is to do your work. People will put up with a lot if you do the work.

"This is a tough week for me anyway," I added. "I'll be out of town pretty much the whole time."

"You'll be in Thursday for the review, though, won't you?" Roger asked.

"Oh, of course. Absolutely. I'll see you then. So long, Roger."

Damn. I would cancel later. Thursday morning. This was going to be more difficult than I thought.

I finished cleaning up the kitchen and then went in and made the bed. It could get to be quite boring, spending one's entire life inside a three-room apartment. Boredom relieved only by fear.

I called up Cathy and asked if there were any messages. There were quite a few. Mostly, it seemed, from people who wanted to meet with me. Cathy herself wanted to show me something she had typed and wondered when I would be in.

"I'm working at home all day today," I told her. "And it turns out that I have to be out of town all the rest of the week."

"What about your meeting with Mr. Leary? Want me to call and cancel him?"

"No," I said. "I'd better handle that myself. Just make sure you tell anyone who calls that I'm out of town. You don't know which day I'll be getting back. Say I'm in Los Angeles."

"O.K. And what about the monthly review on Thursday?"

"I'll call Roger and talk to him about it."

I hung up and thought for several minutes and then called Roger Whitman again.

"Oh, Nick. It's good that you called back. I have an idea I wanted to throw out for you before Thursday. I haven't really seen you for almost a week, and I—"

"Before you get into that, Roger, there's something I wanted to discuss. . . . Do you have a few minutes, now?"

"Sure. Shoot."

"Well, Roger, some things have come up kind of suddenly. . . . Actually, the fact is, I've been thinking through my whole situation, and I've come to the conclusion that I've reached a point where I have to make a major change—"

"You mean moving out of the oils? I know how you feel about that, but we've already—"

"Roger, I'm not talking about just selling some oil stocks. I'm talking about getting out of the market altogether—"

"And just hold cash? You think the whole market is going to take a slide?"

"No. Yes. The market will take a slide. Eventually. It always does, sooner or later. The point is, I'm not trying to predict what the market is going to do. It's a very efficient market, anyway, and it's probably impossible to predict it with any useful accuracy. Anyway, I've decided to stop trying to predict it at all."

"You mean just throw darts at the listings, like one of these random-walk guys?"

"That's not what I'm talking about. I've decided to stop doing this kind of work for a while—"

"Jesus, Nick, I know just how you feel. God knows there've been plenty of times when I asked myself what was the point. Years when you don't even beat the averages. But you can't start thinking that way. For one thing, we've got all this money we have to do something with. I mean we can't send it back to the people and say we don't want to look after it anymore. We need the fees. And anyway, as far as I'm concerned, prices have a long way to go before they reflect the kind of earnings we should be seeing next year. We could be in the early stages of a classic bull market. I'm not saying there won't be corrections along the way. But I think interest rates still have a way to go on the downside, and you've got all this foreign money coming in and pushing everything up to—"

Sometimes Roger loses track and seems to think he is a retail broker again, talking to a dentist.

"Roger," I interrupted, "I think there's a great deal to what you have to say—"

"Do you really?" He sounded startled. "That's great. Listen—"

"Roger, what I'm trying to tell you is that I've decided to resign. Effective immediately."

"Resign what?"

"Resign my position at Shipway & Whitman. Quit my job."

"How do you mean, Nick?"

"I'm leaving. 'Pursuing other interests,' as they say. That's all."

"Nick, do you mind telling me where you're going? What are they offering you? Jesus, Nick. We've known each other a long time. I just don't understand why you wouldn't have come in and discussed a thing like this with me first." He seemed quite genuinely hurt. "I'd be the first to say that you've got to do whatever's best for you," he went on, "and I'm not saying we could necessarily match—"

"Roger, I'm not going anywhere else, and I haven't been offered anything. I'm just leaving. If I ever do anything in the securities business again, you'll be the first person I talk to. In fact, now that you mention it, I'd rather not resign at all. I'd rather request a leave of absence, if that's all right."

"Well, I suppose . . . Sure. Why not? . . . Nick, do you mind my asking why you're suddenly doing this?"

"Roger . . . I'm honestly not sure how I ought to answer your question. It's . . . There've been some fundamental changes in my life."

"How do you mean, Nick? Maybe this is something we can work out."

"Roger, I'm really not sure I'm ready to discuss it at this point."

"Jesus, Nick. After all we've been through together. . . . Is it something to do with the firm—or with me personally?"

"No, nothing like that, Roger. It would take too long to explain."

"God knows I've got all the time in the world, Nick. Is it something personal? I mean, is there any financial difficulty? If there's anything I—"

"Roger, it's nothing that . . . Hell! Look, Roger, I'll tell you what it is. I've suddenly broken through to a new spiritual dimension. I find myself unexpectedly on another plane of awareness, and I need to withdraw from material concerns for a time and reconsider my place in the celestial scheme."

"Jesus, Nick. I had no idea you felt like that."

"I didn't Roger. This is all quite sudden."

"You're absolutely serious about—"

"Couldn't be more serious. I'll tell you, Roger. I had this experience the other day that really set me thinking. A sort of epiphany, slammed me right onto another spiritual plane. I was down in this place in New Jersey—MicroMagnetics—"

"It was in the papers. The place where they had the fire. . . . I heard you were down there when—"

"I was right there, all right. Amazing thing. Changed my life, let me tell you. Just as the whole thing went up, I was standing there watching these two people in front of the building having a sort of dispute about worldly matters of some sort—commerce, politics, whatever—and suddenly, poof! All gone. A wisp of smoke, maybe. Set me thinking—that and other aspects of the incident. Completely changed my perspective on things. Which is why I feel I want to take some time off and take stock of the whole cosmic situation, if you follow me."

"Jesus, Nick, take all the time you need. Get things squared away."

"There is one thing you could do for me," I said.

"Say the word, Nick."

"I'd like to keep this quiet for a while. It's kind of a private thing between me and the cosmos, if you follow me, so if you could just have them take messages for me and not say I've left the firm or anything. And also, if you could find something in the meantime for Cathy. She's a first-rate secretary—"

"Absolutely. No problem. Jesus, Nick, I hope you're feeling better. . . . I mean, I hope you get everything straightened out soon. In your own mind. To your satisfaction. Just let me know—"

"Listen, Roger, I appreciate your accommodating me this way. I knew you'd be the one person who would understand, truly. I always thought you had a kind of spiritual dimension to you that people overlooked. In fact, sometime I'd like to take a few minutes and discuss your own karma with you. We might even take a few minutes now—"

"Good of you to think of it, Nick. Listen, I have to run—"

"A lot of people never stop to think how fragile and fleeting the material world is—"

"But, Nick, if there's ever anything I can do to help, you let me know."

"Roger, thanks again for your understanding. Goodbye."

So much for my job. So much for Roger.

In the corner of my bedroom there was a metal ladder running up the wall to a trap door, which was the only access to the roof from the building. Several times a year I would have to arrange to let some city inspector or workman go through my apartment so he could check a cable or a drain or something. I had never been up there myself, but I climbed up the ladder now for the first time and unlatched the door. I pushed it open several inches to make sure it was free and to have a quick look around the roof, and then I lowered it shut again, leaving it unlatched. If everything else went wrong, and they came for me without warning, this would be my escape route. From the roof of my building I could climb over to either of the adjoining buildings and work my way around the block. From my terrace I could see several routes from roofs down into the interior gardens in the center of the block, and I would surely find more once I was up there. As long as I stayed alert, I should have plenty of time to get clear.

Next I set out working my way systematically through the apartment collecting absolutely everything that connected me with anyone else in the world: letters, diaries, old tax returns, canceled checks, bank statements. I emptied out my desk drawers, took the photographs off the walls, searched through the pockets of my clothing, carrying everything into the kitchen and dumping it in the middle of the room. Then I began crumpling a handful at a time into the oven and setting it on fire. If they did eventually come after me, they would probably be able to find out everything, but I was at least going to slow them down.

It was more difficult than you might think, burning the photographs, seeing the images of people I had known well, had strong feelings for, melt and disappear in the flame, as if they were being obliterated from my life. Which they were, in fact. It would be easy to become maudlin in this sort of situation. Another problem was that the burning paper produced an unpleasant, acrid smoke, and I was afraid that someone might notice it and report a fire in the building. I would have to go slowly, which would give me time for a last look at everything.

There was also a stack of small, black, leather-bound appointment books, each of which contained one year's social and business appointments, with precise notations of travel and entertainment expenses, and, in the back, names, addresses, and telephone numbers. The current year's book was gone forever, invisible, but I had there the previous dozen years or so of my life summarized. I remember that somehow several years were missing—I cannot think how or why. I should, I told myself, stop and study the books and memorize any names or telephone numbers that might be useful. (Useful how?) *Olsen, Orr, Ovinsky.* Odd, the interleaving of people you hardly know—met once or twice in the course of business—and people you have known forever and cared about. *Paulsen, Parker, Petersen.* It is the people you knew as undergraduates that you remember most vividly—even those you no longer see, or even want to see. The madman with whom you stole the clapper of the college bell, or whatever it is you did. The girl lying with you on the grass on a spring night, whom you loved endlessly, past all reason. You never have friendships like that again—I, of course, would presumably never have friendships of any sort again—and although those friendships might not stand up very well under rational adult inspection, you could still find tears running down the face, if you ever let yourself start thinking about these things. Of course, in my case both the tears and the face would have a rather hypothetical quality. The sound made by a tree falling in the forest.

At moments of stress you can be subject to terrible swings in mood.

Still, I could not resist going through those books, reviewing my life in outline form: each business lunch (with cost and method of payment, people present, business topics discussed), each dinner party (with the name and number of any promising new person met), each weekend in the country (with times of trains or of the last ferry). And always the cost of each taxi and ticket. *December 19. 5:30 squash U Club/Carstair 7:30 (LG)dinner/Simons [GU warrants] taxis: $3.75 $4.50. dinner: amex $76.00.* And in the corner: *Martha Caldwell 860-8632.* Gone. It verges on the poignant, seeing your whole existence laid out like that and reduced to numbers—to times, addresses, telephone numbers, and incidental expenses. Driving force: loneliness, lust. Organizing principle: tax minimization. It may seem a banal life to you—I suppose it often did to me—but at that particular moment it seemed to me that it had been quite beautiful, and it was irretrievably gone. Well, that's the thing about all these lives: they pass. We all grow old and die. If we are lucky. And there isn't much chance of even that if we don't stop ourselves from dwelling on these things.

Onto the fire with all of it. I read and burned, drinking as I worked, on into the evening. Beginning tomorrow I would really not be able to drink like this. My last night of safety. Then a new leaf. I went to bed early, trying to ignore the unpleasant sight of the bedclothes suspended over the missing human form. All night long I dreamed of telephones and doorbells ringing.

O N TUESDAY MORNING I WOKE EARLY AGAIN, BUT THIS TIME I CLIMBED out of bed immediately, moving steadily along with grim, fearful efficiency. I washed myself carefully and put on all of my invisible clothing. Then I pulled open the dresser drawer and carefully loaded all the invisible objects into my pockets. From now on, all of my invisible possessions would remain on my person. I reinspected the gun, opening and closing the magazine and testing the safety to be sure I would be able to fire it when I needed to. Three bullets.

I felt no hunger whatever, but I went into the kitchen, sliced some fruit into the food processor, and ground it into a thick, homogeneous slime, which I forced myself to eat, several spoonfuls at a time, for the rest of the morning. My intestines were perfectly clear again, and this way I would be visible for only a few minutes at a time. Indispensable tools, food processors.

It was still too early to call anyone. I made the bed and cleaned up the apartment again. Impossible to read or listen to music. Although I dreaded making the call to Leary, I was eager to get it over with. It would be hours before he would be setting out to meet me, but I could not afford to wait till the last minute. I had to be sure to reach him beforehand, and he might be out of his office all morning. It was presumably his job to be out investigating things. Damn him. The sooner I called the better.

I called at five past nine. The same inscrutable female voice answered by repeating the number I had just dialed, I asked for Leary, and after the same brief warble, Leary was on the line repeating his own name.

"Leary."

"Hello, Mr. Leary. This is Nick Halloway." I paused momentarily to let him say hello in return, but he said nothing whatever, so I continued. "We had an appointment scheduled for two this afternoon."

"Yes, that's right, Mr. Halloway."

"Well, I'm afraid I'm going to have to ask if we can't reschedule. I'm terribly sorry about this, because I know you want to get it out of the way, but something's just come up, and I'm on my way out to the airport right now. Tell me, are you free anytime toward the end of the week?"

There was an unpleasant pause before he replied.

"The best thing would be if I came straight over now. It will only take a few minutes. Are you at your office?"

"Golly," I said, as earnestly as possible, "I appreciate your offering to do that on such short notice, but that really isn't possible. I'm going out the door the minute I hang up. How is first thing Friday morning? Nine-thirty. Or would you rather I called Thursday when I get back, and we can set up an appointment then?"

"Nine-thirty Friday morning will be good. At your office?" His tone had shifted somehow, and I found his compliance more ominous than his former dogged insistence.

"At my office. You have the address?"

"I have the address. Thank you, Mr. Halloway."

"Goodbye," I said.

Fine. I had put him off for three more days. On Thursday I would have Cathy call and say I wouldn't get back to New York until next week. Everyone gives up eventually. In this kind of situation, the most difficult calls are the early ones. After a while they get used to being put off. I might well deflect Leary. And yet I didn't have a good feeling about the call. It was his sudden willingness to wait until Friday. Well, at the very least I had bought myself another day. If Leary did anything right away, it would be to call my office for confirmation of my trip. Cathy would satisfy him. I could relax for today, have a drink even.

But I didn't have a drink. Although over the past few days I had grown used to walking around without clothing, I sat there in my invisible business suit and brooded uneasily about how an entirely invisible human being might quietly live his life unnoticed. Not a trivial question, I can tell you, and I grew steadily more uneasy as I considered it. As long as I had my apartment and my bank account, I could order up food and eat it in safety and sleep in peace. But if they drove me out, how was I to get along? Where was I to go? It sounds as if it ought to be easy, but when you think about it, the desirable nooks and crannies across the face of the earth are pretty well inhabited. Still, there are worse problems. I could be dying. I wondered once again if I *was* dying already from the radiation or whatever had got me. I felt all right. It seemed possible that I was dying at the same rate as everyone else. Perhaps I should leave right now and go to another city. Another country. Which?

I think I must have spent several hours sitting there, turning these tedious thoughts over in my mind. I had been indoors by myself too long, thinking the same things over and over. I should have gone outside and cleared my head. As it was, I don't think I noticed the ringing of the doorbells right away. Rather, I became aware that they had been ringing, but I couldn't say for how long, or exactly where. Right now it was the doorbell in the apartment right below me that was ringing, but I was almost certain that the one in the third floor rear apartment had been ringing before that. And perhaps the Coulsons' bell before that. There was normally no one in the building during the day except sometimes my landlady, Eileen Coulson, and with the building empty, you would hear things like doorbells and telephones.

Suddenly I was perfectly alert. Someone was ringing each apartment in the building. Then he should ring mine too. I braced myself for the sound, but it did not come. If someone were selling something or looking for someone to accept a delivery, he would not omit just one apartment. I was up out of my chair. I went to one of the front windows and looked down through the pane. A stocky, middle-aged man in a short raincoat was emerging from the building entrance. I slid the window carefully up, kneeled down, and leaned out to watch him. Out on the sidewalk he turned and looked up at me. I had to force myself to remember that he couldn't see me. He looked at the building entrance again and then at the neighboring buildings, and then he turned and looked at the buildings across the street. Nothing seemed quite to satisfy him. At this point, Eileen Coulson turned the corner and, with a suspicious glance at the man in the raincoat, pushed her way into the entrance. She was carrying two large shopping bags. The man followed her, and I could see the top of his head as he stood in the outer doorway talking to her. After a moment he disappeared into the building behind her.

I wondered if that was Leary. I had a moment of panic in which I thought that the two of them might be coming up to my apartment. But the Coulsons had no key for my apartment. Leary or whoever he was would just be asking questions. It had been pointless to stall him about the meeting. I should have given up and cleared out. To where? They were probably asking questions about everyone. It didn't necessarily mean anything. And what could they learn from Eileen Coulson that could be of any use? Of course, insofar as Eileen had any damaging information about me, she could be counted on to impart it, her feelings toward me falling somewhere between disapproval and dislike. More nearly disapproval, I suppose. I offended her overdeveloped sense of gentility. She should have been a housemother in a very strict school. I could often hear her, when I was going in or out of the building, lurking behind her door, peering out through the peephole at me. Damn her. Leary, however, was presumably not interested in whether I kept regular hours or had someone of the opposite sex staying with me occasionally.

But Leary must have been learning something. It was almost half an hour before he reappeared on the pavement. This time he left directly, without looking about, walking east. Eileen knew nothing about me that could be of any use to anyone. But in these investigations they ask everyone you know every question they can think of until they run out of questions and people. Would they be back? They were evidently not coming for me yet. They might be back to talk to my fellow tenants about me. But my fellow tenants were seldom in—Eileen Coulson would have told them that. Logically, they should want to talk to someone at my office next. But the moment they talked to someone there, Cathy would let me know. I had to avoid getting too jumpy about all this. These people are only bureaucrats: they probably have trouble tracking down people who are visible. And they probably would never figure out that they should be tracking me down anyway. They would be going through the same investigation of everyone who had been at MicroMagnetics. And then, always in the back of my mind was the reassuring knowledge that, even if everything went badly, I had prepared my escape route over the roof.

Which is why I reacted so promptly when I heard the first footstep on the roof. It had been less than an hour since Leary or whoever he was had disappeared down the street, and it seemed inconceivable that they would already be here for me. There might be children on the roof, or workmen. But I knew instantly that I had to assume the worst case and act on it directly. I had to assume that the roof exit was gone, that the only other exit might not be gone yet, and that I must try to use it at once.

I ran for the apartment door, stopping only long enough to look through the peephole. No one visible in the hall. I opened the door, peered around cautiously without seeing anyone, and started running as fast as I could down the stairs, taking two or three at a time. I could not see anyone, but I could hear people moving around somewhere below. They were whispering, but it sounded as if there were a lot of them. I was running the length of the third floor hall toward the next flight, sliding my hand along the railing as I went, to steady myself. I swung around, strode two steps down the next flight, and pulled up short. At the base of the flight and heading straight for me, were five men. Three of them were Clellan, Gomez, and Morrissey. They were climbing the stairs quickly and they filled the width of the stairway, leaving no room for me to pass. The only thing I could do was turn around and head back up, staying ahead of them.

I took my hand off the railing, because some of them were using it, and I tried to tread as quietly as I could, but they were almost running. Clellan was saying, "Now remember, when we go in, that door closes and stays closed until you hear me say loud and clear I'm about to open it. And if you should see it open without me saying I'm about to open it, you start to shoot, hear?"

I could hear people muttering assent as they huffed up the stairs behind me.

"The moment that door opens. You don't wait to see what you're shooting at, hear? This guy has a gun, and he's already used it once. Gomez will try to get him with the tranquilizer gun, but if he gets out of that apartment, you get him any way you can."

When I got to the fourth floor, I continued several feet past my door to where the corridor dead-ended. The men behind me collected at the head of the stairs in front of the entrance to my apartment. There was no question of slipping past them. Then, at a sign from Clellan, one of the men headed toward me. To get out of his way, I climbed over the railing and hung out over the stairwell. He went right past me and proceeded to inspect a second door, which had been sealed up years ago. Clinging to the balusters, I edged my way back toward the other men at the head of the stairs. The whole railing was wobbling horribly from my weight, but they were too busy with the door to notice. One of them had crouched down and was doing something to the lock.

When I reached the point where the balustrade curved around 180 degrees and began its slope down to the third floor, I stepped across and climbed over the railing onto the descending flight of stairs. I paused and looked back up at the five men by the door. The man working on the lock stood up, nodded at Clellan, and stepped back. Each of the men reached into his suit and pulled out a pistol, except for Gomez, who was already holding an odd-looking gun with a long, thick barrel. Then Clellan nodded, and the door swung violently open. Morrissey, Gomez, and Clellan charged into the apartment—my apartment—and the door slammed shut again immediately behind them. The two men left outside stood watching, their pistols pointed at the door.

I could hear footsteps running through my apartment, and I could hear Clellan's voice speaking to me.

"Mr. Halloway, don't move. We're here to help you. There are armed men all around you with orders to shoot at any noise or movement. Tell us exactly where you are and we will come to your assistance. *Please do not move.* We are here to help you."

When you think about it, it is extraordinary the way these people were always trying to help me. And all these guns for my protection. I did not at the time stop to think about it. Holding the railing, I started back down the stairs, two at a time, as fast as I could go without making noise. As I came down the last flight, I could see that there were two more men standing in the vestibule between the two doors that led to the street. Even if I shot them, their bodies would only block the outer door. And beyond them in the street stood other men holding walkie-talkies. One of them was Jenkins.

I stopped halfway down to the ground floor. I was trapped in the stairwell. The front door was blocked. So was the roof. My apartment was gone. The other tenants not home. But at least one of the Coulsons was home. I walked carefully the rest of the way down, until I was standing just inside the glass entrance door, looking straight at the two men on the other side. On my right was the Coulsons' door. I waited until both of the men were looking away toward the street and began jabbing the Coulsons' doorbell furiously. The men in the vestibule heard it ringing in the background and looked up quizzically. I held the button pushed in so they would not see it popping in and out. Where was she? I pressed my ear to the Coulsons' door so that I could listen for her, keeping my face turned so that I could at the same time watch the men in the vestibule. Over the continuous buzzing sound I could hear someone stirring deep within the apartment. The men in the vestibule were becoming agitated. They were talking to each other now, but they were both peering the entire time through the glass entrance door, their gazes searching the entrance hall. If they had known what they were looking for, they would have had me. One of them turned and went through the outer door to speak with the men in the street.

I could hear footsteps approaching from within the Coulsons' apartment. Why couldn't the woman hurry, damn it. Waddle, waddle, waddle. The man who had left the vestibule was talking to the group of men out on the sidewalk. There was a sort of commotion as one of the men suddenly pushed through the group and started running at the door. It was Jenkins. Eileen Coulson was behind the door now, speaking.

"Is it all right to open up again now?"

I remembered in time that I must not let her recognize my voice. I held my arm up against my mouth and called out as calmly as I could, "Yes, ma'am. We're all finished here. I'd just like to use your phone for a moment, if I may."

Please open the fucking door.

Jenkins was through the outer door and was pushing the man in the vestibule aside. I could hear locks clicking and turning under the incompetent hand of Eileen Coulson. I was lucky her husband wasn't home. He might never have gotten it open at all. Hurry, for Christ's sake. Jenkins was finding that the hall door was locked and was barking at the man next to him to get it open. His voice was still soft and controlled, but I could see the urgency and anger in his face. His narrow little slit eyes.

The door in front of me swung open two inches and stopped abruptly. She had it on a police chain, the stupid cow! Her eyes moved around in the crack, peering everywhere in a futile effort to see me.

"Are you quite sure it's all right to open up now?" she was saying. "I was told absolutely not to—"

"Yes, ma'am," I said, to keep her interest. The one thing I did not want was to have her shut the door again. As the other man fiddled at the hall door lock, Jenkins's gaze shifted up impatiently, and through the glass he saw the Coulsons' open door. He began shouting. "Shut that door! Get that door shut!"

"That's exactly right, ma'am," I was shouting in an effort to drown out Jenkins. Eileen Coulson's eyes became more uncertain. The hall door was swinging open and Jenkins was pushing through it. I took two quick steps backward, almost into his approaching arms, and charged the Coulsons' door, slamming sideways into it with all the force I had. The door swung open, pulling the police chain out of the door frame and smashing the large body of Eileen Coulson back into the wall of her foyer. I had a glimpse of her crumpled on the floor, blood streaming from her face, as I ran by.

I charged down the hall and into the living room, with Jenkins right behind me. He had never been there before and of course he could not know exactly where I was, so that when he found himself in the middle of the large room, he slowed up momentarily and looked around. That gave me enough time to pull open the double glass doors in the far wall and get out into the garden. The garden—only a New Yorker would call it that—was a small, lifeless, paved area with metal furniture, surrounded by high wooden fencing cutting it off from other, similar gardens. I grabbed a chair, slammed it against the back fence, and, standing on the ground beside the chair, began pushing and shaking the fence as violently as I could.

Jenkins was right there. Assuming I was on the chair climbing over the fence, he charged, groping for me with both hands along the fence above the chair. Before he had time to think, I hit him hard with my closed fist in the side of the neck. His body slammed into the fence and twisted around so that he faced me. I hit him again hard, this time in the belly, aiming for the solar plexus. He vomited as he doubled over onto the ground.

I slid the chair to a corner of the fence where a strut made it easier to climb and hoisted myself over into the facing garden. If I could get out through one of the buildings on this side, I would be on Eighty-eighth Street, a block away from the Colonel's men. I looked around. Two windows and a door, all locked. I went over the next fence. It was not so high, but it swayed precariously under my weight as I twisted over the top of it, and for a moment I thought it was going to collapse altogether. As I turned myself around and lowered my feet onto the ground on the other side, I found myself staring straight back at the face of Morrissey, who was peering over the Coulsons' fence. The face dropped out of sight. He knew where I was. I had to get out of here. I looked up at the roof above my apartment. Gomez, staring down at the fence that I had just nearly wrecked, was raising his gun to his shoulder.

I turned and nearly collided with a woman of about fifty in a bathrobe. She had just gotten up from a plastic chair next to a table that held a cup of coffee and a burning cigarette. She was striding toward me, her face horribly contorted with rage. She suddenly began to shriek—so loudly and savagely that her voice cracked.

"Stop it! Stop that right now!"

For a moment I thought she must be able to see me, and I cowered. But then I saw that she was staring right through me at the fence, and I realized it was her fence she was upset about. She thought someone was knocking it down from the other side. I stepped out of her way, as she strode the rest of the way to the fence and glared truculently at it.

There was a small, explosive thud from the direction of my terrace above, and a gash appeared at the base of her neck. Blood began to run out over her shoulder, and she collapsed at my feet.

I ran over and pulled open the glass door into her apartment. There was other gunfire now, and I was aware of glass shattering around my ankles. I charged through the first room and, finding myself in a small corridor, ran the length of it, hoping for a door to the street. The passage ended in a locked door. Damn. They would be here any moment. Jenkins and his men. I turned back frantically and raced up a staircase to the parlor floor. There I found myself in an entrance hall, where I pulled open first one and then another door and charged out onto a stoop. In front of me was a short flight of brownstone steps leading down to the sidewalk. A man I had never seen before was coming straight toward me up the stairs. His face had a look of grim urgency, which was turning to consternation at the sight of the house door mysteriously swinging open, pausing for a moment, and then swinging shut again. As long as Jenkins was unwilling to tell his men exactly what they were looking for, they were going to have a difficult time catching me. Then I saw that Clellan had arrived and was starting up the stairs behind the other man. He knew exactly what he was looking for. As he came he held his arms outstretched to either side so that I would not be able to pass him undetected.

Beyond the metal railings that ran down both sides of the stair was a fenced-in area, which would have made a good cage. The railings were too narrow to balance on, but I clambered up onto one of them anyway and charged down it for all I was worth, so that by the time I tipped off to one side or the other, my momentum would have carried me out to the sidewalk. I hit the pavement with a loud clap and stumbled into a heap almost at the curb.

Clellan knew at once what had happened. Despite his deplorable taste for cowboy hats and brightly colored shirts, he is not a stupid man. He spun around and charged back down the stairs, looking desperately along the sidewalk for some movement or clue to my location. I scrambled to my feet, quickly retreated several steps down the street, and turned back to see what he would do. At the bottom of the stairs, Clellan went into an odd crouch and began dancing around in little circles on the pavement, exploring with his feet for what he hoped would be my injured body. The other man, watching quizzically from the stoop, was plainly wondering whether Clellan had gone mad.

Clellan stopped abruptly. He saw that it was too late: I had gotten clear. He waited for a minute, listening and watching for some sign of me, and then, with his back to the other man, he said quite softly, "You there, Halloway?"

"Yes," I said finally, saving him the trouble of scuttling around anymore looking for me. I spoke softly too, so that the man on the stoop would not hear me. He was watching Clellan with increasing curiosity.

"You all right?" Clellan asked.

They are always so solicitous of my well-being.

"Yes, thanks."

"Is there anything we can do for you?" Clellan asked.

"You could leave me alone. In particular, I wish you would stop trying to kill me. What's the point of that?"

"No one wants to kill you. You don't understand."

"Well, I wish you wouldn't kill bystanders when I'm close by, then. Like that woman in the garden."

"That woman'll be fine, probably. That wasn't a regular bullet. You weren't hit by anything, were you?"

I thought there was a tone of hopefulness in his voice.

"No. It's a difficult shot. I can see why your people went for the woman instead. She's a much better target."

"Mr. Halloway, why are you doing this? What's the good of it? Why don't you save yourself and us a lot of trouble and come along with me now? It'd be much better for you."

Two more men had just rounded the corner from Madison Avenue and were walking fast toward Clellan.

"I don't think so. Not just now," I said.

I turned and saw that there were more men coming down the sidewalk from the other end of the block.

"What is it you want?" he asked.

I did not answer. A black sedan had turned into the block from Fifth Avenue and was rolling down the street towards us.

"Just talk to me," Clellan was saying with his pleasant country accent. "Tell me what it is you want. Whatever you want, we can get it for you surer than anybody."

The men approaching from Fifth Avenue were almost on top of me now. I stepped out between two parked cars into the street to avoid them.

"Halloway, you have nowhere to go. Halloway? You're making a mistake," Clellan was saying. He was talking louder now. "We're just going to have to come get you anyway. We're going to get you anyway. Halloway?"

You can try. But it won't be so easy as you think.

Clellan stood there looking blankly around, talking to the void. The man on the stoop stood staring at Clellan, baffled by his bizarre behavior. The two groups of men approaching from either end of the block stared in confusion at both of them.

I turned and started up the street toward Fifth Avenue. Halfway up the block I had to step aside between two parked cars, to let the black sedan pass, and inside, gliding slowly toward me, I saw the face of Colonel David Jenkins, staring impassively out the left rear window. I felt a flash of hatred and defiance. This man had driven me out of my apartment. And cut me off from everyone I knew.

As he drew even with me, I pulled out my gun, grasping it like a hammer, and slammed it as hard as I could against the window that separated me from Jenkins. The entire pane of glass crazed instantly into thousands of little segments but did not break apart. Stupid. I think I expected the driver to accelerate away in terror, the occupants cringing inside. Instead, the brake lights lit up bright red and the car slammed to a stop. All four doors of the car swung open simultaneously as if it were a jack-in-the-box, and suddenly there were four people standing in the street. One of them was Gomez, holding his odd-looking gun loosely, as his eyes searched the surface of the street for some sign of me. Another was Jenkins. He spoke.

"Halloway, we're here to help you."

I was backing carefully away, watching to make sure that I did not make a noise or create some visible movement.

"Halloway?"

When I was ten yards off, I turned and walked quickly to the end of the block. I took a last look. They were still standing there, gazing hopelessly about, except for the Colonel, who had understood the situation and was walking away from me toward Clellan. I crossed Fifth Avenue and walked south along the edge of the park.

Y HEART WAS STILL POUNDING, AND I REALIZED THAT I WAS TREM-
bling. I would walk for a while, put some distance between me
and my pursuers and let myself calm down. Then I could figure
out what to do next. But I found that weaving my way between loitering
adolescents, bag ladies, and joggers was a precarious and exhausting task,
and I was again startled at how utterly remote these other human beings
now seemed, staring right through me, completely unaware of my existence. I had spent the last five days by myself, hidden inside my apartment behind drawn shades, and now that I was suddenly thrust out into
the glare of the sunlight, everything seemed too bright and too large. I
moved as if in a dream among people and objects that whirled past in
dangerous, unpredictable paths.

Approaching Eighty-fifth Street, I looked back just in time to stumble
out of the way of a boy on a bicycle, who came hurtling out of the park
and across the sidewalk straight at me. It was no longer enough to look
only ahead: I would have to train myself to keep watching all around.
Moments later a small, erratically moving dog suddenly swept across the
width of the pavement, threatening to snare me with the leash that connected it to its owner. This existence requires constant vigilance. I particularly have to watch the people on roller skates, with Walkman earphones plugged into their heads, who glide obliquely across streets and
sidewalks and then abruptly wheel out in broad swooping arcs or little
toplike spins with an arm or leg extended to cut me down. Worse yet are
the runners who, in their silent shoes, continually threaten to pile into me
from behind. But the most dangerous thing of all is a crowd of even a
small cluster of people standing or moving together. Even now, when I
have learned to move confidently through the streets, I will still turn and
retreat from even the smallest gathering of people.

By the time I reached Seventy-second Street I had figured out that I
was safest walking along the curb, between the parked cars and the trees,
where there was less traffic and where I could always escape into the

street or even up onto an automobile. I wondered what Jenkins would be doing now. Going through my apartment. I had been lucky to escape. Recalling my terrified flight out of the building and through the gardens, I felt my heart begin to race again. They would be examining everything I owned, dismantling my home. It came to me that I no longer had a home, that it was unlikely, furthermore, that I would ever have a home again, and, suddenly demoralized, I sat down on one of the benches that line the edge of the park.

I sat there for quite a while. An hour perhaps. I pictured Jenkins and his men handling my clothes, sorting through my desk, and I wished that I could have burned more of it. What would they do next? What would I do next? Jenkins had been absolutely right: it would be very difficult to survive on my own. The afternoon was passing. There were more children now: the schools must be out. More people in running suits. More people moving up and down. I was no longer one of them. Hopeless.

An old man in stained clothes stinking of urine shuffled up and stopped in front of where I was sitting. He turned his head slowly and looked down just as if he were inspecting me, and I looked to see if something visible had attached itself to me. No, he must be looking at the bench. With another sequence of little shuffling movements he got himself turned around with his back to me and began very deliberately to sit down on top of me. I scrambled to one side and stood up as he lowered himself into my place on the bench. He was panting a little from his exertion. A good thing he had come. It got me moving again. The important thing is to keep moving.

As I walked toward midtown it became perfectly obvious to me where I would go. I would go where people traditionally had gone when they found it inconvenient or impossible to go home: I would go to my club. If I had not seen that immediately, it was because that is not the way people tend to think of clubs nowadays; but it was certainly the way the people who built the clubs had thought of them, and it was a point of view that suddenly suited me perfectly. The midtown men's clubs were ideally appointed for someone in my situation. They offered large kitchens and bars, cavernous lounges, libraries, billiards rooms, showers, pools, and private bedrooms. There were enough people wandering in and out of them so that I would always be able to slip through their entrance doors unnoticed, in the wake of a visible member; but their admissions procedures, house rules, and initiation fees guaranteed that a majority of the people who would join would be too old or live too far away to bother coming in much. And the fact that those members who did come in came mainly for lunches or a quick game of squash only made things better for me.

Midtown Manhattan is full of these clubs, and in my situation the issue of membership was no longer of much relevance: I could go to whichever of them happened best to suit my new and rather special needs. Still, I decided on the Academy Club, of which I was a member—partly because of my familiarity with it but also because of its reassuring vastness. It is a large, handsome, six-story building on Madison Avenue, designed seventy-five years ago by McKim, Mead and White, with cavernous public rooms that have not been full in generations. In those rooms I would never be caught in a crowd.

You enter up a short flight of stairs sheltered by an awning. Just inside the entrance and to one side is a desk, behind which Bill sits watching the door, and on the wall behind him is a large board with the names of all the current members. When you enter, he greets you by name and then turns to slide a small peg next to your name from left to right, indicating that you are in the clubhouse. He prides himself on knowing every member on sight, and although half of them seem to live in Palm Beach or London—so that he must get only very infrequent opportunities to fix their faces in his memory—in fact I have never seen him fail. On that day I had to stand waiting for several minutes outside the closed entrance door until another member, someone I had seen often but whose name I did not know, came up the stairs, pulled open the door, and strode through. I slipped in behind him, trying not to crowd on top of him and barely managing to get through before the closer pulled the door shut again. (This is a maneuver at which I have since become quite adept.) Bill looked up and said, "Good afternoon, Mr. Ellis" to the man ahead of me and slid the appropriate peg over. As I slunk by the desk, Bill's gaze drifted back to the door, and I realized that I had taken pleasure in the courtesy of his greeting all these years and that I felt cut off without it now. As if I had been suddenly but discreetly dropped from the membership. No one would say anything unpleasant: my presence would simply be ignored.

I crossed the hall. On my right were passageways to private dining rooms. On my left was a vast, high-ceilinged lounge with high-backed chairs upholstered in leather and long tables arrayed with periodicals. The marble floor was covered with enormous oriental carpets, and lining the opposite wall were tall windows which looked down onto the street. The Club was filling up. Tea had just been put out, and the beneficiaries of trust funds, who had spent their afternoon on the squash courts, were taking small, civilized bites from English muffins. They would be leaving soon, in time to avoid the savage wave of stockbrokers—the first occupational group to leave their offices—who would sweep in and wolf down entire muffins in a single bite on their way to the bar or the courts. The lawyers and investment bankers, who took pride in working long hours, would arrive later. The large, comfortable room easily swallowed up the conversation around the table. I could see people there I knew well.

Melancholy—if I let myself stop to think about it—that I could no longer join them.

I continued up the stairway past the second floor, which housed the main dining room, the bar, and the billiards room, and on to the third floor, which was taken up with card rooms, meeting rooms, and the library, the least frequented areas in the Club. Somehow, perhaps because of the Club's name, someone had conceived the idea—and others apparently continued more or less to hold to it—that the membership would require a large and well-stocked library. This completely erroneous judgment has proved fortunate for me: hardly any of the members seem to notice either the books or the expense, and the place is nearly always deserted except for a few desks and chairs right by the library entrance to which members sometimes retreat to avoid the censure they theoretically should incur for opening briefcases and conducting business in any other part of the Club.

There were two of them sitting there when I came in, poring over some sort of legal document. I went past them and continued all the way around through the library, which consisted of a maze of small alcoves formed by bookshelves. In the most remote corner, I settled into a large leather armchair surrounded by rows of books. I would sit here for a moment and rest. Then I might want to read for a while, take a look at today's papers. That would be perfectly safe. I would go back to the table in the main reading room, where all the periodicals in the English-speaking world were neatly laid out, and bring a couple of them back here. In a few hours I would be able to look around and find something to eat. By six-thirty or seven the Club would begin to empty out, and by nine it would be almost deserted—perhaps a few stragglers in the dressing room or the bar and the people in the guest rooms on the fourth floor. I wondered if there was any sort of watchman or security guard or only someone at the door. It was so extraordinarily quiet. If for some reason someone should wander back here, I would hear in plenty of time. . . . Far in the background—it seemed miles away—I could hear the ancient elevator moving occasionally. . . .

When I awoke it was completely dark. It must be . . . What time was it? I was in the library of the Academy Club. Invisible. It must be the middle of the night. All the lights out. Utterly still now. There had been a lamp beside this chair. I groped about until my hand encountered it, then located the switch and turned it. The light did not go on, but the double click seemed to reverberate through the room like gunfire. I should stop for a moment, be quiet, listen. Make sure there was no one else here. The only sound I could hear was my own movement in the leather chair. The total darkness was claustrophobic. Some master switch must be off somewhere.

I got up and made my way haltingly out toward the middle of the library, guiding myself by running my hand along the rows of books. As I emerged from the bookshelves, I saw that there was some sort of light after all: down toward the other end of the library I could see distinguishable shadows rather than uniform blackness. I stopped to listen again for any movement and, hearing nothing, began feeling my way slowly towards the area of dim illumination. When finally I reached the entrance to the library I found that the light was coming from the main staircase, which wound up through the center of the building.

I would follow the marble stairs down and search for the kitchen. I had not eaten since early morning, and if I were going to be in this club with people wandering in and out all day, then this would be the last time I could risk putting food into myself until tomorrow night. I was startled, however, by the realization that, although I had been in and out of this club all my adult life and eaten here countless times, I did not really know where the kitchen was. I had vaguely assumed that it would be on the second floor with the dining room and the bar, but on entering the dining room, I realized at once that that would be impossible: there was no space left for it in the floor plan. Enough light shone in from the street through the tall windows so that I could make my way easily down the length of the dining room to the double swinging doors through which I had so often watched waiters appear and disappear. Beyond the doors was a small hall with steam tables and dumbwaiters and an open stairway, which I followed down into total darkness.

I groped about helplessly for several minutes in what seemed to be a maze of counters and shelves, until I found the handle of an old-fashioned refrigerator and pulled it open. The small light inside shone suddenly out through an enormous room, creating a patchwork of huge shadows, endless tables, and monstrous antique kitchen equipment. The refrigerator was filled with bottles of fruit juice, and I first gulped down a quart of grapefruit juice, and then, leaving the door open for illumination, set out to explore the kitchen. Glancing down at my stomach, a yellow sack of grapefruit juice, I wondered whether anyone ever came in here during the night. I shouldn't have drunk anything until I had reconnoitered. Too late. Nothing I could do about it now.

I went methodically through the kitchen trying every cupboard and door, confident of finding every food known to man, since, although the food at the Academy Club is less than exquisite, the menu is nevertheless quite comprehensive. Instead I found only locked doors and cabinets and padlocked coolers. It seemed that nothing had been left out in the open but endless stacks of plates and dishes, jumbled masses of flatware, racks of glasses. If I were going to live here, I would need keys. When finally I found a bin of dinner rolls, I greedily devoured three of them without a thought of how they would look collected in my belly. Then on a counter I found a large metal bowl of sickeningly sweet fruit salad, which someone had forgotten to put away, and I unhesitatingly shoveled that into myself as well: it seemed unspeakably delicious.

I was altogether unsightly now, and with my appetite satisfied, I began to worry again about who else might be in the building. There would at the very least be someone at the door all night for the people who were staying in the guest rooms. Perhaps other staff as well. I would have to avoid the ground floor and the fourth floor, where the guest rooms were, but I should be able to explore the rest of my new home in safety. I went back up the stairs, resolved to begin my reconnoitering by finding the staff entrance to the bar, but everything was locked there as well. Obvious: alcohol is always the first thing you lock up. Where would there be a complete set of keys?

I walked back out through the dining room and into the dark, cavernous lounge. With its enormous leather-upholstered sofas and armchairs and its massive tables, and with the ghostly light from beyond the twelve-foot-high windows sending faint but immense shadows slanting upward across the walls, the room seemed meant for some gloomy tribe of giants, and I felt like a small child sneaking through a dark house. Crossing to one of the windows, I peered down into the pale, empty avenue. No sound inside or out.

I walked into the billiards room, a long row of massive rectangular shadows. Nothing of interest here. These vast spaces can be extraordinarily lonely. I turned back and started up the broad marble staircase, which was the only part of these floors kept lit all night. On the landing I paused to look at the grandfather clock. Two-thirty in the morning. Somehow that fact, or perhaps the clock itself, disheartened me, and I stood listening to the tick and watching the abrupt little lurches of the minute hand along the Roman numerals. On the edge of my vision I became aware of something moving, and, looking down, I saw again the yellow and brown filth piled up in my stomach. I should not be standing in the one illuminated part of the building.

Hurrying up to the next floor, I turned down a dark corridor which I thought should lead away from the main library rooms and toward a vaguely remembered back stair, but it turned several times inexplicably, until I had quite lost any sense of which way I was proceeding. When I encountered on my right a small marble staircase with a metal railing, I followed it up. It doubled back several times on itself and then opened into a corridor on what must be the fourth floor, without continuing up any further. This was worse. There were overhead lights running the length of the passage, and anyone appearing now would have seen me clearly. I hurried past a succession of numbered doors, which I decided must be to the guest rooms. I thought enviously of the people safely locked inside, lying in beds with clean sheets. The corridor took a turn and ended at a metal door beneath an exit sign. I pulled open the door, eased it shut behind me, and, finding myself in a fire stair, began climbing again.

Completely disoriented, I had already forgotten my plan of systematically searching the building: I only wanted to find some dark, obscure place where I could rest in safety until I was invisible again. I pulled open the first door I encountered and found myself in a small tiled washroom lined with washbasins and shower stalls. I remembered that in addition to the main dressing room there were several other smaller rooms on this floor, but I was sure that I had never seen this particular room before. I walked through it and out into a narrow passageway. It was darker here, but to one side I could see through an open doorway into a room with windows which admitted enough street light to reveal chairs and tables and mirrors. Why was this so unfamiliar? How was it possible that in all the times I had been on this floor I had never seen these rooms? I continued down the passageway, turned a corner, and came up against a dead end in total darkness. Running my hands along the wall in front of me, I located a door. It was locked. I tried the adjacent wall and found another door. Pushing it open, I stepped through onto what felt like a tiled floor.

I could see nothing whatever. I had set out to search methodically through a building I thought I knew, but here I was, stumbling about aimlessly. Why had everything been laid out in such a maze? It was pointless to do this is the dark. No idea where I was half the time and half the doors locked. Stay calm. Figure out where you are. I listened for a moment. No sound anywhere. I ran my hands over the wall along the door frame until I found a light switch and snapped it on. I was in a small, completely white room with a tiled floor and tiled walls, which I recognized as the anteroom to the steam room. Off to the right would be a door leading into the pool. Straight ahead would be the steam room itself, and to the left would be a small room with massage tables and sun lamps and beyond that a corridor that would lead around to the main dressing room.

I looked down at my viscera, an ugly swirl of vomit, and, suddenly remembering my experiments at the apartment, an idea came to me. Taking a good look at the room and the position of the first door on the left, I switched off the light and made my way across the pitch-dark room and through the door into the massage room. I got the lights switched on and set about studying the sun lamps. There were two long rows of them on a fixture which was suspended over a massage table by a system of pulleys and counterweights, and on the wall there was a control panel with timing dials and separate switches for ultraviolet and infrared light. I switched absolutely everything on, lowered the lamp fixture as far as it would go, and climbed up onto the table underneath it.

I felt the light only as a vaguely pleasant, penetrating warmth, but its effect on my appearance was dramatic and immediate. The filth in my digestive tract began to disappear at once, seeming to melt away like ice under hot water. Soon there were only a few small lumps and swirls of color, and then, within minutes, nothing whatever. It was a wonderful discovery. I would be able to eat and restore my invisibility almost at will. A pity that the sun lamps were not located closer to the kitchen, but still, I felt my confidence suddenly growing into a feeling almost of invulnerability.

Slipping off my clothes and putting them in a neat pile up on top of a cabinet where probably no one had ever before put anything, I walked back through the neighboring room and into the windowless room containing the swimming pool. Next to the door was a row of switches. I flipped one of them up, and a bank of lights came on along one wall, illuminating the small body of quivering, blue, chlorinated water. Kneeling down at the edge of the tiled pool, I slipped quietly in and pushed off into the cool water. It felt wonderful. I swam up to the other end and back. Somehow, the act of swimming seemed almost effortless—as if I now floated more easily than before—and I felt a sort of power and pleasure in my own movement, as I propelled myself up and down the length of the pool.

I could see, though, that to an observer the effect would have a very different quality. I was creating a large amorphous cavity or bubble, which moved awkwardly across the surface of the water, expanding and contracting with my strokes in a rhythmic sequence of convulsions. It was a bizarre effect. One that would certainly hold the attention of anyone who happened into the room. I climbed out. The water beaded instantly on my body and seemed to drain magically from the air like a miniature rainfall cascading down onto the edge of the pool. Footprints appeared mysteriously on the tiled floor as I walked.

Switching off the lights as I went, I returned and put on my clothes again. I felt wonderfully refreshed by my swim, calmer and clearer. Abandoning any idea of further explorations in the dark, I stretched out on a huge leather couch in the main dressing room and drifted into a deep, serene sleep.

At around seven o'clock in the morning, I was awakened by the sound of doors banging in distant parts of the building, followed by voices and the faint clanking and grinding of the elevator. Soon there would be staff here and members getting in a swim or a game of squash before work. I climbed off the couch and went in and washed up quickly. As I climbed up the stairs to the sixth floor, I could hear the whine of vacuum cleaners from the lower floors.

I set out again to make a thorough inspection of the building now that there was light, and by midday I had toured as much of it as I could get at. There were locked storerooms and closets scattered throughout the Club, especially on the top floor and in the basements. And as I moved about, I had to be constantly watching for the Club employees, who by now had spread out through the building to clean and repair it or to prepare in various corners their various concessions—the cigar stand, the massage room, the bar, the laundry, the barber shop. And because behind the huge public spaces there was such a labyrinth of unexpected little rooms and passages and stairs, I was never quite sure what I would find on the other side of a door. It would take days of such expeditions before I grasped the layout of the building with confidence, and it would take many more days of careful surveillance before I began to recognize the dozens of employees and to know roughly where they would be over the course of a day or a week. The members, on the other hand, did not create much of a problem for me. Most of the time there were very few of them in the Club, and their movements were perfectly predictable. No member would ever burst suddenly into an unused room to dust the furniture or replace a light bulb.

When I had begun my tour first thing in the morning, there might have been twenty members who had come in to have breakfast or use the athletic facilities before work, but they hurried out again immediately, and for the next few hours there were never more than a handful of them in the building, most of them reading newspapers in the lounge. But around eleven-thirty, members began to trickle and then crowd in, and, knowing that for the next two hours the Club would be as full as it ever got, I retreated up to the roof, where I sat on the edge of the parapet, watching the traffic and the pedestrians below.

At two in the afternoon, when the Club had largely emptied out again, I went back down to the first floor. There, beyond the doorman's desk and the coatroom, is a small hall with mailboxes and a counter at which members can cash checks or reserve guest rooms or private dining rooms. Opening off that hall is a little maze of offices, in which the manager, the switchboard operator, the bookkeeper, and the clerical staff all work. I spent the entire afternoon there observing the procedures for the reservation and assignment of the guest rooms and trying to determine the schedule for making the rooms up.

At around four-thirty, as the Club was beginning to fill up again, I crept carefully through the open door of the manager's office. He was sitting at his desk copying numbers onto a spreadsheet. Despite my care, he heard me come in—as people so often do—and looked up, but, seeing no one, he returned to his work. I sat down on the floor in the corner and waited. He toiled on for hours. I cannot tell you how agonizingly boring this sort of thing can be: sitting there without moving or coughing or clearing my throat and with nothing to do but watch the man twitch and pick his nose. Even a telephone call would have offered some welcome excitement. With increasing intensity, I prayed for him to get up and leave.

It was almost quarter to seven before he abruptly stood up, folding up the papers on his desk and stuffing them into a briefcase, and scurried out the door. When the lock had turned and I heard his footsteps retreating, I was finally able to stand up and stretch. Sitting down in the upholstered swivel chair behind the desk, I began pulling open the drawers and going through them.

By the time I realized that the office door was being unlocked again, I barely had time to push the drawers shut before the manager exploded into the room and charged frantically at the desk. It is difficult in moments of fear or confusion to remember that you are invisible—even now I am not sure I have absorbed the fact fully—and as he reached right at me, I instinctively drew my right arm back preparatory to smashing him under the chin. He picked up a stack of letters from the edge of the desk, and, with my fist still foolishly poised to strike him, I watched him turn his back to me and scurry frantically out of the room again.

I sat there for many minutes before resuming my search. It is extraordinary how often people will return to a place moments after leaving it—often several times in succession—to retrieve something they have forgotten. You begin to notice these things when you spend your entire waking life sneaking about.

I went back to work on the desk, and in the back of the lower left-hand drawer I found two cardboard paper-clip boxes full of keys of every sort, some grouped together on rings and some loose. I dumped them out onto the top of the desk and picked through them, eliminating two that were clearly automobile keys and several more that were duplicates. I was left with eleven keys, which I hooked onto one ring and slipped into my pocket. That was the problem: they hung there ridiculously in midair. I could hear people still leaving through the main hall. I would have to wait until the Club had emptied out.

I passed the time going through the rest of the office, concentrating particularly on the personnel files and on an interesting breakdown of Club staffing by hour, day of the week, and season. The most important thing I learned was that for most of the night the only employees were the night doorman and a night watchman, who was seventy-one years old.

Sometime after nine, when I had not heard footsteps or voices for twenty minutes, I unbolted the office door and swung it slowly open, stepping out into the corridor and peering around the corner out through the hall. The night doorman was sitting behind his desk, furtively reading something that he held under the counter.

The first thing I did was to go back and try the keys until I found one that locked the manager's office. Then, taking a roundabout route through fire stairs and service corridors, I went up to the top of the building and began working my way down through it again, testing the keys against each locked door I encountered. By now I knew my way through the building reasonably well, and I was not afraid to switch on lights, but it still took me nearly five hours, because I had to spend half my time keeping track of the night watchman, who every hour made a cursory tour of the premises. By two in the morning I had identified a passkey which—except for the guest rooms, the manager's office, and miscellaneous padlocks and cabinet locks—seemed to open everything in the building, including countless closets and storerooms of every possible size, containing goods of every imaginable kind. There were towels, cleaning supplies, athletic equipment, cigars, stationery, wine, clothing, lumber, food, furniture, linen, everything. And in the basement there was a workshop which, although it had a rather deserted appearance, seemed to have been outfitted originally with every sort of tool anyone would ever need to maintain the entire building and all its equipment. The whole place was really far more extraordinary than I had ever imagined: it seemed designed to be almost self-sufficient, a little autonomous world like an old ocean liner, and I became increasingly confident that I would create a secure existence for myself there.

Only two of the guest rooms were empty, but one of the keys opened both of them, and concluding that it would open the others as well, I shoved it into the lining of a chair at the end of the corridor so that it would be there when I needed it. The rest of the keys did not seem to open anything whatever, and I returned them to the manager's desk and locked his office again, hiding the key in a decrepit fire hose by an emergency exit.

Keeping the passkey with me, I went back down to the kitchen, where I had located a small office in which there was a metal box mounted on the wall, containing rows of further keys to all the cabinets and padlocked freezers. I assembled on a tray what by now seemed to be an exquisite, and also rapidly digestible, dinner of bread and cake and cheese and a bottle of chilled white wine and carried it up the back stairs to the fifth floor. If I heard anyone approaching, I planned simply to set the tray down and clear out. The tray of food would look odd sitting there on the floor, but certainly not inexplicable. On the fifth floor I laid everything out and made a sort of picnic under the sun lamp. Then, after a brief dip in the pool, I went down and let myself into the less desirable of the two empty guest rooms, where I locked myself in and went to sleep between clean sheets again for the first time in two days.

OVER THE NEXT WEEKS I SETTLED INTO A COMFORTABLE ROUTINE IN THE Academy Club. Each evening I prepared myself a large meal, which I carried up to the fifth floor and ate under the sun lamp. Then I washed and shaved—the most difficult task of the day. Next to the main dressing room there was a large lavatory lined with washbasins and shelves, on which were arrayed razors, scissors, combs, brushes, and every sort of soap and lotion—but no electric razors. The shaving soap did not adhere well to my face, but—as much to show myself exactly where my face was as to soften my beard—I daubed on huge quantities of it, and, gazing intently into the mirror, carved the lather out of the air. Then, since the noise of a shower would have crashed through the whole building—and would have prevented me from hearing anything, furthermore—I washed myself standing in front of a basin.

Afterwards I liked to slip into the pool and swim repeatedly up and down its length in the darkness. It is odd how much I swim now: I never much cared for it as a child. Lonely and boring but cool and pleasant.

Every week or so I did my best to cut my hair around the edges, flushing the trimmings down the toilet. And every few days I washed out my clothes.

I kept track daily of the reservations for guest rooms, and if there were any empty, I got fresh sheets from the linen closet so that I could make up my bed in the morning and then locked myself safely into a room for the night. When the rooms were all full, which they often were during the week, I stretched out on a couch or on bundles of freshly laundered towels.

During the day I would read in the library, selecting my books early in the morning when no one was about and placing them on the shelves in my favorite alcove. I was beginning a systematic study of physics—or, more specifically, of particle physics—a subject that in my opinion has more in common with theology than with science and that you should probably avoid unless, like me, you find it has some immediate application to your daily life. The Academy Club library was weak in the sciences, but it was adequate for a start, and I spent long hours working my way through encyclopedia articles and periodicals. When I grew bored, I looked at the newspapers half-heartedly, although what they described seemed more and more to be utterly unconnected with my existence. Or I slipped up the fire stairs to the roof and slept under the sun.

At first I made a point of going outside every day, usually at noon, when the Club filled up. I had begun to go a bit mad during those days when I had kept myself locked up inside my apartment. It had affected my judgment, made me delay leaving far too long, and I was determined now to force myself out into the fresh air, where I would get some exercise, keep my mind clear. Not lose all perspective.

I usually walked up Madison, always an exhausting feat in itself, and then crossed over into the relative safety of Central Park. The openness of the park and its emptiness—compared to the city streets, at least—made it easy to move around, and, imagining that I was quite safe, I began to take long walks there, sometimes not returning to the Club until evening.

On an overcast afternoon during one of those expeditions, I found myself on a bench at the edge of the fields north of the Seventy-ninth Street transverse. I had chosen what I thought was a safe bench—one with a slat missing—but when a small group of schoolboys approached, I immediately got up and walked out onto the grass. I aways retreat from groups of people, especially children. And, proving me right, one of the boys hopped up onto the bench I had been sitting on and walked down the length of it. There were five or six of them, most of them black and none of them more than fourteen years old. They were laughing and exchanging taunts as they drifted along, and occasionally they would poke at each other playfully, pretending to fight.

"You call me 'sir,' boy. I'm your father, you know."

I was not paying much attention to them. The sky had suddenly turned quite black, and I was thinking how unpleasant it would be if I were caught here in a shower, miles from the Club. Stupid to be out at all on a day like this. As I stood there deciding how best to make my way back, sheets of rain abruptly emptied out of the sky, and I was instantly soaked. I stood there in the downpour, dully wondering what I should do next and only vaguely aware of the children shrieking behind me.

"Shiiit, boy! You wet!"

"What about you? Shit!"

Two of the boys had run for the cover of a tree, but their clothing was already drenched. The others, like me, stood there helplessly as the rain cascaded down.

"Hey! Look at that! A waterspout!"

I turned to look.

"Look! It's moving."

It took a long instant for me to grasp the awful fact that they were talking about me. The rain was spattering off me and pouring down the surface of my body to create an eerie, but clearly visible form.

"Look at it! What the fuck is it?"

"Hey, it's alive!"

"Some kind of animal."

"Looks like a person. *Shit!*"

We looked at each other for a long moment, the boys and I, not moving or saying anything. I had to get way from here. I turned and hurried off across the grass in search of some sort of shelter.

"It's moving again!"

I had gone twenty yards when suddenly I felt a sharp blow in the back. I wheeled about fearfully, expecting to find something right behind me, but I saw only the boys, following me in a pack twenty feet behind. As I turned to look at them, they held back warily.

"You see that? I hit it! I hit it!"

One of them cocked his arm. They were throwing rocks at me!

"It's stopped!"

They were all watching me, none of them moving now.

"What is it, Bobby?"

"It's an animal."

"No, look! It's got arms! It's a person!"

"It's just a waterspout. Only looks like an animal."

One of them took a tentative step toward me and hurled something.

"I got it again! Fucking rock bounced right off it."

Several of them seemed to be holding rocks. I took a step back, and they all edged forward.

"It's moving again! Come on!"

With fear welling up in me like nausea, I turned and ran. As soon as I started to move, they were after me.

"It's getting away!"

"Get it!"

I felt something sharp hit the back of my neck. It hurt, and I realized that I was now absolutely terrified. I had to try to think. Running was useless: they could run as fast as I could, and I was only drawing them on. And where was I running to? I turned desperately back to face them, holding my arms up to protect myself.

"It's stopped!"

"Watch out!"

They slowed up but continued to inch toward me. One of them had found a short but solid-looking dead branch somewhere along the way, and he held it upraised, ready to swing at me. They began to spread cautiously around me. I hesitated, trying desperately to think what to do. Each step I took in retreat seemed to draw them on. I forced myself to take a step toward them. They backed up uncertainly. No one said a word. I took another step. They backed off further, one of them throwing a stone half-heartedly. The boy with the branch raised it over his head. I charged toward them, waving my arms. Two of them turned and ran. But the boy with the branch darted toward me, swung his branch hard down into my left shoulder, and jumped back. I groaned.

"You got it!"

"It made a sound! You hear that? It made a sound!"

I stumbled back, stunned by the pain.

"Get it!"

The boy with the branch was advancing again. I stepped back, my good arm extended to ward off the next blow. The branch swung hard into my side and, stumbling with the force of the blow, I slipped and went sprawling onto the ground.

"It's down! It's down!"

"Get it!"

They were instantly crowding around me, and I was being pelted with stones. I saw the branch raised high over me, as I rolled over and scrambled frantically along the ground on all fours, trying to get to my feet. The branch came crashing down on my right leg. I was up on my feet and running for my life.

"There it goes! It's getting away!"

The whole pack of them were right after me, shouting.

"Look at its tracks! Get it!"

It was true. I was leaving tracks as I ran, huge gouges in the wet dirt, and, thinking that must be helping them, I turned onto a paved footpath. Ahead of me on the footpath a group of four people had stopped apprehensively, bewildered by the confusion. One of them was a woman in a long flared red raincoat with a matching rain hat. There was a large patterned umbrella; someone had bright yellow foul-weather gear. They were looking not at me but at the black kids beyond, who were running toward them.

One of the boys called out, "Stop that thing! It stole my bicycle!"

The people in the designer rainwear seemed to be looking at me now, uncomprehending.

"Stop it! Knock it down!"

I veered off the path and ran south. Suddenly I was standing at the edge of the Seventy-ninth Street transverse looking straight down at the sunken road cutting across the park fifteen feet below. They were coming up behind me. I half jumped, half slid over the edge and down the face of the wall onto the sidewalk that ran along the road, landing hard and tumbling forward across the pavement.

"It went over the edge!"

"There it is on the walk! Get it."

One of them was already clambering down the wall. As he reached the pavement a little to the west of me, I struggled to my feet and ran desperately east, toward the center of the park. I saw another of them sliding down the wall and others running along the edge above me. Up ahead I could see I was coming to the underpass where the road runs under the park drive.

"It's going into the underpass! It's in the underpass! Cut it off!"

Pulling up in the shelter of the underpass, I watched the rain drain off me, leaving only random beads of water, as if I were made of glass, and I shook myself free of them like a dog. Two of the boys had already entered the underpass behind me, and were peering around intently. Another boy had clambered down the wall somewhere beyond the underpass and was approaching from the other direction, carrying the tree branch. I was invisible again, but I was trapped.

"You see it?"

"Nothing came out this side."

"It's in here. I *feel* it."

The usual massive, deep puddle had formed over a clogged drain and flooded most of the road surface in the underpass. I could not walk through it without giving myself away, so I stood there trembling in the middle of the sidewalk.

The boy with the stick was scanning the ceiling of the underpass.

"Stay there by the edge and watch nothing comes out."

I was perfectly still. The boy waded into the puddle, kicking at it as he went.

"Fucking weird."

"It's just used up," one of them said. "Like a little tornado. Just all used up."

"I hit it with the stick. It's alive." The boy had crossed over to the other side of the road and was studying the wall.

"Might of gone down the drain," said someone else.

"Nothing going down that drain, not even water," said the boy who had hit me.

"Well, nothing in here but us now," said another boy uneasily.

I stood very still.

"Fucking weird," said the boy in the road. "Maybe it lives in the water," he speculated, eyeing the puddle. He started to smash at the puddle with the stick, taking big, savage swings.

"Watch for it to start up again," he said. He was laying about wildly with the stick, banging at the water and the wall of the underpass. I had very little room to maneuver on the sidewalk, and sooner or later he was going to catch me with one of his blows. Or force me out into the rain again.

A Mercedes, its windshield wipers clacking at full speed, loomed up out of the torrent and slowed to a crawl as it entered the puddle. The boy with the stick retreated back up onto the sidewalk to let it pass. I edged over until I was standing next to him on the curb, and as the rear end of the car moved alongside us, I stepped over onto the bumper with my left foot and threw myself up onto the back of the car so that I was sprawled over the top of the trunk and rear window, gripping the rims of the window frames with my fingers. The car heaved under my weight, and there was a metallic thump as I landed on the trunk. The driver looked back to see what was happening and saw a boy frantically slamming a large stick against the rear end of his car.

"The car! It's on the car!"

Another boy was running at him, waving.

"Stop! Stop! Stop the car!"

The driver abruptly accelerated, and the car, with me clinging desperately to the window edges, lurched off, leaving the boys behind.

When the car stopped for a red light at Central Park West, I dropped off the back and stumbled down into the subway. My neck and cheek seemed to be bleeding, and my body hurt everywhere from the clubbing. Feeling like a rat half beaten to death by small boys, I sat on a bench at the end of the platform and tried to collect myself. Eventually I climbed onto a train and rode down to Fifty-second Street and Sixth Avenue, where I stood trembling miserably at the foot of the stairs for another half hour until the rain stopped and I could limp back to the Academy Club.

It was after five when I got back, and the Club was full of people. Not safe to go into a guest room. I slunk into a storeroom on the fifth floor, where I sat on bundles of freshly laundered towels and ran my fingers over my body, trying to determine how badly I had been injured. I decided nothing was broken, although I could not be sure about my shoulder or my ribs. It was hard to tell whether my neck was still bleeding, but I blotted it carefully and wrapped a towel around it. I curled up and fell asleep immediately.

It was morning when I awoke, which meant I had slept through my chance to eat. Two full days without food. I ached everywhere, and it hurt to breathe. When I tried to stand up, I found that my right knee was badly swollen, and I was barely able to get myself down to the kitchen that night. I was sore for weeks, and my ribs continued to hurt for months.

LTHOUGH I CONTINUED TO FORCE MYSELF TO GO OUTSIDE REGULARLY, after that I could no longer leave the Club without a feeling of dread. It was so much safer inside, in those large, quiet, reassuring rooms. No crowds, no running or shoving or shouting. As the weeks passed, I became quite accustomed to my existence there and began to take it for granted, losing sight of how thoroughly odd it was. I was provided with all the necessities of life, and many of the luxuries as well. It was true that I was eating only one meal a day, but I had grown almost used to that, and I had an extraordinarily varied menu to choose from and a wine cellar better than any I could ever have provided for myself. There were books and newspapers, the cool pleasant water of the swimming pool, the acres of leather-upholstered chairs and couches.

The Club had been built with a maze of little corridors and back stairs to allow a vast—and now unaffordable—staff to move discreetly through the building, and soon I knew every inch of it. I knew each employee and where he would be at any time—when the library would be vacuumed, when the dressing room attendants would slip up to the roof to smoke marijuana, and when the kitchen staff would leave each night. I knew which member would fall asleep under a newspaper in the lounge after lunch and which would stay late in the evening. And I moved through the building at will, with complete confidence.

As for Colonel Jenkins, I no longer gave him much thought. I think I assumed that he had given up by now—or if not, that his investigations would lead to nothing. For all they knew, I was dead. In any case, there would be no particular reason for them to suppose that I was in the Academy Club. But even if they did somehow find out where I was, it seemed to me that there was very little they could do about it. It did sometimes bother me that there were only two exits from the building: they might be able to keep me in. But they would never actually catch me inside that warren of little passages and rooms and stairways. Not unless they were willing to send in scores of men who knew exactly what they were looking for.

And it was inconceivable that they would send a raiding party into the Academy Club. The members would not stand for it: they really do have the idea that the place is a sort of sanctuary, and many of them are used to having their way. And anyway, half of them are lawyers. You could probably not send a lone uniformed policeman through the front door without a lifetime of litigation and letters to the editor. They would have people like Anne writing articles on the abuse of police power or the lack of accountability of the intelligence services, and I could not see what sort of explanation Jenkins or anyone else could plausibly give that would come anywhere near satisfying them. Anyway, Jenkins would not do anything that would draw attention to himself or give away my existence: half my value to him lay in the fact that no one knew about me. All in all, I felt quite pleased with my own cleverness in choosing the Club as a refuge, and I think I believed then that I would spend the rest of my life there.

And there was the proximity of friends and acquaintances. There was comfort—at first, anyway—in seeing familiar faces. But then, when you go for weeks without speaking to anyone—only scurrying around the back way, avoiding everyone—your mind begins to go, and you lose any sense of being with other people. No matter how many laps you swim, or how many walks you take. The faces begin to seem like meaningless masks, the conversation a murmur in the background. Just forms drifting past. And you don't really notice it happening to you. You think you are the same person you always were.

I remember one day stepping into the entrance hall and finding myself suddenly face to face with Peter Wenting. He was someone I had always known. Not a close friend ever, but we had gone to the same school, lived in the same house at college. In fact, I went out with his wife Jennifer once, long before he did. But I would normally have walked on past without a thought, except that on this occasion, just as I found myself staring straight into his eyes, he was saying to the other man, whom I knew but could not quite place (you start forgetting the names), "Nick Halloway? No, he wouldn't be interested. Anyway, he's apparently dropped out and joined some sort of religious sect. The Moonies or something."

"*Nick Halloway?* I never really knew him, but—"

"It just goes to show that you can never be sure of anything in this world." There was a pause as Peter reflected on something. "I always liked him, more or less. I know there are plenty of people who didn't."

"The Moonies!"

"Or the Hare Krishnas—one of those sects. . . . Anyway," said Peter, evidently returning to some previous topic of conversation, "it could have gone either way."

"It's like everything else."

"We should get together. Have Marion give Jennifer a call."

"I'll do that, Peter. Take care."

There is always something mildly compelling in an overheard conversation about yourself, even when the people mean nothing much to you and nothing much is said. The trouble was that tears were running down my face, and I could not control the feeling welling up in me that the exchange I had just heard had been extraordinarily moving. It was odd: I would feel perfectly calm and balanced going about my daily routine, but then I would suddenly notice that I was consumed by inexplicable rage or the most maudlin nostalgia, and I began to fear that I was losing control of my reason. It came from scurrying about furtively all day. But it began to bother me that my friends were talking in the next room, and increasingly I would think that I had heard my name. But when I would steal up to them, they would always be talking about something else. And it still bothered me the way Bill would look straight through me as I came through the door. He had, I noticed, acquired a new assistant, who stood next to him, learning the members' names. He would never learn my name. It was living like this, among all these people but cut off from them.

It was also the agonizing worry every waking moment. Can they hear the water running into the basin? Will they notice the food missing, the books out of place, the way the bed is made? You begin to grow paranoid. And when you decide they *have* begun to notice you, you no longer know how much confidence to have in your own judgment. The night watchman had begun to vary his routine so that he would come up to the fifth floor while I was trying to wash up in the evening. The maids had begun to come in to check guest rooms that had not been booked, as if they knew someone was using them. And one night I heard the doorman ask the night watchman, "Is he up there?"

It might have meant anything. You have to try to keep your perspective. But there were times when you could hear the slightest movement in the almost empty building, and perhaps they *were* aware of me. I became more cautious in my daily routine. I always wore all my clothes and carried all my possessions with me, and when I went to bed at night, I wrapped everything up in a single tight bundle that I could pick up and carry off in one hand if anything threatening should happen. I wanted to be ready at every moment to walk out of the room, or out of the building.

As the weeks went by and June approached, there were fewer and fewer people in the Club, especially during the weekends. The maintenance men began to paint and repair the interior of the building—which was disconcerting, because I would come down in the morning to find some part of the Club full of painters and completely closed off for days. The dining room was not open on weekends now, which was also unpleasant, since that meant two full days without fresh food. Then for several days the front entrance was closed off entirely with big sheets of plywood while they performed repairs of some sort on the door. This left only the service entrance, which opened onto an alleyway along the back of the building, and that made me particularly uneasy, because to get through it you first have to pass through a vestibule consisting of a short corridor with a locked door at either end. Running along one side of the corridor is a counter, behind which there is a little storage area for deliveries. A porter sits on a stool behind the counter, and once you are in that vestibule you cannot get out until the porter reaches under the counter and presses a buzzer unlocking one of the doors. Rather than risk being trapped in that space between two locked doors, I stayed inside for three days, feeling more like a prisoner each day.

When one morning I came down and found that the plywood had finally been removed from the front entrance, I felt considerable relief and, by this time, even eagerness to get outside again. They had done surprisingly extensive work. There was new carpeting throughout the entrance hall, and the old hinged door had been replaced by a revolving door. The revolving door was a new problem for me, although it was obvious enough how I would get through it. I would have to wait until someone approached it alone from the other side, and then, when he pushed his way into it, I would jump in just as a full quadrant opened on my side, dance around as the door turned, and jump out again, being careful not to push or be pushed by the revolving glass panels. (I do it all the time now, although I still dislike it.)

I walked through the entrance hall up to the door, keeping on the marble floor along the wall so that my footsteps would not show up in the thick new carpeting. Bill had half an eye on the entrance, and I knew that as soon as anyone appeared, he would be all attention. His apprentice, on the other hand, was staring off at the ceiling with evident boredom. His heart did not seem to be in his work, and it seemed likely that he would not ultimately prove suited for the job of doorman at the Academy Club.

I waited for nearly a quarter of an hour before a member by the name of Oliver Haycroft appeared. He climbed the three steps up to the threshold and then hesitated at the sight of the revolving door, as if somewhere in his rather rudimentary mental machinery there was some recognition that this entrance, which he had passed through regularly for twenty years, was somehow different. He would have liked to be sure: if he could establish with certainty that there had been a change of some sort, he would want to complain about it. This uncharacteristic moment of hesitation passed: whatever may have been the case in the past, there was definitely a revolving door here now, and he stepped forward to push his way through it. I moved quickly, taking one quick toe–step onto the carpet so that I was poised before the opening, ready to enter it when the door was in the right position. I was dimly aware of a faint buzzer going off somewhere in the background. As Haycroft pushed the door and stepped into his quadrant, I took a symmetrical step into mine, at the same time glancing back at the desk, where I sensed some movement. Bill's assistant was suddenly hunched over rigidly, his hands reaching oddly under the desk and his gaze fixed intently on the door. Bill was turned sideways, staring at him with a look of consternation.

All wrong.

As Haycroft pushed the door around, I pulled back out of it, nearly losing a foot, and hopped off the carpet again. The door turned ninety degrees and, with the sharp clicking sound of metal latches snapping into place, came to an abrupt halt, leaving Haycroft caught in the middle. He pushed forward against the door several times, leaning his weight into it, and then leaned backwards in an attempt to push it back the other way. He was trapped, and so would I have been.

Bill looked agonized at the sight of Haycroft shouting and banging angrily on the walls of his glass cage. Suddenly Morrissey was standing there, looking at the situation appraisingly and giving instructions to the assistant doorman, who was inserting some sort of key first into the bottom and then into the top of the door on Haycroft's side. One of the glass panels swung free, and Haycroft stepped shakily out into the lobby.

"Hell of a door," Haycroft said in what seemed meant to be an angry bluster but had a slightly plaintive quality.

"Yes, sir," said Bill. "I'm very sorry, sir. It's new. It's not working properly." He looked resentfully at his putative assistant. "I'm sure it won't happen again."

"I certainly hope not. I don't know what was wrong with the old door."

Haycroft looked darkly at Morrissey, obviously wondering who he was and what right he had to be there, but afraid that he could not ask without risking his dignity. Then, seeing that neither Morrissey nor Bill's assistant was going to show any deference or even interest in him, Haycroft turned and headed for the staircase.

"I'll be on the second floor," he said.

"Yes, sir," said Bill uncomfortably.

"I followed the orders exactly, but I don't get it," the assistant doorman was saying to Morrissey. "The buzzer just went off by itself. I set the door anyway, like I was supposed to, but that guy was outside when it went off. No one was anywhere near the carpet, but it definitely went off." He seemed mainly concerned that he might have done something for which he would be censured.

Morrissey, ignoring him, was talking into some sort of telephone.

"We've got him. . . . In the main door. . . . Yeah, ninety-nine percent sure. . . . He has to be. . . . Sure. The other entrance is secure. We've got him."

It struck me that, whatever I planned to do next, I should offer them some encouragement now, so I leaned over, being careful not to step on the rug again, and pushed on the door, several times, causing it to rattle.

"One hundred percent he's in there. I can hear him."

Outside, a van was backing up across the sidewalk to the steps, and several people dressed as workmen were erecting a sort of plywood enclosure around the entrance. I recognized Clellan among them. As I watched, more workmen appeared inside the entrance hall and under Morrissey's direction began opening out a folding screen across the entrance. As my view was closed off, I saw the men outside dragging a large, cagelike device, the size of a man, up towards the door.

In a moment they would be opening up the other side of the door, expecting to find me inside, and I abruptly realized that if I were not out of the Club by then, I might never get out. The trouble was I could not get the porter to buzz me out the service entrance unless someone happened to be going through.

I ran down the edge of the hall, avoiding the carpet, and halfway up the stairs behind Haycroft, who had almost reached the top.

"Fire!" I called out as loudly and urgently as I could without Morrissey hearing. Still rattled by his experience with the door, Haycroft started and turned to see who was calling. The sight of the empty stairway bewildered him further. I cupped my hands, hoping he would think someone was shouting up from the lobby, and called out again.

"Fire! Please proceed directly to the service entrance and leave the building as promptly as possible." Haycroft stood there immobile, with a baffled look on his face.

"For Christ's sake, Haycroft! There are people dying up there! *Run!*" At that, he finally got it all straight in his mind and ran, thundering down the stairs past me.

"Hurry, for God's sake. Everyone out!" I exhorted, to keep him moving. "It's horrible, people dying like that!"

I turned and followed him back down the stairs, across the end of the lobby, and out through the metal door into the vestibule of the service entrance. The door swung shut behind me, leaving the two of us locked in the short corridor. Haycroft turned to the porter sitting behind the counter, who would have to buzz him out.

It was not the usual porter. It was Gomez. He looked up at Haycroft and said, in a not particularly deferential tone, "This door is closed."

"Well, open it! I know it's closed."

"This door can't be opened now."

"I don't know what's going on here"—Haycroft was screaming now—"but I'm a member of this place, and these doors are here for the convenience of the members, and you'd better open that goddamn door right now or—"

Gomez, seeing that he was creating a problem for himself and being smarter than Haycroft, promptly changed his tone. "That's right, sir. I'm very, very sorry." He sounded extremely earnest, and his accent, which normally is almost undetectable, was suddenly quite pronounced. "We got a security problem here, sir. An unauthorized person in the building. We got orders to keep all these exits closed until we apprehend him. If you could go back in and wait upstairs, sir, it's only going to be a few minutes."

"The building's on fire! Get that door open!"

Gomez looked startled. Watching Haycroft intently, he picked up the housephone, dialed two digits, and waited. Haycroft had stopped shouting and was waiting with anguish on his face for Gomez to complete his call.

I had my penknife out and was trying to identify and extract the little knife blade.

"Hello. This is Gomez." I had the blade open and was sawing into the telephone wire where it ran up the wall at the end of the counter. "I have someone here who says there's a fire in the . . . Hello? Hello!"

Gomez was flipping the cradle bar up and down. "Hello!" He wouldn't notice the little half cut in the wire. Without taking his eyes off Haycroft, he stepped back from the counter to a small wooden desk and picked up another telephone.

Haycroft was shouting again. "The phones are out! For God's sake, do your job and open the door before we're trapped in here!" Gomez watched him warily, but made no reply. He began dialing.

Grabbing hold of the counter, I swung myself over it and slid down onto the floor on the other side. Crouching under the counter, I located the two buzzer buttons, one for each of the doors. The trouble was that if I pushed the one for the exit door, Haycroft would be out and the door closed again long before I could get to it. I got my knife open again and began digging and poking through thirty years of paint until I got the blade under the wires that ran to the button. I prized them loose, ripped them free of the button, and pressed the bare ends together, feeling the electric shock run through my fingers. The moment the wires touched, the buzzer began to sound, and Haycroft pushed his way through the door and was gone. I gave the wires a twist to hold them together and dove over the counter.

"Hey, hold it!" Gomez was shouting. He was still talking to Haycroft,

I think, and there was an expression of incomprehension on his face as he stared at the door and listened to the buzzer. But when I thudded onto the floor and scrambled toward the exit, he understood perfectly what was happening. Gomez was running toward me with a gun in his hand. As I crouched down and pushed open the door, I heard the gun go off once and then twice more, as I raced down the alley and out onto the street.

WAS TREMBLING AS I WALKED DOWN PARK AVENUE. AS MUCH AS I HAD brooded over the past weeks about being noticed, I had never really doubted that I would go on living in the Academy Club indefinitely, and I had never given a moment's thought to where else I might go. It was with an underlying feeling of panic that I tried to consider what to do next.

The panic, I suppose, came from the recognition that the whole thing had been an illusion. Jenkins had never stopped searching for me, and I had never been safe at the Academy Club. There had never been any possibility of my being able to stay there. Just as I had figured out that it was the best place for me to go to ground, he had figured it out too. What was worse, I could still not think of anything better than going to another club—which meant that they would be waiting for me to do just that. I could see that it was hopeless, but what choice did I have? Where else could I sleep and eat and find shelter from the weather? There were the hotels, but they would only be more dangerous than the clubs, brighter and more crowded. I could certainly not go back to my apartment. And I could not risk confiding in anyone.

Perhaps I could have stayed inside the Academy Club and let them try to run me down there. I was still not sure that they could have done it. But I was shaken by the amount of cooperation they clearly had gotten from the Club. A disgrace. I ought to write a letter to the board. Or get Anne Epstein to write something in the *Times*. INTELLIGENCE AGENCY CARRIES OUT ILLEGAL OPERATIONS IN EXCLUSIVE MANHATTAN MEN'S CLUB. It occurred to me that I had no idea what agency it was that Jenkins worked for, or for that matter whether his name was really Jenkins. I had nothing to tell Anne. I did not even know myself who was pursuing me.

Suddenly I conceived an urgent need to speak to Jenkins directly. I had to confront the problem directly, I told myself. I would explain, reasonably but firmly, that I had no choice but to offer him a simple alternative: he would leave me in peace or I would shoot him. I had the means to do it, and he would have to take me seriously. I had, after all, shot Tyler, I reminded myself. And whether or not the threat was effective, I would be better off establishing contact. I would get some sense of what they were thinking and doing. To wander around through the city like this without knowing anything would be unbearable. I had to talk to someone. It struck me that I had not spoken to another human being for over a month. Jenkins, now that I thought about it, was the one person in the world I could really speak to openly.

I remembered again that I had no idea how to reach Jenkins, nothing except Leary's telephone number. Well, they knew that. They would be expecting me to use that telephone number if I wanted to talk to them. They would probably be waiting and hoping for my call. Perhaps Leary's number rang wherever Jenkins worked. Anyway, they would have some way to get him on the line or to put through my call. It was a call Jenkins would be eager to get. I imagined his amazement when they told him I was calling, and I almost began to look forward to hearing the pleasure in his voice when he came on the line.

I assumed they would trace the call, and I wished I had more information than you get from watching movies about how the procedure worked and how long it took. But however quickly they did the tracing of the telephone line, it would take some time to get to wherever I was, and I would call from someplace that would be easy to get out of and hard to close off. I walked west to the Midtown Athletic Club, where I went in through the front entrance and around behind the main staircase to a small hall with four telephone booths in a little dead end. They were real booths, each with a chair and a writing ledge and a glass-windowed door which, when closed, turned on a light inside. There were booths like these scattered throughout the building, but these were the nearest to the entrance. I went into the one on the end, tore a sheet off the pad of notepaper left for the convenience of the members, wrote on it OUT OF ORDER, and slid it between the windowpane and the frame so it would be visible from outside. Unscrewing the light bulb and turning in my chair so that I would see anyone approaching in plenty of time to hang up the receiver, I dialed Leary's number.

The usual woman answered: "594–3120."

"I'd like to speak to Mr. Leary, please."

But instead of the usual warbling ring followed by Leary's voice, I heard the woman speaking again.

"I'm sorry. We don't have any Leary here."

"No Leary?" I said. "Do you have another number where I could reach him? It's important."

"I'm sorry, but I have no listing of any kind for a Leary."

"But I've called him at this number before. Just a few weeks ago. There must be some new number for him. Or someone else I could talk to."

"I'm sorry I can't help you. Please check the number you dialed."

"594–3120," I said impatiently. "Listen, where am I calling exactly?"

"This is 594–3120."

"Yes, but what organization is this? Who—"

"We have no one at all by the name of Leary."

"Do you have a David Jenkins?"

"No, I have no Jenkins either."

"I can absolutely assure you that they will want to hear from me. Tell them that Mr.—"

"We have no procedure for taking a message for anyone not in the directory."

I hung up, stunned. It had seemed so obvious that they would want to hear from me. It should be the thing they wanted above all other things. It was their whole job, as far as I could tell, to find me. They should have had someone waiting by the telephone full time, just in case I should call, ready to hang on my every word. And instead they had inexplicably cut themselves off from me. I tried to think what it could mean. Suppose I had wanted to surrender? How would I reach them? Somehow, it demoralized me far more than being driven out of the Academy Club. Well, the call had been a stupid idea anyway. Self-deception. It was only the feeling of isolation that had made me want to talk to them—all the rest was rationalization. They had done me a favor, really, by forcing me to recognize it. I shouldn't be talking to anyone. Not anyone at all. On my own.

Keep moving. Think about it later.

I got myself out of the Midtown Athletic Club and back onto Fifth Avenue. Too many pedestrians at this time of day. I had to choose some place to go, and I desperately wished I could think of something safer than another club. At least there were a lot of them: they could hardly watch them all. If I were careful and always cleared out at the first sign of danger, I should be all right. I decided, almost at random, to try the Seaboard Club first. It was smaller than the Academy Club, but it had a good kitchen and some guest rooms. Walk into the trap.

Arriving at the entrance on East Forty-eighth Street, I noted with relief that there was a single swinging door that seemed to have been there for fifty years and no sign of any alarms or indeed of anything that had been altered in the last generation or two. The doorman, visible through the glass door panel, appeared to be about seventy. I walked in behind a member who was rather older than that and slipped off into a back stair to begin, without much enthusiasm, my reconnaissance of the building.

I had the idea that I would gradually establish the same sort of secure, regular routine here that I had enjoyed in the Academy Club, and with that aim, I set out to learn the geography and staffing of the building and to get my hands on the necessary keys. I did manage to get into the kitchen, but I slept for three nights out in the open on a couch in the main lounge, never managing to get inside a guest room. On the third morning I awoke to find workmen sealing the windows shut on the ground floor, and I walked immediately out the front door.

I stayed two and a half days at the next club, until, while waiting patiently outside the closed door of the manager's office for a chance to slip inside, I saw Tyler limping down the corridor toward me. I think I must have been relieved to see him alive, but all I felt was dread as I hurried out onto the street.

I kept moving from club to club, but everywhere I went, new locks would appear on kitchen doors, new exit doors would be installed, and new security guards hired. On an employees' bulletin board in the depths of the Republic Club, next to some sort of printed announcement about disability insurance, I found this notice:

To All Republic Club Staff:

Several midtown clubs have recently reported problems with unauthorized after-hours use of their facilities by an unknown intruder. The intruder is apparently able to enter clubs during the day, posing as a member or a guest and remaining in the building undetected during the night. The intruder is believed to be a male Caucasian, approximately 30 years of age.

All Republic Club Staff are asked to report to the Manager *immediately* any sign of unauthorized use of Club facilities and any theft of food or other Club property. Staff are reminded that the House Rules require that all guests be accompanied by a Club member at all times. *No member or guest is permitted to remain in the Club premises after 11 p.m. It is the responsibility of the evening staff to ensure that the Club is empty before leaving.*

I slept someplace different almost every night now. I could not tell how well they were keeping track of me, but more and more I felt that they were right behind me, that people noticed at once that I was there. They noticed the used towels, the wrinkled sheets, the missing food. They heard doors closing, water running, toilets flushing in those cavernous buildings in the middle of the night. Every time I set something down, the little tap would make me jump as if a gun had unexpectedly gone off. Each step I took seemed to make a horribly distinct depression, a perfect footprint in the carpet. Even the faintest, translucent, undigested fiber in my intestine seemed like a flag floating grotesquely in midair. Every sound I made, every movement, seemed excruciatingly gross and obvious, the crudest sort of blunder, and everywhere I saw people watching and listening.

I was out in the streets much more now, as I scurried from one hiding place to another, and I was becoming much better at moving among other people, darting around them as they floated obliviously past. But to me they were all as remote and unreal as a dream. They might as well have been robots or hostile aliens peering malignly out of dead human forms. It had been seven, perhaps eight weeks—I tried to work out the exact number of days, but you begin to lose track and it becomes difficult to concentrate on the calculation—since I had spoken to another human being. That is the most difficult thing about this existence, never exchanging a word with anyone else, the lack of connection. Things seem to drift apart, lose all substance and perspective, as if you were not quite sure whether the wall at the other side of the room is miles off in the distance or so close that you might reach out and touch it. The world fills up with your gigantic, dull thoughts, and when you try to make yourself think clearly, you feel as if you were trying to run underwater.

I knew I had to do something, or I would soon not be able to make any sense of anything at all. I could not go on scurrying from one hiding place to another like some rodent scrabbling into the corners and crevices, nibbling at leftover food, while they blocked up the exits and poked and harried and starved me, until finally they wore me down.

Scuttling through the streets of Manhattan, I could see all around me, for miles in every direction, enormous buildings full of rooms and apartments, into which people locked themselves, safe from the world. There they would eat, drink, bathe, play music, sleep—all hidden from the rest of humanity. I remembered my own apartment, to which I would never be able to return. The trouble was I could not go out and rent another apartment for myself. I needed help, but I did not dare confide in anyone. I had to trick someone into helping me. Since Jenkins would be watching more or less closely my friends and the people I worked with, I would have to turn to someone he could not connect to me, someone I had known only casually, or a long time ago.

I spent several hours in the Ivy Club studying alumni directories and telephone books until I had several promising names. And although I did not expect the calls to be traced, I set out to make each one from a different club, to be safe.

My first call was to a Charles Randolph, whom I had encountered probably a dozen times in my life and spoken to for a total of maybe twenty minutes, probably about golf and interest rates. But we did have some friends in common, and I had an impression of him as an open, jovial sort of person. I thought it likely but not certain that he would recognize my name. I rang Swanson Pendleton, the downtown law firm for which he worked, and a woman's voice came out of the telephone.

It was the first time anyone had spoken to me in weeks—months—and I could hear the voice with extraordinary clarity: it seemed almost tangible, a solid object I might reach out and touch, but I could somehow not make myself focus on the meaning of the words. She had said the name of the firm. Swanson Pendleton. She was speaking again, saying, "Hello. Hello?" over and over.

"Hello," I said. How long had she been waiting for me to answer? She was talking again, asking me whom I wanted to speak to.

"Could I speak to Mr. Randolph, please?"

There was another voice now. Mr. Randolph's office. Asking something.

"This is Nicholas Halloway."

The telephone was silent for a moment, and suddenly a male voice boomed out.

"Nick Halloway! I'll be damned. How the hell are you?"

"Hello, Charley."

"I'm really glad you called. I was just thinking about you the other day."

I was bewildered by the effusiveness of his response. I was calling him precisely because we did not know each other this well.

"I haven't seen you in months," he was saying.

"Actually, no one's seen much of me lately. I've been under a lot of pressure what with one thing and another. Not much chance to get out—"

"Hey, that reminds me. While I think of it, we're having a bunch of people over for drinks on the twenty-seventh. Around six-thirty. If you're still in the city, why don't you come by."

"Thanks very much. I'll probably be out of town, but if I'm here I'd love to. Listen, I'm calling to ask a favor, actually. I'm mainly out on the West Coast these days, and last month I finally decided to sublet my apartment. As it turns out, I have to spend the next few months here in New York, and I'm calling you on the off chance that you might know of an empty apartment somewhere. I'd be delighted to pay anything reasonable . . ."

"Right offhand I don't. . . . Let me think. . . . There's bound to be someone who's away for the summer. Why don't you give me a number where I can reach you, and I'll ask around."

"Actually, it's probably easier if I get back to you. I appreciate—"

"By the way, just what *are* you doing, anyway? I've heard all sorts of things. First, people were saying you'd joined the Hare Krishnas, and then I got grilled by the FBI for your security check. The Hare Krishnas require a security clearance these days?"

Jesus.

"The FBI?" I asked stupidly.

"I guess it was the FBI. It was for a security clearance, anyway. Isn't that the FBI? They must have interrogated me for over an hour. 'When did you first meet him?' 'When did you last see him?' 'Who are his friends?' That was the big thing: the guy wrote down the name of every person I could think of who you might conceivably have ever said hello to. Incredible. Are you infiltrating the Hare Krishnas or something? Do you wear one of those robes? I'd like to get a look at that."

"Charley, I have to run now, but—"

"I guess you can't talk about it. But I'll tell you, everyone is really curious about what you're doing. You've turned yourself into a celebrity. Why don't you try to come by on the twenty-seventh. There'll be a lot of people you—"

"I think it's just that day that I have to go out of town. It's a shame—"

"Well, just come by if you're here. And I'll ask around about the apartment. Tell me, would there be any Hare Krishnas going in and out? That might make a difference."

"Absolutely not. Listen, Charley, thanks a lot. I'll be in touch with you."

I hung up and mentally crossed off most of the other names on my list. Jenkins was being more thorough than I had imagined. Why a security clearance? Why not just say I was wanted for some crime? Arson, for example. Assault with a deadly weapon. But probably this way they were getting more cooperation and attracting less attention. Anyway, I had some names they were not likely to come up with.

At the next telephone I found myself telling one Ronald Maguire, "You probably don't remember me, but my name is Nick Halloway." I paused a moment to give him a chance, but there was nothing but stony silence, so I went on. "We worked together one summer painting houses on the Cape."

"I spent a summer on Cape Cod," he said.

"Beautiful place. That was the time of life. Wonderful summer."

"Yes. How can I help you?"

"Those were the days, all right. I'll tell you, Ron, I think of those days often, and many's the time I've been on the point of picking up the phone and seeing what's become of you." There was no response from the other end of the line, so I plunged bravely forward. "What *are* you doing these days, anyway?"

"I'm chief financial officer for Gurney Shoes." He said it absolutely flat so that you couldn't tell whether it was a cause for jubilation or despair.

"Gee, that's great, Ron. That's really exciting."

"Is there anything I can do for you?"

Friendly devil.

"Actually, as long as I've got you on the phone, there is something I could ask you. I gather you're living in Manhattan. You don't by any chance know of an empty apartment in Manhattan I might sublet for a month or two this summer, do you?"

"I'm afraid I wouldn't know of anything like that."

"Well, it's not important. I thought you might just happen to know of something." I was about to say a final farewell to Ron when an idea occurred to me. "Golly, Ron, I almost forgot my main reason for calling. I'm doing some work for the government that involves a security clearance, and someone might be calling on you at some point to ask a few questions. Standard stuff. Just as a courtesy I wanted to let you know and apologize for any inconvenience."

There was a pause.

"What did you say your name was?"

"Nick Halloway. You remember—"

"Yes, that's right. Someone has already called to ask about you. Several weeks ago. I told them I couldn't be of any help. To be perfectly honest, I don't remember you."

"It's been years, hasn't it?"

"They asked me to let them know if I heard anything from you."

"Well, do let them know, by all means, Ron. Nice to chat with you again after all these years."

With a mounting sense of hopelessness, I also tried a Fred Shafer, with whom I had had tennis lessons at the age of twelve or so and who also didn't remember me or want to help me in any way, and a Henry Schuyler who had just the other day been speaking to someone from the FBI about me. He too was supposed to call them if he ever heard from me, and was that all right, because the whole thing sounded a little odd?

Absolutely all right. Call them right away.

This was all pointless. Jenkins had invaded my past life and cut me off from it completely, and I felt the panic growing inside me as if I were already physically trapped. I was. I was in the trap. They had just not yet reached in to pull me out.

Stay calm and figure out what is going on.

I dialed my office—my former office—and asked for Cathy.

"Nick! Hi! How are you?" She seemed excited to hear from me. The sound of her voice, which had been so familiar to me—not ever very important, but woven everywhere into my former daily life—unexpectedly made the blood drain from my head.

"Hello. . . . How is everything?"

She was telling me who she was working for now and what she was doing. I was trying to talk to her. I should sit down a moment and let my head clear. Where was I calling from, she wanted to know.

"Right here . . . in New York. . . . Well, how is everything going?" Hadn't I just asked that? This was awful.

"Are you all right?" she was asking. It frightened me into something approaching alertness.

"I'm fine. Just got in. Jet lag. It's been good talking to you. I'll try to stop by while I'm in town."

She was asking didn't I want the phone message she had told me about.

"Of course," I said. "Almost forgot."

It would only take her a minute to find it. She had it right there. Yes, here it was.

"Jenkins," she was saying. "David Jenkins." Everything seemed to be going black, and I felt as if I were spinning through the void. Cathy's voice was reciting numbers. Telephone number. "He said you would know what it was in reference to. . . . Please give him a call when you get a chance."

There was a little box of notepaper. Pencil on a string.

"Cathy, could you give me that number again, please." I wrote it down, the pencil trembling. I repeated the number. I should get off the telephone and out of this building. Cathy was saying something about Roger Whitman.

"Cathy, I have to—"

"I'm transferring you right over."

"Nick! How the hell are you? Where are you calling from?"

Great. New York. I stared at the number. I shouldn't call. Memorize it just in case.

"Nick, I'm sorry if I was a little short last time we spoke—I mean the whole story about you and the Moonies. I should have known you wouldn't—"

"Moonies?"

"Spiritual advancement or whatever it was. I should have known you wouldn't get involved in any kind of spiritual advancement. The people were here right after that about your security check, and I gather you're doing some pretty hush-hush, risky stuff, and I want you to know you can count on me not to say anything."

"That's great, Roger. I—"

"I'll back up your story about the Moonies a hundred percent. In a way I really envy you, Nick. I admire what you're doing. I had an uncle in intelligence during—"

"They came and asked a lot of questions about me?"

"Sure. The standard sorts of questions. Pretty thorough, actually."

"What did you tell them about me?"

"Everything. I mean everything I know about you. Shouldn't I have? Was there something I shouldn't have said?"

"Oh, no . . . not at all. You've got to level with them absolutely. Tell them absolutely everything. And they told you I was in intelligence?"

"Well, only in the most general sort of way. Weren't they supposed to do that?"

"No, no. . . . Why not? What exactly did they say I was doing?"

"Nothing specific, really. All classified, right? Just that you were doing some extremely confidential work for the government, and you'd be dropping out of sight for a while."

"Yes, that's right. Anything else?"

"No. I had the impression that it might be kind of dangerous. They said you might be calling me if you found yourself in a situation where you needed help. You're not—"

"And did they tell you to let them know if I got in touch with you?"

"No, they said they would know when you had called."

"Did they? Roger, it's good talking with you. I've got to run."

I was sweating. I took one more look at the number, crumpled it up, and ran out into the street.

DEBATED WITH MYSELF ALL NIGHT WHETHER I OUGHT TO CALL JENKINS, whether I might frighten him off or learn something useful or whether I was only being drawn further into the trap. Whether, in fact, in my state of mind, I could trust even my own resolve, much less my judgment. But in the end I found myself drawn irresistibly to speak to him, and the next morning, feeling like a bird under the gaze of a snake, I walked up Fifth Avenue along the park and selected a pay telephone. It had a good view in all directions and was on the corner of an eastbound street, so that vehicles could approach from only one direction and I could see anyone who came within a block of me on foot. I lifted the receiver from the cradle and laid it on top of the telephone box, adjusting it so that with my head tilted back I could both speak into it and hear it, without having it dance about ostentatiously in midair.

I dialed Jenkins's number, charging the call to my office credit card. Listening to the ring, my mind was frozen with apprehension, as if somehow the completion of the circuit would put me within his reach. There was only one ring, then Jenkins.

"Hello, Nick. Thank you for returning my call."

I had not yet uttered a sound. This line was for me alone. He was absolutely matter-of-fact, as if this were any business call, and his voice had that smooth, exaggerated sincerity that I remembered had annoyed me so much at our first meeting.

"Hello. . . . I'm sorry, is it *Colonel* or *Mister* Jenkins?"

"Please call me Dave. How are you, Nick? We've been worried about you."

"I'm doing reasonably well, under the circumstances. Of course, I do have some difficult days."

"I'm sorry to hear that," he said earnestly. "Is there anything we can do to help you?"

"Yes, there is one thing. You could leave me alone. Let me lead my own life in peace."

There was a brief pause.

"Nick, I know you understand that that's impossible. But we *are* concerned about you, and I wanted to make sure that you were all right, that there wasn't some immediate medical emergency, for example, that we might be able to help you with somehow."

"I'm in splendid shape. I appreciate your concern."

"I know that you're not happy with your situation. I see that you've started calling friends for help."

"I tried to briefly, but you'd already gotten to them and turned them all into spies and informers."

"Nick," he said earnestly, "have you really stopped and thought this whole thing through? You could be injured any time—or become critically ill. If something happened to you, no one would know. No one could help you. Do you appreciate the risk you take just going out in the street alone?"

"Better than you do, I should think."

"Food especially must be a terrible problem for you. It shows when you eat, doesn't it?"

Don't answer. Don't give anything away.

"From what we've observed," he continued, after a little pause, "you have an unusual diet. A lot of carbohydrates and not nearly enough protein and minerals. We're concerned that you may be doing yourself permanent harm."

"Don't concern yourself about me. I'm eating just as well as I ever have."

"I'll feel a lot better when we can do a complete medical evaluation. It's an interesting problem, and we've already put in a good deal of preliminary work on it. You know, your body may not metabolize in the same way as before. Have you been feeling all right? Any dizziness? Violent changes of mood?"

I felt, at that particular moment, dizzy and frightened. It was the telephone call. That insinuating voice. I should hang up right now.

"Nick, what exactly is it that worries you about coming to us?"

"Mr. Jenkins, let me say this clearly. I'm not turning myself over to you. Not ever. You might as well save yourself and whoever you work for the cost and effort. I'm going to—"

"Nick, I just want to assure you—"

"Listen," I said, trying to sound decisive and confident. "I'm not calling just to return your call. I'm calling to explain something to you, and I want you to pay close attention."

"I'm sorry, Nick," he answered smoothly. "Go ahead and tell me what's on your mind."

"Colonel, I've thought this through very carefully, and I've reached the conclusion that I have to offer you the following choice: either you and your people leave me alone, or I am going to kill you. You know that I have a gun. *I'm going to kill you.*"

"Well, Nick"—his voice was even calmer and more earnest than before—"you can try to do that if you want to." He paused. "But I don't think you will. For one thing, you'll have to do it before we get to you, and I don't think that leaves you much time. Furthermore—and, as it happens, I know something about this—most people find it difficult, especially if they start thinking about it ahead of time, to point a gun at another person and pull the trigger."

"Colonel, I just want to remind you—"

"I know that you did shoot Tyler, but I don't think you were trying to kill him. I may be mistaken, but we know quite a lot about you by now, and I don't think so. Anyway, Nick, suppose you do kill me. What do you think will happen then? Someone else will replace me, probably someone who will be harsher in his approach to the problem. And there's one more thing you should consider, Nick. For a number of reasons, I, like you, have an interest in keeping your existence secret. That would probably not be true of my successor. And once your existence is made public, you would be captured in a matter of hours. I think, on balance, you are much better off with me. In a way, we are already allies."

It was true. Everything he said was true.

"You may be right," I said. "But I don't care. That's my strategy. It may not be as compelling as I might like, but as far as I can see it's the best strategy I have. I tell you as forcefully and convincingly as I can that if you don't leave me alone I will kill you. And then I do everything in my power to kill you. It's your choice."

"Well, Nick, you're being very direct with me, and so I hope you'll bear with me if I try to be just as direct with you, because I think it's important that you understand the situation clearly. First of all, it's not my choice. Even if I decided I didn't want to pursue you any longer, whether out of fear for my own safety or for some other reason, it wouldn't make the slightest difference. This thing has its own momentum—in large measure created by you—and it certainly can't be stopped by any one person now. But the really important thing for you to understand is this: we're going to find you. I think we'll be bringing you in very soon now, but even if we don't, I want you to understand that ten years from now we'll be making the same effort as today to find you."

"Colonel, I don't mean to be unkind, but you and I both know that just isn't true. I have some idea of what you're doing now to find me. I can only guess at what it must be costing, but I'm certain you can't go on like this. I know the government has substantial funds at its disposal and that it's not always very careful about how those funds are spent, but this is still a lot of money for what must look to a rational person like a particularly silly enterprise. What do you tell people you're doing, anyway? Some congressman is going to find out that you're looking for little invisible people, and you'll be working at the post office."

"Nick, against my better judgment I'm going to explain this to you so that you won't be under any illusions. First, let me say that for very good reasons this project is classified and very few people will ever have any idea at all what it is we're doing. Secondly, I have—sitting right here on my desk now, as it happens—a small plastic cigarette lighter, which we found on the lawn after the MicroMagnetics fire. It's absolutely invisible. I've shown it to only two people, but it made a dramatic impression on both of them. They see my empty hand move and a piece of paper bursts into flame. And when they take the lighter in their own hands, the sensation is so extraordinary that no other argument has to be made for the importance of what we're doing. It would hardly be necessary to mention you."

"I see. A real piece of luck that you managed to salvage that lighter in all the confusion down there."

"As a matter of fact, we think you probably dropped it on the lawn. I gather you carried away some things from the site?"

"Hardly anything at all," I said immediately. "The gun, of course. A couple of things I found in one of the desks. There *was* a lighter, I think."

If the object he chose to tell me about was something I had dropped on the lawn, did that mean that nothing in the building itself had survived?

"What else have you got?" I asked as offhandedly as I could.

"I'm afraid I'm not at liberty to discuss that," he replied a little stiffly. Perhaps nothing else.

"I still don't see what makes you think you'll catch me. You haven't done very well so far."

"Nick, it's only a matter of time. What you're doing is just too difficult. But I have to say that I admire your resourcefulness and determination, Nick. Not many people could have lasted this long."

In spite of myself, I felt a wave of gratitude for his compliment.

"Time works in my favor," I said. "I'm getting better at being out here."

"We're really only getting started, Nick. Of course, you bought some time by going into the private clubs. We didn't anticipate that at all. It was a good idea. Perfect for you and difficult for us."

"I'm surprised that you get so much cooperation from them."

"We didn't at first. They were quite uncooperative. But we were eventually able to show them that they have quite a serious security problem. Usually they can tell when you're there—or at least when you've been there. Especially now that we've got them watching for this kind of thing, I don't think they'll be a viable option for you much longer. You know, you surprised us from the start. We assumed you would take someone into your confidence."

"I decided I couldn't risk it."

"You were right. We'd have had you right away."

All very collegial. Friendly opponents discussing the tactics of the game. A van pulled up and double-parked in the next block. I had to stop this, get away.

"I've got to go now. Busy day for me. I'm kind of on the run."

"Nick, just one more thing before you go."

"Yes?"

"Nick, you have this number. If there's ever anything you need. Or if you want to talk about what things will be like for you when we get together, please call me. I want to help you."

"That's great. See you around."

A car with tinted windows was pulling up across the street even though the light was green. I slid the receiver onto the cradle and walked east.

My conversation with Jenkins had left me shaken. My threat had been pointless. I knew it, and he knew that I knew it. And it was clearer to me than ever now that I had to get out of the clubs. Of course, Jenkins had wanted to overwhelm me with the hopelessness of my situation, but he was right. The noose was tightening around me, and I could see that if I went on as I was, they would get me soon.

Resigned to the fact that I had to try something new, no matter how unpromising, and reasoning that a hotel would be the closest thing to what had worked for me so far, I set out at once for the Plaza, which was at least large and familiar. As I came within sight of the entrance, my heart fell. Vast numbers of people were crowding in and out, and I knew that it would only be worse inside. Nothing to do. Push on. When there was a brief lull, I scurried through the entrance in the ample wake of an exceptionally fat woman and hurried across to the reservation desk, where I planned to study the allocation of rooms.

There were far too many people, staff and guests, on both sides of the counter, all moving unpredictably, so that all my attention had to be devoted to avoiding collisions. Telephones were ringing; the people behind the desk were punching computer keyboards. It was incomprehensible and dangerous. I had to get off the ground floor and away from all the crowding and movement. If I got to the upper floors, I might learn something by watching the maids cleaning rooms.

I hurried through the lobby and past the Palm Court. The safest route past the floors of ballrooms and meeting rooms would probably be up the broad public stairways, where I would be able to dodge around the human traffic. Everywhere there were clusters of people, sometimes standing around, sometimes moving, and I felt increasing panic.

Eventually I found myself in a long corridor covered with carpeting which showed an unpleasant little depression under each step I took. I stood there for ten minutes, watching as doors to rooms opened at random and people emerged and walked to the elevators. A large metal cart holding fresh linen and cleaning equipment suddenly filled one end of the corridor and forced me to retreat before its approach. Then, in front of me a door opened and a large family of Indians or Pakistanis thronged out and headed toward me from the other direction. Trapped, I turned back in desperation toward the cart and tried to judge on which side I had the best chance of slipping by. Choosing left, I flattened myself against the wall and stood there as the woman pushing the cart slammed its edge into my knee, and then, apparently thinking that a wheel must be caught, gave it another nasty shove before I was able to struggle past.

Hopeless. And it would probably be just as busy in the middle of the night. As I fled down the stairs towards safety, I was temporarily forced back up a flight by a phalanx of Japanese tourists marching up towards me in formation, but I eventually regained the ground floor. There, a large man in a green suit, who was surely a salesman, swung a metal case filled with samples of some particularly heavy widget into the same knee, sending me reeling into an elderly woman. As I escaped out onto Fifty-ninth Street, I could hear her vilifying the man with the case.

My knee hurt and my morale was plummeting. But I desperately needed to find someplace to go, and I had another, even more inane scheme. I had conceived the idea of slipping into Bloomingdale's and waiting for it to close. Which should give you some idea of my mental state. I think I had some sort of vague notion of living in the furniture department. I knew there was a gourmet food department, and I thought that there was also some sort of restaurant or lunch counter somewhere, although I could not remember with certainty ever having seen it.

As I walked across Fifty-ninth Street, I tried to figure out how I would hide from the security guards during the night once I had filled my stomach with food. There would doubtless be sun lamps. (Small Appliances.) And what would I do during the day? No point in speculating. I would push on and figure it out as I went along. I had to try something. And this plan had one undeniable virtue: Jenkins would never anticipate it. I should have considered the reasons for that.

The Lexington Avenue entrance was out of the question. Masses of people swarming in and out. But I slipped in through a door on Fifty-ninth Street without much difficulty and made my way up a short flight of stairs to the main floor. There I found myself in a vast maze of narrow aisles and perfume counters thronged with erratically moving people.

I worked my way cautiously across it. I saw at once that this idea too was ridiculous. Everywhere there were middle-aged women ambling through the aisles in random paths and fantastically made-up salesgirls suddenly popping out from behind their counters. But I was determined to push on. I had nothing better in view.

I had to get off the main floor and up to someplace quieter and more comfortable. As I watched for a clear path, I tried to remember where the stairs were. Over by the elevators, probably. Seeing an opening, I darted past a series of cosmetics counters, their mirrors untouched by my presence, and reached an open area at the base of an escalator.

I watched as two matronly women climbed onto the moving stairs in front of me and glided slowly upward. I tried to think if there was any reason for me not to use escalators. Looking around and seeing no one else approaching, I took hold of the handrail and stepped on. I climbed quietly up until I was riding four or five steps beneath the women, watching them all the time. I would have to be particularly careful at the top. If there was any congestion and the women stopped right after stepping off, I would sail right into them.

As I brooded about potential problems ahead, I became aware that someone was coming up the escalator behind me. Well, that was one unpleasant thing about escalators: you could feel the other people moving on them. I turned and saw a young person—a man or a boy, I think, although other possibilities could not be ruled out—bounding up the stairs two at a time. He had spiky, bright green hair, matching green sneakers, and around the rest of his body, loose-fitting black trousers and a black shirt. His skin was chalky white, and his eyes seemed to be fixed open in a blank, crazed stare. I fled upward before him until I was right behind the women.

"*Excuse* me," he began chanting maniacally as he closed in on us. "Excuse *me*."

Both women turned. There was another bad thing about escalators: their narrowness. Still I hoped, utterly unrealistically, that I might somehow slip past the women unnoticed, by pushing through in the confusion as the women moved aside to let the young thing pass. But just as I edged forward into what looked like an opening between the woman on the left and the escalator wall, she decided to make room on the other side and stepped into me. As we collided, she let out a startled shriek and recoiled upward, blocking my path and almost knocking over her friend.

The young man paused momentarily, and, assuming that he was the cause of the shriek, smiled eerily and said, "Ladies, *please*." The woman who had collided with me threw her hand out to catch her balance and thrust it into my face. She shrieked again. There were people appearing at the top of the flight, staring down at us.

"There's something *here*!" the woman was crying.

I grabbed hold of the handrail and hauled myself over it and up onto the metal strip that slanted down the length of the escalator flight.

"They're absolutely everywhere nowadays," the other woman was saying. "Not just here. I have a niece at Chap—"

I felt myself slipping irresistibly down the smooth stainless steel surface, while at the same time the rubber handrail to which I clung pulled my hand upward, until I lost my grip and went spinning head first downward as if I were on a children's slide. My shin struck some sort of strut, slowing me down enough so that I could get hold of the rail again and pull myself over and back onto the stairs. Struggling ridiculously against the upward movement of the escalator, I managed to regain the ground level.

My shin hurt horribly, and I hobbled desperately out across the floor without looking, wishing I could get someplace where I could scream. Almost at once I found myself trapped again between a couple coming toward me and a uniformed security guard who had somehow appeared behind me. Once things start going badly and you get banged around a bit, you begin making mistakes and everything rapidly comes apart. You have to get clear and collect your wits.

I climbed into an opening under a cosmetics counter where it was hinged to let the salesclerks pass. Huddling there, I could hear the woman sobbing at the top of the stairs and see people flocking to the base of the escalator to find out what was happening. Rest for a moment. Calm down. Watch the long black legs of the salesgirl swishing back and forth, in case she decides to walk into the aisle and crashes into me. There had been a time when I would have enjoyed the proximity of those legs. The whole idea had been ridiculous. Come to think of it, I had always disliked the crowds at Bloomingdale's—as with so many things, this was only a difference of degree. When I saw my chance, I crawled out into the empty aisle and made my way out onto Fifty-ninth Street.

As I walked up Third Avenue, I once again stared longingly at those vast ranges of apartment towers. The greatest concentration of hiding places in the world. People would be going off on summer holidays now, leaving more and more of them empty. The trouble was I needed places with public access where I could get in and out. I had pretty well ruled out hotels and department stores. And private clubs. As summer came on, the clubs were getting emptier and emptier. From Friday midafternoon until Monday morning they would soon be deserted entirely, and I could see that Jenkins might very well close one off without inconveniencing anyone but me. Already, I was terrified every time I opened a door in one of those places at night, half expecting to find them waiting for me on the other side. He was wearing me down. New locks were appearing everywhere, especially in the kitchens, and it was getting harder and harder for me to get at food. I was often eating leftovers now, half-eaten sandwiches or unfinished dinners on plates left out in pantries.

I should get out of New York altogether. Jenkins was everywhere here. Let him try to figure out where I had gone. The trouble was that other cities were so small, and I didn't know them the way I knew New York. I began to think, though, about Boston and Philadelphia. Suburbs were hopeless: no way to get around; no way to get food; no public spaces. Things are difficult when you cannot drive or carry money. Perhaps there was some way to survive in the country. I could go on a camping trip for the rest of my life. A cold and lonely prospect. New York was the best place for me. If it weren't for Jenkins.

Then, two nights later, I came down into the kitchen of the Arcadia Club at 2:00 A.M. and found, sitting out in plain view, a large slice of cake. It was of a sort that would be particularly appealing to me, white with vanilla icing, sweet, and easy to digest. Next to it, sprawled inert on the marble tabletop, lay a large rat, its mouth slightly open, exposing the rows of sharp little teeth. As I stared, its legs twitched once. Whether it was dead, dying, or only drugged, I cannot say.

I knew that I would never eat another bite of food in one of these clubs. I spent a sleepless night on a couch near the entrance, waiting for the first opportunity to get out of the building, and as soon as the morning staff began to arrive, I fled into Central Park.

I had made up my mind to leave New York. I had to get away from Jenkins. Even if I managed to avoid capture, I could not go on living in this state of constant anxiety. Anxiety and hunger. I had to be in a city to have any chance at all, and I tried glumly to calculate whether I would stand a better chance in Boston or Philadelphia. But the vision of that rat kept crowding everything else out of my mind. Fear and loathing. Damn Jenkins. Always knew every move I made. Wherever I went, he was right behind me. But he was wrong about one thing: I could kill him. Although it wasn't clear that I ought to. What I ought to do was throw him off the track somehow. Particularly now when I was about to set off in a new direction.

I walked over to Central Park West and found a pay phone on a corner with a good view. Balancing the receiver on top of the box, I dialed Jenkins's number. It rang three times before he answered. The last time he had picked up on the first ring.

"Hello, Nick. How are you this morning?"

"Good morning, Colonel. I'm a little off today, as a matter of fact. I didn't sleep very well last night."

"I'm sorry to hear that, Nick. Is anything the matter?"

If he would only stop being so solicitous.

"I'll tell you what the matter is. It came to my attention last night that you were trying to poison me. Or drug me. Isn't that right?" For some reason I wanted him to acknowledge it, although it made no difference whatever. I realized suddenly that I was uncontrollably angry.

"What happened to make you think we were doing that?" he asked thoughtfully.

I shouldn't be making this call.

"I came into the Arcadia Club kitchen last night and found a large, ugly rat in very poor condition next to a piece of cake that looked as if it had been set out just for me."

"I see," he said slowly. "That must have been very unpleasant for you."

A cab pulled up half a block north. It picked up a passenger and continued south.

"Nick, I hope you understand that everything we do is entirely—"

"I know. It's for my own good that you do these things. I wish you'd take your kindness elsewhere."

"It must be absolutely horrible for you out there, Nick. I'm sorry. I wish there were something I could say to get through to you right now, because it's only going to get worse. But I know you, Nick. You're not ready to give up yet."

"Jenkins, I'm never going to be ready to give up."

"You know, Nick, we spend a lot of time thinking this through from your point of view. You've surprised us occasionally, and you've shown more determination than we expected, but fundamentally I think we do understand you. Do you know what I personally think you'll try to do next?"

"Go ahead and tell me. I have no one else to discuss my plans with."

"I think you'll try leaving New York in order to get away from us. Boston, of course, is the city you know best after New York, and that would seem to be the most likely place for you to try. Philadelphia would be another possibility."

Damn. Why was he telling me this? To get me to go? Not to go?

"Suppose I do go to Boston? That makes things difficult for you, doesn't it? What do you do then?"

"I think probably you'll find you want to return to New York almost immediately. But you might be able to manage for a while in Boston. We're prepared for that. And for other courses of action you might take."

"How will *you* know where I've gone? Suppose I go to Cincinnati? To Grand Rapids? You can't be everywhere."

"Well, you could do that, Nick. But we'd know very quickly if you turned up in a place like that. I don't think you'd try it anyway. You've never been to Grand Rapids; you've been to Cincinnati only twice."

"Twice?" I asked involuntarily.

"Once last October and once in . . . April of 1959. That was a trip you took with your father. You may not remember. The point is, where would you sleep in Grand Rapids? Where would you eat? There aren't many big private clubs in these places. There aren't even that many in Boston. In most cities people use automobiles to get around. You can't do that. There's nothing to walk to and everything is closed up most of the time. Even if you found a place to sleep, what would you do all day? Wait for us? Who would you talk to? Here you can call your office every now and then. Or even me. You at least see people you know in the streets. That must be some comfort. I would imagine the loneliness must be—"

"I see why you want to make all my plans for me. You think everything out so much more clearly." Tell him something. Doesn't matter what. "But I'll tell you something. I *am* going. Today. Right now. I hope you stay in New York looking for me forever. But even if you don't, it would be an extraordinary fluke if you happened to find me."

"All right, Nick." A beat-up van came to a stop and waited, double-parked, a block and a half north of me. Santini Roofing Co. "You have this number. Just remember, Nick, if you ever need—"

"Tell me, Jenkins, do you trace these calls?"

"Why do you . . . I see. Would it help, Nick, if I gave you my personal assurance that no one will come after you now while we're talking?"

"No."

"I understand, Nick." But he sounded aggrieved.

"Goodbye, Jenkins."

"Nick, wait. Just one thing before you go. We've been extremely patient with you and there's something I'd like to ask in return, as a personal favor. Nick, I'm asking you to stop and honestly consider whether, in all of this, you're not behaving selfishly."

"Selfishly?" What in the world is he talking about?

"That's right, Nick—"

A truck moved up Central Park West into the intersection and without any turn signal wheeled around into the street next to me. The van was starting forward again. As I jumped clear of the phone, there was a little crash within the booth, and a dent appeared on the face of the telephone.

I turned and saw that the side door of the double-parked van was open and a thick gun barrel—probably the same sort of gun I had seen Gomez with before—was pointed at me. I scrambled back from the telephone, toward the building. Cars were stopping everywhere on both sides of Central Park West, and there were people all over the street. The truck filled the side street, its side swinging down as if it were a troop carrier, disgorging men and equipment. It all happened so quickly I could barely take it in. First the nearly empty streets and then suddenly everything opening up, revealing dozens of men all around me.

They were unrolling what looked like snow fencing. Two men seemed to be stapling one end of a roll directly onto the building wall several feet away from me, while two more men unrolled it across the sidewalk and out between two cars into the street. Another section—several sections—were being unrolled out in the middle of the street. There must be more around the corner. I was being enclosed. It was all happening in a matter of seconds. Beyond the fencing, in the middle of Central Park West, I could see other men spreading out what appeared to be an enormous fishing net. Gomez was out of the van, holding his gun, watching warily.

By the time I had collected my wits enough to start moving, twenty, perhaps thirty seconds had passed and the fencing had already been completely joined up so that it ran from one side of the building out into the street, encircling several parked cars and most of the intersection, and then back into the building again around the corner. No time to think what to do. On the half-formed assumption that doing anything—even something foolish—would be better than doing nothing, I started running. I ran straight at Gomez. At the last moment he must have heard me or seen something, because he tried to raise the gun as if to shield himself, but it was too late. I hit him as hard as I could in the neck with my closed fist, grabbed the gun, and heaved it over the fence into the street.

Without pausing, I jumped onto the hood of the parked car behind him, then up onto the roof. Each step caused a loud metallic boom and a sudden, violent deformation of the car body. But for some reason none of the men nearby were coming after me. But why would they? No one would have told them what they were after. So, of course, their attention was focused on Gomez, who seemed to have inexplicably hurled his gun over his head and then collapsed on the pavement. The commotion I made climbing over the car, if they noticed it at all, would be incomprehensible to them. I climbed up onto the roof of the van.

I saw Clellan now on the other side of the fence, running up Central Park West toward me. He was shouting at Morrissey, who was clambering out of the end of the van with his face turned up toward me. I jumped off the edge of the van roof toward the fencing several feet away and a foot higher. I meant to land on it lightly with one foot and push myself up on over it, so that I would come down onto the street on the other side. But the wooden slats buckled under my weight and caught my shoe, and I came crashing down onto the partly unfolded net lying on the street below.

Clellan was screaming. "Stretch out that net! Pull on that net, goddamn it!" The men, with no idea what was going on, moved around the net and began to take hold of it uncertainly. As Clellan tugged violently at one edge and the others began dubiously to spread it out, I felt the net pulling taut under me. I climbed frantically to my feet and then tumbled over again, as the net was yanked under me. Frantically, I half stumbled, half rolled across the spreading net, until I felt myself pitch off the edge onto the asphalt.

I scrambled away between two parked cars and over the wall into the park. I looked back at Clellan. He had let go of the net and was peering toward the park for some sign of me. I climbed up onto an outcropping of rock that loomed above the wall and sat down to catch my breath and observe the commotion in the street below. The nets were already being packed away again and the fences rolled up. The normal traffic was beginning to flow again up and down Central Park West.

As I sat there, a nondescript white sedan pulled up across the street and Jenkins climbed out of the back. He walked several steps down the street towards Clellan, who came up to meet him. Clellan, speaking rapidly, indicated the telephone with a gesture of his hand, and Jenkins turned his head toward it. Clellan's forefinger made little jabs in the air, sketching out the location of the fence, the nets, the men, and then, with an abrupt sweep, tracing out my escape. Jenkins listened to him in silence, his face motionless. Clellan pointed at the wall roughly where I had climbed over it, and both men turned to face it. Clellan made a little shrug and pointed up at the rocks where I was sitting. His face contorted momentarily into a grimace of disgust and he stopped speaking. Jenkins's gaze shifted slowly up the rock and settled there. He made a slight nod. It seemed to me that he was staring directly at me. His face was impassive. Expressionless as a reptile.

I had my gun. I always had my gun. I could climb down, walk right up to him, and blast his brains out. Easy. But he stood there unconcerned, knowing I wouldn't do it. He had everything worked out.

HAD NOTHING WORKED OUT. I NO LONGER HAD ANY IDEA WHETHER I should stay in New York or leave it. I had no idea what Jenkins expected me to do—or even what he wanted me to do. He had had something in mind during that conversation. I was sure of that. He had been trying to push me one way or the other, and if only I could work it out, I would do the opposite. Impossible to know. The main thing in these situations is not so much *what* you decide as *that* you decide. I had not eaten or slept for over twenty-four hours, and for the hundredth time I looked across the park at the tantalizing New York skyline, composed of thousands upon thousands of inaccessible rooms and apartments. All those secure little ratholes. Keep moving.

I walked east to Second Avenue and spent the rest of the morning inspecting buildings until I had one picked out to assault. It was one of those massive white brick buildings which everyone in New York professes to hate but in which almost everyone not very rich or very poor has to live. The one I chose had a particularly lax doorman, whose attention seemed mainly focused on a miniature radio, one earphone of which he surreptitiously kept pressed against his ear until someone approached. He had the main entrance door propped open, which made things easier for both him and me.

Just to the left of the entrance there was a marble counter, and jumbled onto the shelves beneath it and the floor behind it were packages, stacks of mail, uncollected deliveries, a schedule for the exterminator, doorman's caps. And out of sight under the far end of the counter, there were also two metal boxes with keys hanging from arrays of hooks. Most of the keys had little tags tied to them with apartment numbers written on them. I spent half the afternoon crouched behind the counter sorting through everything. Whenever the doorman would amble indifferently over to accept a package or give a key to someone, I would retreat into a corner.

I began with the bundles of mail. Most of them seemed to be from that day and were there only because they contained periodicals or pack-ages which had been too large for the mailboxes at the other end of the lobby. But there were also some stacks which had obviously been ac-cumulating for many days, and from the postmarks and the way the mail was bundled together, I was able to identify several apartments that had been empty more than a week. I turned to the metal boxes full of keys. As far as I could make out, there were keys there for only about half the apartments, and although the rows and columns of hooks were labeled by floor and apartment line, many of the keys were on the wrong hooks, so that I had to search through them one by one, making what seemed to me to be an excruciatingly loud jangling noise. When I had got through both boxes, I had several matches.

I settled on 4C. Mr. and Mrs. Matthew B. Logan. They had both been gone for nearly ten days, which meant that they were almost surely on vacation. Furthermore, there would be only three flights of stairs to hike up, whereas my second choice would have meant seven flights.

Although there was nothing more I could do until that night, I did not want to go outside and risk being unable to get back in through the door. I had to do everything to make this first attempt succeed. I could not go another day without food. I went into a fire stair and dozed fitfully on a concrete landing for the next nine hours.

When I reemerged in the lobby, groggy and dizzy with hunger, it was after midnight and there was another doorman. I watched him for a quarter of an hour. He sat motionless on a chair between the inner and outer doors, looking perfectly catatonic but with his eyes always open and with a good view of the lobby through which I would have to trans-port the keys.

I went back behind the marble counter and carefully extracted the keys to 4C. Getting down on all fours, I crawled out from behind the counter and rapidly slipped the keys under the edge of the carpet that ran the length of the lobby. The doorman's head turned and then turned back. I waited several minutes and then began to crawl along the carpet, sliding the keys ahead of me, keeping them concealed just under the border. If anyone had been looking, he would have seen an odd, jerky little ripple running very slowly down the edge of the carpet.

There was a loud clanking from the end of the lobby, and the ripple halted abruptly several feet from the end. An elevator door opened, and a woman in her twenties strode out and across the lobby, passing within inches of me. The doorman rose, opened one door, then the other, and followed her out to hail a cab. Seizing the opportunity, I spun the keys along the floor the rest of the way to the end of the lobby and then, run-ning after them, kicked them around the corner and out of sight.

The rest would be easy. I picked up the keys and hiked up the fire stairs to the fourth floor. The carpeting in the corridor was laid wall to wall, but I got down on all fours again and slid the keys quickly along the edge, ready to force them under the carpet if anyone came out of an apartment or an elevator. At the door of 4C, I had to pick up the keys and take my chances. It took what seemed like an interminable time to get both locks released and the door opened, but moments later I was stepping into the apartment, pulling the keys free, and pushing the door shut behind me.

I could not remember ever having felt so secure. A physical warmth spread through my body, and I was suddenly free of the grinding anxiety I had lived with continuously for months. I was safely locked inside this splendid little apartment where no one would ever find me.

Switching on a light, I made my way into the kitchen and pulled open the refrigerator door. Ketchup, maple syrup, strawberry jam, five cans of beer, and a bottle of champagne. They had cleared out the refrigerator before leaving. No matter. I snatched a spoon from the drying rack and greedily cleaned out the jam jar. I got the champagne bottle, worked out the cork, and poured myself a large glass. Very special occasion. To my new life. Good champagne. I have experimentally determined that in every refrigerator between Eighth Street and Ninety-sixth Street there is at all times a bottle of champagne.

I turned my attention to the cupboards and found cans of tuna fish and sardines and boxes of spaghetti. That is another thing: there is always tuna fish in the cupboard and usually sardines. There will always be pasta, usually number 9 spaghetti and egg noodles. You can also pretty much count on some cans of Campbell's soup and some boxes of crackers sealed in cellophane—and with luck some canned spaghetti sauce.

I went to work on a sardine can, managing to twist the key just far enough with my trembling fingers so that I could get at the contents with a fork and shovel them into myself. More champagne. To a long and happy life. Safe and sound.

I put some water on the stove to cook spaghetti and made a tour of the premises. It was a standard postwar apartment: two bedrooms and a large living room with a dining alcove. Not enough closet space and the ceiling too low. But it seemed quite wonderful to me. It appeared to be inhabited by a couple with one child of four or five. Mr. and Mrs. Matthew B. Logan. Matthew and Mary and little Jamie. Scattered throughout the apartment were travel brochures for Italy. Another glass of champagne. *Buon viaggio alla famiglia* Logan. I hoped they were enjoying a wonderful and lengthy holiday. How lengthy exactly would it be? I stacked *The Marriage of Figaro* onto the turntable and loaded several bottles of white wine into the refrigerator for the days ahead. Perhaps they were taking the entire summer off.

As I ate my spaghetti I considered my good fortune with satisfaction. I should have figured this out long ago. It was all quite simple. I could forget about Jenkins now. There were hundreds of thousands of apartments all within a short walk, and at any given time there must be thousands of them sitting empty. At this time of year tens of thousands. And there would be no more reason for Jenkins to look for me in this particular apartment than in any of the others. No wonder he had tried to trick me into leaving New York. This must be exactly what he had been afraid of.

I ran myself a hot bath and lay luxuriating in it for an hour with the music playing in the next room. Afterwards I lay in the Logans' vast bed, so comfortable and serene that it seemed a shame to go to sleep.

I slept till midday and then showered and shaved, feeling wonderfully refreshed. On a cork bulletin board in the kitchen was a list of telephone numbers for various emergencies. I dialed the one described as "oficina de Mr. Logan" and was told that Mr. Logan was out of the country and would not be back in the office until a week from Monday. I had another ten days. Nine at the very least. They would surely not return any earlier than Saturday. I would be absolutely safe until the end of next week, and by then I would have established myself in another apartment. One night this weekend I would have to look at the other empty apartments in the building. No reason, really, to look any farther afield.

It was a stunningly clear summer day, and I decided to go out for a walk. After surveying the empty corridor through the peephole, I slipped out the door, leaving it on the latch, and walked over to Carl Schurz Park. The sky was brilliant blue, and even Long Island City looked splendid. Boats moved up and down the East River, and runners toiled along the promenade. When you know you are secure, you can begin to take pleasure in these things again. There were people out on the little fenced-in patches of grass sunbathing, women in bathing suits, almost naked, and I went as close as I could to them and stared at their breasts where the tops of their bathing suits were half peeled away, and at the open thighs. Better not to think about it. Never.

To clear my mind I ran for a mile along the promenade, and it occurred to me how extraordinarily confident I had become about moving around among other people. It would be a melancholy existence, but I began to feel a certain pleasure at the thought of living my entirely separate, secret life in the midst of all these people.

Back in the apartment I showered again and for the first time in weeks washed my clothes. Although it was still afternoon, I made myself a small meal by heating up some clam chowder and toasting a frozen English muffin. It was wonderful to be able to eat more than one meal a day. All evening I watched movies on television and ate and drank whenever I felt like it. It was extraordinary how pleasant my life had suddenly become, when only thirty-six hours before it had been a nightmare from which there seemed to be no escape.

For those two days I imagined I was safe.

On the third morning I was awakened from deep sleep by the insistent, repetitive ringing of the doorbell. I sat straight up in the bed and dully asked myself where I was. Logan. 4C. The bell had stopped ringing and the lock was turning. I looked down at my intestines and saw that they were clear.

"I know there's been someone in there for at least two nights now, and the Logans don't get back for another week."

Two people stood in the open doorway. One was a middle-aged woman in a linen suit and the other was a large man in grey work clothes with the address of the building stitched onto the shirt. Probably the superintendent.

"I can hear whoever it is playing classical music in the middle of the night, and you can see the light under the door. You see? The bed's not made."

I sat there looking at them stupidly. Don't come any closer, please.

"They could of left it like that," said the man. They turned and went into the living room.

"I heard the shower running last night. It's right next to my bathroom. And look in here. The Logans didn't leave out all these dirty dishes. I told Benny yesterday when I went out, but he obviously didn't even tell you. . . ."

They were in the kitchen now. I scrambled out of bed and grabbed the bundle of clothes that I always kept beside me when I slept.

"Look at all this fresh garbage."

"It could be friends of theirs staying in the apartment," the man insisted.

"Well, they didn't tell me, and Benny and Oliver both say *they* haven't let anyone up to the Logans' apartment. Look at the empty bottles all over. Benny says the keys are gone from the—"

Still naked, and carrying my clothes under my arm, I slipped out the front door and down the fire stairs to the street. I had completely misjudged my situation. I had been stupid. Careless. In New York your neighbors may not know you, but they know when you are running the water, when you have a phone call, when you are flushing the toilet. They are always peering out through their little peepholes and peering in through your windows. This would be far more difficult than I had thought. I had not solved anything yet.

OVER THE COURSE OF THE SUMMER I LEARNED A GREAT DEAL ABOUT NEW York apartment buildings. Each one is different, and I began to accumulate lore of a sort that would be valueless to anyone else. I learned which buildings had elevator men, which had fire stairs that exited out of sight of the lobby. I learned where the mail was sorted and by whom, where the apartment keys were kept in the lobby, and better yet, where the superintendent kept his much more extensive set of keys. I got to know which buildings had inattentive doormen and which had a lot of turnover in their staff.

In the beginning I concentrated on large postwar buildings, where there are so many tenants moving in and out and changing their roommates and lovers and families that even the doormen cannot keep track of who is there, much less who ought to be. In these buildings security is often haphazard, and it is usually easy to get at the apartment entrances. But the apartments themselves are small, and the walls paper-thin, so that the neighbors can tell when you are using the toaster, and often there are a hundred people in the building across the street staring right in the window.

As time went on, I tried more and more to stay in prewar buildings. The trouble was that in those buildings it was far more difficult to locate empty apartments and get into them. When people are away, the building staff will put the mail in the apartment or keep it out of sight somewhere. There are far fewer people going in and out, and the main apartment entrances are often accessible only from the elevators. But the apartments themselves are large and comfortable, the walls are solid, and you can feel almost secure inside them.

But after that first apartment I understood that I was in just as much danger as ever, and I would have to think out every step I took. I could not go into an apartment whose entrance was visible from a neighbor's peephole. (Every front door in New York has one of those unpleasant little spy holes, so that you must always assume that you are being watched.) I was careful not to disturb anything or leave any sign of my presence. I would flush as much garbage as possible down the toilet, and I would flush the toilet only during the day, when the neighboring apartments were more likely to be empty. As soon as I got into an apartment, I would search the closets for a sun lamp, so that I could get myself clear again as soon as possible after I had eaten. I never took showers now or played music, and I tried as much as possible to avoid even turning on a light. I crept about in the dark, always listening for the sound of movement in the next apartment or of someone at the entrance.

It was at every moment possible that someone would come through the door without warning: a maid, a repairman, a friend to water the plants. Even in the middle of the night a teen-aged child or a friend from out of town who had been told he could use the apartment might suddenly appear and I would be scrambling frantically into some corner to wait for a chance to get out.

I remember particularly the first time it happened. It must have been three in the morning, and I was sound asleep in an apartment that was supposed to be empty for the rest of the summer. I never heard the apartment door open. The first thing I was aware of was that I was in a room filled with bright light and that I had somehow rolled off the bed and was clutching in terror for my little bundle of clothing. A girl of not more than twenty was standing in the doorway staring at the bed. I had no idea whether she had noticed anything or not. Certainly the bed was untidy, although it did not seem to me that that should bother her particularly. She was short, almost chunky, with dark hair, a rucksack, and the plain, ill-fitting clothing that children in the better boarding schools and universities order through the mail from L. L. Bean, as if they were all on some extended camping trip. Which they more or less are, I suppose.

She walked across the room and around the bed to within a few feet of where I was cowering. She peered under the bed and then glanced about the room. Nothing to see. She must have noticed some movement in the bedclothes when she had switched on the lights, or heard me scrambling onto the floor. I watched her, motionless, afraid of betraying myself by some noise, but the thumping of my heart began to slow to normal, and I became almost calm. She did not know I was there. Nothing was going to happen to me now.

She stared at the bed again for a moment and then, apparently losing interest in the problem, turned and raised the blinds. There was a view of Manhattan rooftops and lights.

Turning back to the bed, she dropped, rather than lowered, the rucksack onto the floor. Then she unbuttoned her plaid cotton shirt, pulled it off, and dropped it to the floor. No brassiere. Full breasts.

My fear was forgotten now, and my mind was filled with the exquisitely agonizing sight of her body. Painful to watch. I knew well enough, insofar as I let myself think about the matter at all, that I would never touch a woman again. Never feel the nipple hardening under my hand, flesh sliding against flesh.

Although she was plump she had a pronounced waist. She was really quite attractive in her way. In fact, she seemed to me at that moment absolutely, excruciatingly beautiful. Probably she was attractive; I have no idea whatever if she was attractive. I had no idea about anything: my mind felt as if it were about to burst.

She pushed off one dirty tennis shoe with the toe of the other, then pushed the remaining shoe off with the bare toes. No socks. They never wear socks. She was pulling down her blue jeans, her breasts extending out as she bent over. Full legs, thin ankles. The blue jeans, half inside out, were left in a crumpled heap on the floor where they had come free. She was sliding down the underpants, stepping out of them, her legs scissoring apart. The tuft of fine, curled hair. The hips and thighs. The short full curves of flesh.

But to say that I was sexually attracted—or even aroused, excited, tantalized, tortured—would be to grotesquely understate matters. I was in love; I would have married her, followed her anywhere, done anything for this woman who inexplicably seemed so extraordinarily appealing and sensible and sensitive and understanding. Which may seem ridiculous, but whoever wired up the hearts and souls of humankind played a cruel and vulgar trick on us all.

There were three short knocks at the front door, and she ambled out naked to open it. I moved back into the corner. She reappeared immediately, followed by a boy also nineteen or twenty. He was blond and slender and wore rumpled khaki slacks and a polo shirt.

"How long have you been here?" he asked.

"Just a little while."

"Any trouble with the doorman?"

"Uh-uh. This place gives me the creeps. Do these people have a cat?"

"I don't know."

He laid his clothes over a chair as he removed them, and when he was naked he turned and embraced the girl. Despite his youth and slenderness, he had a belly, and the flesh on his limbs seemed slightly flaccid. They rolled over onto the bed and grappled at each other for a moment, and then her legs spread open and he pushed into her.

It occurred to me that this was the first time I had ever seen other people performing the act. I understand that people actually pay to see it in some places—although I should think not more than once. To my surprise, I found the whole thing as unpleasant as it was compelling. The two young people were probably attractive—I can't be sure—but there was something distasteful in the sight of all that flesh flapping about. Or perhaps it was rather my standing there, gaping furtively, that made it all seem somehow sordid.

The boy heaved up and down on top of her, panting. Each time he came down, the girl, her blank gaze on the ceiling, would expel a little puff of air from her mouth. I stayed watching to the end, which did not turn out to be much of a wait. The boy began to pump faster, the girl's feet seemed to twitch several times, and they both abruptly relaxed in a motionless heap.

A few moments later the boy rolled off her, already asleep. Her eyes still open, the girl gathered up the edge of the bedclothes in her hand and wiped herself. In that posture, the wadded sheet pressed to her privates, she too fell asleep and began to snore lightly.

Dispirited, I slipped out the front door and dressed myself in the hall.

FTER THAT I WOULD ALWAYS SLEEP IN WHATEVER BED SEEMED LEAST likely to be used by a returning tenant or a houseguest arriving in the middle of the night—usually in a maid's room or a child's room—and I rose early in the morning, because you never know when a cleaning woman or a crew of painters is going to arrive and go through everything. I made a point of getting keys back down to where I had found them as soon as I got an apartment open, because if Jenkins was looking for me in these buildings, missing keys would be the plainest possible way for me to signal my presence. Often I could find a spare set of keys inside an apartment and hide them in a fire stair or basement. Or I would leave a door— preferably a service door—locked on the latch, so that I could get back whenever I wanted to merely by slipping one of my otherwise useless credit cards between the latch bolt and the jamb.

But no matter how careful you are, people notice that you have been there, and I made a point of never staying in any one place more than a night or two. There was no sign that Jenkins knew how I was living, but even if he didn't he surely would soon, and I could not afford to sit still and let him close in on me. I was spending half my time now searching out empty apartments, and as I became more adept at it, I gradually built up a list of safe places that I could go back to. But if anything at all went wrong—if a doorman or elevator man heard something, if a neighbor rang at an apartment door or a maid noticed something out of place, if I returned to find a door rebolted or a hidden key missing—I would leave at once and never return. You have to keep moving.

But as careful as I was and as much as I kept on the move, I knew that I was barely staying even and that in the end I could not stay ahead of Jenkins like this. He would figure it out if he hadn't already. And when cold weather came, things would become more difficult. There would be fewer vacant apartments. Building doors would be kept closed. When it snowed, I would be trapped in whatever building I happened to be in. And once I stopped moving, he would have me.

I had to find someplace secure, a place of my own, where I could stay put and arrange a reasonable life for myself. But I could hardly go out and rent an apartment. I could not even buy a sack of groceries. Whatever I did I would have to do over the telephone. In principle you can do almost anything over the telephone nowadays, and when there *is* something that has to be done in person, you can hire someone over the telephone to act as your agent. The trouble was, Nicholas Halloway couldn't do any more over the telephone than he could do in person. Because of Jenkins. Nicholas Halloway, as a legal person, was defunct.

I would have to start over again. I would have to create a new identity with a checking account and credit cards. Then I should be able to provide myself with whatever I needed. But to open a bank account or get a credit card, you need a credit rating—some sort of financial history—and to get that, you need bank accounts and credit cards. You also need a little something to put into the bank accounts, and it is just about impossible to accumulate any wealth without having an account in the first place. I could, of course, steal any amount of cash and could conceivably even mail it to myself somewhere. But what then? Cash is largely useless in the modern world. It is difficult to pay for anything more than a meal with it. Financial assets exist almost exclusively as bookkeeping entries. If you sent an envelope full of cash to a bank and asked them kindly to open an account, they would probably report you to the police. You need a check to open a bank account, and you need a bank account to write a check.

But that might not be true of every sort of account. A brokerage account, for example. Unlike a banker, a broker might be willing to open an account without meeting you or even having a very solid reference, because the decision would be made by a particular broker with something to gain. The commissions. If there were some promise of real commissions, corners could be cut. And furthermore, you could open a brokerage account without putting any funds in it for a while. You could even get the broker to make a trade if you had him convinced that a check would arrive by the settlement date five days later. He would not be in any trouble until then. It would require a broker who was ready to overlook a few of the niceties for the sake of some commissions, but all my past experience of brokers tended to make me confident that I would find my man.

But what would not be so easy was finding a name with a matching social security number that I could safely use, and I would absolutely need that to open any sort of account. And worse yet, I would need an address and a phone number where I could receive phone calls and statements under that name.

But as it turned out, I got the address almost right away. I had spent a tedious morning looking for apartments in a building on Fifth Avenue and managed to learn only that "the people in 7C are away." Whether for a few days or a few years I could not determine. But there was a set of keys right there in the lobby, and I had no better prospect at the moment, so that night I returned, extracted the keys, and unlocked the apartment. Once I had got the keys safely back where they belonged, I began a thorough search of 7C.

It was a large, comfortable apartment with splendid views out over the park, and it looked from the first as if no one was living there. I found the mail piled up on a table in the foyer, which meant that the doorman or elevator man was probably leaving it there each day, but I was disappointed to discover that it had been accumulating for only about a week. They would be away on vacation, then. Perhaps in the morning I would be able to figure out for how long. I slept in a maid's room that looked as if it had not been inhabited for years.

In the morning, as I was going through the drawers of the table in the foyer, I was unpleasantly startled by the sound of a key turning in the front door. As I hurriedly pushed the drawers shut, an unsmiling woman in her sixties entered and immediately gathered up the mail from the table, as if that were her only interest here. I followed her into a little study off the living room, where there was a small desk. Without ever pausing, she expertly sorted through the mail, making a stack of periodicals, a stack of advertisements and catalogues, a stack of bills, and a stack of personal correspondence. The periodicals she laid out neatly on a table in the living room. The advertisements and catalogues she threw into a wastepaper basket. The personal mail she put into a large manila envelope, which she had already addressed to Mr. and Mrs. John R. Crosby. Somewhere in Switzerland. Then she began opening the bills one at a time and paying them from a checkbook which she withdrew from one of the desk drawers.

I moved a step closer so that I could read the exact address on the manila envelope. The Crosbys seemed to live in their own villa somewhere in Vaud. It all looked very promising indeed. The woman worked for a little more than an hour and then abruptly stood up, returning the checkbook to the desk and inserting copies of the paid bills in a file drawer. She walked briskly through the apartment once, looking in each room to make sure that everything was in order; then she gathered up the paid bills and the personal mail to be forwarded, and left, locking the front door behind her.

I immediately pulled out the checkbook and began examining the register. The woman had been there every Tuesday as far back as the register went. In a state of excitement I spent the next two days going through the apartment finding out everything I could about the Crosbys. I identified a spare key to the service entrance and hid it in the back stairs.

At nine-thirty on the next Tuesday morning I was in another apartment, dialing the Crosbys' number. It rang seven times, and I was afraid she would not answer, but in the end few people can resist a ringing telephone.

"Crosby residence," she answered curtly.

"I'd like to speak to Mr. Crosby, please. This is Fred Fmmmph," I mumbled indistinctly.

"The Crosbys are not in New York."

"Still off in Switzerland, are they? I was afraid of that. When do you expect them to be in New York?"

"I'm afraid I don't know," she said, as if not knowing gave her considerable pleasure. "If you would like to leave a message, I can forward it. If you could spell your name—"

"You must be Mrs. Dixon, aren't you?"

"I am Mrs. Dixon," she said as if it were an affront to be addressed by name.

"That's wonderful. John and Mary talk about you all the time. It's a real pleasure to meet you. You don't have any idea whether they plan to be in New York during the next few months, do you?"

"I really don't know their plans. If you want to leave—"

"Actually, I'll tell you—it's probably better if you don't even mention that I called. The thing is, a bunch of us from Marley School wanted to get together . . . hold a dinner for John . . . kind of honor him for everything he's done for the school and so forth . . . unveil a small statue we've had made of him."

"Oh, I see—"

"And we were hoping he might be in New York sometime in the fall . . . September or October."

"Oh, I'm sorry, Mr. . . . um . . . that is, I'm sorry, but I'm afraid they won't be here before Christmas. They generally come only at Christmas, to see the children."

"That would be perfect. Perfect. Better not even to mention that I called, Mrs. Dixon. So as not to spoil the surprise."

"Of course, Mr. . . . uh—"

"Pleasure finally to meet you, Mrs. Dixon. Goodbye."

LEARNED FROM A TELEPHONE CALL TO THE SOCIAL SECURITY ADMINISTRA-
tion that I would have to "come in in person" for an interview, bringing
"an original birth certificate and two means of identification." The
nearest office was on East Fifty eighth Street. I went in "in person" al
though I had nothing to bring and knew I would do badly in an interview.
It turned out to be on the twelfth floor, which for me meant trudging
up eleven flights of stairs. The office itself was a single large room, one
end of which had been more or less fenced off with a metal desk and
several racks of pamphlets to serve as a waiting room. There were two
rows of decrepit metal chairs, on which half a dozen people sat staring
aimlessly into space. Waiting, probably, for their names to be called.

I went around behind the racks into the main office area, where there
were fifteen or twenty drab grey metal desks, positioned at random on
the linoleum floor. There were very few people applying for social
security cards, and most of them were aliens or minors, so that it took me
several hours to figure out the whole procedure for processing applications.
The applicant would hand in his completed application together with
his birth certificate and "evidence of identity" and wait to be called for
an interview. After the interview, which seemed to serve no function at
all in the process, the interviewer, having noted the documentation
provided, would sign and stamp the application. The application form
then made its very gradual way to one of two women seated in front of
computer terminals, and the information was keyed in and transmitted
directly to a central computer somewhere in Maryland. The application
form itself was then placed in a folder where it was held for several weeks
before being forwarded for permanent filing at yet another office in
Pennsylvania. I spent most of the morning watching the women at the
terminals, paying particular attention when they signed off for lunch and
then signed on again afterward.

At five minutes after five, when the room was entirely empty, I switched
on one of the terminals and logged on, typing in the same password and

information I had seen one of the women use in the afternoon. I called up the format for entering a new name into the system and typed in "Jonathan B. Crosby." That would be different enough from "John R. Crosby" that I would be able to pick out my mail, but not so different as to invite comment from the postman or building staff. I entered the Fifth Avenue address and gave myself a birth date that made me exactly twenty-one that day—old enough to allow me to establish accounts but young enough to make plausible my lack of a credit record.

Jonathan B. Crosby's newly assigned social security number appeared on the screen, and I committed it to memory. Happy Birthday, Jonathan.

I WENT EVERY FEW DAYS TO THE CROSBY APARTMENT TO PICK OUT ANY MAIL addressed to Jonathan B. Crosby, always making particularly sure to get there on Monday evenings, before Mrs. Dixon arrived on Tuesday morning. Of course, at first there was only my social security card to watch for, but I hoped soon to be getting all sorts of confirmation slips and statements from brokerage firms.

But before I got a brokerage account I would have to be ready with some very specific investment ideas. And I had to revise my whole investment strategy radically. I could no longer set myself the goal of being right more than half the time over the course of a couple of years, which had in the past always seemed a perfectly splendid outcome. I now needed an investment that would appreciate a great deal in a short time— and with virtual certainty. Of course, a lot of people feel they need investment ideas like this, and they are consequently not easy to come by, but my condition did give me some advantages.

One place to look for such situations is in the 13D business, named after the form you must file with the Securities and Exchange Commission when you acquire more than 5 percent of the stock of a public corporation. If you are in this business, you look around for a corporation which you think is undervalued by the stock market, or which you think you could make more valuable if only you controlled it. You get together with some friends and start gradually buying up the stock—as discreetly as possible, since you don't want to do anything to drive up the price unnecessarily. Then you cross the 5 percent mark, and pretty soon you have to start telling everyone more or less what you are up to, and probably you make some offer to buy out other shareholders at some price well above the recent market price. You hope in all this either that you will be bought off or outbid, in which case you expect to make a vast and rather quick profit, or else that you will wind up controlling the corporation, in which case you do whatever it is you think will make it more valuable—

restructure it, replace the incompetent management, sell off the pieces, whatever. But no matter what happens—even if you bungle the whole thing—the price of the stock will probably have shot up dramatically, at least for a while.

There are all sorts of people in New York who are involved in this kind of thing pretty much all the time, and I began to spend my days, and some of my evenings, in their offices, watching for promising situations. There are not only the actual principals—the individuals or corporations that actually do the acquiring—but the law firms and investment banks that advise and assist them and that may be involved in any number of takeovers at any given time. They also put together other sorts of trans-actions, such as leveraged buyouts, which can send a share price shooting up suddenly. The investment banks perform all sorts of interesting ser-vices and acts—in fact, any service or act that can be performed in a suit, this being the limitation imposed by their professional ethics.

I would walk down to midtown, or sometimes even to the financial district, in the afternoon and hike up the endless flights of stairs—the more useful the information, the further off the ground it seemed to be—to whatever office I was interested in. I would spend hours listening in on meetings and telephone conversations. When someone was out of his office, I would slip in and read through whatever was on his desk. I spent hours and days this way listening to investment bankers plot takeovers that were never launched. I watched people accumulate huge blocks of stock and then change their minds and sell it. But gradually I began to find out where my time would be most usefully spent and which lawyers and bankers were involved in everything that was going on in their firms. After a while I had several particularly promising situations that I was following closely. And I had become extraordinarily fit hiking up and down all those flights of stairs.

In the meantime, however, I was making no progress at all in finding a broker. Which seemed odd when I considered all the effort I had had to devote to avoiding them in my previous life. The trouble was, I couldn't use anyone who knew me as Nicholas Halloway, but on the other hand, given my condition, it seemed to be impossible to meet new people. But when the twenty-seventh came around, and I remembered Charley Randolph's invitation to his cocktail party, it occurred to me that that might be the answer. Eventually I would need not only a broker but a lawyer and an accountant, and what better place to search for them than at social gatherings where I could observe large numbers of new people half-drunk and talking continuously. I would begin that night at Charley Randolph's. There would even be some people there I knew, and, at the thought, I was suddenly full of eagerness to see familiar faces and hear familiar voices again.

However, standing outside the Randolphs' door at half past seven that evening I nearly abandoned the whole idea. Hearing the roar of cock-tail babble within, I was suddenly filled with dread at the idea of walking into a room full of people, and only my investment of the thirteen-story climb kept me from fleeing the building. The door swung open, and a man I had never seen before walked out. This was my chance, and I instinctively seized it, catching the door before it closed and slipping past it into the foyer.

The foyer opened into a drawing room half filled with people, all with drinks in their hands, talking to each other in little groups. In the opposite wall was a doorway through which I could see people drifting in and out of another public room. It was a good party for me: the rooms were large and not very crowded. When a party really starts to fill up, I have to be on my way. I need some open space between the clusters of people.

I saw, with a flood of emotion which startled me, that there were indeed people I knew. A number of them. There were Bob and Helen Carlson and the Petersons and Corky Farr and Bitsy Walker. Some of them I had known more or less all my life. As I think about it now, there was actually no one there to whom I had been terribly close, but at that moment I suddenly felt an intense intimacy with these people, and I thought for an instant that I was about to weep. I thought of going up to them and announcing my presence, telling them everything. They would swarm around me, amazed. Imagine how they would welcome me. Everyone would want to touch me. Comfort me. They would look after me. It is important not to let oneself begin to think this way.

But it was reassuring to be among them, even if I could not speak to them. And it would be exciting to watch and listen to them secretly. I would see and hear everything. In a way, I would know them better, be closer to them, than ever before.

There was another thing that I noticed right away with pleasure: most of them were reasonably drunk. Nothing does more to put me at ease in these situations than drunkenness in others. Whatever mental capacity these people retained would be entirely devoted to remembering how the sentence they were in the middle of had begun and where it might plausibly go. I can be almost comfortable with people in that state.

I instinctively looked for my hosts. Charley Randolph was standing in the front of the drawing room with an eye on the foyer for arriving guests, half listening to a fat man in a pin-striped suit who seemed to be lecturing rather than conversing. I joined them as best I could, creeping up to within two feet of them and standing there listening.

"They're going to report a dollar fifteen for the second quarter," the fat man was saying. He spoke emphatically but as if he were unaware of Charley's presence, as if he were talking to himself. Perhaps this would be the stockbroker I was looking for. "Worst case, maybe a dollar five," he went on, "which is ten percent off last year." Charley's eyes were shifting around the room as the man talked. "But that includes a one-time write-off of their entire Biloxi operation, and when you add that back in, you're looking at earnings of a dollar forty to a dollar fifty for the quarter and five fifty to six dollars for the year, and that's assuming no regulatory relief whatever."

"What is the regulatory picture?" Charley asked absent-mindedly, his eye on the door. Something about the man was absolutely deadening. But I ought to wait and see if he was a broker.

"Well, that of course is an extremely interesting question. We have a subsidiary in essentially the same business down in—"

I saw Corky Farr on the other side of the room leaning over a girl with a panoramic decolletage, one arm extended past her to the wall to steady himself. I walked over to them: at a party you always tend toward the people you already know—even if you can't speak to them. Although the way the dress was wrapped tight around the woman's breasts, forcing them up and out at the top, may have been a factor as well.

Corky would be drunk. At least at the times of day I saw him, he was always drunk, and getting drunker. But he would also want to sleep with the girl despite the handicap he had set himself.

"But then," he was saying—and he treated the consonants with special care, knowing from experience that they would slip out of control and slur if not watched, "what do these people have in their heads?" He indicated the other guests by waving his gin and tonic in a wide arc, slopping some of it in the process onto the floor. He studied the glass analytically for a moment and then solved the problem by drinking from it.

"Understand me, these are my friends. . . . I love them." Corky, his head inclined forward, was staring directly down at the breasts. He paused, either because he had lost the thread of his argument or simply in order to enjoy a moment of quiet contemplation. "But what, in the end, do they have in their heads . . . in their souls, if you will?"

It was clear enough what Corky had in his: gin, unbridled lust, and a vestigial capacity for speech. I wondered whether he could remove his other hand from the wall and remain standing.

Still gazing into her dress, he went on. "But I can see there's more to you than to the rest of these people." He indicated the rest of the assembly again by tossing a little more gin on the floor. Corky seemed to be making a rather primitive approach, but then, given his condition, he was probably wise to take a strong, well-defined line of attack and hold to it unswervingly. Judging from her rather unfocused expression, his interlocutor had been well supplied with gin herself, so it probably didn't matter much. Someone at some point must have told her what her best feature was, because she kept herself erect with her shoulders back and her torso thrust forward. "There's a good deal more . . ."

She raised her glass to drink from it, twisting her body at the same time so that one breast brushed across Corky's ribs. Corky's entire body shifted in place. He seemed to move into another gear.

"Why," he said, "don't we wander over to Mortimer's for some dinner."

"Brad and Sally and a whole gang of us were going out together for something," she answered vacantly. "Why don't we go somewhere with them. We haven't decided where."

Corky screwed up his features in concentration. He looked as if someone had given him a complex mathematical problem which, if he could hold it in his head, he might try to solve presently.

"Mortimer's," he said with deliberation, "would be closer."

"Closer?" she said uncomprehendingly. "To what?"

"To my place," he replied after a moment's thought. "I'll tell you what. Why not find out where they're going to be and we can always join them later."

Suddenly, out of the tangle of voices coming from the next room, I picked out my own name. I would have liked to stay and follow the course of events unfolding before me. It would be close. a question of whether Corky could retain consciousness and hold her attention long enough to achieve the desired consummation. But the sound of my name—people talking about me—sent a thrill through me. And it created for me a connection with these people whom I had not spoken to—been one of—for what seemed like a very long time.

I plunged into the next room in search of whoever was speaking of me. Standing by a window I saw Roger Cunningham and recognized at once that it had been his voice I had heard. He was talking to Charley Randolph and a woman I did not know. I walked eagerly over to them. Bitsy Walker and Fred Cartmell, who had evidently been talking to each other nearby, had both half turned to join the conversation.

"When did you talk to him?" Roger was asking Charley.

I was quite excited. Here I was with my friends, unseen, the fly on the wall, listening to them talk about me.

"It was just a few weeks ago. He said he'd be here, but I haven't actually seen him in months. Really odd. He was just going along like everyone else and then suddenly—no warning—he just drops out. Disappears. And then you've got all these bizarre stories—"

"Is he the one who joined the Moonies?" asked the woman I did not know.

"That's the one," piped in Bitsy with a smirk. "Only I think it was the Hare Krishnas, actually." I had known Bitsy for years. I had slept with her once when we were in college. "Amazing, isn't it? That it should be Nick, of all people. He's always been so predictable in everything."

Standing there unseen, listening to her—to all of them—speaking about me, I began to feel as if I were taking the tour with the ghost of Christmas Future.

"Well, we probably shouldn't be talking about this, and I don't really know a thing about it," said Charley, assuming the air of one who probably knows a great deal but expects everyone to understand that he is not at liberty to say much, "but I wouldn't be surprised if he was up to something very hush-hush—the CIA or something. And this Hare Krishna thing is just a cover. Some sort of operation or whatever."

"You mean Nick Halloway is going to infiltrate the Hare Krishnas for the CIA?" asked Fred Cartmell with a sardonic little smile. "That's a hell of an idea. I mean, I'm sure it's vital that someone do the job and all, but I'm not convinced that Halloway is the best choice. For one thing he'd need all new clothes, at least if he wanted to go about the thing properly. And even then, if the Hare Krishnas ever get wind of the fact that they're being infiltrated, I should think that Halloway would be high on their list of suspects."

"God, I'd love to see him in his robes banging on his tambourine in the street," said Bitsy eagerly. "We should all make a pact to always be on the lookout for Hare Krishnas and promise to call everyone if one of us finds him."

"In my opinion," said Fred Cartmell, "we would all be well advised to stay clear of him."

"Do you think it's all really true?" asked Bitsy.

"What?" asked Roger. "The CIA thing or the Hare Krishnas?"

"Either," answered Bitsy. "Both."

"Come on, Charley," said Roger. "What did Nick say exactly, when you talked to him?"

Charley again adopted his mysterious air, deepening his voice and weighing his words pompously. "I really don't have any more information than anyone else. However, Nick did indicate that he was involved in some sort of government service that it would be inappropriate to discuss. I'm surprised he hasn't shown up, though. I believe he's traveling quite a lot—he may be out of town."

"Well, I know for sure the FBI or somebody spent a good two hours with me getting absolutely every piece of information I could come up with about him," said Roger.

"You too?" asked Bitsy.

"They've talked to everyone who's ever been in the same room with him," said Charley.

"And they were pretty damn thorough too," said Roger. "Amazingly thorough. Seemed kind of ridiculous, actually, beyond a certain point. But there's probably not a single interesting fact about Nick they don't know."

"Nor a single interesting fact about Nick that they *do* know," contributed Cartmell. "I defy anyone to name an interesting fact about Nick. That's pretty much the whole point of Nick."

"Well, I've never laid eyes on the man," said the other woman, "but from what you say, he seems to have done at least one interesting thing."

"Oh, Nick's all right," volunteered Bitsy without much apparent feeling. "Anyway, it must be something like the CIA. As opposed to the Hare Krishnas, I mean. He was never much on belief of any sort, as far as I could see. I can't imagine him doing anything like that. I went out with him once or twice when we were in college," she added, either to add weight to her opinion or because she thought the fact might in some way make her seem more interesting.

"It's not clear to me," said Cartmell, "in what way infiltrating the Hare Krishnas for the CIA is less weird than simply joining the Hare Krishnas straight out, without any confusion of motives. In fact, both on moral grounds and as a taxpayer, I think I prefer the latter. Not that I like the idea of my taxes being used to fund Halloway's spiritual development."

"Why shouldn't Nick have your money?" said Roger. "They're not going to put it to any better use."

"I'd rather have it put into missiles or welfare fraud. Halloway has never evidenced much capacity for spiritual development. And anyway, why can't I have my money? Now that they revise the tax laws every year, it's a tricky business hanging on to anything at all."

"I wish I'd been a tax lawyer," said Roger. "It's incredible what you have to go through just to figure out what you owe. I don't know how people do it. I have this dispute with the IRS now—actually, there's not even that much money involved—but I have these oil royalties—not much, but naturally one fraction is 'tier one non-Sadlerochit oil,' whatever that is, and another is something called 'incremental tertiary oil'—I wish I could show you the reporting requirements on this. . . ."

I noticed after a while that I was not following Roger's anecdote, although a few months ago I would probably have found it perfectly entertaining. I was, I realized, a bit shaken by this discussion which I had so eagerly anticipated. It was the tone that had been somehow disheartening, the lack of warmth. Or of affection. I tried to remember how I had talked of absent friends in such situations. It probably meant nothing, really. Still, these things can engender a feeling of emptiness. Remoteness.

I wandered in a bit of a trance out into the hall and down to the empty bedroom that had been left open so that guests could dump coats and briefcases on the bed. The weather was vaguely threatening so that, despite the time of year, there were a number of raincoats and shawls scattered about. I sat down on a chair by the window. Someone had left half a gin and tonic on the sill. I sipped at it, watching the liquid run down my esophagus and form a faint outline of the bottom of my stomach. I think I half hoped that someone would come in and notice before it faded. It would be a relief in a way. Have the whole thing over with. Free of all the decisions and anxiety. People would look after me. The tonic was flat and unpleasantly sweet, the gin like a chemical. Soon the glass was empty. I thought that I should probably leave, but I continued to sit there.

I heard someone approaching down the hall. Helen Carlson walked in followed by Tommy Peterson. I have always liked Helen: quiet, but sensible and solid.

As they entered, Tommy was saying, "I've arranged it with Bob"— Bob Carlson is Helen's husband and a friend of mine—"so that the four of us are going out together for something to eat." The Petersons and the Carlsons have always done everything together. Best friends.

"This is Jane's, isn't it?" said Helen, picking up a long raincoat from the bed and handing it to Tommy. Tommy took it and folded it over his left arm. Helen placed her open hand on Tommy's shirt front and slid it down into his trousers. Tommy's eyes closed momentarily and he expelled the air from his lungs with a faint sound that was almost a grunt or a sigh. He tried to embrace her, but with her arm twisted beneath his belt, they remained awkwardly turned apart from each other. Tommy ran his right hand down her back, still holding his wife's coat over the other arm like an attendant. He bent his head and kissed her.

I must have made some noise. I don't know. But something made them both pull abruptly apart and look around. No one to be seen. They had impassive expressions on their faces again. Helen picked up a bag and, moving toward the door, said, "Why don't we try Parma?"

I listened to their steps and voices fade down the hall. Difficult to know what is in the hearts and minds of other people. Difficult, now that I think of it, to know always what is in one's own heart and mind. Anyway, I found myself a bit demoralized. Partly it was finding out about Helen and Tommy, although you are always finding out these things about other people. But it was also the way I was finding out. Without their knowing. Spying. Sneaking. You find that this sort of illicit, intimate information about people only separates you from them.

I walked back through the hall. In the front rooms there were only half as many people as before. They were all loud, grinning crookedly, drunk. I slipped out the service entrance and down the stairs. The air outside was close and dirty. I should force myself to hurry, before it started to rain. I should really never have gone out in this weather.

AFTER THAT I FOUND MYSELF AVOIDING PEOPLE I HAD KNOWN IN MY former life, but in my search for a broker I continued to go to parties of every conceivable kind almost daily for the next several weeks. It was the perfect time of year for it. The people who are still in the city in July, especially if they are single or their families have left for the summer, will often go out every night of the week, eating in restaurants and wandering from one gathering to another. I would spot little bands of them in the street or climbing out of taxis, and I would follow them to their celebrations, or sometimes I would simply walk into one of the big postwar apartment buildings with hundreds of apartments and go through the corridors until I heard the roar of a party behind a door. It never took long. I would drop in sometimes on three or four parties in an evening, until I found one that looked promising, and then I might hang about for hours, drifting from conversation to conversation, sometimes sipping cautiously from an abandoned drink in a corner, using as a straw the plastic shaft of an otherwise useless, invisible ball-point pen from which I had removed the ink cartridge. At these moments I think I sometimes lost sight of the fact that I was not really a guest at the party.

By the middle of July I had taken a careful look at several likely-looking brokers, finally settling on one Willis T. Winslow, III. I had first encountered Willy, as he is known to his friends, at a party on Seventy-second Street, where I spotted him aggressively telling another young man a story about an exciting disk-drive manufacturer selling at forty or fifty times earnings. I could see at once that he held promise. For one thing, although it was early in the evening, he had already drunk a great deal and showed no signs of easing off. Willis, I was soon able to observe, drinks almost continuously when in company. But unlike a lot of people, he does not lose his bearings when he is by himself: he keeps on drinking. I stayed with him the rest of the evening, and long before it was over he was having trouble moving about. Over the next few days I found out where Willy lived, where he had gone to school, who his friends were. I

(255)

attended more parties with him. I even went in one day and stood next to his desk for several hours, listening to him talk to his customers over the telephone and watching his sporadic attempts to read research reports. At around eleven in the morning he came back from the water fountain with a paper cup and, slipping it into a desk drawer, managed to pour a shot of gin into it from a pint he had secreted there.

In the third week of July I saw my opportunity. One of the offices in which I had spent many tedious hours over the past month was that of Myron Stone, who was one of the most successful and feared of the corporate raiders—and this is a business in which a history of past success is by far the most useful weapon in securing future success. Over the course of seven months he had quietly accumulated, for various anonymous accounts that he or his associates controlled, just under 5 percent of the stock of Allied Resources Corp., at prices ranging from $9.50 to $11.00 a share, and then, having reached that point, he had paused for several weeks to marshal his forces for the final onslaught. During the time I had been watching him, he had been assembling a war chest of something around $100 million in commitments (which he would later describe to the press as $300 million) and working with his lawyers to prepare for every legal attack or defense that might conceivably be undertaken. In the second week of July I could see that this activity had reached a new level of intensity and that he would soon have to move in for the kill. I could always find Stone in his office, night or day, and, growing increasingly fascinated with his campaign, I spent far more time there than I really needed to for my purposes. What particularly astonished me was how much he had learned about Allied Resources and the people who ran it and how thorough his plans for its dismemberment and reconstitution already were. He was, however, not a sentimental man, and there would clearly be some anguishing moments for the current stewards of the assets of Allied Resources. It was perhaps only humane and best for everyone that the current management had so little warning of just how much more Myron Stone was going to do for the shareholders than they had thought necessary.

When the markets opened on Monday of the third week in July, Stone began buying Allied Resources shares again, quickly running over the 5 percent limit. He would now have ten more days to buy shares in secret, before he would have to file his 13D with the SEC and announce his intentions to an innocent and unsuspecting world. In those ten days, using brokers and accounts under various names which people would not connect to him, he would amass as much more of the stock as he could, before the public announcement drove the price up and before Allied Resources management realized what was going on and tried to stop him. But his massive buying would itself force the price up, and inevitably more and more people would figure out what was happening—or at least that *something* was happening—which would also tend to send the price soaring upward during the days before the announcement.

The day after Stone crossed the 5 percent mark, I was at the Crosby apartment, waiting for Mrs. Dixon to leave. As the door shut behind her, I was dialing Willis T. Winslow's number.

"Hello, Willy? This is Jonathan Crosby. . . . We met last night."

"Oh, of course," he replied. "How are you?" Willy's memory of the night before, as of all nights before, would be sketchy at best.

"Fine, thanks," I said with as much boyishly ingenuous enthusiasm as I could generate. "I really enjoyed our discussion, and I wanted to follow through on opening the account with you. Is this a good time for you? I don't want to bother you if you're busy now."

"Oh, no. Not at all. . . . I mean, any time will be busy, but this is as good a time as any. I just . . . Uh, let me get some information here, Jonathan. . . . Get the paperwork out of the way. . . . Just a second. . . . Let me find the forms here. . . ."

"It was good," I said, while he searched for the account application, "to hear about Jim Washburn again. Although I was really more a friend of his brother Bob's. Awful about Bob."

"Terrible," said Willis absently. "Let's see. No, that's not it. . . . People drive much too much. . . . Sorry I'm taking so long here. You went to Hotchkiss with Bob?"

"Actually, I knew them before that. Before we moved to Switzerland. Great people, the Washburns. You must know Peter Andrews from school as well."

"Sure. Absolutely. Great guy. I gather he's living out in California now."

"That's what somebody told me. Were you the same year as Peter?"

"Year after. Great guy. . . . Here it is. Let me just get a few pieces of information from you. Now, how exactly do you want your name to appear on the account?"

I spelled it out for him. Jonathan B. Crosby. He asked for my home address. I gave him the Fifth Avenue address, and I could tell he liked it. He asked for the business address. I told him I wasn't really doing anything right now; I was just here in New York staying with my uncle while I figured out what I wanted to do. Social Security number? I gave him my new number. Bank references?

"Gee, to tell you the truth, I don't think I've ever had a bank account. Not that I know of, unless you count the trust fund. I mean, whenever I need money, I call Herr Wengler—he's someone who works for my father—and he handles it. He handles everything, really. I mean, I'm about to open a bank account here. It's one of the things I mean to do right away. I just haven't really got myself organized here yet."

Willis wondered if my father had a bank he used here in the United States.

"Well, I don't think he actually has his own account, but I know that years ago when he would still come here, there was a bank that had some arrangement where he could have money sent to him from Switzerland. Is there a bank called Morgan something?"

He told me there was a bank called Morgan Guaranty. He asked what I meant to open the account with.

"Open it with?" I asked. "I was hoping I could open it with you. Over the phone. Actually, I hoped to buy a stock today."

"I mean what sort of money or securities did you mean to put into the account to start with?"

"Well, that was one of the things I wanted to ask you. How much money do you think I ought to have in there?"

"Well, I . . . How much do you . . . Jonathan, it might be helpful to begin with if we briefly went over your investment goals in the context of your overall financial picture. That way we could develop an integrated—"

"I was thinking maybe just one or two hundred thousand dollars to start with and then see how it goes. Do you think that would be enough?"

"Why, yes," he said quickly. He would be mentally computing his share of the commissions on $200,000 worth of trades. "That is, of course there are some sorts of strategies that you couldn't really implement effectively without a more substantial commitment of capital, but, yes, that would be a prudent level to begin with. Tell me, Jonathan, how are you going to be making payment? You don't seem to—"

"Oh, right. It's good you mention that. I'm going to have it wired or transferred or something. I don't know exactly how it works, but I've already talked to Herr Wengler about it. I'm supposed to get an account number from you so he can take care of it."

"I'm going to get that for you right away, Jonathan." I could hear him punching keys on a terminal. "Let me just get a couple more things I need to open this account. . . . What are your investment goals for this account?"

"I guess making a lot of money, mainly."

"Yes, but—"

"My grandfather and my father both did that, and I think I'd like to accomplish the same sort of thing too."

"Yes. Well, that's very good, Jonathan. But I meant more your particular strategy for this part of your assets. That is, are you interested in preservation of capital or yield or long-term appreciation or trading or what?"

"Trading, I think. I'd like to get in there and really get an active feel of the market. I mean, I'd be prepared even to lose money at first just so I could learn the ropes. I think I'd want to trade as much as I could."

There was a pause. Willis T. Winslow, III, was not speaking. He must be dizzy with greed thinking about the commissions. I went on.

"I mean that's why I was so interested last night in hearing your ideas. You've obviously given this a lot of pretty serious thought. Could you tell me—I suppose this is really the sort of thing I ought to be asking you—do most of your clients make money? I don't mean to be rude, but—"

"Not at all. Not at all. That's a very sensible question." His voice was a good octave deeper. "I think I can say that my clients are pleased with whatever role I have been able to play in their investment programs."

In a way, these people are telling the truth when they say this sort of thing. The clients who are still with a given broker at a given moment in time are inevitably people who either happen to be ahead so far or else don't open their mail.

"Great. I'm sorry to be in such a hurry, but as I said last night I want to buy this one stock right away today that this friend of my father's told me about."

"Well, we really ought to have some funds in the account to—"

"Oh, gosh. I must have misunderstood what you said last night. I thought that just so the money was there within five days . . . That's really why I was in such a hurry to open the account."

"And I don't have your signed application—"

"Golly," I said. "I'm creating problems for you, aren't I? I didn't realize. Actually, I have the name of someone who my father knows at . . . Kidder, Peabody?—is that the name of a brokerage firm? I think it's Kidder, Peabody. Anyway, he could probably handle this for me now, and then in a few weeks when I have a bank account and everything, I could give you a call again. Would that be better for you?"

"Jonathan, what exactly did you want to buy today?"

"Well, I wanted to buy"—I wondered one last time how far I dared push him—"two thousand shares of a stock called Allied Resources. This friend of my father's said I should do it right away. . . ."

I could hear him punching the keys in the background.

"That's at 10-¾ bid, 11-¼ asked," he was saying distractedly. He would be doing the multiplication. Say $22,000, in a listed stock trading at six times earnings and within a point and a half of its low for the year. Not much downside there. But I was ready to compromise if he balked: I would settle for 1,000 shares. I would settle for 100. The critical thing was to get somehow from zero assets to any assets at all.

"The thing is, you'd absolutely have to have the funds here within five business days."

"I think it only takes twenty-four hours to wire it. That's what Herr Wengler told me. Are you sure this isn't too much trouble? I just don't want to let this opportunity go by."

"As long as the funds are wired tomorrow . . . Jonathan, I'm looking at some information on this stock right now. Do you know exactly why your father's friend recommended it? It's not something I follow myself, but I see it hasn't been much of a performer this year."

By that he meant that it seemed too cheap, and he would prefer something that had already become expensive. This is the way brokers think. I explained to him that the recommendation came from a very good friend of my father's and I was pretty sure that it was going to work out. He told me he was sending some papers up by messenger for me to sign. I said I would be out when they arrived, but I would put them in the mail tonight.

Five minutes after we had hung up, he called back to tell me he had bought my 2,000 shares at 11-½. You sometimes wonder how these things are possible moments after you have been quoted 10-¾, 11-¼. Well, that's the advantage of paying full commissions: I had not only the benefit of Willis T. Winslow's thinking but the skill and muscle of his firm's trading department when it came to the executions.

On the other hand, it might be that Allied Resources was already moving, as Myron Stone busily bought up enormous gobs of it for his various accounts. I hoped so. I had put a lot of work into this, and I was giving it my best shot with Allied Resources, which was as close to a sure thing as I could imagine. Even without the acquisition activity, it seemed as undervalued to me as it did to Myron Stone, and I could not see much downside. But you can never be sure. If over the next few days Allied Resources inexplicably dropped—or even if the price stayed the same—I would have to forget all about Jonathan B. Crosby and Willis T. Winslow, III, and start over again.

I waited in the Crosbys' apartment all day. The account application was delivered to the doorman around three o'clock, and he brought it right up and left it in the vestibule. I signed everything and took it out to the mail chute.

I have never been a tape watcher, but I turned the television on to the cable channel that runs the tape and watched eagerly until the end of trading. Allied Resources closed at 12-¼, which was not a bad start. I had already more than covered the commissions on the turnaround. Of course, tomorrow it could drop to 10 and stay there for a year. Not that a year mattered in this case. I had a little over a week, with luck. There is probably no sure thing ever, but there is certainly nothing so sure that it can be counted on to come through within a week.

I waited until Thursday afternoon before calling Willis again. I told him that I had spoken to Herr Wengler and that the money was being wired and it should arrive sometime in the next two business days. "I guess that means sometime tomorrow or Monday," I added, as if I had just worked out a difficult idea for the first time.

"That's fine," Winslow said absently. He was not worried yet. It would be interesting to see how he felt around Wednesday or Thursday of next week.

"I'm going away for the weekend and I won't be getting back till Monday afternoon. I'll give you a call then, just to make sure everything's arrived."

"O.K. I see Allied Resources has moved up a little bit here. It's trading around 12-½. Your friend seems to have put you into a good situation. Who exactly did you say he was?"

"Uncle David? He's a friend of my father's. Some sort of banker. I think he's on a lot of boards of corporations or something. I have to hurry to get my ride out to Southhampton. Have a nice weekend."

Allied Resources closed at 13-½. I had forgotten the elation that could come with making a winning bet. Especially when you have put a lot of work into it. I was on my way. It would all be easy after this, I thought.

On Friday it closed at 13, inexplicably back off half a point. I hoped this was going to work out. Pointless to think about it. The market would be closed for two days. Nothing to do but wait.

I called Willis again on Monday afternoon.

"Hi, Willy. I was just calling to make sure you got back my application and everything."

"Oh, Jonathan. I'm glad you called. I've been trying to reach you. Your account application arrived today, but we haven't—"

"And did the money get there all right?"

"We haven't received anything yet. I've left instructions for them to notify me as soon as it comes in. What I'd like you to do is give me the exact name of the bank at which the transfer is originating and the wire route, so that we can—"

"Gee, that's awful. I don't know what could have happened. Herr Wengler said it should be here by now."

"Well, Jonathan, if you could just give me the name of the bank, we'll try to track down the problem."

"Gosh, I'd have to ask Herr Wengler about that. I don't really know anything about it. . . . Maybe I should have him call you. Do you think that would be a good idea?"

"That might be the simplest way to get it straightened out. Now you're sure he had the funds transferred? There wasn't any question about his issuing the instructions?"

"Oh, no. He was absolutely clear about it. He's awfully precise."

"Well, I'm glad to hear that, Jonathan, because I've kind of stuck my neck out personally on that Allied Resources transaction, and tomorrow's the settlement date."

"Gosh, I'll get right on the phone to Herr Wengler. I mean, he's always absolutely reliable. . . . By the way, how is Allied Resources doing?"

"It was up a point from where you bought it last time I looked. . . . Wait a moment . . . 13. Up a point and a half from where you bought it."

"Gosh. That's great, anyway. But I'm really sorry about the money not arriving. I don't know what could have happened. I'll call Herr Wengler first thing in the morning and then get back to you as soon as I've found out something. Will you be there at one in the afternoon?"

"I'll be right here."

"I'll talk to you then. I'm really sorry about this."

Still only a point and a half. And with Stone gobbling up every share he could find. I hoped this was going to work out. I probably had another two or three days before they closed me out. I thought of starting a rumor about Myron Stone and Allied Resources to push things along, but I was unwilling to take any risk, no matter how slight, of bringing on an SEC investigation. What I had to do was deter Willis and his employers as long as possible from selling my shares. And I also had to make sure that Willis did not talk to Mrs. Dixon. Tomorrow would be Tuesday.

I slept at the Crosbys' apartment that night. At seven in the morning I got up and switched off the bell on every telephone in the apartment. Mrs. Dixon arrived at nine exactly, and I stood next to her desk the entire time she was there. If she happened to pick up the telephone just as Winslow was calling, I wanted to know about it. There were no calls. She left a little before eleven.

I left right after her and went to another apartment to make my telephone calls. I didn't like to use the Crosbys' phone any more than necessary, because Mrs. Dixon looked like the sort of person who would immediately notice a few dollars in extra local units on the monthly bill.

When I got to the telephone, I wrapped the receiver in a washcloth and for good measure held against it a portable radio, which I had tuned to pure static. I dialed Willis's number.

"Hello, Mr. Vinsslow?" I said rapidly and brusquely, as soon as he picked up the receiver.

"Hello?"

"Rudi Schlesslgemuenze here, from the Schildkreuzige Landsschleier-schafts Bank."

"Hello, I'm sorry but I didn't—"

"I am calling about the transfer of two hundert tausend dollars U.S. funds originated by us to an account in the name of Jonathan Crosby."

"Yes, that's right," said Winslow eagerly. "Could you give me your—"

"Also, I vould vant to confirm the account number if you don't mind."
I read off the number he had given me in as fast a staccato as I could manage.

"Yes, that's . . . I mean, I think that's . . . Could you read that off again?"

I read it again, less distinctly and perhaps even faster.

"We seem to have a rather faint connection here. I'm going to read the correct account name and number off to you." He fumbled for a moment and then read it all off.

"Precisely," I said. "Ve are seeking to trace the funds now. Ve believe them to be somevhere in New York since yesterday."

"That's very good. I hope you can track it down, because we really should have those funds today."

"Ve should have the entire matter resolved vithin a matter of hours—and in any case as you are dealing vith the Crosbys, I hardly think you need be concerned. I shall call you tomorrow to confirm the transfer."

"Could you give me your name and number in case someone on my end has to get back in touch with you on this?" said Winslow.

"Of course," I said. "Talk to you tomorrow. Goodbye." I hung up.

I waited five minutes and called back again as Jonathan Crosby.

"Hi, Willy. It's Jonathan. I just talked to Herr Wengler a few minutes ago and he said he was going to get the bank to straighten everything out about the transfer. He said to tell you that someone from the bank there would be calling you today."

"He's already called. By the way, could you give me the name of your bank in Switzerland?"

"Darn," I said. "I meant to ask Herr Wengler for the name."

"Well, they seem to have things in hand. It's just that today is the settlement date for those shares of Allied Resources you bought. They seem to be doing surprisingly well, by the way." I heard him clicking at his terminal. "14 bid, 14-½ asked."

"Gosh, that's great. But I'm really sorry about this confusion. I really hope I haven't caused you any trouble. I'll call back tomorrow and make sure everything is straightened out."

He seemed fairly calm about it, but just to make sure he would be in a good mood, I let him tell me about some of his plans for my $200,000. His basic strategy seemed to be to look for stocks with very high P/E's and a history of never having paid any sort of dividend whatever. He seemed particularly to like issues with a recent run-up in price, which indicated to him that a stock had "already started to move." All in all, it was for the best that the $200,000 would never appear.

Allied Resources closed at 15-⅛, and I knew I had pulled the thing off. It was just a question of how much further I could take it. I called Winslow again the next day. He was getting edgier again and pressed me more insistently for information: the name of the Swiss bank, Herr Wengler's telephone number, anything. I told him I would call Herr Wengler right away and then call him right back. Meanwhile, people were buying and selling Allied Resources at 16, which took the real pressure off us all.

I called back just before four, so that the market would be closed by the time our conversation was over. I told him gosh, I was sorry about all this, but Herr Wengler was absolutely amazed that the money wasn't there: he thought it had all been straightened out. Willis T. Winslow, III, sounded unhappy.

"The trouble is, Jonathan, I got called in on this. Opening a new account, I should really have waited until there were funds actually in the account before initiating a transaction. Now in the course of the conversation, Jonathan, I think I may have told some people here that I've known your family for years, which in a way is not inaccurate, but if it should ever come up, you might just keep it in mind . . ."

"Gee, I'm really sorry about all this," I said. "I don't know what to do."

"Well, Jonathan, I think we're going to have to sell your shares of Allied here. The market's just closed, but tomorrow morning . . . I don't want to get caught here."

"Gee, absolutely. Do whatever you think is best. I feel terrible about this. It's nighttime in Europe now, but I'm going to call up once more, and I'll let you know first thing in the morning. It would be great if you could wait for my call, but you should go ahead and do whatever is best. I just hope I haven't made any trouble for you. Because I'm really counting on working with you. Maybe I should just have them send another two hundred thousand. What do you think?"

"That might be a very good idea, Jonathan. I don't want you to worry about this. I'll be able to sort everything out on my end. This won't in any way impair our working relationship. These things happen."

When they finally sold my shares the next day, they got 17-¼ for them. After commissions I would net almost $10,500, which was an excellent return on an investment of zero. And although it was not enough in itself to accomplish much, it was more than enough to build on. Jonathan B. Crosby suddenly had a positive net worth. He was acquiring substance. At that moment I was absolutely sure I had won. They would never get me now. I could lead my own life, do whatever I liked.

In my elation I was eager to push ahead immediately. Soon I would be opening a bank account, buying an apartment. Just as I had gone out and found Willis T. Winslow, I would now go out and find lawyers and accountants to do these other things for me. Let Jenkins try to find me then.

WALKING DOWN THIRD AVENUE, I SAW A GROUP OF FIVE PEOPLE TURN-ing into a building, and I could tell that they were on their way to some sort of party. They were loud, shouting rather than talking to each other, and there was a good deal of friendly shoving. The men had their shirt collars open and their ties untied, the two ends looped once loosely around each other—a style which I associate with bond traders. These were people who would hire exactly the sort of professional help I was looking for. Also, they would probably throw fairly lively parties, and I was in a celebratory frame of mind.

The doorman directed them to the penthouse, and they climbed into the self-service elevator. I watched the numbers on the dial click up. It would be a thirty-four-flight hike for me. Another elevator opened beside me and a man walked out, leaving the elevator empty. I stepped through the open door. Why not take the chance? My recent triumph in the market had filled me with confidence that whatever happened, I would be more than quick enough and clever enough to deal with it. I pressed the buttons for both the penthouse and the floor below and got off on the floor below: however reckless my mood, I knew that I could not risk being on an elevator that was opening to admit descending passengers—especially not some large group leaving a party.

When I had climbed up the last flight of stairs and slipped into the apartment, I found myself in a large room filled with people resembling those I had followed into the building. From their conversation it was apparent that many of them were commodities traders. If you do not already know, I am not going to try to tell you what these people do at work—in the "pit," as it is aptly termed—because no matter what your point of view, you are apt to find it more distasteful than what they do at play. However, I will offer you my uneducated opinion that in the long run the only way to make money in commodities is by collecting commissions on other people's losses.

But one of the appealing qualities of these people is their unlimited, manic energy. They are pushing and shoving and shouting all the time—both at work and at their social gatherings—and if they sleep, which I doubt, they probably shout in their sleep as well. Their voices as a consequence tend to have a gravelly hoarseness, and in the middle of a conversation with someone standing right next to them, they are apt to shout suddenly at someone across the room. "Hey Ronnie! Ronnie! Listen to this! At ten o'clock this morning Norman starts closing out his pork bellies. . . ." Their instinct is to stuff themselves with every sort of sensory input, which leads to a high incidence of obesity and a lot of annoying background music. They tend to live on a far more lavish scale than the rest of humanity, something that they accomplish by careful budgeting: they make an estimate of what they expect to earn if everything goes perfectly, and then they spend more than that only if they really feel like it. This keeps them active in the markets, as they feel that lots of risk taking is the only way to lots of profit.

Through the windows of the apartment I could see a vast terrace and beyond that breathtaking views for miles in all directions. Although I have no idea what the apartment was worth, the value of the cocaine inside it was certainly greater. These people tend, at regular intervals, to roll up a dollar bill—or probably it is a fifty dollar bill—and suck some powder up through it into their nostrils. Then to keep things in perspective they knock back tumblers of rum or vodka mixed with soft drinks. Whether all this is seen by them as relief from their workday activities or more as a continuation of them, I cannot say.

There were a lot of people spread out all through the apartment, and you could hear the shouts and laughter floating in from the other rooms and the patio. The women, although they were perhaps not exactly beautiful and often had a little more bulk than one might ideally like, nevertheless had a fundamental appeal. Furthermore, unlike a lot of gatherings in New York nowadays, there was nothing at all problematic here about distinguishing the men from the women.

I walked outside, where the sun had just set, leaving the sky filled with extravagant colors. The terrace extended around three sides of the apartment. On the west and south it formed a broad expanse, which was filled with guests sitting on deck chairs and leaning against the railings, drinking and talking. But on the north side it was only wide enough to form a narrow walkway, and it was there that I sat, sipping furtively at a deserted gin and tonic through the plastic shaft of my ball-point pen. In the twilight even I could not see the thin column of clear liquid rise into the air and dissipate. Around the corner I could hear other guests boasting cheerfully of their exploits in the trading pit, and all about me I could see the spectacular canyons of concrete and glass. Even if you live your entire life in New York, these views out over the skyline never lose their excitement and power.

A woman appeared around the corner, and I backed away so that she would not stumble over me. Then I saw that she was being pushed along by a man behind her. When they were both out of sight of the others, he maneuvered her up against the wall and kissed her. She languorously folded her arms around him and twisted her open mouth hard against his. His body pressed hers against the wall, and she seemed to wrap herself around him.

Suddenly, in the background, there was a chorus of voices shouting exuberantly.

"Leo!"

"Hey, Leeeo!"

"Let's go, Leo."

"Annie's looking for you, Leo!"

"Better get it together, Leo!"

With a vaguely startled look, the man next to me disengaged himself from the woman. He hurried around the corner, where he was greeted with laughter and more shouting.

"Hey, Leo!"

"Where you been, Leo?"

"All right, Leo."

The woman ambled tranquilly out after him to the group on the terrace, and I followed to see if anything interesting would happen. Leo was already gone, but one of the men standing on the terrace put an arm casually around the woman's shoulders, and then, as he talked with the others, he ran his hand down her body, clapped her on the bottom twice, and gave her an absentminded hug that looked as if it might crush the ribs of a less resilient creature. She accepted all this quite passively. It was hard to say whether she really noticed.

I walked back inside to take a tour of the premises. In the main room there were two men sprawled over a sofa that took a ninety-degree turn, their feet up on a glass coffee table. A woman lay across one of the men, inert, face down; she might have passed out or she might just have been listening to the music. The men were talking in subdued, gravelly tones.

"Anybody seen him since?" one of them asked.

"First few weeks no one knew what happened to him," answered the other. "He just disappeared. Then he turns up in Chicago, talking about maybe trading on the Merc. But then he disappeared again. No one knows where. He owes too much money to too many people. Maybe the wrong people too."

"Too much coke. It's one thing now and then, but Mel toward the end had his brains completely fried. Lot of these people get in trouble that way. You gotta have some moderation so you know what you're doing. Mel was crazy."

"No, all the coke was because he was already in trouble. He was just tapped out, that's all. Could happen to anyone."

There was a moment of gloomy silence. To be tapped out is to go bust, in their world. Ruin. These people do not just lose *your* money while raking off commissions. They lose their own—it is really their main interest. And, some would argue, their only truly endearing trait.

"I don't believe that," said the first man. "You gotta be careful. You can't go home every Friday holding some enormous position. Next thing you know, you get your lungs ripped out. Mel was crazy at the end."

"Maybe. It's too bad, anyway. Hard. He had the whole thing for a while there. The Mercedes, the boat, wife and kids in New Jersey. All gone, like that."

The first man winced, whether out of sympathy for Mel's loss or because he was reminded that he too possessed such accessories, it was hard to say. He stretched out the hand without the drink and ran it over the bottom of the girl lying across him. Her head stirred in his lap and she pushed one hand along his leg in what might have been a caress.

The girl from the patio wandered by. She had had a good deal to drink and perhaps to smoke as well: her progress was deliberate, almost stately. I watched her pass through the room, her hips swaying to bring her weight over each step. I turned and followed her. She walked partway down a corridor, pushed open a door, and went through. I followed her. There were two men on the other side of the room standing beside a woman, who was sitting on the edge of a bed. She had the trousers of one of the men open and was performing or about to perform an obscene act. The other man seemed with one hand to be engaged in a complicated drug operation on a table next to the bed, involving the spreading and mixing of little heaps of some powder, while with the other hand he was pulling at the woman's skirt.

I took several steps towards them so that I could see more clearly what they were doing with each other. Unpleasant to be both attracted and repelled by these scenes. But I myself was never going to be able to touch another human being in my life, and although gaping at people like these is an admittedly poor substitute, you make of life what you can.

Watching people fumble with each other in real life is not quite like watching a film, where you see human beings of extraordinary physical perfection, photographed very carefully. These particular three people were, for example, fairly plain and distinctly overweight. Out of curiosity I looked at the powder on the table. It was a grainy orange substance entirely unfamiliar to me. Even in matters of drug abuse, these people have no respect for convention.

The man who had been working with the powder looked up and squinted at the woman I had followed into the room.

"Hey, Janie!"

Janie continued toward a door on the other side of the room. The tableau by the bed did not seem to make any impression on her one way or the other. She tried the door handle and found it locked. She turned and looked at the people by the bed.

"Hey, Janie! Come here!"

She paused for a moment, a vague expression on her face, and then turned and proceeded out of the room. I watched as the second man directed his attention back to the woman on the bed, reaching up under her skirt and pulling at her underpants while she labored at the other man with her hands and mouth. I turned and followed after Janie, not knowing what I had in mind. The slow, graceful swaying of her hips.

She was already disappearing through a door farther down the corridor, and by the time I reached it she had crossed through another, smaller bedroom and was closing the door to a bathroom behind her. Stepping into the bedroom and shutting the door to the hall behind me, I switched off the overhead light and went over to the bathroom door to wait for her.

I knew that it was in every way a bad idea. But at that moment nothing seemed as important as putting my hands on her, my arms around her. Just to touch her would be worth more than anything I might be afraid of. How would she ever know in the darkness that I was not really quite there? My heart was pounding, as I tried to screw up my courage. I was like some trembling adolescent unsure of whether it was the right moment to reach over and kiss the girl. Was the whole thing even remotely plausible? How, in my state, could I judge? That or anything.

Trembling with indecision and anticipation, I listened to the stream of urine, the flush of the toilet, the water running in the basin, clothes being straightened. There was an inexplicable pause and then two slow steps across the tiled floor. She pulled open the door and switched off the light, leaving the two of us facing each other in total darkness.

Before she could reach back and switch the light on again, I put my arms around her and pulled her towards me, twisting my head down so that my cheek was against hers and then drawing my mouth across her face until it pressed against hers. My tongue pushed between her lips, and her mouth opened wide. I felt her arms wrap tight around me, and my ribs ached with pleasure where they touched me. Her mouth seemed to open for my tongue like a vast cavity. The feeling of her thighs and breasts, flattened compliantly against me, was agonizing, exquisite.

I had until this moment believed that I would never know these sensations again, never feel a woman against me. My entire body seemed about to explode.

I slid one leg over so that it was between her thighs, pushing them apart. I felt her twist up her pelvis, rubbing the tender flesh and the hard bone beneath it against me. I was walking her across the room, kissing her and holding her tight against me all the while. She moved as I directed her, with a languorous passivity. Still holding her, I toppled her over onto the bed and we lay there, writhing slowly, legs entangled. She hardly moved except to pull me toward her or to open her mouth or her legs. I lay between her legs, feeling her through the layers of clothing, twisting, heaving against her, her limbs around me. I was running one hand over her body, over her large floating breasts, between her thighs, feeling through the thin fabric of underpants the downy hair. The moist lips.

Somewhere, physically close by but at the remotest edge of my consciousness, I heard a door open. There was light flooding through the room.

I saw her vacant, uncomprehending eyes staring through me, and for a brief moment her body went utterly slack beneath me as though it were no longer a living thing. Then, instantaneously, it hardened into something rigid and alien, and she began to emit a horrible, piercing scream. Her face was contorted with terror and revulsion. She was pushing me away. Now she was flailing at me with her arms, hitting me over and over. The awful screams were coming like the rhythmic blasts of a siren. I was scrambling off the bed and across the room into a corner. There were people pouring into the room, crowding around the bed.

"Take it easy, Janie. Take it easy."

"What's wrong with her?"

"Was anyone with her?"

"Too much to drink."

"Someone get some water."

The screams became convulsive, then transformed themselves momentarily into dull, gurgling explosions, and I realized she was retching on the bed.

"Is she all right?"

"Let's get her into the john."

Shaking, I picked myself up and scurried across the room, hardly caring whether I stumbled into anyone or not. Down the corridor and out of the apartment. In the hall outside you could still hear her screams.

FOR THE REST OF THE SUMMER I WORKED LONG DAYS AND STAYED IN evenings, avoiding other people as much as possible and changing apartments every day or two. I devoted all my time to searching for new opportunities in the stock market, and although the work was dull and a bit shabby—ranging, as it did, from eavesdropping to outright burglary—I worked far harder than I ever had in my days as a conventional securities analyst with a handsome salary. But of course the potential reward was so much more compelling now. Survival.

After giving Willy and his employers a couple of weeks to settle down and turn their thoughts to other matters, I called and delivered once again my apology for the $200,000 which had still not arrived. It was not a problem, Willy assured me—although with a bit more reserve and wariness in his voice than formerly. He also wondered whether the funds were eventually going to get there.

"My father's filing some sort of lawsuit having to do with the whole thing," I said. "I was supposed to call and let you know that someone from the law firm will probably be getting in touch to verify a few things. By the way," I added, "I have a little bit of money in my account, don't I?"

"Yes. Let me see. . . . Ten thousand four hundred seventy-six and some change. You might as well do something with that in the meantime. I'm just looking at an interesting situation, as it happens, a biotechnology company out in California called Orex. It's true that they've never reported any earnings, but they've been around for over three years, so they have a track record that—"

"Actually," I said, "I had some suggestions from a friend of my father's . . ."

"Would that be the same friend who put you into Allied Resources? Because that had a nice move. It's too bad you sold so soon. The next day there was an acquisition announcement that pushed it right up to 19."

"This is a different friend, actually. I wonder if you could get me four hundred shares of Westland Industries. That's 'over the counter'—is that the right expression?"

"Yes, it is, Jonathan. Let's see. That's 6-½ bid, 7 asked. Now, I'm not sure if I went over this with you before, but we can put in an order to buy that at a certain price or we can just go ahead and do the best we can, which means putting it in at the market. Do you follow me?"

"Yes, that's a very clear explanation. That sounds fine. Just get everything at the market." The last thing I wanted was Willy calling the Crosby apartment at a random moment to report the execution of some standing order. "This next one is on the New York Stock Exchange. It's called RGP. Are just those initials enough?"

"Yes, they are, Jonathan."

"If you could get me three hundred shares, that would be great. I'm sorry to make this so complicated."

"That's perfectly all right, Jonathan. That's what I'm here for. Let's see—"

"And then the other thing was, I wanted to buy some calls, someone explained to me that you can make a lot more money that way—"

"Options can play a useful role in structuring an overall investment strategy, Jonathan. You do understand that with a call you can lose your entire—"

"I wanted them for a company called Great Appalachian. . . . Wait, I've got this all written down here. . . . I wanted two thousand October forty-fives. Is that the way you say it? At the market."

Fifteen minutes later Willis called back to report on the executions. They had bought the calls at 1-⅝. The Westland and the RGP did not much interest me. They were just the sort of rational, well-researched, long-term investments I would have made as Nicholas Halloway, but now I thought of them only as camouflage for the Great Appalachian calls. On that day the shares of Great Appalachian were trading at 44, but having spent many hours in the offices of Distler Corby, the investment bank which was working with the management of Great Appalachian on a leveraged buyout, I happened to know that before the end of the month an offer would be made for those shares at around 70. Buying the shares themselves, I could have had a return of over 75 percent in roughly three weeks, which you might think ought to be enough for anyone. However, that move in the stock would take the calls, which are an option to buy the stock at a stipulated price, from 1-⅝ up to around 20, for a return of over 1,000 percent in the same period. Even so, I was uneasy about buying the calls rather than the shares, because I was afraid that it was more likely to attract attention, but I had to go ahead with it anyway. I had so little time.

For the moment it was easy to find places to sleep. In August whole buildings can be virtually empty in New York. And in the warm, dry weather it was easy to move around. But I knew that I had only a few more weeks before people began to return and reoccupy their apartments, and then I would again have to spend most of my time searching for places to stay. And the risk of being noticed would be greater. Then the weather would become steadily wetter and colder, and I would need more clothing than the suit I had been wearing for the last four months. I would have to get back to New Jersey for some of the clothing I had left there. But that was another reason why I desperately needed my own apartment: I had to have someplace to keep my invisible possessions; if I had more things in New York I could not go on carrying everything with me all the time. Furthermore, I was sick of sardines, tuna, and noodles. I wanted desperately to eat fresh food again, but I could not risk having it delivered to one of these apartments that was supposed to be empty.

Then there would be an absolutely inflexible deadline in December: the John R. Crosbys would return to their apartment. By then I had to have at the very least another telephone number and mailing address if I wanted to keep Jonathan B. Crosby in existence.

And there was one more thing that kept me moving. Walking down York Avenue one afternoon, I saw, or thought I saw, Gomez coming out of a building a block and a half further south. It might have been Gomez, anyway, and it sent a shock of fear through me. It was a building I had stayed in two nights before. As I ran to catch up with whoever it was, he climbed into a car and pulled away.

It might be nothing. A mistake or a coincidence. They were probably not even sure whether I was in New York. But it was pointless, absolutely pointless, to speculate and brood about what they might be thinking or doing. There was nothing I could do differently. I had to keep moving, as quickly as possible, and hope to stay ahead of them.

In the last week of August, on the morning of the day on which the management of Great Appalachian would announce their leveraged buy-out at 69, I called Winslow.

"Willy, I think I'd like to sell those Great Appalachian calls."

"There seems to be some activity here in Great Appalachian. You might think about holding on to your position and seeing if something is going on with it."

"Gee, I've done pretty well with it, and I think I'd like to sell it this morning." The stock was at 63 and the calls were at 19. The SEC claims that it scans transactions in these situations, looking for possible insider trading. Even if that is true, I doubt that they look at people who have sold out before the announcement.

"Also, I've been watching this Westland you bought. It hasn't done anything here," he told me. He always talks about these things as taking place "here," as if the market were located in one of the drawers of his desk. Next to the pint of gin perhaps. "When you've been in the market for a while," he was explaining to me, "you get a feel for when a stock is going to move and when it's not. Kind of a sixth sense that goes beyond just number-crunching. Really, it's fair to call it an art. . . ." I badly wanted to ask him why, with this talent, he was wasting his time as a registered rep, sneaking drinks from his desk drawer, while Warren Buffett accumulated all the wealth and fame. But I needed him. I told him I would be sure to heed his advice next time. And really, the fact that Willy never seemed to notice how well I was doing was one of his most endearing and useful qualities.

I got 19-⅝ for the calls. My portfolio was now worth a little over $49,000. A very satisfactory performance, considering that I had started less than two months before with zero. Very few things produce such a feeling of well-being as success in financial markets. It combines the best features of contemplating a difficult job well done and of winning the lottery. And there is something particularly pleasing about being able to look in the newspaper each day and receive a grade, a numerical score, for your work. Sometimes the score would be lower than the day before—it is impossible for anyone, even me with my extraordinary advantage, to predict a market with complete reliability; the markets are too efficient for that— but more often than not my score would be higher. Come to think of it, I was, in my small way, contributing to the efficiency of the market, seeing to it that useful information was transmitted a little more quickly through the price mechanism. The invisible hand taking its own small cut, as it were. And success makes one labor even harder. Tedious as the work might be, I became absolutely absorbed in it. I was happier than I had been since the accident, although occasionally I would remember how in the old days I had liked from time to time to call some friend and discuss what I was buying or selling and how I had won or lost.

Then September arrived and Labor Day weekend, and suddenly, just as I had feared, there seemed to be no more empty apartments anywhere. I would spend whole days now searching for them, and I found myself frequently forced to remain in the same apartment for several days, although I knew how dangerous that was.

One day I saw Tyler. I was sure it was Tyler, even from a distance. A large black man, walking with a limp up Third Avenue. I had no idea where he had come from or where he was going to. He walked half a block, climbed into a grey sedan, and drove away. There was no way of knowing what he was doing there. Perhaps he lived there. Perhaps they had all forgotten about me and were working on something else. In that block there was an enormous white brick apartment building—just the sort of building I would be likely to stay in.

One thing was certain: they were not looking for me in some other city.

Jenkins had probably worked it all out—where I was staying, how I was doing it. But it was possible that they knew nothing definite at all. They might still be unsure whether I was even in New York. I wished there were some way of knowing. Or at least of stopping myself from turning it over endlessly in my mind, until I could hardly think of anything else. It would have been easier if I could have talked to someone—anyone. About anything.

I thought of going to Boston and calling Jenkins from there. The call itself would mislead him, and perhaps I would get some sense of what he thought and what he was doing. Ridiculous. The only thing was to keep absolutely quiet: give them nothing to go on, nothing to lure them on. If they went long enough without a trace of me, they would have to give it up. For all they knew I might be dead.

A few days later I thought I saw Gomez again. I began to see all of them all the time, until I was no longer sure if I had ever really seen any of them. Always, when I would rush after them, they would be gone before I could get to them. They would disappear around the corner. The car would be just pulling away as I got there. I was watching for them constantly now.

Sometimes a telephone would ring in some apartment I was staying in, and I would become convinced that it was Jenkins calling me. He knew I was there. Or that I might be there. He was tempting me to answer. It would be almost a relief to speak to him. The telephone would go on and on. Then the ring might stop and start again a few seconds later, until finally I would have to flee the apartment to get away from it.

I hated the feeling of them gradually, steadily closing in on me, and waves of rage and hatred would surge up in me until I could not think of anything else. I had the gun. I would imagine myself patiently watching for them and picking them off one by one. I would imagine myself stepping up to Jenkins and saying, "I'm here, Jenkins." And then I would fire into a joint, an elbow or knee, which would shatter horribly. He would collapse, his face contorted in unendurable pain. I would fire again at the writhing form, and he would watch the blood spurting out of the holes in his chest. These scenes of revenge would take possession of me, and I would live through them over and over again, powerless to turn my thoughts in any other direction.

But in practice, as Jenkins had so helpfully pointed out, it is difficult to raise the gun and shoot down the other person. One needs a sudden access of hatred or desperate terror—feelings which, although they seem to be forever crowding useful thoughts out of your head, are never there when you really need them. I still shuddered at the memory of Tyler, bleeding before me. And as Jenkins had also pointed out, there was nothing to be gained by shooting any of them. It would hardly diminish their determination to get me. My only choice was to go on as I was.

Then, late one morning as I was setting out for the day from an apartment in a large white brick building on Second Avenue I saw Clellan at the other end of the lobby, talking to the doorman. Although I was constantly watching for them, constantly expecting to encounter them, the sight of one of these people always stopped my heart and filled me with dread. Trembling, I walked very slowly and carefully up to where they were standing.

Clellan was saying in his hearty way, "Now you know and I know that in a building this size, there's no way you're going to be able to monitor one hundred percent who comes in and who goes out. Which is why this city-wide task force has been set up."

The doorman spoke with an Eastern European accent. "The people that come through here, I could tell you things, you wouldn't believe it."

"Well, that's it," Clellan said. "That's why we're here. We can work with you. The thing is, we need your input. We need to know exactly where the problems are, whether you're seeing any sign of unauthorized access to any of these apartments. Any keys missing or out of place. You keep keys to apartments down here in the lobby, don't you?"

"The keys I could tell you. The night man, Freddy—Puerto Rican guy, you know what I mean? All you gotta do is put the keys A to C or D to F for each floor on that hook, you know what I mean? But after Freddy's been on, you can forget it."

As the doorman spoke, Clellan's face suddenly took on an intent expression, and I saw that he was staring down at the floor. Following his gaze, I looked down too. He was staring directly at my feet, or rather at the two footprint-shaped depressions in the carpet beneath them. For a moment neither of us moved. Then, very carefully, I lifted my right foot and put it quietly down again on the marble floor beyond the edge of the carpet. Clellan and I both watched as the carpet pile gradually straightened itself in the footprint. He continued to stare down. Then his hands twitched at his sides and his fingers opened indecisively, as if he were unsure whether to lunge in my direction. I withdrew the left foot, and the other footprint began to disappear from view. Clellan's hands relaxed at his side. He looked up at where I was standing, an uncertain expression on his face.

The doorman, having noticed that Clellan was no longer listening to him, had stopped talking. He was watching Clellan now with a look of mystification.

"Halloway?" Clellan asked softly. I said nothing, made no movement. Clellan was staring intently toward me. I tried to decide how certain he was of my presence. His gaze went back to the carpet. No sign left there. "You there, Halloway?"

The doorman was watching Clellan very closely now, through narrowed eyes. "You mind if I have another look at your identification?" he said suddenly. Clellan was not paying any attention to him. "You'll have to wait here until I call the superintendent," the doorman went on.

"Halloway?" Clellan repeated.

Quietly, slowly, I backed away.

"Halloway, we want to help you."

I backed out through the open front door. Clellan's gaze was moving all around the lobby. He took a good look at the open door, screwed up his face, and turned back to speak to the doorman, who was trying desperately to call someone on the housephone.

I waited there in front of the building for Clellan. He came out several minutes later and walked purposefully down the street to the next block, where he climbed into a grey sedan parked in front of a fire hydrant. I followed him right to the car, peering into it in vain for anything that might give me some sort of useful information about them. As Clellan drove off, he had a telephone receiver in his hand and was talking animatedly.

COULD NOT GO ON HELPLESSLY WATCHING THESE PEOPLE CLOSE IN ON ME. There must be something I could do to stop them. Or even just to slow their advance. Or to hurt them. My mistake was that I was always running, always retreating passively out of their way. Everything I did was defensive, a response to some move Jenkins had made. That was why he was always in control and why he would eventually get me. I had to find some way to seize the initiative. I had to strike directly at Jenkins somehow, take some forceful and unexpected action against him.

But where exactly was he? Somewhere these people would have some sort of headquarters, some office from which Jenkins organized his search for me. What I had to do was track Clellan or Gomez back to it. There I would find my opportunity to strike back. At the very least, I might learn something that would enable me this time to anticipate their next move, instead of letting them once again anticipate mine.

Then I suddenly understood why Clellan and Gomez and the others always arrived and departed in their grey automobiles. It was precisely so that I would not be able to follow them. It was to keep me from doing just what I was now trying to do. Jenkins had, of course, already thought all this through, and even if he did not expect me to try it, he would, as a matter of course, make sure that I could not get at him. I would never be able to track Clellan or Gomez or Tyler or Morrissey. They knew exactly what they were guarding against. They knew all about me. But Jenkins was conducting a massive investigation, and he would have to be using a lot of people who had no idea that they were searching for an invisible man and who would have no reason to think that anyone might be following them. I had to do something just interesting enough to draw one of those people but not interesting enough to warrant sending Clellan or Gomez.

The next morning I called my old office and, disguising my voice, told the receptionist that I would like to speak to Mr. Halloway. She told me that I was no longer employed there.

"He's not?" I said. "There you are. I had no idea he'd changed jobs. You just start to lose touch with people as the years pass. Do you have any idea where he's working now? I've tried his home number, and I never get anything but an answering machine."

She said that she had no number or forwarding address to give out, but that if I wanted to leave a message, she would see that I got it.

"Will you?" I said. "That would be very kind. You could just tell him that Howard Dickison called. Nothing urgent. I just ran into a mutual friend, and I have some news that I thought might interest him. Nothing important. But he might give me a call." I gave her Howard Dickison's number.

I had encountered Howard Dickison at a party in July and recognized him as someone I had once been introduced to. I chose him now for two reasons. First, I did not know him, so that Jenkins's investigators either would not have talked to him at all yet or would not have wasted much time on him—it really did not matter which. Secondly, he had no office—he was a writer, or said he was—which meant that I would not have to stake out both an office and a home.

Dickison lived in a brownstone in the West Seventies off Central Park West, and I went there immediately upon making my call and camped out on the front stoop for the rest of the day. He seemed to have the first two floors of the building and probably the garden, although I never saw the inside of his apartment. He must also have had a trust fund, since he seemed to work a fairly light schedule. He emerged at a little after ten-thirty, and I followed him over to a coffee shop on Broadway, where he consumed a prodigious quantity of eggs and bacon, while slowly reading the *Times*. I stood outside in the street and watched him enviously. He was back home again, ready to start his day, a little before noon.

I sat on the stoop and waited. Nothing whatever happened the rest of that day. Between five-thirty and seven, the tenants of the apartments on the upper floors straggled in. First a girl in her early twenties, not unattractive. Then a man in his fifties, who looked like an accountant. Next a middle-aged woman with both a briefcase and an enormous bag of groceries. Then another young woman in her twenties, who was probably the roommate of the first one. By seven-thirty they were setting out again. First the accountant; then the two young women, together. At exactly eight, a sweating, bald man carrying flowers arrived and rang one of the bells. The woman with the groceries presumably. He was buzzed in and set off up the stairs.

Dickison came out a little after eight-thirty, wearing a blazer and a silk tie. I followed him over to Central Park West and watched him get into a taxi. Then I walked north to a building in the Nineties where I knew of an empty apartment in which I could spend the night.

I was back at Dickison's the next morning before eight. Not that Dickison would be up, but the visitors I was waiting for might well be. I watched the other occupants scurry out between eight-thirty and nine. The high points of the day were the mail delivery; the arrival of the superintendent, who vacuumed the hall and rearranged the garbage cans; and Dickison's breakfast expedition at eleven. I hoped he would at least take a walk in the park, but he went straight home again, leaving me to sit out front on the stoop. By nine in the evening I had seen everyone come home from work and go out again for the evening, and I decided that I could leave too. No one would be coming to talk to Dickison this late.

On the third morning I was back once again in time to watch them file out as usual, except that one of the girls came out a little late with a young man, pink faced, not much over twenty-one. Out on the sidewalk, he squeezed her hand, a bit embarrassed, and turned quickly toward Broadway, while she hurried off the other way toward Central Park West.

At exactly nine-thirty the man I was waiting for appeared, walking up the street from Central Park West. He was middle-aged and stocky and wore an ill-fitting brown suit. He stopped in front of the house, checking first the house number and then his wristwatch before walking past me to the door and ringing. I followed and stood next to him, waiting. It was some time before Dickison appeared at the door, wearing a purple robe and evidently still more asleep than awake. He seemed confused by the presence of the visitor, who began at once to get through the formalities, speaking in a slow, mechanical monotone almost devoid of any pause or inflection.

"Good morning, Mr. Dickison, my name is Herbert Butler, I spoke to you yesterday, thank you very much for meeting with me, we're performing a routine investigation of Nicholas Halloway in connection with the granting of a security clearance permitting access to classified materials who we understand is a friend of yours and I'd just like to ask you several questions about him which should only take a few minutes—"

"What did you . . . Didn't you call yesterday?" An expression of comprehension began to take form on Dickison's face. "Yes. . . . I tried to tell you yesterday, I don't know Halloway, and I couldn't be of any help to you at all. And as it happens you catch me at a bad moment."

"Well, I appreciate your arranging to meet with me now," he said, looking at his watch. "I just have a few questions I have to get through that shouldn't take more than fifteen minutes. How long have you known Mr. Halloway?"

"That's right. I remember. You did say you'd be here this morning," said Dickison with annoyance. "But I don't know him. I haven't ever known him. Or met him. Whatever the expression is."

"On the telephone yesterday you indicated that you had met him socially—"

"I said I might have met him. I thought I recognized the name, possibly. But that's absolutely all. I have no recollection of him. I'm not even sure whether I actually did meet him on that occasion. I mean whether there was such an occasion."

"Well, I'd like to ask a few questions about that occasion and any time more recently when you might have contacted or attempted to contact Mr. Halloway."

"I have never contacted or attempted to contact Halloway, whoever he is, whether or not I ever met him. Look, I'm going to get myself some coffee." Then as a grudging afterthought: "You had coffee yet?"

Holding the door for Butler to follow, Dickison retreated inside.

"No, thank you. To the best of your recollection, how long ago was your last meeting with Halloway?"

The door shut behind them and I could no longer hear what they were saying. I had, really, no interest in what they said. I watched through the window as they appeared in the kitchen and then withdrew into another room. I waited nearly an hour before the two of them reappeared in the doorway, neither of them looking particularly pleased. Butler's farewell took the form of a statement that he would probably be getting back to Dickison with a few more questions. Dickison opened his mouth as if to protest and then thought better of it.

Butler trudged out onto the sidewalk and turned east, with me following a few steps behind. One of the surprisingly small number of things an invisible person can do better than other people is to follow someone unobserved through empty streets. It rarely comes up in daily life, but on this particular occasion it was quite useful. He turned south on Central Park West, and after we had walked another block, I was confident that he had not come with a car. It was still possible that he would climb onto a bus, and if he did, I would have a difficult decision to make. I never take buses. There is no safe place in them to retreat to. You can slip into an empty one and have it suddenly fill up at one stop—every seat, every foot of standing room. Furthermore, to get out you have to push open the rear doors. And even if you try to slip out behind someone else, you have to hold them open unnaturally. Still, on this occasion I might have risked it.

At Seventy-second Street Butler descended into the subway, and after a long wait on the platform, we boarded the AA train together. I like the West Side IND lines: they are the least crowded in the city. Butler got off at Chambers Street, and I almost lost him there in the station, because people lined up to get out through the exit turnstiles, and, unlike Butler, I could not establish a place in the line. By the time I got up to the street he was nowhere to be seen. Desperate, I climbed up onto the hood of a car, generating a metallic thundering noise and causing the people around me to turn and stare in bewilderment at the dented car body. I spotted Butler a block away, walking north, and charged after him, weaving recklessly through the pedestrians.

Several blocks further on he entered a large, institutional building which could have been built only by a government. The spirit plummets at the sight of these places. I followed right behind him through the lobby, counting on his bulk to shield me from a collision with someone else. He turned and scanned a bank of elevators for floors 2 to 17, locating the car about to depart. It was half full of people: it was inconceivable that I should risk following him in, but I stepped to one side of the door and craned my head in behind him as he entered, so that I could watch him push the button for his floor. Seven.

I turned and ran. It took me a full minute to find a stairway and forever to charge up the six flights. As I paused momentarily behind the metal fire door at the seventh floor to listen for the sound of anyone on the other side, I realized that I was panting audibly. I pushed the door open just far enough to slip through and found myself in a narrow hall by the elevators, facing a doorway in front of which a uniformed guard sat. Struggling to hold down my convulsive breathing, I tiptoed past him into a vast warren of little cubicles and offices. The corridors and open areas were crammed with filing cabinets and metal desks at which women were typing and sorting papers and talking to each other. There was no sign of Butler. I began working my way through the maze of desks, peering into the little cells wherever I could and inspecting the numbers on the office doors and the occasional black plastic name plates next to the door frames.

It was unspeakably dreary, the metal furniture and partitions and opaque glass jumbled together under long white fluorescent lights without any human or aesthetic organization. The noise of the people and the typewriters clattered against the bare walls and ceilings.

After wandering this labyrinth for a quarter of an hour I finally found Butler sitting in a windowless cubicle, jabbing steadily at an old mechanical typewriter. His door was open, but the cubicle was so small that I was unwilling to go in. I leaned in far enough to make out the name Dickison at the top of the page he was typing and then retreated outside to wait.

It took him an hour on the typewriter and then another ten minutes reading it over and penciling corrections. He brought out his work and handed it to an extraordinarily fat woman with greasy hair and dirty fingernails who was reading a book with a picture of a couple in fanciful velvet clothing embracing in front of a castle. She put down her book, fed a sheet of paper into the typewriter, and to my amazement began typing faster than I had ever seen anyone type. Almost by the time Butler was settled at his desk again, she had finished and was proofreading her work, apparently taking in an entire page at a glance. Remarkable. Almost anyone would refuse out of hand to hire this woman, and yet she was evidently splendid. I found myself wondering whether she had made any errors. She, in any case, seemed satisfied. She brought in the report and laid it on Butler's desk. He turned directly to the last page and signed it.

"With this we're supposed to send two copies up to Special Liaison in fourteen-oh-seven—take the case number from the first page—and don't file anything down here."

That was all I needed. I left them and walked back out to the stairway to begin my hike up to the fourteenth floor. I did not race, but I did push along fairly briskly, since I wanted, if possible, to be there when the report arrived. As it turned out I was able to beat the internal mail system by twenty hours.

Room 1407 was actually two rooms, one of them a real office with windows and the other an outer office in which a secretary sat. At first I expected to see the report arrive at any moment and I waited standing by the secretary's desk, until so much time had gone by that I began to think something had gone wrong. Perhaps the number 1407 had referred to something other than a room number. But I could see other correspondence on the secretary's desk addressed to Special Liaison. Perhaps there had been a change in orders, and the report had been sent somewhere else. But I did not dare go back down to Butler's office and risk missing the more likely arrival of the report here. I sat down on a wooden chair to wait it out. In the inner office I could see a man of about forty-five reading typewritten reports one after another. At four-thirty people began leaving the building. The secretary left at five, and a few minutes later the man came out of the office, locking it behind him. I gave up and went home.

I was back at seven forty-five in the morning, ready to wait all day if necessary. Everyone else returned to 1407 at exactly eight-thirty. A little after nine-thirty an old man in a grey jacket came through wheeling a large cart containing scores of small compartments stuffed with mail and paperwork. He pulled out a stack and dumped it onto the secretary's desk. She sorted through it, opening most of the envelopes and stacking everything neatly. It was there: two copies. When she carried the stack in to the man in the inner office I was right behind her.

I stood by the window and watched him go through it all at his desk. He put my report to one side until he had finished with everything else and then read it carefully from beginning to end. He picked up the phone and tapped out a number.

"Hello, can I speak to Mr. Jenkins, please?"

I took a step forward so that I would be sure not to miss anything.

"Well, then, can I speak to Mr. Clellan?"

There was a pause and then a voice at the other end, which I could not make out.

"Hello, Bob? Jim O'Toole. I've got a stack of stuff here waiting for you. . . . You know the guy who tried to get in touch with Halloway? . . . Dickison. . . . Well, we sent a man over to talk to him, and he denies ever having tried to reach him. Says he might have met him years ago but isn't even sure of that. . . . I don't know what the story is. Why don't you take a look at the report, go over the transcript of the call, and see what you think. We can go back and push this guy a little harder if you think there's any point. . . . We've also got the primary school records that they thought no longer existed. They were in boxes in a basement. . . . No, it doesn't give us any names that we didn't already have. . . . Pretty much the same as the later school stuff: didn't work very hard. He did get in a fight on the school bus in the fourth grade once, but that was about the most exciting thing I could find. Someday you'll have to tell me why you're interested in this guy. Whatever it is, I sure can't see it. . . . O.K. It'll all be here at the mail room on the second floor for pickup any time. . . . Sure. So long."

He got up, taking one of the two copies of the report, and walked over to a file cabinet, from which he extracted two large manila envelopes. He took everything out to his secretary and handed it to her.

"Put all this into one package and address it to Global Devices—no address—and leave it with the mail room for pickup. And could you take it down yourself? Otherwise, it could take days to get it all the way to the second floor."

I hurried back down the stairs to the second floor in time to see the secretary leave the package for Global Devices. Just inside the entrance of the mail room was a long, broad counter behind which three people were sorting envelopes and packages. I retreated to the end of the counter and waited. After three quarters of an hour, a Hispanic boy of eighteen with a strapped canvas bag slung over his shoulder stepped up to the counter.

"Pickup for Global Devices."

A woman behind the counter turned and looked at him. "You from Global Devices? I need an ID."

"I'm from Speedwell Messenger Service. Call in if you want." He held out a slip of paper to the woman. I moved closer, hoping to be able to read an address, but it was only the address we were at scribbled on a piece of Speedwell stationery.

The woman handed him a clipboard and said, "Sign on the last line— your name, the date and time, and the addressee." I watched as he wrote "Global Devices." She went back and got the package for him.

While he took the elevator, I raced down the stairs to the lobby and waited for him. We walked together out to his bicycle. Nothing could be more hopeless for me than a bicycle. He unchained it from a no-parking sign and climbed on.

I had no clear idea of how it would help me or what I would do next, but seeing my entire plan coming suddenly apart, I reached out just as he shifted his second foot onto the pedal and pushed the bicycle onto its side. The rider, completely unprepared, hit the street hard. Before he had a chance to take stock of the situation, I jumped onto the spokes of the rear wheel, crushing them hopelessly out of shape. As the boy looked up uncertainly to see what had happened, I retreated a few steps. He twisted free and studied the damage to the bicycle, wheeling it carefully up onto the sidewalk. The rear tire jammed against the frame with each revolution.

Perhaps we would now be able to walk together to his destination. I hoped he was not allowed to take taxis.

He leaned the bike against the building and walked a bit unsteadily to a pay telephone, where he dialed a number. As he waited for an answer, he began swearing.

"Goddam fucking shit! Damn!" Then, "Hello, this is Angel. . . . No, I'm still downtown. Somebody trashed my fucking bike while I was inside making my pickup. . . . No, I didn't leave it in the fucking street! . . . On the fucking sidewalk chained to a post. They just trashed it. Like everything in this fucking city. You look the other way, they fucking trash it, just like that. No reason, man. . . . One wheel's all bent out of shape. What you want me to do? . . . Global Devices, One thirty-five East Twenty-seventh Street. . . . Sure, I know how to walk. You want me to leave the bike here or what?"

I was on my way, full of triumph. I had tracked them down while they thought they were tracking me down. I was not altogether easy about walking in on them, but I had seized the initiative. I hoped I would think of something to do with it.

35 EAST TWENTY-SEVENTH STREET WAS AN OLD, SLIGHTLY SEEDY TWELVE-story office building, built in the twenties or thirties. From the vast directory in the lobby I could see that it contained scores of small, marginal businesses of every sort: dentists, graphic designers, one-man accounting firms, and an uncountable number of "import-export" firms, whatever they may be. "Global Devices" fit in perfectly. The office number was listed as 723, which would mean a relatively easy climb for me.

If this worked out, I might be making the climb often. How convenient it would be if, with an occasional visit to Jenkins's office, I could find out exactly what he knew about me and what his plans were. I should, I thought, really have done this sooner. People are too inclined to be passive.

But as I mounted the marble stairs, my confidence began to give way to apprehension and then to outright dread. I was taking an enormous risk. I could go anywhere in the world to escape these people, and yet I had chosen to come here.

When I reached the seventh floor I walked the entire length of the corridor, which wrapped around on itself in a large rectangle, with offices on either side. There would be a courtyard in the center. I found a door marked 723 and below that Global Devices, Inc., and then studied the markings on the neighboring doors, trying to determine how many rooms Global Devices occupied. Then I went down to the sixth floor and entered the offices of an advertising agency directly below, walking through them several times until I was sure I had the floor plan clear in my mind.

I went back up and waited in front of 723. Normally, I am willing simply to push open a closed door and slip through, because often no one even notices a door opening a few inches and then closing, and if someone does notice, harmless explanations always suggest themselves: someone starting to enter and then changing his mind, a sudden draft, something. But the people behind this particular door would instantly draw the right conclusion. Any incongruous little movement or noise would make them think of me at once. And they would have me. Here, I could not take chances.

After about twenty minutes a young woman came down the corridor, carefully holding out in front of her in both hands a brown paper bag from which coffee dribbled. Without letting go of the bag, she managed to get one hand onto the doorknob and pushed the door open with her shoulder. Staying as close to her as I could, I followed her in.

I was in a large office containing several shabby secondhand desks. A woman sat at one of them typing. When we came in, she looked up and said, "Oh, you're back." Along the walls were file cabinets of unrelated shapes and a large Xerox machine. There was a closed door in the left wall, which would lead to the other offices. I watched the first woman unpack five containers of coffee and several pastries on her desk. After putting one cup on her colleague's desk and leaving one on her own, she carefully gathered up the remaining cups, balancing the pastries on top, and headed for the door, which she managed to get open, with some difficulty. I hesitated. It would be more dangerous on the other side of the door. Well, why was I here? I stepped up to her and slid through the door with her.

I stood now in a short corridor lined with doors. I watched as the woman pushed the first one open. Gomez sat at a desk with his back to us, looking at a computer display. There was a second computer in the room and what appeared to be a number of very elaborate tape recorders. Several large pairs of headphones lay on a table. On the wall opposite Gomez was an enlarged photograph of me in a bathing suit, holding a drink. I did not recognize the photograph: probably, I decided, I had never seen it. I had an odd—perhaps ridiculous—expression on my face. It struck me that this must have been part of a larger picture with other people in it. The photograph was pinned to the wall with a metal dart skewering the crotch of my bathing suit, and it had been spun forty-five degrees so that it looked as if I were beginning a long fall. Gomez turned around in his seat and counted out change to pay for his coffee and Danish.

Next we delivered a cup of coffee and a doughnut to Clellan, who as always was full of good-old-boy chatter: "Thank you, Jeannie. That's very kind. Well, don't you look fine today." She blushed and smiled.

Then, carrying the last cup of coffee, she knocked on the third door, and I heard the voice within, although I could not make out the words. She pushed open the door, and from my position in the corridor I saw Jenkins sitting at a desk writing, his pallid face expressionless. And although he did not stop writing or even look up when the woman entered, I felt like a bird gazing into the eyes of a snake.

I was startled, perhaps even frightened, by the drabness of the office. The desk and chair were the sort you would find piled three high in a used-office-furniture warehouse. There was nothing on the walls, which some time ago had been sloppily painted a dirty white color, and there were two filing cabinets, dented and scratched, one green, the other brown. The window looked out over black rooftops and water towers. On Jenkins's desk were several large piles of papers and an inexpensive plastic cup holding pencils and ball-point pens. The only sign of status or power seemed to be the presence of two telephone receivers. It struck me that one of them would be for the number he had given to me.

She put the coffee slowly down on his desk. Still without looking up or pausing in his writing, he said, "Thank you, Jean."

"You're welcome, sir."

She stepped briskly out of the room. I considered momentarily whether I should slip through the door before she shut it. Better not to risk it. One involuntary cough or sniff, and I was finished. I had to wait until I could go in alone.

She pulled Jenkins's door shut and walked back out into the front room, shutting that door behind her as well. I was trapped in the little corridor, surrounded by six closed doors which I did not dare open. I stood—and after a while sat—there for the rest of the day. Occasionally, I would hear a telephone ring somewhere behind one of the doors, and once, leaning with my ear pressed against Jenkins's door, I was sure I heard the murmur of his voice, but I could not make out any words. Excruciatingly boring, sitting there looking at those closed doors. Well, I had no choice now.

When after two hours the door at the end of the corridor opened and Morrissey entered, I was almost glad to see him. He paused, holding the door open, and looked back into the outer office, and I quickly picked myself up off the floor and moved toward him, thinking I might take this opportunity to escape from the corridor. One of the women was speaking to him.

"The meeting tomorrow is changed to two in the afternoon, because Colonel Jenkins has a meeting with someone from Washington first thing in the morning."

Morrissey pulled the door shut before I got to it, and I retreated again to let him pass down the corridor. He knocked at Clellan's office and went in, closing that door behind him as well.

Someone from Washington. I should be there for that. That might be the way to learn something useful. In the meantime, though, what should I be doing? So far I had accomplished nothing. I put my ear up to Clellan's door and heard a meaningless, unarticulated drone of low voices. I was certainly not learning much this way. A waste of time. But I had to try everything. It was around four o'clock: soon they would be leaving, and I would be able to look around. After a quarter of an hour Clellan came out and went into the outer office for something. Through the open door I could see Morrissey sitting motionless on a wooden chair next to Clellan's desk. Five minutes later Clellan returned and closed the door again.

At around four-thirty Morrissey came out and left. Then, at what must have been about five, Gomez came out. I watched him lock his office behind him. Damn! If they were all going to do that, this really was a waste of time. Perhaps it was just the computers and the tape recorders. Anyway, there would still be the outer office. A little later Clellan emerged. He locked his office. Outside I could hear the women in the outer office packing up for the day. As Clellan passed into the outer office, there were loud good-nights, and then everything was still.

It was another two hours of waiting until Jenkins emerged, carrying an old, inexpensive briefcase. He set it down and double-locked the door to his office. Hopeless. He picked up his briefcase and walked down the corridor and out through the door at the end. Then I heard him lock that door as well. I was locked up in this little passage for the night. A moment later the light went out, and I was left sitting on the floor in darkness.

I waited what seemed like a very long while, although it is difficult under such conditions to judge the passage of time. Then I felt my way down to the end of the corridor, where I could see a little crack of light under the door, hoping—although really I knew better—that there would be some way to unlock the door from this side. Nothing. I worked my way back down the corridor, trying each door as I went. One after the other was locked. I got out one of my credit cards and tried to jimmy them open, but I knew that it would not work. They were bolted. There must at least be a toilet. My bladder was by now painfully full. My mood took another nasty plunge, as I realized that there would be no toilet: the toilets would be out in the public hallway. That was why Clellan had gone out earlier. No. This door was unlocked. Must be a toilet after all. At least that.

I pushed the door open very slowly. There was still some light coming through a window that looked into an air shaft. It was a long, narrow room, almost entirely filled by a large, oval conference table, around which were half a dozen metal chairs. Shoved into one corner was a grey metal desk with no chair in front of it. The only other furnishing in the room was a wastepaper basket. As a matter of principle, I went over to the desk and slowly pulled each drawer open. All empty. With some difficulty I forced the grimy window open and urinated into the air shaft.

I went back out into the corridor and stretched out on the uncarpeted floor, where for the next twelve hours I tried to sleep.

Jenkins was the first to arrive in the morning. I was on my feet and wide awake before he was through the outer door. I felt myself trembling from hunger and from having lain half-awake on that floor all night. And also from fear, I realized. But I was there. I would stay with it through the morning meeting with the person from Washington. I could certainly go a day and a half without food.

I watched as Jenkins came through the door and walked down the corridor toward me. I knew that there was no reason in the world for him to continue past his office, and yet it terrified me to see him coming straight at me, and I felt as if it had been a narrow escape when he stopped and unlocked his door. This time he had left both his office door and the door at the end of the corridor open behind him. It was early—before eight—and you could hear every little noise reverberate through the empty building. I waited where I was, absolutely still. From Jenkins's office came the sound of drawers being opened and closed and then the scratching of a pencil on paper.

A half hour later an electric bell sounded in the outer office, and Jenkins reemerged and walked out to the entrance. This was the moment. I crept into his office. I could hear him in the distance unlocking the entrance door again and greeting someone. Fragments of two voices approaching. Something about the Eastern Shuttle, I thought. I looked rapidly around the room for the safest place. The corner away from the door. No one walks into a corner. I sat down with my back leaning against the wall, trying to find a comfortable position so that I would not have to move. I prayed that this really was whomever Jenkins was meeting with, because the worst thing that could happen would be to find myself closed into a room with one person—and that one person Jenkins. I would not be able to sniff or cough or clear my throat; I would hardly be able to move, perhaps for hours. These situations are bad enough when there are two people, but at least then they are paying attention to each other, and they are shifting around in their seats and sneezing, and each has someone else to attach a random noise to.

Jenkins stopped at the door to let the visitor precede him. The man was in his fifties, immaculately groomed and wearing a suit that had been made for him at great expense. His eyes skipped around the room as he sat down in the scuffed wooden chair next to Jenkins's desk.

"Temporary quarters?" His thin lips twisted easily and automatically into an urbane smile each time he finished speaking. As he settled himself on the chair, he crossed his legs and adjusted his tie.

Jenkins, who had opened his mouth as if to say no, paused abruptly and closed it again. For an instant he seemed to scrutinize his visitor's face.

"Yes, I suppose so. We're always in temporary quarters, really."

The visitor, who had been peering curiously at the battered front of the metal desk before him, looked up, startled.

"Yes, of course. You are, in a way, aren't you?" He turned his eyes to the green metal file cabinet standing awkwardly against the wall beside him and then looked suddenly back at Jenkins again. "I was speaking about you just the other day with Bob Neverson. He sends his best. He has an extraordinarily high opinion of you. Said you were the most capable person he'd ever had assigned to him." The man smiled.

"That's extremely generous of him," said Jenkins without any hint of emotion. "It was a privilege working under him. Those were valuable years for me." As Jenkins spoke, the other man's attention seemed to wander, his eyes flitting distractedly about the room. "I rarely see Bob now," said Jenkins. "Please give him my best."

"I will. I certainly will." The smile formed. The stranger uncrossed and recrossed his legs. Then he started speaking again, in a changed tone of voice which indicated that the real discussion would now commence. "I wanted to take this opportunity to meet alone with you this morning because, as you are doubtless aware, there are so many rumors floating around about your operation, and before we find ourselves facing a full attack on the budgeting for this, I wanted to be clear in my own mind exactly what our goals and priorities are here." He paused and ran his index finger delicately along his lower lip. "The budget, in fact—that is, the portion directly attributable to your operation—seems likely to run over twelve million dollars. And then there are the various indirect and support costs . . . and above all the requests for interagency cooperation. These are real costs . . ."

"Of course," Jenkins said. "And you naturally need to assure yourself that these expenditures are justified. Let me say I'm glad—"

"It's not only that. . . . Although of course we do have a responsibility to evaluate and oversee these expenditures. Still, the fact that the costs are reaching this order of magnitude creates a kind of vulnerability. The fact is—and this is only based on what little I know of this operation—I would not want to be put in the position of having to defend these expenditures to a Congressional committee, for example." He paused again, twisting his head uncomfortably. The thought seemed to cause him genuine distress. "I find that when these things reach a certain level of funding, no matter what security precautions are taken, we can no longer be confident that we won't find them suddenly being used as a vehicle for a political attack." He ran his finger along his lip again, tapping it lightly at several points. Perhaps he was checking for cold sores. "And so I particularly wanted this chance to review the situation with you directly."

"Yes," said Jenkins. "I understand perfectly. I've tried to keep Nick Ridgefield fully informed about how we were spending money and how much. I think—"

"Well, you have. You absolutely have."

"And I've tried to present an honest picture of the very real possibility that we will ultimately fail in our efforts."

"Failure is not really an important issue here. Nor, up to a point, is cost. Public scrutiny is really what we have to be concerned with."

"Of course," said Jenkins. "I understand your concern perfectly. The political risks are high and the costs are unquestionably high. But the value of what we are doing, if we are successful, is incalculable."

"I'm sure it is. I'm only concerned that the political risks here may be so great that no amount of value could justify them."

Jenkins's eyes widened momentarily, as if something in this startled him. "Of course," he said slowly. "I see that perfectly. That's why I'm so glad to have the opportunity to go over this with you in person. So that you can judge for yourself what is at stake." He paused for a moment and then resumed. "I assume you've talked to Ridgefield."

"I *have* talked to Ridgefield, of course, but . . . Let me be frank, umm— your name is David Jenkins just now, isn't it? Perhaps it would be best if I called you that as well. Let me be perfectly frank, Jenkins. Ridgefield doesn't want to talk to me about this. He strongly recommended that I speak with you directly. He doesn't want the responsibility. He doesn't want to be on record as having stated clearly—or having known—what is going on here. He has the highest possible opinion of you. Everyone does. Brilliant record, nothing odd or erratic—otherwise this wouldn't have gone as far as it has. But Ridgefield wants to make sure that you have the whole responsibility for this. Or that I have it. And I'll tell you quite frankly that I almost refused to talk to you at all. But, on balance, I felt safer informing myself, so I allowed myself to be prevailed upon. But whatever you may have told Ridgefield, you should assume that I know nothing about all this. You should present—and you should understand that this will be strictly off the record, for the time being at least—you should present me with all the facts." He glanced involuntarily at his watch.

Jenkins's face wrinkled up. He walked over to the filing cabinet and withdrew a folder of large photographic prints. "This building housed, until last April, a small corporation called MicroMagnetics, Inc., which was engaged in research funded by various agencies of the DOD. I apologize for the quality of the photograph: it is the only one we have; it was taken in connection with an application for a mortgage, by the wife of the man standing in front of the building. We are still, after many thousands of man-hours of interviews and scientific review, not sure about the precise nature of the research being performed there. However, inside the building there was a laboratory in which had been constructed some sort of magnetic containment device—that would be the next photograph—similar to those used in the development of nuclear fusion devices. . . ."

Jenkins was giving a set speech. He recited the curriculum vitae of Bernard Wachs, Ph.D., including a critical bibliography of his published work. He listed the names of the people who had worked for Micro- Magnetics, what they had done there, what they understood of Wachs's device. Jenkins's visitor showed a polite interest in the photographs, examining them in much the same way he would have examined photographs of distant cousins in whom he was not much interested, during an obligatory visit to a great-aunt.

Jenkins began to describe the press conference. He had a floor plan of the building and grounds. There was a picture of Carillon. I found myself getting to my feet so that I could see the photographs, and I realized that I was quite unsteady. I reminded myself that I had not eaten for thirty-six hours. But seeing those pictures and hearing those events recounted in that insinuating monotone was having an overwhelming and unexpected effect on me. I was startled by the realization that it had all taken place only five months before. Somehow I had put it all out of my mind, and it had come to seem, until this moment, quite remote. But now, looking at these photographs, I felt the blood draining from my head, and I pictured again the final pulsing incineration of Carillon and Wachs. I had to keep hold of myself. Jenkins was talking about the Students for a Fair World and what else they had done and then how everyone had filed out onto the lawn in front of the building. Why hadn't I filed out onto the lawn like everyone else?

Jenkins was walking across the room. He pulled open a closet door, revealing a metal safe the size of a small refrigerator. I knew that I must get over there no matter what. One, two, three careful steps, lowering the heel onto the floor and then rocking onto the edge of my foot. He was turning the knob around and around, clockwise. He stopped at fifteen. Fifteen, fifteen, fifteen: remember fifteen. Back around to thirty-seven. Fifteen, thirty-seven. Fifteen, thirty-seven. Forward to eighteen. Back to five. Fifteen, thirty-seven, eighteen, five. Fifteen, thirty-seven, eighteen, five. Easy, but my mind threatened to go blank with panic at the possibility of forgetting.

Jenkins pulled open the door to the safe and carried over another little folder. He laid it on the edge of the desk in front of his visitor and lifted the cover. There was a small pile of black and white photographs. The one on top showed a lawn with what appeared to be a large hole or crater. It might have been the excavation for the foundation of a new building.

"And this is how the site appeared shortly after the explosion. If explosion is the proper word. Fortunately, there was a transient condition of high radioactivity, which resulted in immediate evacuation of the area." The visitor was flipping through more photographs of the site. He reached a photograph of a man in a spacesuit floating over the crater.

"I don't quite make out what's going on in this one," said the visitor, turning the picture at an angle and furrowing his brow. "There's a man being lowered somehow into this pit."

"Actually, that's not what's happening," Jenkins was saying. The other man was flipping through the remaining photographs. He stopped at a picture of three men suspended in midair, one on his hands and knees, one standing, and one in the posture of a man sitting on a chair. It looked like some improbable pantomime. Throughout the space in which they floated, there was a network of lines forming squares and rectangles, as if someone had tried to draw in the outline of a building.

Jenkins was trying to explain. He had pulled out the photograph of the building before the accident and the floor plan, and he was pointing from one to the other. "This picture is taken at a slightly different angle, unfortunately, but this man is standing in the room next to this door in front, and the man crouching above him is in the room directly above."

Jenkins's visitor was looking at the pictures with total concentration now. "What you are asserting here is that the entire building is still there, only invisible." The man licked his lips nervously and blinked. "Ridgefield left me with a more modest impression—some extraordinarily transparent objects. . . . Have you had these photographs authenticated?"

"Well, from our perspective there wouldn't really be any point. One of my men took those photographs. The person standing in this first room is me."

"I see." He went back through the photographs, looking at them intently now and saying nothing. "Tell me. . . . It's of course hard really to tell from these photographs . . . how convincing, exactly, was the illusion . . . the sensation of invisibility? That is to say, did you see the outlines of things? Was it as if everything was made of glass? Did . . . How exactly does it work with glass? Does the light reflect off it differently? . . . With these photographs it's impossible to—"

"It was not at all as if everything was made of glass. You could see nothing whatever. No outline, or shape, not the slightest opacity or visual distortion. When you touched something, you could feel it. That was all. Everything was exactly as it had been, except that it was completely invisible. I know it sounds incredible. It's too bad that the photographs aren't better. We took others with much better equipment."

"What happened to them?"

"They were destroyed."

"Destroyed how?" asked the man. He seemed to feel some outrage that such a thing had been permitted to take place. "Is that part of the . . . I gather from Ridgefield that there is some issue of sabotage here. How much of this remains? Can we visit this site?" He was still squinting at the photographs.

Jenkins had walked back across the room and was carefully groping inside the safe. He walked back towards the desk, holding his hands out oddly before him, palms upward, as if in supplication to some deity. He was carrying something, something invisible, and there was a little clatter as he deposited it on the surface of the desk in front of his visitor. Fifteen, thirty-seven, eighteen, five. It was several objects, and as he arranged them, his hands moved mysteriously over the surface of the desk as if he were performing some magical incantation.

Jenkins was holding an empty hand out toward his visitor and saying, "You might examine this." The man looked at Jenkins with an expression of discomfort and perhaps annoyance. Either he was like the member of the audience who is suddenly singled out by the magician and told to take a card or else he was being forced to humor a madman, and whichever it was, it made him feel foolish. His eyes shot momentarily back toward the door as if in contemplation of escape. But there was Jenkins's hand under his nose. He moved his own forefinger self-consciously toward it. Just before it reached Jenkins's forefinger, he started, jerking back as if he had been stung. He reached out again and took whatever it was and began to manipulate it, as a look of astonishment spread over his face.

"It's . . . it's a cigarette lighter. . . . It's quite unbelievable. . . . And is the whole thing like this? The whole building?"

"It was. It's been burned down."

"*Burned down?* How in God's name could that have been permitted to happen?" He was staring intently at his own hand. The thumb was jerking up and down comically and you could hear the scratch of the flint. He moved the fingers of his left hand in a little circle over the right hand. Suddenly he emitted a half-stifled little shriek, and his hands flew violently apart.

"I see it still works perfectly."

He sucked momentarily at the fingers of his left hand and then leaned forward from the edge of his chair to search for the dropped lighter.

Soon both men were on all fours feeling about for the lighter. "Tricky keeping track of a thing like that, isn't it?"

"Very tricky. That, in a way, is our main problem."

"How much survived this fire? What do you still have?"

"I'm afraid that this—" Jenkins located the lighter somewhere under his desk. "Here it is." The two men stood up and Jenkins carefully deposited the lighter on the desk. "I'm afraid that what's here on this desk is all that we have. There was probably some sort of explosion during the course of the fire. It may have been a fuel tank, or it may even have been something in the laboratory, but there was essentially nothing left of the site. We spent several weeks sifting the ashes and raking the surrounding area." The other man was groping over the surface of the desk in front of him. "You'll find, in addition to the lighter, a portion of a glass ashtray, a screwdriver, and a bullet."

The visitor picked something up and held it in his hand, which was shaking.

"That's all that survived the fire? This bullet has been fired," he said, turning it over in his fingers. "Have you had anyone look at this . . . I mean, from a scientific point of view?"

"We've sent pieces of the ashtray to Riverhaven and to the Radiation Labs. They refer to it as 'superglass.' For security reasons, we haven't for the time being told them that we have any substance other than glass with these properties. At some point a decision will have to be made about how we want to proceed on all this." Jenkins frowned, his face contorting in folds. He seemed to be thinking about something.

"And have they come back with anything? I mean, do they know how it's done?" The man's voice had a little quaver of nervous excitement to it. So would mine have, if I had tried to speak then. I was trembling as I waited for the reply.

"If you mean could they re-create the phenomenon, make other objects like these, no. They have come back with a great deal about the properties of 'superglass.' But when you come down to it, they are mainly just describing the lack of properties you might otherwise expect to find. I'll give you the reports, and you—"

"Well, if they can't do it themselves yet, do they know . . . do they have some general idea more or less how it must have been done?"

Jenkins wrinkled up his face. "You should look at the reports. I would say the answer to your question comes down to no. But they would give a much lengthier, more complicated formulation. The fact is, they have many different ideas how it must have been done. Too many." He stopped as if considering whether to pursue the question. "The theory seems to be that these objects are not built up out of the same subatomic particles as other physical things. Instead, they are composed of different particles, or perhaps units of energy, but arranged in the same structure as before. Or perhaps they are largely the same particles, only interchanged somehow. There are differing schools of thought. In any case, you have an object with roughly the same properties as the original, except that light passes through it without any refraction. Specific gravity is slightly lower. Mechanical bonding seems to be poorer. But basically you have an invisible version of a given object."

"It's really quite extraordinary." He had the cigarette lighter in his hand again and was tapping it against the top of the desk. His hand was still trembling. "Incredible. It's difficult even to take in the possibilities. . . ." Although he made a point of maintaining his detached, urbane manner, his voice was an octave higher and his speech had a disjointed quality. "Surely they have some idea. . . . What about the papers of this man Wachs. You say he was funded by the DOD. What about his reports?"

"We have people trying to reconstruct his work. But if he was working on anything like this, it doesn't show up in any of his submitted reports.

All his recent published work is on magnetic containment devices for nuclear fusion. He does seem, near the end, to have stumbled on some new phenomenon that he thought was significant, but in what way—or even whether—it was related to the properties of these objects we can't tell. He certainly had constructed some magnetic device that caused these transformations—probably as the result of a malfunction. Whether Wachs could have anticipated—or even have understood—any of this, we can't say. The people working for him seem to have less idea of what he was doing than we do. We're working on it, but so far it doesn't seem to be leading anywhere. It's difficult. He's dead. His notes, his papers, his laboratory, this device, whatever it was, all went up in flames. The answer is that to date no one has any useful idea of how these objects were produced, much less how we might produce more of them. And furthermore, the only experimental techniques that yield any information about the structure of this material seem also to destroy it in the process. Our supply is being rapidly consumed, which will soon force another difficult decision on us. I've had copies of these reports prepared for you."

Jenkins turned to a stack of papers in plastic bindings arranged neatly on one side of his desk and proceeded to go through them, explaining which scientific team had produced each report and what promise or lack of promise it held. And this, he explained, was a dossier on Wachs. And these are all his published papers. And photocopies of what few drafts of unpublished work we have.

"It's all here in summary. We've sifted through every inch of dirt and ashes at that site. We've been through Wachs's personal life day by day, and we've done everything we can think of to try to reconstruct his scientific work. We have the best laboratories in the world looking at the actual material we've recovered from the accident site. And that," said Jenkins with the air of someone summing things up, "is pretty much where we stand."

"So that is where you stand," said the other man quietly. "And this is all there is?" With raised eyebrows, he peered up at Jenkins and tapped the surface of the desk where the unseen objects lay. "A pity. Because you started with an entire building. And then, several months and many millions of dollars later, you have only this. A sudden and, to me at least, mysterious fire, and everything else is gone. How, by the way, did this fire begin? And why do you have a bullet there? Your narrative raises so many more questions than it answers."

Jenkins stared at the desk as if he could see the objects there, his face compressed in folds. He seemed undecided about how to respond. His visitor elected to end the silence and continue.

"In any case, based on what you tell me, this seems like a problem for physicists. An interesting and difficult problem, without doubt, and one that requires the strictest security, but not one that requires a massive intelligence operation, surely. And not one that requires these vast expenditures."

"There has been a great deal of investigative work . . . ongoing investigative work. . . ." Jenkins paused, frowning. "Is there any further information you would like about what we are doing?"

"Is there any further information I would like." The man did not repeat the words as if they were a question. "Really, you will have to tell me if there is any further information I would like."

"I am, of course, here to give you any information I can. I just want to be sure I don't tell you anything you would rather not hear—that is, anything more than you need to evaluate this project. When you discussed coming up here with Ridgefield—"

"Perhaps I failed to express myself clearly before. It is not that Ridgefield has told me all about this yet out of prudence wants it on the record that I have been briefed directly by you. Ridgefield shows the same reluctance to speak about this matter that you do. That is why I am here. Perhaps you had better tell me whatever else there is to this. Was there something else in the building that you people have somehow lost track of? Or does someone else know about all this? What is the problem exactly?"

Jenkins was silent for a moment and then said, "Both those things are the problem." He paused again. "To begin with, there was a cat in the building. . . ."

"A *cat*? And was it . . . was it like the cigarette lighter?"

"Yes. Unfortunately, it escaped."

"Escaped?" He did not seem to understand at first. "You mean it survived the explosion? Or whatever it was?"

"That's right. One of my men had it in his hands briefly. It struggled free and ran off." Jenkins turned his head and gazed at the bare wall.

"And have you tried . . . Of course you have."

"We've done everything conceivable to capture it. We're still trying. You may want to look at those reports as well. We've seen no sign of it since the first day."

"Well, presumably it's dead. Even if it did survive initially. You say there was a lot of radiation?"

"We have reason to believe it may still be alive."

"How can you—"

Jenkins was handing over a photograph of me. Taken a little over a year ago at a wedding. I remembered it.

"This man is named Nicholas Halloway. The photograph is no longer really relevant. He was inside the building, and we've lost track of him as well. Although not so irretrievably as the cat."

"Good Lord. You mean this man is also . . . like the cigarette lighter?"

"That's right."

The man stared blankly at the photograph as if it might contain some useful piece of information that he had not yet been able to pick out.

"What is . . . Where is he now?"

"Right here in New York."

"And that's what this is really all about? A human being has become invisible. . . ." He looked toward the objects on the desk. "Totally invisible. And you're trying to capture him."

"Yes."

"I see. Good Lord." They both sat in silence. The visitor gazed at my photograph, turning it at different angles, and then spoke again.

"I take it that he burned down the building in Princeton. And that he is armed."

"That's right."

"He's hostile, then?"

Jenkins appeared to reflect on this question.

"I would say rather that he is uncooperative. In burning down the building and even in his physical attacks on us, his motivation has been escape. Almost exclusively, I would say."

"Why? Why is he running away from you?"

"He's afraid of what will happen to him. He's afraid of being 'a laboratory animal.' Those are his words. Once we get him, he doesn't think he'll have any control over the situation."

The visitor looked startled.

"He's quite right, isn't he? It hadn't occurred to me. It won't be very nice for him at all, will it?"

Jenkins was silent for several seconds.

"Perhaps not. But we have to catch him."

"Yes," said the visitor. "Of course we do. We absolutely have to catch him. The mind reels at the possibilities. . . . And furthermore, we really have no way of knowing what he might do on his own, do we?"

"That's right."

"Do you have any reason to think he might be actively working for any other intelligence group?"

"No. Not at this point. I'm virtually certain of that. And if he ever did work with anyone, it would probably be with us. But you're right. The risk is always there. He's unpredictable."

"This is incredible! You've actually seen the man with your own eyes . . . or rather, not seen him. You've talked to him? Touched him? How sure—"

"I've been in physical contact with him." (That would be in the garden below my apartment, when I hit him as hard as I could.) "And I've talked to him on a number of occasions. This second telephone is for his exclusive use. At this point he hasn't many people to talk to at all, and I'm probably the only person he can talk to freely. I encourage him to call me as often as he likes. Although we haven't spoken lately. He has been pretending that he has left New York, and I have been pretending to believe that.

The man looked up slowly from the photograph and gazed at Jenkins.

"Jenkins, you will understand that this is not meant in any way to reflect the slightest lack of confidence in you, but you say that some of your men have also seen . . . have also had . . . direct evidence of this person?"

"Yes, very direct. One of them was shot by him and another physically assaulted. Would you like to talk to them? I would understand perfectly."

"Perhaps later. I'm . . . I want to get my bearings in this whole thing first." He looked down at my photograph again. "Who is he? What was he?"

Jenkins began to recount from memory my curriculum vitae, leafing, as he spoke, through page after page of mounted and labeled photographs. He had an extraordinary quantity of information about the circumstances of my life. I could see that he knew far more than I knew or had ever known. I learned how much money my father had earned, where each of my parents had grown up, who their friends had been, whom they had slept with, what they had died of. There was a picture of my father as a young man, with another man and two women, none of them people I knew. My mother expressionless at the railing of a ship. And there I was, spindly legged, at summer camp, circled in a row of boys. Jenkins's fingers flipping over the pages of photographs, the school report cards, letters I had written to people I could no longer remember. The lukewarm comments of my teachers, the qualified opinions of my colleagues regarding the quality of my work and friendship. Whom I had slept with and when. And whom in turn they had slept with. Pictures, dates, names. All irretrievable. No way back to any of that now.

My whole life was, as the expression goes, passing before my eyes. As rendered by a policeman. Better not to consider the violent mob of emotions it stirred up. I was, from beginning to end, transfixed.

The rest of the audience, however, seemed less caught up in the narrative. More than once, Jenkins's visitor seemed to be gazing out the window, as if he were thinking about something else altogether, and at one point, looking down with a frown at my picture, which he still held in his hands, he abruptly interrupted.

"Where is he living? Who has he gone to for help?"

Jenkins looked up from his folders full of documentation.

"He's been sleeping in private clubs or breaking into empty apartments. I'm going to get to all this."

"How many of his friends and family know?"

"None of them. He wouldn't risk telling them. We're the only people who know."

"I'm sorry. Go on. I didn't mean to interrupt."

Jenkins went on. There was a picture of Anne. Stunning. Speculations on how I might have escaped from MicroMagnetics. Pictures of my apartment and an inventory of the contents. He listed, with demoralizing accuracy, which clubs I had slept in and which apartment buildings they were sure I had used. He stacked up on the desk the transcripts of our telephone conversations. He described each encounter and each attempt at capture.

When it was all over, the other man said, "You people have done an extraordinarily thorough job here."

"I think it would be fair to say that I know more about Halloway than I've ever known about another human being. But I'm not sure at this point that it's of much use."

"Yes. Exactly. The long and short of it is that it doesn't add up to much of anything. Your friend has attended some good schools, where his performance was consistently respectable and undistinguished. He seems to have approached his career and his personal life in much the same spirit. Never married. It would appear that he has a great many friends without being particularly close to any of them. Not even a hobby. An occasional game of squash or tennis. All in all, there really doesn't seem to be much to him. Surprising, in a way, that someone like this turns out to be so much trouble."

"It's always difficult," Jenkins replied, "when you get people like this— no strong emotional ties, no political beliefs, no particular interests of any sort. You can't find a handhold."

"Yes, I suppose you're right. But you think, even so, that you'll get him?"

"We'll bring him around," said Jenkins, wrinkling his face pensively and nodding to himself. "It won't be long now. It can't be very pleasant for him out there. There are so few choices for him, and he knows we're right behind him. If we don't catch him soon, he'll give up. Without even admitting it to himself, he'll stop trying so hard. He'll let us close in. His situation is hopeless." Jenkins closed his eyes until there were only the narrowest slits. "It should be very soon now. He can't get away with this sort of thing much longer."

"Well, you're probably right," said the visitor, gazing at Jenkins with an appraising look. "You know, you've put a lot of work into this, and sometimes there can be a danger of a thing like this becoming an obsession. . . . Well, you'll be the best judge of that." He paused reflectively and then recommenced. "Tell me, assuming that you weren't successful in capturing Halloway and that for some reason it was considered unacceptable that he remain at large, out of control, how feasible—"

"Of course we hope we can bring him in, but if it became necessary, it might be easier to terminate him than to capture him."

"And there's one other thing," said the visitor. "Do you have any incontrovertible proof—I mean, other than your testimony and your men's—that Halloway didn't die in that accident? Proof that he's alive . . . in this condition?"

"We have tapes of him speaking on the telephone. To us and to people who knew him before."

"Tapes, unfortunately, are not the most compelling demonstration of invisibility."

"Would you like to talk to the other men who have dealt with him? Some of them will be here now." Jenkins moved his hand toward the telephone tentatively.

"No, no. I think not. That really isn't what I meant at all. I'm only concerned about my position—and yours, of course—if we have to justify all this at some point. Never mind. It doesn't matter." He was running his finger along his lip again, and his eyes avoided Jenkins as he spoke. "What you're doing here is extremely important, and I want you to know that I'm going to do everything I can to back you up as far as budgeting goes. However, for the time being—until you've actually apprehended Halloway—I think it would be better if we both took the position that we had never discussed this matter. I think you should go on reporting to Ridgefield on whatever basis you both decide is appropriate. As far as I'm concerned, you are working on an extremely difficult and important scientific problem. Which is indeed the case. . . . I will take along this lighter, however. It might be of help if any questions are ever raised about all this."

He found the lighter on the desk and slid it into the side pocket of his suit jacket.

Jenkins's eyes widened and he opened his mouth as if to voice an objection. He paused for a moment and then said, "Of course. I can see that that would be sensible. Be careful, though: these things can get lost very easily."

"Yes, I imagine so. Well, thank you for your time." His well-bred smile had reappeared, and he was looking straight at Jenkins again. "This is really quite extraordinary. Incredible. Well, good luck to you."

Jenkins walked with him out to the elevator. I walked with them too, slipping through the doors right behind them, but once I was in the hall, I raced to the stairway and charged down the six flights to the lobby. When the elevator door opened, I stepped right up beside him and walked out into the street with him.

I had to do something right away. There would be no second chance. He walked east, his right hand in the side pocket of his jacket, fingering the magic cigarette lighter. Across the street I saw what was probably his car. A uniformed driver. As he stepped off the curb, I planted my right foot directly in front of his, so that with the next step it caught, pitching him face forward into the street. His hands flew out in front of him as he went down.

I was right there beside him on the ground, reaching into his pocket. My hand found the lighter immediately, and before he had begun to collect himself, I had slipped it out and stepped quickly off to the side to watch. People were helping him to his feet. He was dusting himself off, while other pedestrians paused to see whether he was all right—or perhaps whether he was sober. The light had already turned and cars were driving through the crosswalk again before he checked the pocket.

Suddenly, he was waving the cars to a stop. "Hold it! Hold it! I've lost something. . . . No, no, I don't need any help. Just hold the cars back. . . . That's right, a contact lens." He was down on all fours, crawling through the street, feeling with the palms of his hands. His driver appeared but was waved impatiently away. Soon traffic was backed up the length of the block and horns were sounding. He was muttering anxiously. His driver, standing dutifully in front of the intersection to block the traffic, seemed perplexed.

Eventually a car pushed through. "Look, I'm sorry, buddy, but contact lenses are widely available. I'm not gonna grow old and die here so you can save fifty bucks." The cars behind followed him through the crosswalk.

The man stood up, tight-lipped, and stared morosely at the street. He looked back toward the building where he had left Jenkins. It would be difficult for us both if he decided to go back and tell Jenkins what had happened. But why should he? It would be embarrassing. Perhaps more than embarrassing ultimately. It would be safest to say nothing, not admit to a mistake. But if he did start to go back, I would have to stop him somehow. I waited. He looked despairingly down at the crosswalk where the cars were rattling through. When the light turned again, he walked over and climbed into his car.

I stood out in the street for several minutes debating what I should do. I wanted very much to get away from there. I desperately needed food and rest, and the thought of going back inside the offices of Global Devices filled me with dread. But if I were ever going to go back up there at all, I had to do it right away. Jenkins's visitor could have a change of heart at any time and decide to tell Jenkins about the loss of the cigarette lighter. Jenkins would understand at once everything that had happened, and after that I would never be able to enter those offices again. Furthermore, they were all about to have a meeting, presumably to discuss the latest information they had acquired about me and what they would do next to capture me. I might learn enough in that meeting to put me out of their reach for months. But above all, I knew I had to go back and try to do something about the contents of Jenkins's safe.

Fifteen, thirty-seven, eighteen, five.

I climbed back up to the seventh floor and waited in front of the door.

It was nearly an hour before Morrissey arrived and let me in through the entrance door. I followed him straight to the room with the conference table, where I stepped quietly into the corner nearest the open door.

Everyone was there except Jenkins. Tyler sat erect in his chair, not taking part in the conversation of the others. Gomez was helping Clellan set up a sort of wooden easel on the other side of the room, to which a stack of large drawings was clipped. The one showing on top was a map of Manhattan marked with little red rectangles. I counted six of them. They would be buildings I was known to have slept in during the last month. There seemed to be more maps in the stack, and I could see a large floor plan protruding. Several floor plans. Particular apartments that they were watching? I would soon find out. I wondered what the housing situation was like in Queens.

"This guy sure does get around, doesn't he?" said Gomez. "Every night in a different place."

Clellan smiled his good-old-boy smile at Gomez. "Now, from what I understand, Gomez, that's not so different from you."

"The hours you got me working, I'm lucky to sleep anywhere at all."

"When we get your friend, we'll all get some rest."

Tyler was staring at the chart. "These are the places he's been staying?"

"These are places we're pretty sure he's been," said Clellan. "Not always one hundred percent, but pretty sure. The thing is, he seems to keep moving. Never more than one, maybe two nights in one place. Which is a good sign, because it shows he's feeling the pressure. It means he's all the more likely to make a mistake. I'll go through the whole thing for everybody as soon as the Colonel's here."

"I hear you talked to him," said Tyler softly.

"Yeah, I talked to him, all right," said Clellan with a loud laugh. "I talked myself blue in the face. Only he didn't talk to me. I was standing in this lobby"—he found the building on the map and pointed at it—"and suddenly I'm looking down at two footprints in the carpet, and there I am talking and talking, telling him how much we all love him and miss him and what a treat it is to run into him this way. I'm doing everything but sing to him, and all the time I'm thinking, 'Nicky boy, maybe it's time to take a big jump at you,' when one, two, the footprints step away, and I'm talking at thin air. The doorman thought I was a real wack-job. Wanted to have me taken away."

"Anyone finds out what we're doing, they'll think we're all wack-jobs," said Morrissey unhappily. Morrissey is always whining. "We're not going to get this guy. How can we? He's fucking *invisible*."

"We're going to get him real soon now," said Gomez. "Wait'll you see one of these apartments I'm fixing up for him. Once he's inside, I got sensors in the apartment set up to drive the dead bolt home on the main door and freeze it. At the same time it transmits a radio signal to us."

"Furthermore, these apartments can also be used by Gomez in his busy social life. Gomez does a lot of entertaining." Clellan's laugh boomed out.

"Look, that was one time I had to talk to a friend—she has very difficult problems—and I happened to be in that apartment. Anyway, the hours we're putting in, your private life is bound to get mixed in with your work sometimes."

"That's a fact, Gomez," said Clellan, his smile disappearing and his eyes narrowing. "I meant to speak to you about that. You got to leave Carmen alone. It's easy for you to find women, but not for me, especially ones with big breasts who can type. The same for Jeannie. I want you to leave both those girls alone, hear?" He fixed Gomez with a threatening look.

"Shit, I'm just trying to help Carmen out. She has a very difficult situation with her husband."

"And you're going to help her out with that?" The exaggeratedly stern expression on Clellan's face exploded into laughter.

"What's more, it's very difficult for a Hispanic girl working with people like you guys, and I'm just trying to help her, talk to her a little." Gomez seemed to be growing uncomfortable with the discussion. "Anyway, this door mechanism is gonna get this guy. I mean, this is a cheap system. I can do an apartment for five—tops, six—thousand dollars, and you don't need any human surveillance. We can have any number of these places just set up waiting for him."

Tyler looked up. "What about the apartments?"

"What do you mean, 'what about the apartments?' "

"What do you pay to rent the apartments? I've been looking for an apartment in Manhattan, and one bedroom can run you over two thousand a month. Even over in someplace like Park Slope it's bad." Tyler thought for a moment. "Maybe I could use one of these places while you're working on it."

"Gomez couldn't spare even one. You're talking about real *throughput* with Gomez." Clellan laughed. Gomez looked away, embarrassed but with a little smirk showing. "Anyway, we'll soon be taking some time off, I hope. Once Nicky boy comes to our party."

"How many apartments are there in New York?" asked Morrissey. "Maybe a million? You gonna set up five or ten and then just wait until he walks into one of them? Those are piss-poor odds. We're never gonna get him."

Clellan tilted his head and looked appraisingly at Morrissey. "There aren't a million apartments that Halloway would go into. There are not many at all. And there'll be fewer now that summer is over. He goes certain kinds of places. We know a lot about him by now."

"We know a lot about him all right, the fucker." I was startled by Morrissey's vehemence. Frightened. "Mostly we know what a smart-ass he is.

It could have been anyone in the world in that building, and we had to get that asshole. I'll tell you this: if we ever do get the fucker, I hope it's me. I'd love to get a shot at him."

They were all silent at this. I thought Tyler nodded, but it might have been my imagination. It was Clellan who started talking again.

"Morrissey, you just aren't giving him a fair chance. You and Nicky boy might get to be real good buddies. You just need a chance to get to know each other. Have a few beers together. Kick things around. Maybe Gomez could fix the two of you up with a couple of girls. You've got to give people a chance—"

"He's such an asshole. Thinks he can do whatever he fucking feels like, like he's the only person in the world. You ought to see that school he went to. They got a gym there you could hold the Olympics in—hockey rinks, swimming pools, indoor baseball diamond—for maybe three, four hundred kids. All smart-asses like Halloway. You could—"

Morrissey broke off and sat up straight as Jenkins entered the room. They all seated themselves around the table, Jenkins at one end, with Clellan next to him. Everyone looked at Jenkins, waiting for him to begin.

"I want to say first of all that I've been talking to Washington—I had a meeting here this morning, and I've just been on the phone for the last half hour with someone else—and the pressure to produce some results is gradually mounting." I remembered how much I disliked the earnest, insinuating quality of Jenkins's voice. "Our budget is beginning to attract attention. There is very little we can do about that—we have no choice now but to push ahead. The trouble is that virtually no one really knows what we are doing and what is at stake, and the few people who do will not acknowledge it. This operation is still being represented as an investigation into the incident at MicroMagnetics and an attempt to reconstruct Wachs's scientific results, intentional or accidental. Only a handful of people have any real idea of what those results were. There are inevitably rumors, however, and those rumors could catch up with us eventually. As you can imagine, it would be unpleasant to have to justify this operation if ultimately we came up empty-handed."

Jenkins paused and looked at his hands.

"I might as well say this now. If the moment should ever come when we are in that situation and facing a political attack or some sort of investigation, each of you will have to decide how you want to handle it. You could, of course, describe events exactly as you saw them. However, I would think that you would probably feel safest taking the line that you were following my orders and that you really had no sense of the overall scope or direction of the operation. And you would probably be vague or unsure of exactly what you had seen. Or hadn't seen. I would, as I say, understand anyone's wanting to approach the thing that way. Furthermore, I'm not even sure that it would make my own situation any worse if you did that."

The others were all absolutely still, their eyes fixed on Jenkins. He had continued to study his hands as he spoke, but now he decisively placed them both, palms down, on the surface of the table and looked up.

"In any case, I don't envision our facing any such problem. I think that my discussions today have secured our funding for the moment and may have bought us some time as well. And time works in our favor. We may take Halloway this week, or it may be next week, but it will be soon. I know that at times it may seem discouraging to some of you, but we've all put extraordinary effort into this, and we can't allow ourselves to let up now, when we're on the verge of success. Halloway is completely alone. He's under enormous pressure day and night. He only has to be careless once, make one mistake. If we stay on top of him a little while longer, this will all be over.

"I know I've said this over and over, but it bears repeating: he has very limited choices; all of us have to try to put ourselves in his place and figure out what he's going to do, what he *can* do. You're the only people I have to call on. That's why I've kept every one of you fully informed about everything we've found out and everything we're trying to do. I realize how hard you're working and how frustrating it is, but I'm counting on you. Together we're going to succeed, and I don't have to tell you what that will mean for us."

Having finished his exhortation, Jenkins looked at Clellan, who began to speak.

"As you all know by now, I ran into Halloway on Monday. In addition, we have fairly good evidence of several other places he's been in the last two weeks, and a pretty clear picture of his movements is emerging. . . ."

Clellan related a more sober version of our encounter, indicating the location of the building on the first map. He had pictures of the apartment that they had decided I must have been staying in. Everything he said seemed correct. He indicated the location of two other buildings where there had been reports of activity in empty apartments. There were more photographs of apartments and floor plans. There were descriptions of what I had probably eaten and drunk, what my hours might have been. It all seemed quite accurate. Accurate and useful.

Clellan went on to relate the recovery of certain missing school reports and what they said about me. He described the odd telephone call made by a Howard Dickison to my office and the subsequent interview of Dickison, in which he had denied having made the call and had tried to disclaim any knowledge of me.

"Do you have the write-up of that interview there?" interrupted Jenkins. "I haven't had a chance to go over it."

Clellan leafed through a stack of papers, pulled out the report, and handed it over. Clellan began to describe what Gomez had contrived to trap me.

Jenkins was reading the report. His eyes would travel quickly down each page and then he would fold the stapled sheet back. When he got to the end, he went back and reread two passages, locating them immediately.

Gomez was now standing at the end of the table, showing everyone a section of a door. It contained some sort of battery-driven device that drove home a dead bolt and locked it in place. While he talked, Jenkins turned to Clellan and asked in a lowered voice whether he had the transcript of Dickison's telephone call to my office. Clellan leafed through a folder until he found what he was looking for. Holding his finger on the middle of a page, he slid it over to Jenkins, who took it and read it through intently. Gomez was pointing at the floor plan of an apartment. If you moved any of several interior doors in the apartment, the locking mechanism in the front door would be triggered. Jenkins opened the interview and began reading it again, the creases in his face contorting into a frown. Clellan was standing next to Gomez now. They were showing on a map the locations of the apartments that had already been fitted with Gomez's device and of those that were going to be fitted. It was information I very much wanted.

Jenkins put down the report of the interview and picked up the transcript of the call, reading it through from beginning to end once more. He narrowed his eyes and tapped his mouth with his forefinger. He looked up from the transcript to Clellan and interrupted him.

"Excuse me, but do we have the tape of this phone call or just this transcript?"

"Just the transcript. But I can have the tape sent over if you like." Clellan had an inquiring look on his face. He waited for Jenkins's reply.

"Yes, I think you'd better do that." Jenkins made a little gesture with his hand for Clellan and Gomez to continue. Gomez was holding some sort of transmitting device, but I was having trouble paying attention to what he was saying. Jenkins had laid both hands flat on the table and had closed his eyes in thought. Gomez glanced at him uneasily but continued to speak. The eyes opened, and Jenkins, ignoring Gomez and his speech, asked Clellan directly, "How do they send over these reports?" He placed his forefinger perpendicularly on the two reports lying on the table in front of him.

Clellan blinked uncomprehendingly. The room was silent.

Jenkins spoke again. "Do they mail them, or have one of their people deliver them, or what?"

Tyler answered the question. "We arrange for a commercial messenger service to pick everything up and bring it over. Their internal service is slow and unreliable. . . ."

Jenkins nodded. He was pressing two fingertips hard against his forehead so that the skin turned white under them, and his eyes were closed again. Gomez looked at him with a slightly uncertain expression and resumed speaking. Jenkins sat like that for several minutes. Then he opened his eyes suddenly and took a long, careful look around the room. He stood up and walked over to the door. I edged carefully along the wall until I was nearly next to him. He turned so that his back was to the door and he was facing the others. He spoke rapidly but very clearly.

"I want you to pay very careful attention to me. We've overlooked something important, and it is possible that it will have immediate consequences. By the way, are any of you carrying guns? Just out of curiosity, could you show them to me?"

The effect of this was that suddenly both Tyler and Morrissey, although they seemed a bit mystified, were holding guns in their hands.

"Good. Halloway may be right—"

I hit him as hard as I could just below the breastbone so that he made a nasty grunting sound and his head and shoulders jerked forward. I got one hand behind him and the other on the back of his neck and pitched him forward, away from the door, with as much force as I had. As I pulled open the door and charged out into the corridor, I saw Jenkins diving head first against the edge of the table, while the others stared at him astonished. Blood was pouring over his face, and I was running down the corridor and pulling open the door to the front office. As I entered the room, the two women looked up, startled to see the door swing violently open on its own. Someone was behind me. I heard a gunshot. The women were both screaming. Another gunshot. I pulled open the door out to the public corridor. Morrissey and then Tyler were in the front office with me now, both holding guns in their hands. When they saw the open door, they raced out through it into the hall.

I stepped aside to let them pass and moved quietly back across the room. I could hear Morrissey and Tyler charging around outside in the hallway. A moment later Jenkins appeared with Clellan and Gomez on either side steadying him. He was holding what looked like a shirt crumpled up against his face. Blood was dripping from it.

"My God! What happened?" one of the secretaries shrieked. "My God!"

Jenkins turned to the other secretary and asked calmly, "Do you have a pocket mirror?"

She fumbled in her bag. Gomez said, "We should go into the men's room." The other woman continued to chant, "My God. My God."

Jenkins took the mirror that was extended anxiously to him. He looked up at the open door to the hall and said, "Could you close that door, please?" He removed the wad of fabric from his face and began to study himself in the small mirror appraisingly. There was blood everywhere. It streamed down his face and dribbled over his shirt and necktie. He blotted his cheek with the crumpled cloth, and for a moment a patch of white bone appeared below his eye and was then flooded with blood again.

"You'll have to go to a doctor," Clellan said.

Jenkins nodded. He pushed the wad of material up against the side of his face again. It covered one eye. With the other, he peered around the room. The woman was still chanting, "My God. My God."

Morrissey and Tyler reappeared in the doorway looking out of breath and unhappy.

"Anything?" Jenkins asked.

The men both shook their heads. "We followed him into one of the stairways, but after that we lost him," said Morrissey. "It's no use. All the exit doors are kept unlocked, and it's only six flights to the lobby, anyway. Is there anything you want us to try?"

"No. Any indication that you might have hit him?"

"Can't tell."

"All right," said Jenkins. "Come inside and keep that door shut. And get those guns out of sight. Tyler, I'd like you to come with me to the hospital. Someone in the building may have heard the shots and called the police. Clellan, you stay here and deal with them. Also, get all the locks changed today. And then start looking for new office space. I want to be out of here as soon as possible. In the meantime, someone should be guarding that door at all times, including during the night. We have all our records here. I want to be sure that he doesn't get back in."

"My God, who was it? What happened?"

Jenkins turned toward the woman and asked her, "What did you see?"

"Nothing! I saw the doors fly open like anything, and there was nobody there, and then you all came running out and shooting."

Jenkins turned to the other woman.

"I didn't see anyone!" she said. "Who were you shooting at? What happened?"

There was a long silence. The men looked at each other. Then Clellan spoke, a little tentatively.

"He's very fast."

There was another little silence and Gomez spoke.

"*Fast?* Fast isn't hardly the word for him. Fast is not the half of it. He is one fast mother."

"Lord, he is fast," said Clellan. He turned to the woman who had been babbling. "You say you didn't get a real look at him? But would you say he was medium build, light brown hair?"

"I really didn't see him. I couldn't say anything for sure," she said uncertainly.

"Gomez," said Jenkins, "could you see that Jean and Carmen get home all right? As soon as possible. This has been very trying for them. Tyler, could you take these keys and lock up my office before we go?"

I was right down the corridor ahead of Tyler and through the open door into Jenkins's office. He pulled shut the door, fitted in the key, and turned the lock. It did not matter to me. There was a simple knob to unlock it from the inside.

Fifteen, thirty-seven, eighteen, five.

I waited several minutes to give Jenkins a chance to leave and then went to the safe. Three full turns to the right to fifteen. Back around all the way to thirty-seven. Eighteen. Five. The door clicked open. I pulled out a stack of photographs of the invisible building and then ran my hands over the shelves until I found the invisible objects. I slipped the ashtray, the bullet, and the screwdriver into my pocket. Just as I thought, Jenkins had kept something in reserve. On another shelf there was a pair of scissors. I pocketed them too.

I went over and crumpled up several sheets of paper on Jenkins's desk and, with my new pocket lighter, set them on fire. I added the photographs to the blaze, one by one.

There was a strong, acrid burning smell. I opened the window. Then I pulled open the desk drawers and the drawers of the filing cabinets, and emptied their contents onto the fire. Seeing that everything was well in hand, I unlocked the door and slipped into the corridor. The door into the front office was closed, so I went up to it and waited.

I could hear their voices on the other side. Clellan was talking on the telephone to a locksmith. Morrissey was saying that he was sure he smelled something burning. After a while Clellan said that actually he smelled something burning too. In a moment the door swung open and the two men charged through.

"It's in one of the offices!"

As soon as they passed, I slipped into the outer office, which was completely empty now. I unlatched the outer door and opened it. I could hear Clellan and Morrissey behind me.

"It must be in the Colonel's office!"

"Tyler locked it."

"Wait, try the doorknob."

"Jesus Christ!"

Since they were leaving me the free time, I set fires in the two wastepaper baskets in the front office and dumped whatever papers I could find into them.

"He must still be—"

"The main door!"

They were running back down the corridor towards me. Best to run now. It would be a difficult moment for Jenkins when they told him what I had done. I scurried down the stairs and out through the lobby into the street.

I HAD DONE JENKINS AS MUCH HARM AS I COULD CONTRIVE IN THE LIMITED time available to me, and I knew that I had made his situation far more precarious. But as I thought it through, I saw that I had done almost nothing to slow him down. They would have to abandon the apartments that Gomez had prepared for me, but they would set up others soon enough. And in fact, by destroying his invisible objects and making him more vulnerable, I had only made it that much more important that he catch me as soon as possible. At least for the present, I had only put more pressure on myself. They would now step up their efforts, and I had to step up mine if I hoped to say ahead of them.

The first thing I did was to begin reconnoitering buildings like the Olympic Tower and the Galleria, which are full of apartments belonging to South Americans and Europeans who are almost never in residence. There is never enough food in these places, and the building security is oppressive, but they might provide me with shelter through the worst of the winter.

My most urgent task, however, was to get Jonathan Crosby solidly established in the world, and to do that I had to find some way to open a bank account. It was not just that I had no way to get at the money accumulating in my brokerage account. Almost everything I wanted to do would require bank references. Without a bank reference I could not get a credit card or open a cash management account or even qualify for a department store charge account, much less enter into a real estate transaction. But a bank officer would not want to open an account without first meeting me in person. And when the bank ran a credit check and found that my entire financial history consisted of a brokerage account opened a few months earlier, the discomfort would become acute. If I showed the slightest reluctance to come in and say hello, they would be convinced that they were dealing with some major new drug dealer—and the banks will only do business with the old, established drug dealers.

The only way around all this was to have an introduction from someone the bank knew. I needed an accountant or lawyer who regularly handled other people's affairs and who already had the right relationship with a bank.

When I first came upon Bernie Schleifer, C.P.A., at a party in late September, he was manically extolling to a fellow guest the merits of a particularly bizarre tax shelter. The scheme itself seemed well outside the law as I understood it, but Bernie's attitude and ingenuity struck me immediately as just right for my needs. Furthermore, he was good-humored and likable, and I always assume that people like that will do better for you in tax audits—and tax audits would be an inevitable feature of any financial identity worth establishing. Also, I could see right off that Bernie was not a stickler for rules, which was an absolute requirement in my situation. In fact he is about as easy-going, when it comes to rules, as you can be without winding up in prison. It is true that Bernie wears a great deal of jewelry and drenches himself with a deplorable cologne, but as I only talk to him by telephone, these faults do not concern me.

"Hello, Bernie? My name is Jonathan Crosby. You may not remember, but I met you a couple of months ago at a party—it might have been given by someone named Selvaggio—does that ring a bell? Anyway, I remember being intrigued by a tax shelter opportunity you were describing that involved erecting windmills on historical buildings for some sort of double investment tax credit—"

"Oh sure, Jonathan, I remember now. How are you, anyway? I'm glad you called! We're not doing that particular deal anymore, for technical reasons, but I have something I think might really interest you. This is being syndicated by—"

"Actually, Bernie, I'm not so much looking for shelters. What I really want is someone who can handle all my personal bookkeeping and records and do my taxes."

"O.K., Jonathan, let's *do* it! When can we get together and go over everything? How about Friday?"

"Actually, Bernie, we can probably handle everything over the phone right now. That way I wouldn't waste too much of your time. Basically, I've just moved to New York this year. I've been living with my family in Switzerland and different places—"

"Tell me, Jonathan, are you a U.S. taxpayer?"

"Yes, that's right."

"Oh, I'm sorry to hear that, Jonathan." He said it as if I had told him I had leukemia. "Still, we may be able to work around it. How much of the year would you have to say you were here, if someone asked you?"

"I plan to be resident here pretty much permanently. And I am a U.S. citizen."

"Well, maybe we should approach this from another angle, Jonathan. Can you send me copies of your returns for the last two years? That'll give me an overall picture. By the way, are you keeping a diary of your expenses?"

"No, I'm not. I—"

"Well, that's not so important. You can always take care of that afterward, if you're audited, but I'll need the back returns."

"This will be my first return."

"Great! That'll give us a lot more flexibility. And you might be able to let the state returns slide for a while as long—"

"Actually, Bernie. All I've got here is some short-term capital gains. Under a hundred thousand for the year. And I'm not employed. In fact, I don't think there should even be a Schedule C."

"Don't worry, Jonathan. You'll have a Schedule C. We'll find something. And there's still plenty of time to get you into some shelters. I have—"

"Bernie, let me just give you a little background on my situation. My family all live in Switzerland, and they have some fairly substantial assets outside the country, and I think some of those assets may actually be mine, or intended for me or something. Maybe they're in trust. I'm sure it's all perfectly all right, but still, I'd rather not do anything that would get the IRS interested in me or my family—especially not just to save a few dollars. I'd rather do everything according to the rules and not attract any attention."

"I get you, Jonathan. On the stuff out front you want to pay every penny you owe—go strictly by the book. There are situations where that's a really smart strategy, although it can be pretty costly. But it could work. Let me just make a note of that one. But one thing you're sure right about is offshore assets. We have a number of foreign clients in the office, and we're very familiar with these problems."

I had made a visit to his office, and I knew that he did in fact have a number of foreign clients, some of them surprisingly respectable.

"That's great, Bernie. Do you mind my asking what your fees will be?"

"Jonathan, of course not! I only bill you for the time I actually put in. It's a hundred dollars an hour, which is pretty standard."

Having seen Bernie's billing, I knew that it was not standard for Bernie, anyway. At $100 an hour, I would be his best client, but, under the circumstances, that would be an excellent thing for both of us.

"That sounds very reasonable, Bernie. You know, I'm kind of busy with a lot of different personal things and traveling a lot, and I think I'd like to have your office just handle all my financial stuff for me. I'm going to have all my brokerage statements sent to your office, if that's all right."

At $100 an hour, it would presumably be all right. I gave him Willy Winslow's name and number and told him to expect a call. Then I called Willy and told him to call Bernie and to change the mailing address on my account.

(315)

I waited a few days to be sure that Bernie and Willy had chatted about me and then called back.

"Jonathan, baby! I'm glad you called! I've been going over your account with your broker, what's his name, and you know, you've been having a pretty good year."

"I've been quite lucky."

"We've got to get you into some shelters right away! The end of the year is coming up, and you're going to be paying fifty cents on the dollar in taxes. It's like throwing money out the window! I want to send you something I've worked up that could be just the thing for you. It's a newsletter start-up. Basically, you've got the thing on an accrual basis and you treat the unused portion of each subscription as a liability, so no matter how fast income increases, the liabilities have to increase faster, and it all passes straight through to the limiteds. The one I'd like to put you into is an economic forecasting letter—it's very good. I have this guy I work with out on Long Island who writes them—"

"Bernie, it sounds very interesting, but I don't think I'd really want to invest in an economic forecasting newsletter."

"He's also about to start putting out one on fly-fishing in—"

"Bernie, I really don't—"

"And I have another thing here—this isn't for everyone, but it's an attractive deal—soft-core video production. This is very different from what you're used to seeing here in New York. This stuff is produced for the midwestern market. You don't actually see any genitals. More tasteful, and I'll tell you, it's still surprisingly good. I mean, you look at these movies, and who wants to see some guy's schlong projected on a screen eleven feet long? In a way, it's almost better not to—"

"Bernie, I think we're in agreement on that. But the reason I called is that it suddenly occurred to me that I hadn't paid you any retainer. Do you think two thousand dollars would be fair?"

"You know, Jonathan, that might be a good idea, come to think of it."

"Well, then it suddenly struck me that I don't even have a checking account here in New York for things like this. You don't by any chance know a good bank I could use, do you?"

"Sure, Jonathan. We keep a lot of our client accounts here at Mechanics Trust."

"Well, that would be great if you could arrange it all for me. I could have Willy send over a check for ten thousand dollars to open the account, if you think that would be enough."

"More than enough, Jonathan. I'll set up everything, and then you can just stop by the bank and sign the signature cards. Let me give you the address and the name of the bank officer we work with—"

"Gee, if there's anything to sign, why don't you just send it to me here at my uncle's apartment. You know, now that I think of it, I'd rather have you get all the bank statements and everything too. And put your name on the account so your office could pay bills for me and so on. Would that be all right?"

"Jonathan, leave it to me. We'll take care of everything."

By the end of the week I had my checking account. In a few weeks, when the printed checks arrived, Bernie would mail me one book, which I would hide in a storage closet in the Crosbys' apartment. At about the same time, I would receive my first credit card. Jonathan Crosby was nearly a person.

THEN, ONE EVENING IN EARLY OCTOBER, AS I WAS WALKING UP CENTRAL Park West, I saw a girl I had known once, not very well. Ellen something—it would come to me. Ellen Nicholson. Almost the only thing I remembered about her was that she had been very attractive, and now I was abruptly seized with an awful longing for her—whether because she seemed familiar or because she seemed beautiful, I could not say. But when you go for months without speaking to another human being except over the telephone, and for days without speaking at all, it becomes difficult to think clearly about the people and things drifting across your field of vision. The emotional contours begin to blur, and it is not so easy to distinguish between loneliness and lust.

There was no point, because I could not talk to her or touch her, but I followed her for several blocks anyway. She wore a sort of jersey dress and nothing much else, and I stayed alongside her, so that I could watch her breasts move as she walked and the fabric stretching across her thighs with each stride. In the middle of a block she stopped in front of an awning and smiled.

"Hi!" she said. "I didn't expect to see you guys at this thing." A man and a woman came up to us, also smiling.

"Hi, Ellen! Still all alone?"

"Eating my heart out. You guys *still* married?"

All three of them turned into the building, and a doorman sent them to the tenth floor. I could see that it would be a party, and while they rode up on the elevator, I hiked up the stairs. It took me much longer, so that by the time I pushed through the door of the apartment, they were already long inside, and Ellen was being hugged and pawed by an enormous man in blue jeans and a tweed jacket. Aside from her, I did not see anyone I knew. Most of the guests were younger than I, and some of them looked vaguely academic. You could tell at once that they all knew each other well. They had probably all gone to the same college not many years ago. I wondered what I was doing there.

As a matter of principle, I made a tour of the apartment, pausing a while in the kitchen to sip some white wine—probably too much. The noise in the other rooms was overwhelming. People in these situations do not notice how excited they have become or that they are shouting rather than speaking to each other. It was probably a good party, but really it had nothing to do with me, and I wandered back out into one of the rooms full of people, intending to make my way to the front door.

But then, glancing a last time over the crowd, I happened to see Alice. It is always difficult to say why, in these situations, you are suddenly so struck by someone—there are attractive people everywhere—but I started at once through the room to her without giving the matter a moment's rational thought. She was tall, in her late twenties, with strawberry blond hair, and she wore a silk dress that clung to her and spread open as she moved, in a way that was almost painful for me. Standing in a semicircle around her were several men, who seemed to be staring at her as much as talking to her, and whenever she spoke to one of them, she would bestow on him a dazzling smile which seemed full of warmth but which included two sharp canines that gave it a slightly feral quality at the same time. She moved about animatedly in their midst as she talked, and when I came up, she had just stepped out of her shoes so that she stood there barefoot. Because it was the only way to get close to her, I walked around the wall of other gawking admirers and stood behind her.

"It seems awfully rude of you, Donald," she said good-naturedly, "to say these things against my grandmother, when you don't even know her."

"I'm not saying anything whatever against your grandmother." The man who spoke was dressed in khakis and a blazer. He had long hair and, despite his youth, a pedantic, professorial manner. "I'm only saying that you can't go about asserting the existence of ghosts."

"But why not?" she asked ingenuously.

"Because there is no satisfactory procedure for verifying or refuting such an assertion."

"Well, you could talk to my grandmother."

"I . . . With all due respect to your grandmother, I have to weigh her reports of sense-data she has experienced and the interpretation she has put on them against the reported experiences of a multitude of other human beings, and I may have all sorts of reasons for giving one person's reports more weight than another's—"

"Yes, that's right. In the case of my grandmother, you have my word. She's the most honest person I know of. And the nicest. It isn't at all some subtle question about interpreting sensory data or anything like that, you know. She's perfectly clear about what she saw. Either she's telling the truth or she isn't." The smile seemed to have some mischief in it, but the eyes were wide open and bright blue with innocence. Who knows what evil lurks in the hearts of men? Much less of women.

"It has nothing whatever to do with your grandmother. It has to do—"

"But it's my grandmother we're talking about. And anyway, why shouldn't there be ghosts and all sorts of things, just because you've never seen or touched them?"

Another of the men, who was wearing a grey pinstriped suit and rocking forward and back a bit drunkenly, smiled maliciously.

"Yes, Donald, why this abusive attack on Alice's poor old granny? What's she ever done to you?"

Donald, knitting his brow with irritation, ignored the other man and continued in the logical track of his argument. "Because I have never needed the notion of a ghost to explain any sense-data I have experienced and because I can only posit existence for those entities necessary to the most economical and predictively powerful explanation of the sense-data I experience."

"Why?" asked Alice, smiling beautifully.

"Because it's an underlying principle of all rational thought. It's a precondition—"

"You know, I'll bet you're a Capricorn," said Alice. "You think like a Capricorn."

From the annoyance that flickered momentarily in Donald's face, I decided that he probably was a Capricorn—whatever that might be.

"Anyway," Alice continued, "what would you do if a ghost appeared to you now? I mean, with incontrovertible sense-data and all that? Suppose it stepped up and gave you a good pinch so there wouldn't be any doubt?" She gave Donald's cheek a playful pinch, causing him to blush brilliantly.

For all Donald's pompous certitude, his reasoning was absolutely correct, and I felt a bit sorry for him. Apparently, no one had ever explained to him that reason does not win arguments. Or for that matter, that winning arguments is not everything—or even much of anything. He should have counted himself lucky to be standing there basking in Alice's smile.

"Well," Donald replied, "I would be quite amazed, to begin with. I would have to extend and reorder the categories and concepts with which I think, in order to accommodate sense-data that were inconsistent with—"

"So you see my point of view is much more useful and flexible. If a ghost pinched me, I wouldn't have to be amazed at all, and I wouldn't have to rearrange a thing, or—"

I have never before or since pinched a woman's bottom, and I am not precisely sure what moved me to it on this occasion—whether it was to vindicate Donald's unfairly discredited argument, whether it was the attraction of her hips moving beneath the silk as she incessantly shifted her weight, or whether it was only the irresistible opportunity offered by the course of the conversation—but I reached out and took a fold of silk and flesh between my thumb and forefinger and held it for a long delicious moment.

Alice stopped speaking, and her entire body stiffened, especially the bit of it in my fingers, which I now released. Then with an effort she resumed.

"I wouldn't be amazed . . ." She was looking at Donald resentfully, as if he were guilty of employing an unfair tactic. She looked down at his hands, which, as he was standing directly opposite her, could not possibly be culpable. Her gaze turned uncertainly to the men on either side of her.

This is wrong in every way, I thought. I should not be doing this. But lust and the logic of the situation drove me on. With my two hands I gripped her upper arms, pressing them against her sides. Her gaze traveled over the hands of the men standing around her. All in plain view, holding drinks or just hanging there harmlessly. She continued shakily.

"There are more things in heaven and earth . . ."

She turned about suddenly, and I withdrew my hands. No one there. Nothing. She turned back to face the others with a look of vaguely defiant puzzlement. I gently took hold of her arms again. She looked down at her right arm where my fingers made little indentations in her flesh, and she turned quite pale. I leaned over and kissed her exquisite neck. She shivered.

"Are you all right, Alice?" one of the men was saying.

"When you say something exists," Donald was going on, "what you're really saying is that it—"

"Do you want to sit down for a moment?"

"No . . . . No. I have to go . . ."

"Do you want me to get you into a cab? Or take you home? I could—"

"No. . . . I'm . . . I'm meeting someone now. I have to go."

She walked straight out of the apartment, as if in a trance. I stayed right with her, my hand on her arm.

"Bye, Alice!" someone was shouting. "Where are you off to?"

"Is anything the matter?"

Alice kept going without looking back or answering. When the door closed behind us in the corridor, I turned her around so that she faced me and kissed her. She was utterly limp in my arms. Then, tentatively, she raised her arms and felt with her hands to see whether there was indeed some more or less human form there. Finding one, she folded her arms around me uncertainly.

I kissed her forehead.

"Oh God," she said, "I can't believe this is happening to me."

I kissed her again on the mouth and suddenly she clutched me tight. I held her to me, feeling the entire length of her body, her thighs, her breasts, her ribs, pressed hard against me. I too could not believe this was happening to me.

Down the corridor I heard an elevator door slide open.

"We have to go," I said.

"Oh my God!" she said, and I realized that this was the first time she had heard me speak. It seemed to startle her more than anything else that had happened. I put my arm around her and felt her trembling. As I walked her toward the elevator, she kept looking at me—or through me.

"Don't speak to me in front of other people. You have to act as if I weren't there."

She nodded dumbly. Someone passed us going down the corridor, but neither of us paid any attention. I never even considered walking back down the stairs. I didn't care what risks I took now. I pressed the elevator button, and when it came we got into the empty car together. A woman got in at the seventh floor, but Alice went on staring straight ahead in a daze.

What could she imagine? What had she imagined standing there at that party and feeling the invisible hands touch her mysteriously, then grasp her, pinning her arms to her sides? Feeling the mouth, somehow alive in the transparent air, kiss her neck. And what could she have thought when she fled, only to feel the inexplicable presence following at her side, seizing her in the hall, the unseen force crushing her, the phallus swelling up against her, the tongue pushing into her mouth. And then when it began to command her. "We have to go." A voice out of the air. "Don't speak to me."

We walked through the lobby together and out into the street, both of us half delirious. I still had my arm around her, and I kept looking at her. She was extraordinarily beautiful. I turned and kissed her there in the street, and she must have looked quite odd with her head tilted back and sideways and her mouth strangely flattened and gaping open, because there was suddenly a doorman beside us, saying, "Are you all right, Miss?" I took her by the arm and led her down the street.

"Do you live alone?" I asked.

She nodded and then said. "Oh God. I can't believe this."

I kissed her again and she ran her hands around my body—as much to verify again that I was actually there as out of any passion.

"You should hail a cab," I said softly.

We are not going to get into a discussion of the ethics of all this. If we did, I would be relying mainly on the argument that consenting adults can do as they please, although you might want to raise the question of whether it would be strictly applicable here and whether her consent could be described as informed. You might argue that I was taking advantage of my situation—although I had to date found precious few opportunities to take advantage of it—or that I was only interested in my own gratification and I did not even know her, but the last argument would not be pertinent for long, and besides, Alice was very beautiful. And my desire was enormous and just about the only thing in my mind.

When the taxi stopped, out of habit I opened the door for her. Fortunately, the driver did not notice, and it seemed to add to the dreamlike quality of the whole episode for Alice. I climbed in after her and pulled the door shut. The driver turned and waited and then finally had to ask Alice where she wanted to go. As soon as she had told him, I leaned over and kissed her again. She moaned and wrapped her arms around me, and I completely lost sight of where I was.

The driver—some time later I became aware of his eyes, but I could not bring myself to care—watched in the mirror as the girl in the back seat writhed about in the most extraordinary positions, twisting over to one side and extending her arms up into the air. Her mouth opened strangely. She stuck her tongue out and twisted it around grotesquely. Her bosom seemed to flatten inexplicably as she writhed. She panted and grunted. Somehow the front of her dress pulled open and a breast was exposed and deformed itself, assuming one shape after another. Her dress was up almost around her waist, and her legs spread open, and her hips tilted and twisted. She was emitting a succession of little moaning sounds, and when we pulled up in front of Alice's building and I turned and looked at the driver, I saw that his eyes were wide open and his face was contorted with some unusual combination of sexual excitement and terror.

I pulled Alice's handbag down out of sight behind the back of the seat, found a five dollar bill, and shoved it into the tray. Alice gathered herself more or less together as the doorman appeared, and I pulled her out of the cab, so that she appeared to lurch impossibly across the sidewalk and through the lobby into the elevator. I was beyond caring what kind of impression we made. I did not for that matter care if this was the last night of my life. All I wanted was this woman, right away, and I might have made love to her in the elevator or the corridor, but somehow we made it into her apartment.

When she saw her clothes lifting off her body and flying across the room, she began half laughing, half sobbing. "Oh God. Oh God." As for me, I almost wept to feel her smooth skin under my hands—her breasts, the hardened nipples, her buttocks, her thighs. I kissed her body everywhere. And when finally I spread her legs apart—it was the most exquisite moment of my life—and pushed slowly into her, she was half hysterical, quivering with fear or pleasure or amazement, until she began to explode,

(323)

her hips and loins convulsing rhythmically. She was emitting screams or sobs and holding me as tightly as she could. Mind and body, I felt like a bomb bursting into oblivion, into a thousand irretrievable fragments.

I found, eventually, that I was lying dazed upon a bed, and Alice lay next to me, weeping softly.

"Who are you?" she asked through her sobs.

"No one," I said, for some reason imagining that this would comfort her.

Her sobbing intensified. I laid an invisible hand upon her breast to soothe her. She gasped. She propped herself up on one elbow and, with an anguished look upon her face, stared at the space I occupied. There was a light on somewhere across the room, and she could clearly see that she could see nothing.

She reached over and began to run her hand over my body to verify again that it was all really true. And as her hand slid over my groin it collided with the rigid protrusion. She started skittishly, then grasped it, and in a moment I was over her and inside her again, and we were rocking slowly into each other. I could see her looking at herself, at her knees up in the air and her hips tilting forward. She wrapped her legs around the small of my back, and she watched herself, opened up, rolling forward and back. She got her hands around my head and suddenly found my mouth and began kissing me frantically. What could she have thought? Mastered by the brute blood of the air. Or whatever. I cannot remember that that pleasure ever subsided, but it must have, because I remember it starting up again, and we went on and on until we lost track of everything.

I N THE MORNING I AWOKE TO THE SOUND OF ALICE STRAIGHTENING UP THE apartment and picking up the clothing she had been wearing the night before. It was the most miraculous awakening I had known since the morning I had discovered my invisibility. There before me I saw, almost naked in underpants and brassiere, a beautiful woman, with whom I had made love just a few hours ago. Yesterday it would have seemed inconceivable that I should ever again enjoy such a moment. I would have liked to speak to her, but we had said hardly anything to each other the night before, and finding myself unable to think of anything sensible to say now, I lay there in silence, watching her.

From the way her skin glistened, I decided that she must have just bathed. I was struck by the practicality with which she busied herself about the apartment so soon after what must have been the most bizarre experience of her life. But as she moved around the room, she kept looking over at me—or rather at the bed covers where they molded the lower half of my body—with an anxious frown. She hung up the dress she had worn the evening before and came out of the closet with another, which she pulled on, depriving me of the sight of her long, naked legs. The dress had buttons up the back, so that she had to reach behind to fasten them, arching her breasts forward, tilting her head, and unfocusing her eyes the way people do when they are concentrating on a manual task they cannot see. She stepped into her shoes, walked up to the bed, and stood next to me, looking down at the mound of bed covers and the depression in the mattress. She put out her hand uncertainly, as if deciding whether to touch me or not, whether to assure herself once more that it was all true.

"Good morning," I said finally.

She started. "Good morning. I thought you might be awake. How did you sleep? I mean, you *do* sleep, don't you? . . . Of course you do. I know that."

"I slept very well, thank you. . . . How did you sleep?"

"Very well. . . . Thank you."

The conversation did not seem to be taking flight. There was a long, uncomfortable pause, during which I lay there supine, staring up at her, feeling quite awkward, and she stood staring uneasily down at me—roughly at my sternum, as it chanced.

"My name is Alice Barlow," she ventured finally. "Maybe you already knew that."

Without thinking, I started to tell her my name.

"I'm Nick— Just Nick, really. I only use the first name now." For some reason my name seemed to distress her. She opened her mouth and hesitated, as if she were having difficulty formulating her question.

"What's going to happen to me?"

I struggled to understand what she might mean by the question, but the only thing that occurred to me was that she was somehow concerned about possible gynecological consequences of the night before.

"Happen to you?" I asked inanely.

She seemed extraordinarily nervous. She was looking away from me now.

"I mean. . . . It sounds ridiculous. . . . But then it *is* ridiculous—in some way or other. . . . I mean, have I forfeited my soul or something?"

"Oh, no, no, no," I hastened to reassure her. "Certainly not . . . or, actually, I have no idea—I'm not very well informed theologically. . . . But only in the normal way—if at all."

A nervous smile flickered over her face. "Then you're not . . . I know it sounds silly, but the whole thing is so . . . I mean, you're not the devil, or anything like that?"

"Good heavens, no." It flitted across my mind that by my honesty I was giving up a valuable advantage: for those who believe in these things, the devil, despite his faults, has some real stature in the world—and a certain romantic appeal, furthermore. "Not at all. I'm just like everybody else."

This concession evidently struck her as preposterous, because she laughed, and although the laugh had an edge of hysteria, it also seemed to contain a measure of relief. "Are you? Just like everybody else?" Her laughter began again, and she seemed to be having difficulty checking it. Tears began to form in the corners of her eyes.

"Well, of course there are differences. . . ."

"Are there really? You know I *thought* I noticed something. . . ." Still laughing, she sat down on the edge of the bed and put her hand on my knee.

"You know, I don't think you should be taking this so lightly," I said. "For all you know, I still might inflict some terrible curse or suck out all your blood."

"Or turn back into a frog," she suggested. She pulled the sheet up to my shoulders and smoothed it over my body so that my trunk took form. Her expression grew suddenly serious again. "Who *are* you? . . . *What* are you? If you don't mind my putting it like that."

The question, although perfectly obvious and inevitable, somehow caught me unprepared, and my mind raced in complete confusion. What should I tell her? Nothing. I didn't dare tell her anything. The first rule of survival for me was never to tell anyone anything.

"There's really nothing interesting to say about that. I *am* actually just like anyone else. . . ." What sort of answer would satisfy her? "That is to say, I exist in a different material modality. . . ."

"I see," said Alice—which startled me, since I didn't.

"You mean you were here before? I mean inhabiting a material human body, or however it works?"

"Yes. That's exactly right. I used to have the same sort of body as everyone else."

"And you've come back."

"It's more that I'm still here." By the skin of my teeth.

I reached out and ran my hand along her leg. She got to her feet again but remained standing next to the bed.

"Is there something you have to do here? I mean, before you can be released from the world?"

"Not that I know of. Just the ordinary things, I suppose . . . like everyone else." This discussion made me uncomfortable. "If I'm careful and don't make any very serious mistakes, I may manage, with luck, to grow old and die."

I sat up and put my hands around her right leg, just above the knee, sliding them up over the thigh and pushing up the hem of her dress. She shuddered but remained standing there.

"Actually, there *are* things I am compelled to do," I said.

I pulled her over onto me, and I heard one of her shoes clatter to the floor.

"I can't. I have to go to work."

But she made no effort to move. The full length of her body lay pressing on mine, and I could feel her heart pounding. I ran my hands up the backs of her thighs and over her buttocks. I kissed her and heard the other shoe tumble onto the floor. With a shudder, she kissed me. Her hands began exploring my body, and we made love.

Afterwards, she sighed, and then laughed.

"No one will ever believe this."

I was suddenly filled with dread. This had all been a mistake.

"Alice."

"Yes?"

What should I say to her? A threat would be best. I was still in a position to inspire some terror. I should tell her that if she ever said a word about me to anyone, she would be struck dead. The earth would open up and swallow her.

"You must absolutely never speak of me to anyone. No one can know about my coming here."

"Why not?"

"I . . . It's not something I can talk about." Somehow, despite my good intentions, this was not taking form as much of a threat. "I'm asking you not to say anything at all about me to anyone. It's very important."

"If you don't want me to say anything, of course I won't. But can't you give me some idea what it's all about? Why are you here at all?"

There was a long silence, during which I again tried desperately to think what I could tell her. I suddenly realized that I wanted to tell her everything. Odd the way physical intimacy engenders these confessional urges. Well, what difference would it make if I did tell her? I would never see her again. I certainly could not risk ever coming back here. This had all been an utterly extraordinary incident, a freakish, improbable turn of events that should never have occurred and would certainly never occur again. There would surely, the way my life had to be lived, never be anyone else to whom I would want to tell anything. Still, you have to be rational. What could I safely say to her? Nothing.

She climbed out of the bed and then turned back and looked down where I lay, her eyebrows raised skeptically.

"Do you mind if I ask you something?"

"Of course not," I said—uncomfortably, since that is a question to which the true answer is probably always yes.

"Will I see you again? . . . I don't mean see you. I mean, will I hear from you, or do you just fade into the sunset—or wherever it is you fade to?"

I was floundering in panic.

"I don't know. . . . It's not entirely within my control. . . ." The one thing I knew was that I could not possibly come back here. "Of course I hope so. I'll have to see." It was the sort of risk I must absolutely not take. I had to keep moving.

She laughed, and her laughter seemed to contain a note of mockery. "You know, you're right. You *are* like everybody else."

"You don't understand," I objected. "It's not at all that—"

"You needn't worry. You're not the sort of person a girl is going to pin all her hopes on—not based on the first impression, anyway. There's a kind of elusive quality to you, if you want to know. I was just curious. And anyhow, the question is built into the female soul: *Will he call?* It's an involuntary mental reflex. It doesn't mean a thing."

She had disappeared into her closet, and now she reemerged in a fresh dress. "In fact, usually you're better off if he doesn't call," she added.

She stood before a mirror, drawing a brush through her hair with long, fierce strokes. She looked neither at her own reflection nor toward me but gazed instead out the window, so that I had a view of her profile, which, although for the moment expressionless, seemed altogether perfect to me. During the—for me, at least—uncomfortable silence, I tried to contrive a reply.

"I can't imagine that anyone could ever have failed to call you."

She glanced skeptically in my direction, but I thought she might be blushing.

"Maybe you're some kind of alien. You probably ought to go out and get to know some of the other folks in the brave new world."

"I find that lately I'm having a lot of trouble getting to know people."

"You seemed to be managing last night."

The corners of her mouth turned up to form the beginnings of an ironic smile. She was still not altogether comfortable addressing these looks to someone she could not see, and I watched as her eyes searched for some sign of me. She put the brush down and smoothed her dress over her body. The thing was—if only I could think clearly about it—that no matter what calculations I made of the risk and no matter what decisions I took, I was, beyond any question, going to come back here.

"It's difficult for me to call, actually, but I thought that I might come back here this evening if you're free." Having said that, I found that I felt suddenly quite elated.

"I'll be home a little after six."

She had turned her full dazzling smile on me. She walked over and, after inadvertently flattening my nose in the search for my face, kissed me once on the lips. Then, as she drew back and turned to leave, she reached out and touched my chest with her fingertips.

"Amazing," she said with a little laugh.

As she went out the door, I called after her, "Remember not to say anything about me."

I waited several minutes to be sure that she was gone before going into the kitchen. I could not risk letting her see my digestive tract in operation. I had not eaten anything in thirty-six hours, and I greedily devoured several slices of bread. I knew that I was taking an unconscionable risk remaining here at all, much less making myself visible, but I was finding it difficult in my present mood to worry about anything.

I went through the apartment, taking an almost physical pleasure in touching Alice's possessions. An open closet full of dresses, blouses, skirts, underwear. Skis. Tennis racket. The walls of the bedroom were covered with unframed sketches and paintings, many of them signed with the initials A.B. I was startled by the almost photographic quality of the draftsmanship. I had somehow thought that people no longer learned to draw that way. There were a few landscapes and some full human figures, but most of the sketches were studies of isolated objects or anatomical fragments.

At the end of the living room, by the door to the balcony, I found a drafting table. To it was pinned a pencil drawing which appeared to be an absolutely precise re-creation of the view out the adjacent window. And yet the effect was altogether different—more benign somehow, almost humorous. Perhaps it was some trick of perspective that I did not understand. Perhaps it was only my mood.

One wall of the room was covered from floor to ceiling by shelves filled with enormous art books. The books without pictures took up less than a single shelf, and looking through the titles you could see every course Alice had ever taken in college outside the art history department. Chase and Phillips, Liddell & Scott. Cambridge Shakespeare. *Ulysses. The Collected Poems of W. B. Yeats.* I pulled out a book. The name Alice Barlow was written along the top edge of the flyleaf in italic script. *Stately, plump.* Notes neatly lettered into the margins everywhere with a drafting pen. *I am the boy who can enjoy invisibility. . . . Yes.*

Once my stomach was clear again, I went out and walked to midtown in such an exultant mood that I wanted to stop the other people in the street and speak to them, tell them what a pleasure it was to be among them on that beautiful autumn day. I spent several hours in the offices of a law firm, learning about the proposed acquisition of an insurance company in Kansas, but finally I decided that I could not stand there any longer in silence, and I went outside and walked back uptown. Mainly just to talk to someone, I called up Willy and discussed my portfolio. Even he could not undermine my mood. On the contrary, he only reminded me that as Jonathan Crosby I was growing more substantial by the day, with a net worth now over $80,000. I was barely able to restrain myself from making some trades. Never buy anything when you are in a good mood.

I was outside the door to Alice's apartment before six, expecting to wait for her there in the corridor, but I could hear her already inside unpacking groceries in the kitchen. When I knocked, she came and looked through the peephole. Seeing no one there, she opened the door and kissed me.

"You don't walk through walls?" Her voice echoed through the hall. I put a finger on her mouth.

"You have to be more discreet," I whispered.

"Are you married or something?" Her voice was a bit mangled because of my finger, but still loud and bright. I pushed her back into the apartment.

"You're married to someone right on this floor?"

I got the door shut behind us.

"Alice, this is serious. No one must know anything about me."

"I'm sorry. I forgot. I'm not a secretive person." She ran her hands up through my hair and then down my body, as if to make sure that I was entirely there. I felt her left hand encounter the gun in my pocket. Her expression clouded momentarily, but she kissed me, and I embraced her, feeling her body pressed against mine and her breath on my neck.

"I went and bought all sorts of food for dinner, but then I realized I don't even know if you eat."

I hesitated. Should I let her see what happened when I ate?

"Yes, I eat. Not very much."

"Then why don't you open the wine while I get dinner ready."

As she prepared the meal, she kept glancing over at the bottle tilting at impossible angles on the tabletop and at the corkscrew wrenching itself violently into the cork.

"It's just incredible," she said excitedly, and she came over and ran her hands all over me again. We embraced again for several minutes, and I ran my hands over her. I was so intoxicated by her physical presence that there hardly seemed any point, but I made myself let go of her and poured some wine into the glasses. Then, full of apprehension, I let her watch the first sip of white wine going down.

"Amazing!" she said. She seemed genuinely delighted by the sight. "Drink some more!"

She ran her hand down my chest in front of the esophagus.

"It's absolutely magical."

And when later I ate my first bite of the pasta, she was unaccountably even more entranced.

"Incredible! You can see everything! You know, you would be marvelous in an anatomy class."

"That is unfortunately true," I replied glumly.

"Would you mind eating a little more? God, it's beautiful! You can see it disappearing before your eyes. What's happening exactly? I mean is it being absorbed into some non-material dimension or something? What *is* happening?"

"Nothing. . . . I just have an unusual metabolism. I can't discuss it. To tell you the truth, I find it a revolting spectacle."

But Alice did not, not at all. She watched with fascination as I absorbed one bit of the material world after another, unable to take her eyes off my digestive tract. She might have been staring at a particularly splendid tropical fish tank.

Then, abruptly, she furrowed her brow.

"Why do you have a gun?"

"Oh . . . that's not anything. It just happened to be there when . . . I just happen to have it."

"Nick, is it true what you said this morning, that you have to die again?"

"As far as I know," I said uncomfortably.

"What *do* you know exactly? Are you in touch with other ghosts?"

"I am definitely not in touch with other ghosts."

"Well, is 'ghost' the right word for what you are? I mean, what are you exactly?"

I felt again the temptation to confide in her, to tell her everything. Too dangerous. I saw now that it had been wrong to come back at all. Tomorrow I would really have to leave for good. I could not afford to take these risks.

"Does it matter what I am? I could be anything. The Spirit of Christmas Past, a visitor from Venus, the devil—"

"I have to admit to a twinge of disappointment that you weren't the devil. That would have been the most wickedly romantic, although I suppose the terror and the despair would be awfully wearing in the long run."

"Or I might be like anyone else—a bookkeeper who happened to fall asleep under a defective sun lamp or who stumbled into the wrong vat on a tour of a chemical plant."

"Well, that wouldn't be very romantic at all. I think I definitely prefer you as a ghost. You said you had lived in the material world before in a normal human body. Isn't that—"

"Yes, probably it's best to think of me as a ghost."

"Well, what can you tell me? I mean, about what happens when we die. Or what there is beyond the material world."

"I can't tell you anything. I don't *know* anything."

"Oh!" she gasped. "That's such an extraordinary sensation—to feel a hand suddenly inside my clothing. Oh God."

Buttons began to unbutton themselves.

"I know exactly what you are, you know."

"You do?"

"You're an incubus."

"I am not an incubus."

"It's perfectly obvious that you're an incubus. An incubus is a spirit that—"

"I know exactly what an incubus is—or would be, if there were such a thing—and incubatory functions regrettably constitute only a very small part of my activities."

"Oh yes? Well, you seem pretty vague on the rest of your activities. In fact, incubusing seems to be the only thing you know anything at all about. Ohh! You see? That's *just* the sort of thing an incubus does."

> *I am the boy*
> *Who can enjoy*
> *Invisibility.*

I HAD ABSOLUTELY RESOLVED TO LEAVE FOR GOOD IN THE MORNING, BUT somehow I found myself staying with Alice again that night, and the next night as well, until eventually, without there ever having been any decision taken or even any discussion of the matter, we both took for granted that I was living there. I told myself constantly that I should not be staying in one place and that I should above all not be putting myself at the mercy of another person. On the other hand, I also told myself that really I was safer now than before. I no longer had to worry each day about where I would sleep that night or whether I was walking into some trap prepared for me by Gomez. At least for the time being, I would be much harder to find. So long as Alice didn't say anything to give me away. But although I remember that the question gnawed at me continually, it seems perfectly obvious, looking back at it now, that I could not possibly have done anything other than go on living with Alice.

She worked in the East Thirties as a commercial artist, and when the weather was good—and I remember it as a particularly clear, brilliant autumn—we would go out together in the morning, walking from her building on York Avenue down through the East Side to her studio. She would bump into me or lean against me as we walked, to confirm my presence, and she would frequently break into a smile.

"It's so amazing. I mean walking down the street with you like this without anyone knowing."

"Alice, you can't talk to me in public like this."

"It's such an incredible secret. No one would ever believe it."

"Just be sure you don't give anyone the chance."

I would usually spend those days in law offices or investment banks or corporate headquarters, performing my securities research, if it is fair to call it that. We kept a key hidden under the edge of the hall carpet so that I could always get back into the apartment, and when it rained I would stay home reading and listening to music—without ever having to worry about being heard by the neighbors.

Alice would pick up groceries on the way home from work. This was the first time since I had been driven from my own apartment that I had been free from constant hunger: suddenly I could eat and drink whatever I liked and as much as I liked rather than what I happened to find and could digest quickly. With Alice's help I began to learn how to cook, and together we prepared elaborate dinners each night. I had Alice buy the most powerful sun lamp she could find, and I installed it in the bathroom so that I could go in and burn myself clear again whenever I needed to.

Those evenings we spent together in her apartment were the most pleasant I had known in my new life—or in my old life, come to think of it—and it seemed to me that I had everything I could ever have wished for. It is impossible for me to explain how wonderful it was just to be able to talk to another human being again. I would spend hours drawing Alice out about her childhood, her parents, her friends, her work, her opinions on popular music or Baroque painting or whatever I could find that she had an opinion about. And although for my part I was more interested in the intimacy than in the information itself, looking back on it now, I can see that it must have all seemed quite strange to Alice, as if she were the subject of some mysterious inquisition.

And the fact that I would not tell her anything about myself must have made it seem stranger still. It was bad enough that Alice knew about me at all and that I seemed, against my own better judgment, to be staying with her. But I could at least be careful not to give away any more about myself than I had to, and whenever she would ask me about my former life, I would immediately deflect the topic of conversation back to her. Even so, I could see that I must have been more careless than I thought, because she had somehow gathered that I had grown up and worked in New York and even that I had been in my present state for less than a year. No matter how fond you find yourself becoming of someone, I told myself, there is no reason to take them recklessly into your confidence and to put your fate in their hands. Especially not in the hands of someone who believes in ghosts.

That was in a way the thing that made me most uncomfortable—all the embarrassing nonsense about my being a ghost. And the more so since it seemed to constitute a major part of my appeal to Alice. Understandably, I suppose, she had many questions to put to me about other spiritual realms. The trouble was that I had no answers, and I felt foolish and more than a little guilty at the thought of inventing them, so that I found myself being more evasive than dishonest. Which, of course, did nothing to lessen Alice's curiosity.

It was not long before Alice was bringing home books with titles like *Realms of Psychic Being* and *Astral Selves and Others*. For several days I managed to ignore it, but in the end I could not stop myself from commenting.

"Alice, I dread even asking this question, but why are you suddenly possessed to read about ghosts and voices from Beyond the Great Divide?"

"No reason. It just seemed like an interesting topic. I can't think why I suddenly got the idea of reading about it."

"Well, I notice that there weren't any books like this in your library before I arrived, and I hate to think that I might be the cause of anyone reading this sort of thing."

"Well, you know how it is. You go out with a plywood salesman and you want to read up on plywood. You start going out with a ghost and you find yourself getting all interested in ghosts."

"Well, I can tell you that these books are a very poor source of information on this or any other subject. *Bridges to the Beyond.* This is nothing but the crudest superstition."

"Nick, have you ever considered that by not believing in ghosts, you put yourself in a kind of awkward position?"

"Alice, have you ever heard of Occam's razor?"

"Yes, I have. And in my opinion it cuts a little too close for someone in your situation."

"And what about this? *The Hermeneutics of Ghosts and Apparitions: A Psychocultural Approach.* This doesn't even rise to the level of superstition. It genuinely distresses me to see you reading these books."

"Well, I might not have to rely on them, if I had some other source of information. Perhaps you'd like to recommend some more authoritative source. Or you might even consider telling me something about yourself."

"There is, unfortunately, nothing to tell. What you see is what you get."

T FIRST WE STAYED HOME EVERY EVENING, THERE BEING NO REASON I could think of ever to go anywhere else. But the telephone would often ring, and I would hear Alice saying, "No. No, I'm really sorry, but I can't. . . . No, I'm seeing someone—sort of. . . . No, it's not that. It is serious. . . . I'd love to have you meet him, but we just can't on the seventeenth. . . . Why don't we give you a call. . . . Sure. Bye."

"You know, Alice," I said, "maybe you shouldn't be turning down all these invitations. You ought to get out more and see your less ethereal friends."

"You think you'd like to have dinner with Myra and Bob?"

"I'm not having dinner with anyone except you. But I'm beginning to worry that you'll go stir-crazy sitting home every evening. It's an entirely selfish concern. I'm afraid it will make you cranky and difficult to live with."

She said nothing but walked over to her drawing table and, frowning, made some impatient strokes with her pencil. It seemed to me that she might be annoyed or unhappy, although I find that there is no way of knowing such things with any certainty.

But I decided that I had to do whatever I could to make our curious life together as normal as possible, and so at the end of October I had Alice accept an invitation to a Halloween costume ball. She chose to dress herself as a witch, with a black robe and cape, which only set off the wholesome radiance of her features, and a black conical hat, from under which masses of strawberry blond hair spilled out incongruously. But her smile, when it revealed those savagely pointed canines, really did seem to have a magical quality. Bewitching.

Whereas I, showing a lack of judgment which still takes my breath away whenever I think of it, had Alice wrap yard upon yard of white gauze bandaging around my head, leaving only two little slits for the eyes. In some thrift shop she found an old suit that fit passably, and she made a trip to Brooks Brothers for gloves, socks, shoes, and a shirt and tie. When

I got everything on I looked just like Claude Rains doing H. G. Wells. I might as well have worn a sign saying "Invisible Man."

Alice found the whole thing in poor taste. "Why do you always want to make yourself less interesting than you really are? You could be anything. Why pretend you're a bad chemical experiment? And besides, I'm the only one who can get the joke."

It was actually quite an uncomfortable arrangement. It was difficult to breathe, and I finally decided to puncture the bandaging at each of my nostrils. Speaking was even more awkward, but there was nothing at all I could do about that. My voice was muffled and probably sounded a bit sinister, and the bandaging over my mouth became almost immediately wet, so that by the end of the evening my lips were rubbed raw. But worst of all were the eyes. If I stood where a light shone toward the slits, you could see straight into what seemed to be an empty cavity where my head should be. A sickening sight. But Alice bought me a pair of mirror sunglasses, and I bent the metal frame back so that no one could see in from the sides.

I think there must have been something compelling about my appearance, because as Alice and I walked across the East Side through streets filled with Halloween costumes of every sort, I got many admiring looks and several compliments. And although I was already discomforted by the wetness of the bandaging over my mouth and nose, and I had trouble seeing through my dark glasses in the lamplight, I was exhilarated by the experience of being seen once again by other people and once again occupying a full human place in the world. I found myself striking up pointless conversations with other passers-by in fancy dress and giving away all of Alice's change to trick-or-treating children.

At the ball itself I attracted less attention, since it was a benefit for something called the New York Institute of the Arts, and many of the several hundred guests had created fabulous costumes for themselves. Alice seemed to know an extraordinary number of people there, and as she led me gradually across the room, introducing me to her friends, I could feel her quivering with delight at my side—delight, presumably, at the magnitude and audacity of our secret.

"This is my fiancé, Nick Cheshire."

"Nice to meet you, Nick. Congratulations. Wonderful girl, Alice."

"I was beginning to wonder why we never see her anymore. . . ."

"Good to meet you, Nick. That's great about you and Alice. We'll have to get the two of you over for dinner. Can you—"

"Nick's living in San Francisco, so we hardly ever—"

"Tell me, Alice," said a girl dressed, I think, as some sort of nymph or fairy queen—it was difficult to tell exactly, as she was virtually naked— "what sort of pig have you got in that poke? Is he good-looking?" Titania, or whoever she was, winked at me and reached up for my glasses, pressing into my side a bare breast onto which several small golden spangles had been pasted at random.

" 'Good looking' isn't the word for it," said Alice as we spun out of Titania's reach and off across the dance floor through crowds of pirates, angels, vampires, and gangsters.

"You stay away from her, Nick. I don't want her getting her hands on you."

"I'm not interested in anyone but you. And if I were, I would absolutely deny it. It was only her costume that appealed to me."

It was dizzying to be able to speak again in the presence of other people, and I decided that Halloween was my favorite holiday.

Alice slipped her hands inside my jacket and around my waist.

"I apologize for introducing you as my fiancé. It just seemed like the easiest way to put everyone off."

"I'm delighted at the honor. I'm sorry that out of costume I'm so hopelessly ineligible."

"You do seem to be a rather poor prospect in some ways. Out of curiosity, are you permitted to get married?"

"Permitted? As far as I know, I'm permitted to do whatever I please. . . . But I'm not sure how it would be possible. There are usually other people around on these occasions, and they might find my appearance a bit wanting. Normally you have to meet the parents of the prospective bride. There would at the very least have to be someone to perform the ceremony. It wouldn't be the sort of event to which you can come swaddled up as the Invisible Man." A large spherical yellow Pac-Man caromed off us in the embrace of Cleopatra. "Or as Pac-Man."

"Before you say that, you should have a look at some of the weddings these people have," she said, turning her head to indicate the people around us. "Can ghosts father children?"

Into my mind came the image of a wan, infantile form, translucent, with all color bleached out like a leaf left for a winter in a swimming pool.

"I have no idea. . . . I don't see how. . . ."

Alice laughed. "You know, you have a kind of will-o'-the-wispy quality. It's just as well there's no question of taking you seriously." A waltz started up, and suddenly taking the lead, she set us whirling across the floor at breakneck speed.

THE NIGHTS WERE PAINFULLY COLD NOW, BUT AFTER OUR SPLENDID Halloween outing I was all the more determined that Alice and I should not stay holed up like fugitives in her apartment. Invitations to costume balls come only very infrequently, but I hit upon another idea. We picked out a film near the end of its run at one of the movie theaters on East Eighty-sixth Street and arrived twenty minutes early for the last showing. There were not enough people there to form a line, much less a crowd. Alice bought her ticket while I waited off to one side, and then, when no one else was going in, she stepped up, handed over her ticket for tearing, and strode through, with me right behind her. In the lobby, to avoid being crashed into, I stood against a wall, and Alice stood right in front of me with her back pressed against me, looking out across the crowd as if she were waiting for someone. Then, when the film was about to begin and everyone else was already seated, we hurried in and picked out seats off to one side. Sitting in the half-darkened theater, we both felt a childish pleasure in getting away with something that we were not meant to enjoy, and we opened each other's clothing and embraced and caressed each other like teenagers.

We went to the movies often, and then after a while we started to attend exhibitions at museums and galleries, usually in the morning when they first opened for the day. Eventually we even began to go to concerts and to the theatre. I would try to choose unpopular times and events, but with Alice there, I found that I could go almost anywhere. It was odd when I considered that not many weeks before, my life had consisted mainly of cowering fearfully in corners. Really, the main danger now seemed to be that Alice would inadvertently give me away. At my insistence, when we were in public places, she would speak to me under her breath, almost without moving her lips, like a stage ventriloquist. With all the practice she got, she became quite good at it, but there seemed to be nothing I could say that would convince her of the importance of it, and from time to time, as we were walking down the street surrounded by other people, she would suddenly turn and speak openly to me as if we were completely alone.

"What difference does it make?" she asked. "People will think I'm talking to myself. New York is full of people talking to themselves. And why is it so important, anyway?"

"I can't explain it to you now."

"Well, if it really were so important, you *would* explain it to me. Nick, where do you go in the morning? What do you do all day?"

She had stopped on the sidewalk and was facing me. She was talking under her breath now, but her face was animated and she really did look like a madwoman standing there muttering to herself. A man walking along the opposite side of East Eighty-eighth Street turned and stared at her curiously.

"Nothing at all. What I do during the day wouldn't interest you, I promise you."

These discussions were always a torture, and this particular one was made worse by the fact that it was ten at night in the middle of November. Alice had on an overcoat, whereas I had only the clothes I had been wearing since last April.

"Why are you here?"

"I've told you. No reason."

"Everyone's here for some reason. Otherwise why would anyone be here?" She turned her brilliant smile on me, but I could not make up my mind whether it was full of warmth or only mockery.

"Well, then, there probably is some reason, but it's the same reason everyone else is here for, and although I'd like to stop and work it out, it's very cold just now, and if I don't keep moving, I'll freeze to death."

We walked on in silence for several blocks.

"Those are the only clothes you have, aren't they?" she asked.

"For the time being, yes."

They were indeed the only clothes I had and they were hopelessly inadequate for winter. I thought of the random pieces of clothing I had hidden in Basking Ridge and of the curtains and other fabric out of which I might be able to fashion some sort of outer garment against the cold. If I took Alice into my confidence, she could drive me down there tomorrow to get it all. No. Impossible. If there was one thing I could never afford to reveal to another human being, it was the existence of that store of invisible objects. I wished I could stop having this argument with myself. This had all been a terrible mistake. I should really contrive some decent explanation for Alice and say goodbye for good. But not until after winter. It was only rational to wait now until the weather was warm again.

"You're cold all the time, aren't you? I feel you shivering next to me. How are you going to get through the winter?"

"I was hoping you wouldn't throw me out till spring."

"I really ought to, you know."

She wrapped her arms around me as we walked, perhaps out of affection, or perhaps to keep me warm. It looked quite odd, and when I saw a police car turn down the block, I had to tell her that she could not hold on to me like that.

B Y LATE NOVEMBER, IT WAS TOO COLD FOR ME TO BE OUTDOORS MORE
than a few minutes at a time, and I could no longer walk to work
with Alice in the mornings, but I still managed to get out when
the weather was good by waiting until after rush hour and then running
from the apartment into the subway and from the subway into some office
building. Despite the increasing pain I experienced whenever I was outside, I felt more secure than ever in my new life. Through force of habit
I still bundled up my clothes each night and kept them beside the bed,
and I stayed away from the clubs, but I had long ago hidden my gun away
in the furnace room of Alice's building, since it seemed to upset her each
time she felt it in my pocket, and I was no longer constantly watching
for Jenkins and his men whenever I went about the city. Really—so long
as Alice did not say or do something indiscreet—it was hard to imagine
how Jenkins could ever find me, and I had almost stopped thinking about
him at all.

In fact, it occurred to me one day, as I sat rifling through a desk in an
empty law office, that I had almost stopped thinking about my past life
entirely. It was all quite remote now, a jumble of memories and concerns
to which I no longer had any connection. There was a telephone in front
of me on the desk. Large law firms and corporations are the best places
for me to telephone from, because even if I dial some number that Jenkins's people are monitoring, the call can be traced back only as far as
the PBX, and they can't tell anything more than that I am on one of half
a dozen floors of some vast office building. Without anything particular
in mind, and knowing that it was a mistake, I picked up the telephone
and dialed my old office. I would be giving away the fact that I was in
New York. But Jenkins would already be working under the assumption
that I was in New York anyway. And I felt an inexplicable urge to talk
to someone from my former life.

Cathy greeted me enthusiastically and asked the usual questions, hoping
for some exciting piece of gossip about whatever exotic life she imagined

I was leading, but it seemed to me that she was no longer really interested in talking to me. She had very little news. Someone I did not know had joined the firm. As I listened to her voice, I tried to remember how well I had actually known Cathy. Not very well.

"No, there haven't really been any calls for you for a long time. Just what's-his-name. Dave Jenkins. I guess he's a friend of yours? He said you'd know what it was about. . . . He's called several times. In fact he called just this week. He said—"

"This week?"

"He said if you called in. . . . Can you hold on just a second? Someone's buzzing me."

I was left on hold. I should hang up. It had been completely wrong to make this call.

"Isn't that amazing? That was Dave Jenkins! He said to tell you it was extremely important and you had the number. Isn't that an incredible coincidence?"

"Yes it is, Cathy. Thanks. I have to run now."

I should not call him. I could not possibly learn anything of use. Whatever Jenkins told me would be carefully calculated to his advantage, and anything I said could only help him. I had already needlessly let him know that I was still alive and still in New York. I was only encouraging him. And in addition, to be perfectly honest, the sound of his voice is frightening to me. And yet I wanted to hear it. I felt impelled to call him and find out what he had to say to me.

I dialed the number, and just as always, it was answered on the first ring by the silky, earnest voice.

"Hello, Nick. How are you?"

"Swell. I've missed you. You called?"

"Nick, that was an extremely foolish and unfortunate thing you did when you destroyed government property in my office."

"Gosh. I'm sorry if I showed poor judgment."

There was a pause.

"Nick, I'm asking you—I'm begging you—to listen carefully to what I have to say and to take it seriously. This is the most important thing anyone has ever told you. I want to help you, Nick, and I'm very much afraid that this is the last chance I have. You've put me in a corner. You're going to have to surrender immediately. If for any reason you don't, we have no choice but to kill you."

"That's your important message? Gee, I'm glad I called. I have to run now—"

"Nick, this is deadly earnest. I want to be sure you understand the position you've put yourself and us in. Before, we could afford to wait. We *preferred* to wait rather than to put you at physical risk. But by destroying that evidence, you've placed all of us, and indeed an entire organization—a vital organization—in grave political danger. We need you now to assure our own survival. If not alive, then dead."

"You mean you guys might get in trouble? Gosh, I never thought of that. I hope it won't in any way interfere with your work with me."

"Nick, I don't like this any more than you do—"

"I'm almost certain you're mistaken there."

"And I beg you to come to your senses now. You're leaving me with no choice."

"I really have to go. You know how it is when we let these telephone conversations drag on."

When I walked out of the building, Morrissey and Gomez were already climbing out of a grey car parked at the curb. This was the first time I had seen any of them since my visit to their offices, and looking at them, I imagined, at least, that they were grimmer, more desperate. After all, I had hurt them badly. In fact, I seemed to be winning. They were under attack from the people they worked for, and at the same time their chances of catching me were decreasing all the time. This was almost certainly the first trace they had had of me in months. How could they ever find me now? As long as Alice didn't give me away.

Still, the conversation with Jenkins left me uneasy. He had sounded just as deadly earnest as he claimed to be. Of course he had wanted to frighten me, but the fact was he had succeeded. I believed him when he said that he would try to kill me. And the fact that these people could trace my call and arrive in less than ten minutes meant that they were still able to devote their full attention to me. I had to be careful not to grow complacent and careless while they gradually tracked me down again. I had hurt them before by striking out directly at them where they had least expected it. But having done that once, I could never do it again. I could never risk going near them again. I was back to where I had been before. I had to keep moving and hope that I could stay ahead of them. I wondered again how long I dared stay with Alice.

I brooded about Jenkins for several days. Although it was true that I could not go near Jenkins himself, I reasoned that it might still be possible to outflank him once again by going after his superiors. I might find some way to undermine his efforts further or I might at least learn something useful about what he was doing.

"Alice, I'm going to be away for a couple of days."

"Where are you going?"

"I can't say. There's something I have to do."

"Why can't you say? You have your gun again. Is it dangerous? Will you be back?"

"I'll be back, almost surely. I seem to be incapable of staying away."

I boarded the Metroliner to Washington, choosing one in the middle of the day that was fairly empty. I hated attempting this expedition in the late autumn weather, but with each passing hour I saw more clearly that Jenkins had been exactly right. I had left him no choice. I had to do everything I could to defend myself.

The trip was a complete failure. I spent three and a half days hiking through the streets from one intelligence agency to another, trying to find the people to whom Jenkins reported and to learn anything at all about Jenkins himself. The weather was milder in Washington, but that was not much comfort, because there is very little public transportation there, and I had to walk for miles, twice all the way over to Virginia and back, shivering miserably from the cold the entire time. I could not risk entering a club, because Jenkins might have them watched, and I spent my nights shivering on the floor of a cafeteria, not daring to eat more than a few scraps of bread for fear of being seen.

In the end I located the office of a man named Ridgefield, who seemed to be Jenkins's immediate superior, but I was unable to find so much as a piece of paper with Jenkins's name on it. Everywhere I encountered locks. Offices were locked; file cabinets were locked; corridor doors were locked. There were people on duty at all hours of the day and night, and in any case I did not dare stay in these places overnight, because I would have no way of safely feeding myself the next day.

After four days of this I was so weak and cold and hungry and disheartened that I could not go on. I rode back to New York on the train physically debilitated and completely defeated, having learned nothing, and sustained only by the knowledge that I would soon be back home, where Alice would take care of me. It came to me, perhaps for the first time, that Alice had saved my life. I should tell her and thank her. Sometime when it was safe.

It was bitterly cold when I arrived in New York, and the subway ride up from Penn Station was an agony. I ran as hard as I could—which in my condition did not amount to much of a pace—from the subway stop to Alice's apartment to keep my body from succumbing altogether. It would be so much better when I got to the apartment. I had been continuously miserable and afraid for the last four days, but now I would be able to stay inside where it was warm and secure and Alice could feed me.

The key was not in the usual place. Could she have gone somewhere? I had told her I would be gone two days and it had been four and a half. I should have called.

But before I could knock, the door had swung open, and she was standing there.

"Nick!"

I was too relieved or overcome to speak.

"God, I'm so glad you're back. Where have you been?"

"I . . . I'll tell you another time."

"I was afraid you were gone for good. You're shivering! What's happened to you?"

Alice ran a hot bath for me. Then, while she prepared dinner, she gave me a mug of hot soup. She wrapped a blanket around me that looked like a child's tent erected over the couch, and I sat there warm and safe, wondering how I could ever have imagined that I could get through the winter on my own. At the realization that—at least until next spring—I no longer had to consider whether I ought to leave, I felt an enormous wave of relief and gratitude.

I N DECEMBER IT BECAME SO COLD AND IT RAINED AND SNOWED SO MUCH OF the time that I could hardly go out at all, and I did most of my work in the apartment now. I had Alice subscribing to all sorts of financial publications and receiving a steady stream of annual reports and 10Ks. I still tried to get to the Crosbys' apartment once a week to be safe, but all my statements were now mailed to me care of Bernie Schleifer, who handled all the paperwork. I managed my accounts and made the actual trades by telephone while Alice was at work, so that she did not really know what I was doing, but the sight of all those financial statements spread out over the dining room table in the evening and of the pencil magically jumping through the air to compute cash flows and rates of return seemed somehow to offend her sense of propriety.

"Why do you spend all your time studying these things? Are you hoping to be an accountant in your next incarnation? It's awfully unromantic of you."

"It just happens to be what I'm interested in."

"I thought you were supposed to lose interest in earthly riches when you passed on."

"Maybe it's because I seem not to have passed very far on."

"Well, it doesn't seem right for a ghost to be in trade."

"Beneath my spiritual station, you think? Anyway, I'm not in trade at all. I'm an investor."

"Really? Where exactly do you invest? And why?"

"Actually, it's mainly the intellectual challenge of the thing that interests me."

"Tell me, Nick, on a scale of one to ten, where would you rate yourself for *candor*?"

"Ghosts have to make a living like anyone else." A thought struck me. It was a thought that ought to have struck me long before, and I wondered momentarily why it hadn't. "Alice, it suddenly occurs to me that it must be quite expensive feeding me and buying all this expensive wine."

"It hasn't been a problem."

"Tell me, do you have a brokerage account?"

"No. I have some AT&T stock I inherited from my grandmother, though."

"How much?"

"I'm not sure, but I can show them to you. They mailed me a lot more stock certificates afterwards for different telephone companies."

She pulled out a stack of certificates interleaved with countless mailings and booklets detailing the intricacies of the AT&T divestiture and the probable tax consequences to shareholders and the disputed position of the IRS. There must be tens of thousands of people in the same situation as Alice. If they ever sell their shares, they will have to use all the proceeds to pay accountants to compute the tax on the transaction.

"Alice, take these certificates to this address tomorrow—it's a discount broker—and tell them you want to open an account and sell these shares. They'll show you exactly how to endorse them over. Then put in an order to buy these stocks—I'm writing everything out on this piece of paper."

"Then you can predict the future!"

"I cannot predict the future. No one can predict the future," I said with some irritation in my voice.

"Then why are you telling me to buy these stocks?"

It must have seemed as if I could predict the future though, because Alice's account prospered at once, and she no longer commented on how unromantic she found the study of financial statements. Furthermore, as time went on she pressed me less and less with questions about myself.

And in the warmth and security of Alice's apartment I began to forget again about Jenkins. In fact, the only thing that marred that winter for me was being kept constantly inside by the weather. But in early January a new possibility was suddenly suggested to me by the sight of a child bundled up in a parka and gloves and a wonderfully sinister woolen ski mask completely covering his head. I immediately made reservations at Stowe and had Alice outfit me with clothing and equipment from a ski shop in the city.

Alice set out early on the day of our departure to fetch her car from its garage somewhere in Queens. On her return she found me waiting in front of the building, fully arrayed in gloves and ski mask and dark glasses. The doorman had been a bit startled to see me emerge like that from the elevator—the lobby being maintained at a steady eighty degrees—and as he helped me load the skis and the luggage, he kept glancing at me suspiciously, but I was too elated to care.

The snow was only fair and the weather unspeakably cold, but I had a wonderful time. I acquired an extensive wardrobe of face masks. When the sun came out and the temperature rose, I explained to people that my skin was sensitive to the sun. It is true that we had to eat most of our meals in our room, but otherwise I was just like everyone else, able to go anywhere without worrying about coughing or inadvertently colliding with someone. It was Halloween all over again. I would strike up conversations with strangers in lift lines. And Alice would suddenly become quite exuberant as she walked in some public place on my arm.

HE WINTER WAS A SUCCESS FOR JONATHAN CROSBY AS WELL. BEFORE THE end of October I had accumulated $100,000 in his account, and by the end of the year I had amassed more than a quarter of a million. I was showing a rate of return that would, if maintained, rapidly render me rich beyond all imagining. Of course, in practice, you cannot go on doubling your money every month for very long without attracting all sorts of attention, and attracting attention was the one thing that I absolutely could not afford to do, so as the amounts involved grew larger, I began to make less obtrusive investments, avoiding especially the acquisitions and buyouts in which the SEC is always eagerly looking for signs of insider trading. As a result, I found myself more and more making the sorts of investments I had made in my former life, only with much more accurate and timely information now. This change in investment strategy should have slowed down my rate of success dramatically, even in the kind of buoyant, rising market we had then. But somehow, whenever I bought something, it would move right away, and although I was no longer enjoying enormous windfalls, one solid success followed another with uncanny reliability.

By the beginning of March my account was worth over $500,000. Although an account that size is nothing out of the ordinary as brokerage accounts go, I still should not have let even that amount of money accumulate in one place. It was an entirely unnecessary piece of carelessness. But my life with Alice had come to seem so secure. And furthermore, I had such confidence in Willy's inability to notice anything unusual about my performance. Really, he had never seemed to notice much of anything at all. But I underestimated him.

If I had been paying attention I would have seen that Willy's attitude toward me had gradually changed: at some point he had started asking me questions rather than trying to sell me his ideas. Then, one afternoon, glancing through a glossy magazine that had appeared in Alice's mail— GOTHAM, *The Monthly Chronicle of Upper East Side Living*—I saw a picture of someone who looked vaguely familiar, a bland looking man in his thirties, wearing a club tie. The caption identified him as "hot young superbroker, Willis Winslow—a rising star on Wall Street."

I was astounded. Reading the article, I found that Winslow was "one of the creative new breed of young brokers." In today's more competitive financial markets, I learned, a broker had to be able to do more than take orders: he had to be someone who could understand market forces and even shape them. This was disturbing news: it is all right with me if stockbrokers want to try their hand at understanding something—although they might start with something easier than market forces—but I am frankly shocked at the thought of their trying to "shape" anything whatever. Some examples of Winslow's wisdom were quoted. "There are no shortcuts in this business. The only way to find value is to put in long, painstaking hours looking for it. You can't just be swept along with the crowd. Now, I put a lot of my customers in Hutchison Chemicals. To most people it looked like a pretty unglamorous, uninteresting situation. But if you did your homework you knew that besides its basic business of producing chemical feedstocks, it had one of the most creative research laboratories in the industry. Now, that was a stock that we started buying at twelve and watched go over thirty...."

Hutchison was something I had come upon, and it had indeed been selling at twelve at the time, although I remembered with annoyance that most of my original order had been executed at thirteen. I had learned that someone at Hutchison had discovered some sugar substitute that, unlike other sugar substitutes, would purportedly not break down when raised to temperatures high enough actually to cook food. I doubted that the stuff would ever be manufactured: there would be years of force-feeding rats with it until they developed cancer or died of despair. But I correctly concluded that the thing was plausible enough to run up the stock for a while in this kind of market. Now I wondered how far and how quickly my trading orders were propagating.

I called Willy up immediately.

"Jonathan, hello," he said enthusiastically. "How are you? Can you hang on just a second. I have two calls on hold, and I just want to get rid of them. . . . Hello, Jonathan? Sorry. I'm really busy here. What can I do for you? I see that your ACL has had a nice move. Do you think it's got anything more in it?"

"Willy, I want you to sell everything, and—"

"Sell all the ACL?"

"Not just the ACL. I want you to sell everything."

"*Everything?*"

"That's right. I've been talking to some friends of my father's and they told me I should be in cash right away. So I think you should sell everything today. Put a hundred thousand dollars into a tax-exempt money market fund and send me a check for the rest at Bernie Schleifer's office."

"Jeez, Jonathan, your friends think this market is about to go over the cliff? I guess they've called some things pretty well in the past. . . ." Willy sounded concerned.

"Well, Uncle David said, 'It could be tomorrow, it could be next year, but you'd better be a hundred percent in cash.' "

I figured this might be the kindest thing I could do for Willy's other clients, who would otherwise now be entirely at the mercy of his analytical skills. Long term, however, they were probably doomed anyway.

I immediately had Bernie open cash management accounts for me with two other brokers. In the future I would be careful to keep everything broken up into discreet pieces that no one would notice.

It was living with Alice that had made me so confident and careless. I reminded myself that spring was almost here, and I realized that I had been dreading its arrival. But I had no choice: I would have to leave Alice as soon as the weather turned warm. I had to keep moving.

But soon March was gone and the season had changed, and yet somehow I had not moved out. It would actually be safer, I told myself, to go on as I was until I had established a secure place of my own to live in. Really, living with Alice was the prudent course of action for the time being, and I could put off thinking about leaving for a few more months.

In the middle of April I would have to give a large part of the money I had amassed to the federal government and the State and City of New York, but I would still be left with almost eight hundred thousand dollars—far more than I needed to establish a safe existence for Jonathan Crosby, and I set Bernie to work on the next step.

"Bernie, I've decided I'd like to own my own home."

"That's very smart. There are a lot of tax advantages to ownership, and you're throwing away way too much money in taxes. By the way, I have a deal on my desk—"

"Bernie, do you have someone in your office who could go around with the brokers and see what's available? I'm kind of busy just now. When you've got it narrowed down, I'll arrange to look at the choices myself."

"Sure, and I also have a very good real estate broker—in fact I'd like to get you together with him sometime. You know there can be tremendous profits in buying up single-room-occupancy hotels. There's a lot of unrealized value in these situations, and it's not as big a deal as people think clearing out the—"

"That's great, Bernie. Let me tell you exactly what I'm looking for. There are some things that might not be important to someone else. . . ."

I had Bernie and then his broker describe all sorts of properties to me over the telephone, and although I was never able to get inside any of them, I went and looked at several buildings from the outside and peered in the windows. In the second week of April we signed a contract on a brownstone on East Ninety-second Street, and at the end of June we closed. Bernie produced a lawyer, and the two of them handled the entire transaction, including the financing, with a power of attorney. One of Bernie's great virtues is that he is not pedantic about notarizing signatures.

The top three floors of my building were broken up into apartments occupied by rent-stabilized tenants, leaving me with a large apartment consisting of all of the first two floors, a small basement, and an entirely useless garden. I was not at all happy about becoming a landlord, but it was out of the question for me to live by myself in an apartment building, where the front door, and probably the apartment door as well, would always be visible to someone. And furthermore, since I could not safely use elevators, there would be stairs to climb, and the stairways would have doors that would probably also be in public view. And doormen always know when you come and go. I could not so much as have the groceries delivered without them knowing that I was there, but they would also know they had not seen me come in. Within a matter of days they would realize that something was terribly strange.

In my own brownstone, on the other hand, I could come and go as I pleased and have whatever I wanted delivered without anyone knowing anything. Outside there was a broad stone stair leading from the pavement up to a door on the old parlor floor, which still served as the building entrance for my apartment as well as for those on the upper floors. However, underneath the stair and out of sight of the street was another door, which the former owner seemed to have used only for taking out the garbage, and I made this the main entrance to my apartment. From the sidewalk I would step over a little waist-high metal railing and then down two steps into a recess under the stair, where I would be entirely out of sight. In the beginning I kept a key hidden there so that I could unlock the door and slip through unseen by anyone in the street.

Although the apartment had been completely redone just two years before and was in perfectly good condition, I had Bernie hire a contractor to redesign it for my special needs, and each evening I would let myself in and inspect the work, so that I could phone in my instructions the next morning. To start with I had the front door reversed so that it opened on the side furthest under the stair and out of sight. Then, upstairs in the front room, I had them cut through the wall behind the mailboxes, which were in a small entrance hall at the top of the outside stair, so that I could remove my mail from inside my living room. I had special blinds installed and heavy curtains, and I put in a complete alarm system and grates on all the windows. Of course I knew that if Jenkins ever found this place, nothing I could do would keep him out, but I could eliminate the risk of some random burglar or vandal making an extraordinary discovery. I had them redo the largest bedroom as a workroom completely outfitted with woodworking and metalworking tools and a full set of locksmith's equipment.

I had already spent many days in a locksmith's shop, watching the work and reading books and equipment catalogues, and I now set about practicing what I had until now only been able to observe. As soon as the work was finished in my apartment I inserted new cylinders in the locks with tumblers that would open with the invisible keys to my old apartment and office. This was such a convenience that I mailed two cylinders to Alice and installed them in her locks as well.

For some reason this made her uneasy. She wondered why I had keys at all and where I had gotten cylinders for them suddenly. Perhaps it all seemed too practical for a ghost. But then lately Alice often seemed uneasy.

"What are you doing these days, Nick?"

"Same as always. Trying to buy cheap and sell dear. What makes you ask?"

"Nothing. You seem preoccupied lately. As if you were thinking about something else."

"Alice, I find it difficult almost to the point of impossibility to think about anything else but you."

"Oh yes? Well, I'm sure you'll give it your best and manage somehow. But I'd like to ask you something."

"Anything."

"If you should have to leave for some reason, would you do me a favor and let me know first?"

Why was she asking this?

"Solemn promise," I said. "But you know I wouldn't leave . . . unless it was absolutely necessary."

Very likely it already was absolutely necessary. Every day I stayed increased the risk. Sooner or later something would happen to give me away. Alice's friends asked all the time about her fiancé. And her neighbors knew someone was actually living with her in the apartment. Did they ever wonder why they never saw him? Still, I could put off leaving a little longer. Until I had my new life completely set up. I would, I reflected cheerlessly, have the rest of my life to live alone.

I spent most of the summer furnishing the apartment. I got credit cards and opened accounts at department stores and had everything delivered: furniture, kitchen appliances, cooking utensils, silver, books, records. It was a wonderfully pleasant home I was setting up, and really I would have enjoyed doing it all with Alice. But, of course, the whole point was that I must not do it with anyone. At last I had a telephone under the name of Jonathan Crosby, and I could now have all my mail sent to me at the apartment. Each day I would go and collect it and sit at the desk in my new study and conduct my business. I even provisioned the kitchen with all the staples. I could at any moment have begun to live there on my own.

But each night I would go back to Alice's apartment.

"ALICE, WOULD YOU DO ME A FAVOR? THERE'S A SHOP IN MIDTOWN THAT has a clown suit to which I've taken an irresistible fancy. I want you to buy it for me. For some reason they won't take telephone orders. I've picked out a mask to go with it and some handsome puffy white gloves."

"Why? Do you have a date? The Invisible Man bandaging suits you better, you know."

"I thought you didn't like it. And I don't have a date. Just an errand to run. I'd like you to rent me a station wagon for twenty-four hours as well."

"You're awfully mysterious lately."

"That's just a ghost's job."

"Is it? I'm glad you tell me that, because I've been wondering what a ghost's job is, and this is really the first information I've been able to get."

On a Thursday afternoon in early August I drove the rented station wagon down to Basking Ridge. My clown suit was of professional quality, although it would have looked better with real make-up instead of a mask. But make-up does not adhere very well to my skin, and anyway I had to be able to shed the disguise and flee if something went wrong.

And there were all sorts of things that could go wrong, I reflected uneasily: the car could break down, the police could stop me, someone could drive in to clean the gutters just as I was loading up the car. But I did not need extraordinarily good luck for everything to work: I just needed not to have extraordinarily bad luck.

People were extravagantly friendly the entire way. Whenever I passed a car with children in it, I would wave inanely and blow kisses, and everyone would wave back. When I got to Richard and Emily's house, I turned into the drive and drove straight up to the door of the icehouse. I had called several times during the last few days, most recently ten minutes before from a gas station, to make sure no one was there. I was out of the car, into the icehouse, and back again with all my invisible possessions in under fifteen minutes. I crawled around on the sawdust floor for several more minutes to be sure I hadn't dropped anything, and then I was in the car again, heading out the drive and back to New York.

Then, a few miles from Basking Ridge, everything began to come apart. A state trooper pulled up behind me, the light on the roof of his car spinning and his siren emitting little warning blasts. I pulled over onto the shoulder, trying to decide whether I should be frantically tearing off my costume or whether I should wait for a better opportunity. But if I fled now, I would certainly lose all my invisible things for ever. Better to see if I could somehow salvage the situation. I had barely brought the car to a halt before the trooper was standing there staring in at me through the open car window.

"Sorry to wave you over like that. I was just wondering what it would cost to have you work my daughter's birthday party. . . ."

I took his number and promised to call.

When I got to New York it was already dusk. I parked the car several blocks from my house, on the park side of Fifth Avenue, where I could grind the windows of the station wagon up and down without being noticed. I slid over to the passenger side, squeezed myself as far down onto the floor under the dashboard as I could get, and pulled off the clown suit, stuffing it under the seat for Alice to retrieve later. Invisible again, I climbed out the open window by the passenger seat and set about unloading my invisible possessions through the tailgate window and carrying them, one load at a time, back to my brownstone.

I HAD ALREADY BEGUN PRACTICING WITH THE EQUIPMENT IN MY WORKSHOP, using visible materials. I was an indifferent craftsman with wood and had never so much as drilled a hole in a piece of metal in my life, and even with the motivation I now had, my work was still primitive and unpredictable. Furthermore, because I could not see exactly where my hands were, I was constantly slicing and scraping my fingers on saw blades and files and chisels, and no matter how careful I was I found it impossible to avoid wood splinters and metal shavings. When I began working with invisible materials, these problems became even worse, and I had to stop regularly to examine my hands, for fear I was bleeding.

I tried to compensate for my lack of skill and the difficulty of the materials by doing everything extremely slowly and carefully, but I could see that it would take years of practice before I would be able to fabricate some of the things I would want, and I had to be careful to conserve my limited supply of raw materials until I knew exactly what I would most need and had the skills to produce it. Above all, it was essential that I not make mistakes. I executed each project with visible wood or metal first so that I could see exactly what I was doing and what might go wrong.

To start with, I manufactured an extremely light, collapsible ladder that could be easily carried around when I wanted to go somewhere I wasn't meant to. It was usually more than enough to get me up to a first floor window or even a fire escape. Then I fabricated a set of simple lock-picking tools and went about experimenting with them until I was quite proficient at opening locked doors and filing cabinets.

I had several invisible telephones, and after many days of research I was able to determine their brand and model and obtain a visible duplicate. I disassembled the visible and the invisible sets in tandem, putting each piece in a labeled envelope for future projects. With part of one of the receivers and some of the electrical wire I had salvaged, I set up a supplementary alarm system. It was far less elaborate than the commercial one, but then you could not see it, so that no one would ever disable it. I knew that the commercial alarm system would not mean anything at all to Jenkins: he would go right through it without leaving a trace. But no matter how carefully Jenkins entered the apartment, there were certain things I knew he would have to touch. Such as the pages of this manuscript, neatly stacked on a table in my study. He would see the first words, "If only you could see me now . . .," and understand at once that it contained everything he wanted to know. He would have to look at it, and once he did, he would trigger my alarm system, and I would know he had been there. In the frame of the entrance door was an old doorbell that had been painted over many years ago. I cleaned it out and wired my alarm into it. Each time I arrived at the door, I would press the bell, and there would be a single, just audible click, which told me that nothing had been disturbed. One day, I might push the button and not hear the click, and I would know that Jenkins had been there. I would turn away from the door and never return again.

Not that I thought Jenkins would find this apartment. I had worked it all out so carefully, and I could not see what could ever lead him here. Furthermore, I had not given up on my plan to counterattack again, and toward the end of August I decided that I was ready to attempt another trip to Washington.

This time I had the advantage of all my new, invisible equipment, and, even more important, I had Alice with me, which meant that I had a hotel room to retreat to whenever I needed to eat or sleep. Alice had a number of acerbic things to say about the idea of visiting Washington in August and about my failure to explain the purpose of the trip, but she seemed, actually, almost enthusiastic about it, and once we were there, she spent her days cheerfully in the National Gallery and the Corcoran.

I spent my days finding out everything there was to know about David Jenkins. The long walks from agency to agency were at this time of year almost a pleasure, and the locks I encountered everywhere presented no problem now that I had my invisible lock-picking tools. I had been afraid at first that I might be walking into a trap, but it quickly became clear that for the second time Jenkins had failed to anticipate me. I found everything I was looking for, although it took me not several days as I had expected but almost two weeks, and I had to spend many nights locked in offices or archives.

I found out almost immediately that Jenkins had moved his operations to the fifth floor of a loft building on West Thirty-eighth Street and that he had no promising lead whatever. At least none that he was reporting—and surely he would want to report anything he had. Thanks to my helpful telephone call, he did know that as of last November I had still been alive and probably still in Manhattan, but beyond that he had lost my trail completely. He had people watching empty apartments and clubs and Nick Halloway's friends and business associates, but there had been no verifiable sign of me for many months now. I wondered how long he could go empty-handed before his funding would begin to dry up.

More difficult was the task of tracing Jenkins's career through a succession of name changes and through a hierarchy of assignments and reassignments from one agency to another and back again, so that no one file contained anything approaching a complete or even accurate account. In the end, I think I may have been the only person who knew everything about him. I knew, come to think of it—the files these organizations maintain on their employees are extraordinarily detailed—almost as much about him as he about me.

But just what use it all might be to me was not clear. Jenkins did not seem to have told anyone that I had destroyed whatever evidence he had once possessed that might have made my existence credible. Only I knew that he was left with nothing but a few fragments of "superglass." I might be able to embarrass him by informing his superiors or some Congressional oversight committee that they were funding a search for a will-o'-the-wisp. Or I might tell Anne Epstein, who could tell the public. But the fact was that Jenkins had not really done anything or even said anything on the record that he could not explain away with a minimum of awkwardness. As I went over the problem, I saw that he had hardly exposed himself at all. I had found out everything there was to find out, and there seemed to be nothing more I could do. Only keep moving. If I got caught, it would be from staying too long in one place and confiding too much in Alice.

WE TRIED ONCE THAT SUMMER TO GO TO THE SEASHORE, BUT THE FIRST time I walked out onto the beach, I saw that it would be impossible. No matter how carefully I brought my foot down, each step churned a nasty little cavity in the dry sand; and, worse yet, when I reached the wet sand along the water, perfect footprints began to appear beneath me. I insisted on getting into the car and driving straight back to Manhattan.

But after our trip to Washington, we drove up to the Berkshires, and Alice rented an old farmhouse not far from Sheffield. There was no other human habitation within view, only fields and woods, and we could take long walks outside without any fear of being seen or heard. During what was left of summer and the beginning of autumn, we went up every weekend.

During the week, while Alice was in her studio, I toiled in my workshop, mastering the tools and trying to figure out how I could make the best possible use of my supply of invisible materials. As I saw the summer drawing to a close, I turned to the most important project of all, the fabrication of new clothes. I had an assortment of random articles of invisible clothing, most of them too small for me, and a collection of window curtains and upholstery pulled off the MicroMagnetics office furniture. I had never in my life held a needle and thread in my hands, and I did not even know the names of the different kinds of fabric, but I hoped to stitch together whatever I had into a workable wardrobe for the rest of my life. I had assumed that sewing would be much easier than the woodworking and metalworking I had been doing, but I quickly saw that it was in fact much more difficult. I abandoned almost at once any idea of working with a sewing machine—although I had purchased what was described as the most versatile and usable machine in existence. Even with visible thread and cloth I found it to be the most unmanageable piece of equipment I had.

Next, I experimented for several days with needles and visible thread, at the same time reading various incomprehensible books on needlework and tailoring. Then, when I thought I was reasonably proficient at sewing by hand, I unraveled part of one of the invisible drapes and tried to use the thread to stitch together some of the other material. It was slow, nasty, infuriating work. It is almost impossible to thread even the largest needle with invisible thread, and no matter how careful I was, it always seemed to pull free again immediately. My fingers were soon raw from pulling on thread. Furthermore I could tell it was coming out badly. Whenever I would run my fingers along one of my seams, I would find that it was hopelessly crooked and that it pulled open at random places.

I could not face another winter without more clothing, but I could see that, at the rate I was learning to sew, I would never outfit myself in time. Furthermore, I was particularly unwilling to risk wasting my small supply of cloth on more botched attempts. After considerable debate with myself, I finally turned to Alice for help.

"Alice, do you know how to sew?"

"Of course. But why? Are your clothes beginning to wear out?"

"They seem to be holding up surprisingly well, actually. There is a tear in this shirt that I'd like to repair, but what I—"

"And what about you? Are *you* wearing out?" she asked. "Or are you going to stay the same . . . the same age. . . . Are you going to stay the same for hundreds of years?"

"Based on the aches and pains and the wobbliness in certain joints, I would say I was getting older in the usual way. Hard to judge the wrinkles by touch—and I haven't had enough time yet, anyway."

"I'll tell you why I ask. I'm wearing out, myself, and if you're not, I'm not sure I can count on holding your interest through the winter years."

I always hated conversations like this. But that is the trouble with asking people for favors: you have to be civil.

"So far, I see no sign whatever of any waning of my interest in you. And anyway, as I keep telling you, I hope, with luck, to die of old age at around the usual time. The only plausible alternative would seem to involve dying much sooner."

"And when you next die. What will happen then?"

"I don't know, and I try my best to avoid thinking about it. But I have adopted as a working hypothesis that absolutely nothing happens. I lie in cold obstruction and rot. Anything more would be in the realm of the miraculous and entirely inconsistent with everything I have so far seen in the world."

"Well, you're here now," she said, reaching out and poking a finger into my belly. She caught me by surprise and it felt quite unpleasant. "In whatever form you're in. Wouldn't you call that miraculous? Most people would."

"I suppose it is miraculous in a way, but not now that I've grown so used to it. It's really no more miraculous than your being here. Actually," I added, kissing her forehead, "your being here is altogether miraculous."

"Speaking of things you've grown used to." She smiled, but her eyes did not take part in the smile, and I wondered if tears were forming in them. Alice had been increasingly moody these last weeks.

"You know, now that you mention it, *you've* grown used to *me*, haven't you? The novelty of living with an invisible spirit has pretty much worn off. And the thrill is gone even from the secret, isn't it?"

"Well what's the point of a secret you can't tell anybody?"

"Do you sew?"

"I told you I did. What would you like me to sew?"

"I just want you to show me how."

"You have new clothes, don't you? After wearing the same things every day for almost a year, you suddenly have all sorts of new things. But of course you can't discuss that at present. That, or where you keep your new clothes, or what it is you're doing, or why you're away so much now. Or what it is you're so preoccupied about all the time. Why don't you just show me what you want me to sew. You won't have to tell me anything you don't want to."

After several unsuccessful experiments, Alice worked out a technique in which she basted pieces of visible tissue paper onto the pieces of invisible fabric. Then, once she had sewn everything together, she would remove the paper. Out of the various fragments of cloth I had salvaged, Alice stitched together a patchwork overcoat, lining it with pieces of material cut from a sweatsuit; and with other bits of fabric she lengthened the trouser legs and sleeves of the invisible clothing which was too small for me. The garments she produced in this way felt quite odd, being pieced together out of scraps of different textures and weights, and no one piece of clothing, not even the coat, was in itself very warm, but by wearing several layers at once I was going to be able to survive the winter in reasonable comfort.

S I THOUGHT ABOUT IT, I REALIZED THAT ALICE REALLY HAD GROWN USED to me. She was no longer amazed at the sight of the pencil dancing over the paper, the glass of wine floating through the room and tipping itself into thin air and then evaporating. She would no longer suddenly reach out and run her hands over my body, marveling to find the solid human form invisible in her grasp. These things had become part of her daily life and no more miraculous than the kitchen table or the view from her window or anything else in creation. In fact, she seemed at times rather to regret that I was not like everyone else than to marvel at my uniqueness. I wondered whether it was all gradually becoming boring for her. She would realize that she was harboring a defective fugitive rather than some magical being.

She would often run her fingers over my face, in what I thought at first was a sort of caress, but was, I one day realized with a little shock, her way of trying to see my features. And one evening, when I had fallen asleep on the bed, I awoke to find her smoothing the sheet over my face.

"I was just curious to see what you looked like," she said.

"I don't look like anything," I said with annoyance, pulling the sheet abruptly away.

But when I saw her staring down at me, I at once felt remorseful and as a show of good will drew the sheet over my face again.

"All right, then. What do you think? A good face, or just as well that you can't see it?"

"A difficult call," she said appraisingly. "But the sheet doesn't suit you at all. Too much like a death mask."

"Just the right effect for a ghost, I should have thought."

She pulled the sheet away and ran her hand over my face and down onto my chest. "Yes, that's definitely better."

"Alice, you haven't ever told anyone, have you? About living with a ghost?"

"I've never said a thing to anyone. I gave you my word."

She seemed genuinely aggrieved at the question. But something about her answer made me uneasy all the same.

"And anyway," she went on, "who do you imagine I would tell? I sit alone all day in my studio, and I spend the rest of the time with you. You're the only person I ever see. Or you would be, if I could see you."

"Well who is 'James,' then?" The question escaped me before I was quite aware that I was asking it—it is never a good idea to ask this sort of question. "The one who keeps calling up and leaving messages on the answering machine."

There was a little pause.

"That would probably be *Father* James," she said, "calling about the exorcism. Did he leave an estimate?"

I did not reply, and there was another pause.

"Or then again it might just be James Larson," she resumed, "calling about the book jackets I'm doing for him. . . . What's the matter? Don't you like exorcism jokes?"

"Not particularly."

"Sorry. But frankly it seemed like just the sort of remark *you* might make."

"Did it? Anyway, it doesn't matter. The important thing is that you never tell anyone about me."

"Is that the important thing? It's good you tell me, so I don't lose sight of what's important and what isn't."

Alice seemed unhappy out of all proportion to whatever it was we had been talking about. But her moodiness was hardly surprising, I reflected. It must be a rather odd and unsatisfactory life that she was leading with me, cut off from everyone she had known before.

One day, I remember, as we walked together down Madison Avenue, a man, well dressed, in his thirties, stopped and greeted Alice, a vast smile breaking out on a pleasant, handsome face.

"Alice!"

Holding her by both arms, he kissed each of her cheeks. Alice was uncomfortable.

"How are you," she said.

"What's become of you? All of sudden there, you just disappeared from my life. Stopped returning my calls. And now I hear you're engaged to someone no one has ever seen."

"Sort of. How are you?"

Alice shifted her weight uneasily from one foot to the other and glanced nervously at where I had been standing beside her. I stepped away. Perhaps it would be more considerate to walk out of earshot, although it would hardly help Alice, since she would have no way of knowing I had done it.

"Why don't we have dinner. I gather this guy is out of town a lot." He still held her left arm.

"I really can't. I—"

"Or we'll get together for lunch. Very discreet."

"Maybe when Nick is in town we can all get together—"

"I'll call you at work, Alice." His fingers slid down her arm and he gave her hand a squeeze. "Take care."

We walked together in silence for several blocks.

"You know, Alice, you probably ought to get out and meet some nice, visible young men. You're going to waste your youth hanging out with wraiths."

Her eyes narrowed.

"You think so? Maybe you should concentrate on your own affairs. Whatever they may be."

For everyone's sake, this was really the proper and decent moment to say goodbye to Alice. I had created another existence, another place in the world, completely private and impenetrable. I had only to say goodbye and walk a few blocks west to where everything was set up and waiting for me to live out my life alone. I would be safe, and Alice would lead a real life.

But the trouble with this carefully reasoned conclusion was that it overlooked the only really important fact in the whole debate, which was that I loved Alice and I was going to go on living with her. If only I could have seen it then: I might have mentioned it to Alice. But I find that sometimes, in my concern with solving the immediate problems, I miss altogether the heart of the matter. And in this instance I somehow went on telling myself that I would only be staying with Alice another few days. In a few days I would do the prudent thing and disappear forever through my secret bolt-hole to where Jenkins could never find me.

But really, I no longer worried about Jenkins in the same way. It had been so long since I had felt him pursuing me. And I think the fact that I now knew so much about him made him seem somehow less threatening.

Perhaps that is why, when I encountered him one October morning on Seventy-second Street, I arrogantly turned and began to walk alongside him. I should never speak to him. It can only help him.

"Good morning, Colonel."

I was impressed by how well he contained his surprise: his head jerked perceptibly, and his hands tensed momentarily, but he relaxed again immediately and spoke, never altering his stride.

"Good morning, Nick. Are you ready to come in with me?" He seemed not to care about the answer as he always had before. And furthermore, he had not asked me how I was. That should have been a warning.

"I'm actually quite pleased with my life as it is. Please keep your hands at your sides and especially not in any pockets. Otherwise, I'll have to leave, and we so seldom have a chance to chat anymore."

"Yes, we really seem to have lost track of you, Nick. I was mistaken. I didn't think you could make it through the winter."

"What are you up to these days, Colonel?"

"The same things, Nick."

"Still looking for me?"

"Yes. Among other things. Are you sure you wouldn't like to come in with me now?"

"I think not. Goodbye."

"Goodbye, Nick."

He never threatened me, never told me that they would have me soon. I should have paid attention to exactly what Jenkins was saying. I should have seen that something was wrong.

DIANE
SOFT and TENDER
YOUR EYES
A PRESENCE of SWEET
FLOWERS

IT WAS ONLY A FEW NIGHTS LATER THAT ALICE CAME IN FROM WORK WITH A large portfolio of the sort that artists use to carry their work, which was unusual, because Alice never brought back anything from her studio. She would sometimes tell me that she was working on an illustration for a magazine advertisement or a book jacket, but she had never shown me anything except the drawings she did for herself at home.

I saw that she was going to much more trouble than usual in preparing dinner, and I wondered if she was celebrating some professional success. I should make a point of asking her about her work more often.

"Nick, could you open the champagne?"

"Certainly, if you'll tell me why we're having it."

"You don't know what day this is, do you?"

Could it be her birthday? I realized unhappily that I did not know when her birthday was.

When I did not reply, she said, "It's the anniversary of our meeting." She was still elated, but there was no missing the disappointment in her voice.

"I'm sorry. That's stupid of me. I'm terrible about these things."

"It's all right. I know you by now. It doesn't matter."

Based on my experience of women in general and Alice in particular, it did matter.

"Of course it matters. I'm glad you remembered, anyway."

"Never mind. Open the champagne. I have a surprise for you."

While I worked the cork free and filled two glasses, she went to her portfolio and took out a flat package wrapped in colored paper with a ribbon.

"This gift can be for both of us," she said.

She watched eagerly as the wrapping paper tore itself off, and then she watched the place where I stood. I did not grasp at first what it was I was looking at, and it must have been some time before I spoke, because the expression on Alice's face had already turned from excited anticipation to uncomprehending disappointment.

It was an ink drawing of a naked man, which seemed an odd gift until I realized that it was a portrait of me. I stared at it stupidly, trying to judge how good a likeness it was. I had never had any very exact picture in my mind of what I looked like, and in any case I had not seen myself for a year and a half, but it was quite a good likeness, I should think. I was trembling with fear and anger.

"*Alice, what made you think you could do this?*"

"I don't understand. . . ."

"This has to be destroyed."

"I just don't understand."

"I want to know if you have any sketches or any other versions of this?"

"No. . . . This is the only one. . . ."

Once again I had the feeling that there was something wrong about Alice's answer. Tears were running down her cheeks.

"I thought you'd be so pleased."

Alice fled to the next room. I could hear her methodically tearing the drawing up into little pieces as she sobbed convulsively.

The world seemed suddenly a very bleak place, and I would gladly have given up anything else in it to have my words and Alice's drawing back.

I followed her into the bedroom and kissed her. She turned away, her mouth set firm, and her body rigid.

"Alice, I'm horribly sorry. Of course you couldn't possibly have known how dangerous that drawing could be for me. But everything I said was still inexcusable."

"Damn you," she said. "Damn all your secrets. Why don't you just go away? You're going away anyway, aren't you?"

"No. I'm not going away. . . . Alice, listen to me. I was completely wrong. Why don't the two of us go away together for a while?"

She did not answer. I kissed her again. She had stopped sobbing, but as we made love, I felt the tears running down her cheeks the entire time.

However, the next morning Alice seemed to have put the incident out of her mind. When I tried to apologize again, she dismissed the whole matter with a shake of her head, and when I proposed again that we drive up to Sheffield, she agreed at once, although I knew she had a lot of work.

We stayed almost a week. It was already quite cold there, but I had a jacket with an enormous floppy hood that I kept pulled over my head, and I would go outside fully dressed in visible clothes. If anyone had got up close and seen the empty hood, he would have thought he had run into the Grim Reaper. But I could not see the effect, and I enjoyed being able to walk about freely with warm clothes on. However, it may be that my appearance affected Alice, because she would be cheerful one moment and then look up at me and begin weeping the next. Or in the middle of a conversation she would suddenly become silent and preoccupied for no reason.

We went for long walks through the countryside, and as always, being able to talk openly out of doors gave me a wonderful feeling of liberation. More than once I was on the point of telling Alice everything. Despite Alice's moodiness I felt happier each day. And yet, when it was time to return to New York, it was Alice who wanted to stay.

"Why couldn't we spend the winter here? Why go back to the city at all?"

"Don't you think the local residents would begin to wonder about the sinister hooded figure that never speaks to anyone?"

"You could use the invisible things I made for you. I could pretend I was living alone."

I had a vision of my footprints appearing mysteriously in the snow.

"We could stay up here for good," she went on. "We could have a completely normal life together all by ourselves."

"It's not safe for me here, Alice. We have to get back to the city."

But as soon as we returned to New York, Alice's mood seemed to recover. She had apparently forgotten entirely about the drawing, and to my relief, she no longer asked me where I went during the day or whether I was about to leave or who I really was, so that our life together was if anything more pleasant than before. And of course I now enjoyed the security of knowing that whenever anything went wrong, whenever Jenkins began to close in on me again, I would have my identity as Jonathan Crosby and my apartment on Ninety-second Street to bolt to. But in the meantime I was perfectly happy living with Alice.

THEY CAME EARLY ONE MORNING, JUST AT DAWN. A MOMENT AFTER-wards I realized that in my sleep I had heard the hissing sound made by whatever gas they were pumping in under the door and I had been aware of Alice climbing out of the bed and walking toward the entrance to see what was happening. But the first thing I heard consciously was the throttled scream and the awful gasping as Alice breathed in the fumes.

I remember stumbling out toward her and seeing her turn back from the door, her face convulsed, her mouth opened wide to reveal a gro-tesquely contorted tongue. It may be that she was trying to speak. She took a step toward me and seemed to reach out for something with one hand, when her legs abruptly gave way and she collapsed onto the floor. Locks were turning in the door.

I was wide awake now. Panic had brought me instantaneously from deep sleep to a state of total consciousness in which everything all around me was brilliantly clear to my senses but in which my mind remained in a trancelike state, capable of comprehending only one thought at a time. But at that moment there was only one thought that required compre-hension. From the instant I saw Alice, I held my breath. I was running past her now. The front door had swung open, and men in gas masks that made them look like giant insects were pushing into the apartment. One of them held a short hose with a flat nozzle connected to a large canister mounted on wheels. He was aiming it into the apartment, and the hiss of escaping gas was quite loud now. Somehow, although I thought I was not breathing, I got a whiff: it was as if a bus had slammed into me. Two of the men were picking up Alice. The others were charging toward the bed-room.

I was running across the living room and sliding open the glass door to the balcony. I have no idea whether any of them saw it move. They were piling into the bedroom. I remember leaning over the balcony railing and gasping for air, sucking in enormous lungfuls. I found that, miraculously,

I had my bundle of clothes in one hand, the little bundle I had made each night and always kept by my bedside in readiness for this moment.

I leaned out and threw it onto the balcony below. The balcony was fenced around on all three sides with opaque glass panels mounted in a framework of steel rails. I climbed over and, holding onto one of the steel posts, lowered myself down, so that I was dangling off the end of the balcony. The view down was horrible: a repeating pattern of balconies like endlessly reflected forms in facing mirrors and then the pavement. There were people gathered beneath the building—too far down to make out clearly—and police cars double-parked everywhere. Dizzying. If you start to think about that long, sickening drop, you could find yourself spinning down. It was particularly horrible for me, because I could not see my own grip, my hold on life.

With my forearm wrapped around a post, I lowered myself further, so that I was dangling below the balcony. I remember thinking that I could now probably not pull myself back up. I kicked my feet about, trying to find the railing of the balcony below. Nothing. If only I could see my foot. I could see the railing right there, right beside the vertiginous view down to the pavement. I should surely be able to reach it, to find it with my foot.

Above me I heard voices.

"Was this door open when we came in?"

I heard the door slide further open. I had to keep going. I slid down the rest of the way until I was holding onto the post by my hands. The toes of my right foot came to rest on the railing. I slid another fraction of an inch, until I was clinging by my fingers. My left foot found the railing. I got the balls of my feet onto it and let them take some of my weight, then all of it. I was poised on the railing, steadied only by my tenuous hold on the balcony above. If I fell forward, I would tumble down onto this balcony; if I fell backward, I would plunge down to the street. I took my right hand off the railing post and slid it under the bottom of the balcony above me. Trying to dig my fingertips into the concrete, I pulled myself forward until I had to let go of the post with my left hand too. I felt myself tilting forward. I came down on the balcony floor on all fours.

I heard footsteps on the balcony above.

"Anything out here?"

I did not move. Looking up, I saw two gas-masked heads appear over the edge of the balcony above and peer down. One of the heads and then the other twisted around to peer upwards. "The door was open when we came in. Better check the apartments above and below. Below first."

It might have been Clellan.

I was pulling on my clothes frantically. The moment the heads withdrew, I slid over the railing and began lowering myself to the next balcony.

It was easier this time. For one thing I knew it was possible. For another I now had rubber-soled tennis shoes on my feet to help me get my footing and clothes to protect my body as I slid against the concrete edge of the balcony floor. But by the time I had descended three more stories, my fingers were trembling with exhaustion. And terror probably. I paused to rest them. Heads appeared above me again, peering out over the edge of a balcony. They were unmasked, and I recognized one of them as Morrissey. I tried to count back and figure out exactly which floor they were on, but my mind was seized with panic. This was awful. I was not sure I could do this sixteen more times. Was it sixteen now? No, fifteen: there was no thirteenth floor. It didn't matter. No choice. I went down two more stories and on the second came crashing through a canvas beach chair.

Then, looking out at the prospect below, I saw several yards away the column of balconies descending along the neighboring line of apartments. Below the third floor there were no balconies! Of course not.

I tried the door of the balcony I was on. Locked. I went down another level, my panic mounting again. Also locked. Down one more. Here the door moved under my hand. I slid it open just a fraction of an inch and paused to look inside. A middle-aged woman stood in the kitchen in full sight of the balcony, cooking something. Brewing tea. I waited. Please hurry.

Finally, when she had filled her mug and walked, ever so slowly, out of the kitchen, across the living room, and into the bedroom, I inched the door carefully open and slipped through. I pushed it shut again behind me and latched it, hoping that would make it more difficult for them to figure out where I had gone.

I crossed to the entrance door and paused. I could hear water running. I pulled open the front door, which emitted a piercing creak.

"Hello?" the woman called out.

Slip through and pull the door shut again. Nothing to do about the noise.

"Hello? Who's there?"

I ran down the hall and into the first fire stair. I thundered down it as fast as I could, five, six, seven stories, three and four stairs at a time.

Somewhere below I heard a door open, and voices. I slowed up abruptly, still proceeding toward them frantically, two stairs at a time, but carefully now, quietly, holding onto the railing so that I would not stumble and betray myself.

"How many of these stairs are there?"

"Just the two."

". . . main entrance on the avenue and the service entrance from the basement to the side street . . ."

Two flights from the bottom, I caught sight of part of Clellan's face below. I stopped altogether for a moment and then crept forward. Tyler was there too, and someone else.

"Why don't they lock?"

"They're fire exits. . . ."

"Well get some armed men in from the street and put one on each of these doors right away. On the second floor too. We should have both floors evacuated within a few minutes. If he tries to leave the building, he's got to do it from either the first or second floor. I want to see the other stairway. . . ."

I slipped out through the fire door and into the lobby right behind them. At the other end of the lobby I found Jenkins and Gomez. Gomez was letting people out through a revolving door, one at a time.

A policeman was calling up residents on the housephone: "This is the police. We have to evacuate the building. Don't open your door until police officers come to escort you from the building. . . . That's right, we got an armed fugitive."

Jenkins was talking into a radio. "How many men have you got outside? . . . All right, if you can bring up more. . . . Make sure they're ready to shoot at anything unusual. . . . Watch especially the second floor windows. . . ."

That made sense. The service entrance was hopeless, and there were no apartments on the ground floor. Maybe the third floor, but it was so high above the pavement. I walked back across the lobby. Through the large windows of plate glass that ran from floor to ceiling I could see police cars everywhere and uniformed men wearing bulletproof vests and holding rifles. They were staring up at the second floor. The situation was only going to get worse.

I walked up to a light, upholstered armchair with wooden legs. I leaned over and shoved my hands into the crevices between the sidearms and the seat, which bent my fingers back the wrong way but gave me a good grip. Hunching forward with my head down, I tilted the chair toward me and heaved it up so that the back rested on my head and shoulders and the four legs pointed ahead like the horns of a charging animal.

I heard a shout, then more shouting. I was running full tilt straight at the plate glass window for an endless, excruciating moment. Unable to see anything with the chair over my head, I could not tell exactly when the collision would occur, and I had no idea whether I was strong enough to smash through.

When I hit, there seemed to be an explosion all around me. I felt something brushing against my legs, and there was a dense shower of broken bits of glass. I heaved the chair forward off my shoulders and free of my hands and immediately scrambled off to one side. I heard guns firing everywhere and wondered whether I was being hit as I ran down the sidewalk and then scurried between parked cars into the middle of the street.

"Where is he?"

"He never came out."

"He's under the chair. We got him!"

"I never saw him."

Despite the earliness of the hour, a crowd had gathered across the street. There were faces at the windows of the surrounding buildings.

"Move those people back, God damn it! He's still in the building!"

"Is it one guy, or what? How many people we dealing with?"

I stood in the middle of the street, panting, and watched. Morrissey and Tyler were moving the police back from the building. Morrissey had a long, thin metal cane of the kind blind people use, which he was sweeping back and forth over the sidewalk in front of the shattered window. Tyler was down on his knees feeling the pavement with his hands. He looked up as Clellan approached.

"Blood, maybe."

"A lot?" asked Clellan. Hopefully, I suppose.

Tyler shook his head. "Not here, but that doesn't mean much. He must have been moving pretty fast."

Clellan looked at Morrissey, who had reached one corner and was doubling back to work his way to the other.

"Look's like he's still moving," said Clellan morosely.

I was about to leave when I saw two men come out of the building carrying a stretcher. Someone must have been hit by the gunfire. But then I saw—they had left her face and bright hair uncovered—that it was Alice they were carrying. Alice! I was in a frenzy, unable to think any clear thought, aware only of wanting desperately to get her away from these people. Was she alive? This was all my fault. I discovered that I was running toward the stretcher, which, for some reason, they were holding in front of the open door of an ambulance.

Then I saw that Gomez was standing several paces away, his eyes moving warily. He was holding a gun. Further off and to the other side, Jenkins stood watching with his right hand in his pocket. The stretcher bearers continued to stand motionless, as if exhibiting their load for public inspection. The peculiarity of it stopped me, and suddenly I realized that they were doing this for me, and I felt the rage swell up uncontrollably within me like some violent chemical reaction until I was delirious with hatred. They were waiting for me. Trying to provoke me. I wanted more than anything in the world to inflict some unspeakably painful punishment on them.

Alice stirred. I managed somehow to make myself understand that there was nothing I could do. Her mouth opened. Jenkins made a sign, and suddenly the stretcher was in the ambulance, the doors slammed shut, and the ambulance moved off. Gone. (If I had had my gun, Jenkins, I would have shot you then.) Jenkins turned indifferently and walked over to another man, who appeared to be some sort of police official. Jenkins began speaking, too softly for me to hear, but he seemed to be indicating the police cars with a dismissive movement of his hand. The other man answered animatedly.

"Look, we'll do whatever you want. We've got plenty of other things to do. But whoever you guys are after is still in that building. *No one* came out through that window."

Jenkins said something in reply and, turning away, walked over to where Tyler was still crouched over the pavement. I could not hear either of them, but I saw Tyler nod and point toward the place where I had crossed between two parked cars into the street.

It suddenly struck me that I must still be leaving a trail of blood. I knelt down and felt the street at my feet. There was a pool of thick, sticky liquid all around me. I moved my hands up my body. There was blood running down my legs and soaking through my torn trousers. I tried to determine where it was coming from, but now there was blood all over my hands and everything felt sticky.

Run.

I raced down the avenue, past policemen and police cars and onlookers, and then turned west, still staying in the middle of the street as much as I could. I imagined that I was leaving a clear track of blood for them to follow, and I wanted it obliterated by the traffic and the sun. I pulled up several blocks later, realizing that that was a ridiculous idea and worrying that by running I was only making myself lose blood faster.

Walking now, I arrived at my apartment on Ninety-second Street several minutes later. I walked past it up to the next corner and then back again. No sign of anything unusual. I climbed up the outside stairs and, leaning out over the railing, pushed the old buzzer button next to my door underneath. I heard with relief the little click. They had not found this place. I waited several minutes to be sure. No sound or movement anywhere. I went back down the stairs and around to my entrance, pushing the button once more, to hear the reassuring click again.

Inside I found everything undisturbed. I went into the bathroom and stripped off my clothes. The trousers were torn and would have to be patched and resewn, but it was my body I was worried about now. I stood under the shower for less than a minute and then carefully dried myself all over. Then, beginning with the scalp and working down, I explored every inch of my body with my fingertips. I am used to inspecting myself this way, because every time I stumble badly or crash into some sharp object, I have to check laboriously that there is not some unseen fracture or cut. But usually I am only checking one part of my body, whereas now I had to go over every bit of it to make sure that my life was not bleeding away out of some gash or bullet wound.

Everything was all right until I got to my calves, but there my fingers encountered the moist, thick stickiness of open wounds. I ran the shower over them again and blotted them dry with the towel. I could feel the blood well up immediately and begin running down the outsides of my legs again. It is almost impossible to tell by touch how serious wounds are, but I decided that I had one bad horizontal gash on my left calf and two on the right.

I got out the first-aid kit that I had carried away from MicroMagnetics and found a roll of adhesive tape and some gauze. I hated to use it up; normally, I would have used visible bandaging and stayed out of sight until I had healed, but I was in a hurry now. I had to get moving. I cut a series of strips from the roll of tape and laid them out in a row along the edge of the bathtub, where they would be ready when I needed them. Then I cut off a large hunk of gauze, folded it to what seemed like the right size, and laid it over the first wound. I quickly applied the adhesive strips, using them to pull the wound together and fasten the gauze in place. I used too much tape and too much gauze, but I had to be sure to contain the bleeding so that I could go out.

When I had finished bandaging both legs, I propped them up on a chair and waited almost an hour, to make sure the wounds were closing. I would have to walk to midtown and I was afraid of pulling them open again. I put on fresh clothes and, slipping my gun into my pocket, set out walking carefully down Madison Avenue. In the sixties, I stopped to use a pay phone.

"I have a collect call for anyone from Mr. Halloway. Will you accept the charges?"

"Of course," said Jenkins in his most unctuous, sincere voice. "How are you, Nick?"

"I'm fine. I mainly called to let you know that. I thought you might be concerned."

"That seems an imprudent thing for you to do. Unless you need help. Or unless there was something you wanted to find out from me."

That wasn't the way Jenkins talked. He was trying to provoke me into losing control. But I was already so angry that nothing he said could have affected me.

"Why did you take Alice, Jenkins?"

"She'll be safer with us. And of course we'll want to talk to her."

"Jenkins, she knows nothing that will help you. Nothing. I was very careful about that."

"I'm not surprised. You're almost always very careful when you can afford to be. But we're concerned about you. Are you sure you weren't hurt by the gunfire or the broken glass? If you're bleeding, you should have medical—"

"What are you going to do with her?"

"We're going to talk to her. And we're going to make sure that she's safe. We'll be looking after her."

"What do you mean, you'll be looking after her? She doesn't know anything. You can let her go right now."

"Nick, I don't doubt you when you say you didn't tell her anything. I know you. In fact, I'll tell you something: if you'd told her the truth about yourself, we might not have found you so quickly."

"How did you find me? Did Alice tell someone about me?"

"Take a look in any bookstore. You brought this on yourself. You have to learn to trust people, Nick. As for Alice, she may know more than she realizes. And it can sometimes take us a while in these situations to be sure that someone has been perfectly frank with us. In any case, she'll be safer here with us until we have you. Then, of course, there would be no reason—"

"Now I'll tell *you* something, Jenkins. If I could trust you, I'd make the trade: me for Alice. But as you point out, I'm not good at trusting people. Just as you're not much good at inspiring trust."

I hung up. The conversation was exactly what I had expected, and they had had plenty of time to trace the call.

Had Alice given me away? I tried to make sense of what Jenkins had said about looking in a bookstore. I walked into the next one I came to, simply pushing the door open, not much caring at this point if anyone noticed. I saw it almost right away. It was some sort of romance. *White Lies*, by D. P. Gengler. It must have been quite popular, because there were several stacks of copies, with one copy propped upright on top so that you could see the cover. It was actually Alice that I recognized first, although she had drawn herself with her face turned away, swooning in the arms of an elegant but rather untrustworthy-looking man in a dinner jacket. I could see that it was an excellent likeness of me, one that Jenkins or any of his men would recognize immediately. On the back flap of the jacket were the words "Jacket illustration by Alice Barlow."

Jenkins was right: it was my own fault. But that was all beside the point now. I had to get Alice back. While doing as much damage to Jenkins as possible. I tried to think what they would be doing to her. Whatever they thought might be useful. Well it would not be useful to them to kill her. No point in thinking about it. I had to keep moving.

I walked several blocks further south and went into the offices of a large law firm to get at a safe telephone. I found an empty conference room, closed the door, and dialed the *Times*.

"I'd like to speak to Michael Herbert, please." Michael Herbert was to me nothing but a name that I had seen over occasional and uninteresting articles in the *Times* and that I had heard Anne Epstein mention in conversation as if he were a friend.

There was ringing, and then a voice said, "Michael Herbert."

"Hello," I said. "I urgently need to talk to Anne Epstein."

"You have the wrong extension. Let me—"

"I have some extremely confidential information for her and I don't want this call to be routed to her extension." I was talking extremely rapidly and softly, trying to create a sense of secrecy and urgency. "Could you possibly go to her desk and ask her to take this call at your extension? It's very important."

There was a pause, and then he said, "I'll see if she's there."

Several minutes later, Anne's voice came on. "Hello, this is Anne Epstein. Who is this?"

"Hello, Anne. Do you recognize my voice?"

"I . . ."

"Don't repeat my name. This is Nick. Do you recognize me now?"

"Yes. How—"

"It would be *extremely* dangerous for me if anyone found out I had called you about this. You cannot tell *anyone* where you got the information I'm about to give you. Do you understand?"

"Yes."

"What I'm about to tell you is going to seem utterly incredible. Then it's going to seem utterly silly. But it's not silly. It's deadly serious. A highly ranked intelligence officer, a man with extensive power within the intelligence community and with extraordinary personal discretion over large amounts of virtually unsupervised and secret budgetary funds, has become mentally deranged. He has gradually become convinced that we are threatened by invisible aliens from another world. On a personal level it's a tragedy the way this man is being destroyed by his illness. But the greater tragedy is that he is using not only public funds but the entire machinery of American intelligence to combat his own paranoid delusions. Vast sums of money are being spent, valuable human resources are being diverted, illegal acts are being committed—burglary, arson, even abduction. Lives are being ruined. And because there are no safeguards, no real oversight or monitoring of intelligence activities, this continues unchecked. In fact, it's expanding in scope, and officials at the highest level of government, having initially failed to bring this thing under control, are being drawn into a massive cover-up. This whole thing goes to the heart of how citizens in a democracy place limits on the institutions through which they govern themselves. Anne, do you know where the Academy Club is?"

"Yes . . ."

"You should get over there within the hour. Bring a photographer. I'm going to describe this man to you—he's currently using the name David Jenkins. He is about to cordon off the Academy Club and search it for imaginary enemies. You probably can't quite believe what I'm telling you, which is why I want you to be there to see this particular incident. I also want you to see how the authorities will move to cover this up. Without you, this—and God only knows how many other such acts—

will be carried out with impunity. When you spot Jenkins, make sure you have him photographed there.

"All I can do over the phone now is sketch out the basic facts of this story, but I'm going to see that you receive extensive background information on this man in the mail. I'm also sending you information you can check out on some of the illegal activities he's supervised. . . ."

By the time I had finished with Anne, she had a vision of herself as the next Woodward and Bernstein. I had to move quickly now. It was eleven, and I wanted everything to reach its peak during lunch hour, when the Academy Club would be at its fullest. From a telephone booth across the street from the Club, I telephoned my old office and got Cathy on the line.

"Cathy, I can't talk now, but do you happen to remember the name of that doctor I saw three or four years ago? Eisenstein? Einstein? Something like that. I've lost my address book and I need the name. . . . I know him well. The name has just slipped my mind, exactly when I need it. . . . No, I'm fine. Could you look on one of the insurance claims or something. . . . I'll call you back in five minutes."

I walked over to another pay phone and called again several minutes later.

"Essler. That's it. You don't happen to have his number there do you? . . . Thanks. . . . No, I'm fine. I'll have to stop in soon. Bye."

That should do it right there. But to make sure I walked in through the front entrance of the Academy Club. There was an electric eye across the front hall. I positioned myself directly in its path and stepped on the carpet. Jenkins had scattered things like this around the places where I had hidden myself last year. I had no idea if he was still bothering to watch for me in the clubs, but if he was, this should generate some excitement. Especially after the telephone calls to my office.

But to be absolutely sure, I went upstairs to a telephone booth inside the Club and called Essler.

"Hello, Dr. Essler's office."

"Hello, I'd like to speak to Dr. Essler, please."

"The doctor's not available now. Is it about an appointment?"

"Well yes, I'd like to see him, but I have to speak to him—"

"The first available appointment I have is in December."

"December would not fit in with my needs. I have to talk to him. It's an unusual situation. I mean . . . it's urgent."

"If you'll leave your name and a number where you can be reached, I'll try to have the doctor call you when he's free." She sounded unpromising. Try to get your children into medical school. No other service profession is in a position to treat people like this.

"I'm not anywhere I can be reached. I think I'd better hold."

"I'm sorry, sir, but you can't do that. The doctor may be—"

"I might have to step away from the phone for a moment, but I'll be right back."

"Hello? You can't do that. Who is this? Hello. . . ."

I left the phone off the hook and headed downstairs to slip out of the Club again before Jenkins arrived. But halfway down the stairway I looked through the front hall to the entrance and saw that I had underestimated Jenkins. The outside of the entrance was already completely covered over with a tentlike structure, and there were several people gathered by the door wearing gas masks.

I quickly turned into one of the lounges off the hall with the half-formed plan of forcing open or breaking through a window again, but there I saw another man with a large canister on wheels, which was emitting a loud hiss. I had seen one just like it that morning pumping gas into Alice's apartment. In the second before I turned and ran, I saw that three men were moving quickly through the room, waving long blind men's canes through the entire space, poking under every piece of furniture, stabbing into the window frames and over the tables, quickly and efficiently checking every place I might be.

Charging up the stairway, I came up short behind several more men in gas masks. There were two members and three or four Club employees looking distraught, and they immediately clustered around the men in gas masks. One mask was removed, revealing the face of a man I had never seen before.

"Everyone stay calm. We have a leak in a gas main. You'll all be evacuated as quickly as possible using the gas masks at our disposal. In the meantime, everyone should move into the small room in the northeast corner with doors. You'll be evacuated from there one at a time. Nobody is in any danger if you remain calm and follow directions."

More employees were appearing from the dining room, and several members appeared from the staircase in squash clothes. It was still only eleven-thirty, and there were very few members in the Club. This was not working out at all the way I had planned it. I had expected this to happen an hour later, when the Club would be full. I had assumed that they would announce that a fugitive was in the Club. I had pictured them leading out hundreds of indignant Academy Club members and then beginning a destructive search of the building. Anne would be there with photographers, and when the whole fiasco was well underway, she would go after Jenkins directly: *Colonel Jenkins? Anne Epstein of the New York Times.* Photographer clicking up near his startled face. *Can you tell us the reason for this search of the Academy Club and the name of the agency you are representing? Or Would you care to comment on reports that the federal government is engaged in a search for invisible aliens?* Jenkins would blink and retreat. Even if I were trapped in the building, he would have to give up and leave before they could find me.

But it was not like that. The Club was still nearly empty. The story about the leaking gas main seemed to satisfy everyone. And they were moving quickly through the building. More people were straggling down the stairs to be evacuated. I could tell from the way they held towels and napkins over their faces that gas was already seeping up to this floor.

I charged up the stairway and down a corridor on the top floor. I would wait this out on the roof. I would be safe there. But the door to the roof was locked. It never used to be locked. What now? Try the door again. Hopeless. There must be a thousand places to hide in this building. Try to think of one. Go back through the building. There will be some place.

I found myself in a small room with card tables. If I could get a window open. . . . No, that would draw them immediately. Looking out, I could see ambulances in front of the building and people standing around outside watching. Where was Jenkins? Perhaps he was inside the building, and Anne would never find him. Would she wait for him to come out? Would she miss him entirely? I looked for Anne, but I could not see her.

I turned from the window and ran out of the room. This was all a mistake. I could hear the men moving around on the floor below. I ran through a doorway and found myself in one of the private dining rooms. There was a long table running down the length of the room and above it an enormous chandelier with elaborately curved arms branching out from a shaft which ran up into the ceiling. It was all I could think of. I climbed up onto the table and grabbed hold of one of the metal arms close to the shaft. It swayed a bit, and there was a cracking sound up at the juncture with the ceiling, but it held as I pulled myself up. The whole thing was shaking. I was agonized by the exertion and by the fear that the whole thing would come crashing down onto the table with me under it.

I managed to hoist myself up and get first one leg, throbbing with pain, over a metal arm, and then the other leg. I twisted around until I was sitting with my chest and face right up against the central shaft. The whole thing was creaking. I unbuckled my belt and rebuckled it around the shaft so that I was held firmly against it. Then I unbuttoned the front of my shirt, slipped my arms out of the sleeves, and rebuttoned it. I wrapped the sleeves over one shoulder and under the other arm and knotted them tightly around the chandelier post so that I was lashed in place. I raised my legs, which were still dangling straight down over the table, and hooked them around chandelier arms as securely as I could.

I heard people moving in the corridor. I tried to relax my body, so that when I went under, I would not suddenly slump and cause the chandelier to lurch. The giant insects were moving in with their canister, and I had just enough time before passing from consciousness to feel how horribly painful and insecure my perch in the chandelier was.

T HE FIRST THING I FELT WAS THE PAIN UNDER MY ARM AND ACROSS THE side of my neck where I hung by my shirt from the chandelier. That brought me very quickly to a level of consciousness where I also felt the extraordinary pain across my lower back where my belt cut into it and a cramping discomfort in my thigh where it lay across a thin metal branch of the chandelier. My body had sagged down and now hung inertly from the chandelier like a sack of grain.

"Nothing."

Two men dressed in grey work clothes stood in the doorway staring straight at me.

"It sounded just like someone moaning. You know, like someone didn't get out in time."

Try not to move. These men could not be working for Jenkins, anyway.

"Let's take a look next door."

When they disappeared from the doorway, I tried to pull myself up so that I could untie the shirt and the belt. At first I did not have the strength—or rather it felt as if I did have the strength but I was too groggy and miserable to summon it. Then my fingers seemed too stumpy to untie the knot. Careful. You could hang yourself. When I had finally somehow freed myself and dragged my limbs off the chandelier arms, I lowered myself laboriously until my feet reached the table top. I stood up and fainted.

"It's not in here."

The two men were in the doorway staring in again. I lay in a nasty heap on the table. Jesus. Better just lie here for a moment. Feels much better than before anyway.

"Maybe it's upstairs. Someone probably dropped something onto the floor right above us."

Please go away.

But even when they did, I went on lying there for quite a while. Then I slid myself onto the floor and lay there. It must have been almost an hour before I stumbled downstairs and outside into the bright afternoon. The Academy Club was full of members again. In the street, people walked by without a glance. It was as if nothing had happened. But I had been tied up in that chandelier: my body ached horribly. . . . I should call someone. Jenkins. Or Anne Epstein. They have Alice. Better get it straight in my mind first, get home.

At the entrance to my building I pressed the button, on principle, but I didn't much care. I staggered in and collapsed on my bed. If they knew about this place, let them come. I would be here sleeping.

NEXT MORNING, I HAD A *Times* DELIVERED. NOTHING ON THE FRONT PAGE. I went through the whole thing, page by page, column by column. Nothing. The whole thing had gone wrong. Anne probably hadn't found Jenkins. I had to call.

I checked over my bandages as well as I could. Scabs had formed over the wounds, and the gauze seemed to have dried into them. One wound had partially reopened, but nothing more than a few drops of blood was oozing out. I cut two more strips of adhesive tape and patched on another piece of gauze.

I walked all the way down to midtown to get to an office with a safe telephone system and called Anne. Or rather I called her friend, Michael Herbert, and when he answered, I asked for Anne; her voice came on right away, as if she had been waiting there for the call.

"Hello," she said eagerly. I was pleased that she remembered not to use my name.

"What was the matter?" I asked her straight off.

"What do you mean?"

"Why isn't there anything in today's *Times*. Couldn't you find Jenkins?"

"Of course I found him. Your description was perfect. Everything was just the way you said, except for the Con Ed stuff."

"Con Ed?"

"The story about the gas leak. I wasn't expecting that from what you said. But we watched for almost half an hour. Jenkins was standing there the whole time, right in front of the building. Then when he was just about to go into the building, we went after him."

"Did you get a picture?"

"Great pictures. He blinked like a mole when Jimmy stepped up to him with the camera. I introduced myself, told him I was from the *Times*, and asked him if he was Colonel David Jenkins, alias Donald Haslow, alias—"

"What did he say?" I asked eagerly.

"Nothing. He stopped dead and just kind of blinked. He just stood there as if he couldn't hear me anymore, as if he were thinking about something miles away. Then he gave a little nod, not to anyone—more to himself, really—and walked back to his car."

"Didn't you ask him anything else?"

"Sure. All sorts of things. Why he was there, who he was representing, whether he had a search warrant for the Academy Club, whether the federal government officially believed that there was evidence of extraterrestrial life, all sorts of things."

"And what did he say?"

"Nothing. Once he gave me a look as if he were memorizing my face. But basically he just walked to his car, got in, and drove away. It was amazing. Within, I would say, ten minutes everyone was gone—police, Con Edison, everyone."

"And did they have a search warrant?"

"No. There was no search warrant. They're staying with the story of the gas leak. They're insisting Jenkins just happened to be driving by and stopped to take a look like anyone else—"

"So there's no story?"

"Of course there's a story. It's a fantastic story."

"Then why didn't they run anything in today's paper?"

"It's not like that. You can't run something like this without checking the whole thing out. Did you send that stuff you were going to give me on Jenkins?"

"I'll put it in the mail for you," I said.

"Everything you gave me over the phone checks out perfectly. The entire editorial board and the legal department have been meeting on this practically around the clock since last night. Two people flew down to Washington this morning, but the intelligence people are sticking absolutely to their story and at the same time screaming about the peril to national security if we print anything. It's wonderful! I'll be working on this full time."

"That's great, Anne. So there seems to be some discomfort about all this in Washington?"

"It's unbelievable. They've gone into an absolute frenzy of not knowing anything, not commenting, not returning calls. This is obviously something big."

"When do you think there might be an article, Anne?"

"I don't know. A week, a month. Six months even. There's an enormous amount of research to do on this. I want to give you a number where you can reach me any time you have information of any kind that could be useful. This is a very patriotic and brave—"

"Good luck with this, Anne. I can't stay on this line too long."

"Wait—"

I tried to think it all through. I was not sure exactly where all this left Jenkins, but it could only be bad for him. I went to another office several blocks away and spent some time getting ready and going over exactly what I would say, so that I could keep the call short no matter what tack Jenkins took.

I dialed Jenkins's number, but it never rang: there was a click, and suddenly Jenkins was speaking to me.

"Halloway!" His voice was as soft as ever, but I could hear that it was contorted with anger.

"Good afternoon," I said.

"Halloway, you don't know what you're doing." His voice had a whining quality that seemed on the verge of turning into a snarl.

"Not exactly," I conceded. "Nothing ever seems to come out exactly as we plan it. You probably find the same thing in your work—"

"Halloway, you're ruining the careers of dedicated, decent men."

"So you keep telling me. I want you to—"

"You act as if you were the only person in the world that mattered, as if you didn't owe anything to anyone. These men have only tried to do their jobs and help you, but you—"

"Jenkins, do you mind if I give this number to the *Times*? They've been having the devil of a time reaching you."

"We're going to have to kill you now. I wanted you alive, but now I have to settle for you dead, just to survive."

"That's another thing you keep telling me. I want you to let Alice go."

"There can be no question of that." His voice took on an unpleasantly vindictive tone. "She'll be with us until we have you. If she survives that long."

"Jenkins, that's enough. A hundred people saw your men carry her off. The *Times* knows—whether or not they can prove it is not clear yet—that you've ransacked the Academy Club without any warrant and half poisoned several distinguished and contentious members of the New York Bar, but they don't yet know that you've abducted someone and are holding her hostage. But they *will* know unless Alice is out within half an hour. You let her go, and I'll be reasonable. There are all sorts of things I won't tell the *Times*. It's not in my interest to make a fuss either."

"Halloway, you can't get away with this. I have all sorts of evidence of what you are."

"I doubt it. Not evidence that would make anyone believe the story you want to tell about me."

"And I have tapes of every one of these telephone conversations."

"I never doubted it. I have some recordings too, by the way. I make them on some tape cassettes I happened to carry away with me from MicroMagnetics. Would you like me to play back the part of this conversation where you make the threats about Alice?"

There was a silence. I let him think for a while and then followed up.

"Jenkins, I wish you well. The situation is straightforward. You have to let Alice go. If you don't, you'll very shortly be in prison or a lunatic asylum—it's not clear to me which. Maybe the quality of my life will be a little worse too, but it will still be my best choice. Besides the things I know about directly, I've found out where you were trained, where you've worked, every name you've ever used. I've also found out some interesting things about people you've worked with. I'm ready to give it all to the *Times* to use as they in their wisdom see fit."

"Halloway, if you destroy me, there will be someone else. People know about you by now. Sooner or later, we'll get you."

"Do you have Alice at Thirty-eighth Street?"

Silence.

"I want you to tell her to walk straight up Fifth Avenue. You understand. Against the traffic, to make it a little harder for your people. But I don't want to see any of your people there. Do you understand? This is best for everyone."

I waited, but he did not answer.

"Jenkins, I have to hang up. You have her out there within half an hour. I can't call back and discuss it."

I WAITED FOR HER ON A BENCH IN THE SIXTIES FROM WHICH I HAD A GOOD
view of both sides of the avenue and from which, by standing up on
the seat, I could also get a good view of anything happening in the
park behind me. I had no idea whether they would let Alice go, but I
certainly intended to keep turning the screws on Jenkins. When I had
waited nervously for forty-five minutes without any sign of Alice or of
Jenkins's men, I found myself considering exactly what information I
should turn over to Anne next. Certainly the location of Jenkins's office.
Then I might start implicating other people above Jenkins. That ought
to turn them against Jenkins and his project quickly enough.

Probably Jenkins was thinking through exactly the same possibilities.

I got up and walked slowly down Fifth Avenue, watching for her. A
woman with blond hair emerged from a cluster of pedestrians several
blocks down. No, not Alice. What would she be wearing? Might be anything: Jenkins's men would have brought some clothes from her apartment. Could she have got past me somehow? Unlikely. How would
Jenkins make this decision? As far as I could tell, he did not have to discuss
these things or get approval from anyone else. Or probably he did now.
Now that the *Times* was on top of him, he was probably discussing everything with his superiors all the time. Best to go back and wait at that same
bench. That way I would notice the arrival of any unwelcome people or
vehicles. That was the other thing: even if they did let Alice go, I would
have no way of knowing whether they were using her to set another trap
for me.

I had given Jenkins half an hour, and it was well over an hour now. If
he were going to release Alice at all, he would already have done it.
Otherwise, he would be running the risk of being too late to stop me from
releasing the next piece of damaging information. I had nothing to lose
by waiting longer. Give it another fifteen minutes. Even another half
hour.

I saw her coming two blocks away, on the park side of the avenue, and

I rushed down to meet her. When I was within ten yards of her, I stopped by the park wall and waited for her to come up even with me. She looked dazed, as if she had not slept for a long time. When she was alongside me, I turned and started to walk in parallel with her but several feet away. I could not decide what to say or do.

"Nick?" she said, turning her head.

"Keep walking," I said softly. "And don't turn toward me."

Tears were running down her face.

"Oh, God," she said.

"Alice, I'm sorry. I'm sorry that I got you into all this. What did they do to you?"

"Nothing." She was shaking her head. "They just asked a lot of questions. Mostly the same questions, over and over. They were so awful at the end."

"What did you tell them?"

"Everything. I didn't realize it made any difference. You never told me anything, you idiot." She started sobbing out loud. "I'm so sorry, Nick. I didn't know it mattered."

"It doesn't matter. But don't turn toward me. They may be watching, and I don't want them to know exactly where I am."

"They're not here," she said quite definitely.

"How do you know?"

"They're all at that *place*. At Thirty-eighth Street. They were all meeting when I left."

"How many of them?"

"Seven or eight."

"Seven or eight?"

"Yes. Some more people came this morning. From Washington, I think. Something happened yesterday evening. They started getting phone calls and meeting all the time. They still kept asking me questions off and on all night, but it was as if they weren't really interested any more. They're worried about something else."

"Themselves."

"Nick, I'm so sorry. It's my fault they found us, isn't it? It was that stupid book jacket. I should have told you about it."

"It doesn't make any difference."

"You're such an idiot. You should have told me everything. Or you should have just left, if that's what you wanted to do."

"Based both on generally accepted ethical precepts and on the empirical evidence, you would seem to be right about that."

"Why couldn't we have just gone off together?"

"That wouldn't have been much of a life for you."

"Idiot. That's my business."

"Did they give you any message for me?"

"The one in charge, Jenkins, said to tell you they would get you eventually."

She was weeping again.

"That was all?" I asked.

"Yes. He said, 'Tell him we'll get him, whether it's me or someone else, eventually we'll get him.'"

We turned off Fifth and walked into the park. She told me about her interrogation. They had taken turns, all five of them, going through the same questions over and over. Where had Alice met me? When? What did I do all day? Where did I go? What did I wear? What did I eat? Did I ever talk to anyone else?

"At first I thought they were friends of yours. That's what they kept saying. That they were friends of yours and they were just trying to find you so they could get you the help you needed."

They told her all about who I was and how I had become invisible.

"They tried to get me to help them catch you, and when I wouldn't, they began to threaten me. I'm sorry, Nick. I told them everything before I ever realized."

"It doesn't matter. They didn't find out anything they didn't already know. No, that's not true. They did find out one thing. The most important thing. They found out about you."

Alice began to weep again.

"That means we can't live together anymore, doesn't it?"

We walked in silence for a while.

"Also there's one thing they didn't tell you about me. I kept meaning to tell you myself, but I never quite got to it."

"Of course not."

"I keep meaning to mention that I love you."

"A fat lot of good that does me if you're just going to sneak off without me."

"Alice, I'll do whatever you want, no matter how preposterous. It's a solemn promise."

A stunning smile appeared on her face, and she wrapped her arms around me and kissed me, which made her look quite odd. We were standing in the middle of Central Park, and people were turning and staring, but it seemed like the wrong moment to say anything about it to Alice.

JENKINS HAD A DIFFICULT TIME FOR A WHILE. HE SPENT SEVERAL MONTHS in Washington answering questions in his earnest, plausible way. He explained, not entirely to everyone's satisfaction, that his investigation was primarily scientific in nature, an attempt to reconstruct the intriguing results—whether intentional or accidental—of Professor Wachs. To talk of "invisible matter" was surely unwarranted. He himself would never characterize the objects found at the MicroMagnetics site that way, or if he had used such an expression on occasion, it was only informally and in discussions with other people who were quite familiar with the actual phenomena under investigation. It was unfortunate that random comments and facts had, despite every effort to maintain the appropriate security, somehow leaked out, because taken out of context they had inevitably generated outlandish rumors that were now endangering potentially invaluable research and that were furthermore needlessly calling into question the credibility and competence of the men working under him—men who had performed magnificently under extremely difficult conditions.

There was, of course, the "superglass," which was being studied in two different laboratories; everyone interested in this whole incident should be sure to examine it. Anyone who did would certainly understand why such an extraordinary effort had been made to reconstruct Wachs's work and to investigate the troubling circumstances surrounding the explosion of his laboratory.

But it was the fantastic rumors of "invisible men" that were particularly regrettable. It was true that there was at least one person still at large who had been clearly identified as having been present at the site of the explosion and who was known to have been responsible for acts of arson both then and subsequently; and an extensive effort had quite properly been made to apprehend him. It was also true that certain aspects of the whole incident would probably remain obscure, partly because of the difficulty of reconstructing events and partly because of considerations of security. There was the known involvement of certain left-wing radical groups, and conceivably of foreign powers. There were other issues that might be raised at some time in the future, but which it was not Jenkins's place to introduce into the discussion now.

Jenkins's subordinates were equally vague. It had been difficult to see much of anything at the MicroMagnetics site. Damage had been extensive: the whole area had been swept by a succession of fires, and a fuel tank had exploded. As to the scope of the subsequent investigation, it had really been in Colonel Jenkins's hands, and they did not have enough information to make any useful judgment. They had been following orders. Nothing had seemed really out of the ordinary, and there had certainly been no reason to question the appropriateness of any of those orders. One thing everyone insisted upon—and for some reason the assertion seemed to reassure the investigators and compilers of reports despite its rather tautological quality—was that no one had seen any invisible men.

Clellan was shortly thereafter assigned to the staff of a training camp in North Carolina. Morrissey was sent to a succession of exotic places to participate in the surveillance of drug traffickers linked to officials of foreign governments. Tyler, who was probably the most inscrutable of all during the investigation, was quickly promoted. He lives in a Virginia suburb now and supervises the collection and analysis of vast quantities of obscure political information from obscure parts of the world. Only Gomez continued to work for Jenkins in New York.

As for Jenkins, I was surprised when I saw that his career would not be left in ruins, but on reflection I see that the actual outcome was perfectly logical and predictable. In the end, after they had all finished subjecting each other to the most careful and searching scrutiny, they decided that, although in retrospect certain individual decisions might be questioned, on the whole everyone had behaved appropriately and within the scope of his authority, and no useful purpose would be served by the broadening or prolongation of the investigation. However, everyone was of course to be reassigned, and care was to be taken that no further operation or investigation would be undertaken in the immediate future which might draw further attention to potential problems raised in the course of the current inquiry. Jenkins, it seemed, had substantial support somewhere. He ended up in charge of monitoring the shipment of strategically sensitive technology through New York Harbor to hostile countries. This may or may not have been a demotion, but I follow these things, and I note that he has had several successes and people are pleased with the job he is doing. His budget has begun to increase dramatically, and he has more people under him. He is beginning to devote more time to looking for me again. I cannot tell whether he has support in this from his superiors or not. I could make more trouble for him, of course, but it is not clear to me that I would not be making things worse for myself as well.

When Anne's article on the Academy Club incident finally ran, it lacked excitement. It was composed of sentences like "However, despite these official denials, the incident leaves in its wake a host of unanswered questions." A spokesperson reaffirmed on behalf of Jenkins, who was not available for comment, that he had been driving up Madison Avenue, when, seeing ambulances in front of the Academy Club, he stopped to see if he could be of assistance. There was a lengthy discussion of the location of gas mains and of Consolidated Edison's service records, which appeared to be incomplete. However, Anne and her employers soon saw that the story was going nowhere, and, losing their initial enthusiasm, abandoned it. Anne has since been assigned to the Washington bureau, which, unaccountably, pleased her enormously.

Several left-wing journals then took up the matter, and radical academics began to acquire encyclopaedic expertise in the routing of gas lines and the membership of the Academy Club. It was hypothesized that a liberal member of Congress, who had fortuitously just left the building at the time of the incident, had been the target of a covert right-wing action. The main result of this was that the Congressman was forced to resign his membership, as it became known that he belonged to a club that did not admit women. A right-wing group saw a plot by the KGB, the Rockefellers, and the Trilateralists, whoever they may be, and began gluing posters detailing their intricate reasoning to the walls of the Academy Club on a regular basis, which was an annoyance to both the membership and the maintenance staff.

HAVE VERY LITTLE MORE TO TELL YOU AND VERY LITTLE TIME, I SHOULD have liked to be able to sum up the whole experience for you, to offer you, from my unique vantage point, some valuable insight into the human condition—or at least some greeting more poignant than "You can't catch me!" The trouble is, I have grown so accustomed to my vantage point that its uniqueness is lost on me, and although you might hope that an invisible man could offer you some intelligence of an invisible purpose in the world, if it is there, I have not yet found it. No doubt I am looking right at it and just can't see it. Like the pattern in the carpet. Like me, for that matter. If I ever work it out, I'll be sure to let you know.

In the meantime I can tell you that the bad points of this existence are that it is often lonely and arguably pointless. The good points are its not being over and Alice.

I know now, as I write these final words for you, that Jenkins is closing in again. I can tell—never mind how—that he is about to find Jonathan Crosby's apartment. But I don't care. I will be gone. And this time I will be much more difficult to find. Like the leopard, I am going into other spots.

The trouble is that Alice expects to come with me. I have tried to show her why that would not make sense for either of us. The risks would be awful. Of course, anything is possible, and I have given it some thought. Perhaps it could be done.

Perhaps one day, as Alice is riding home on the subway, she will step out, just as the doors close, onto the platform of a station where she has never got out before, and she will dart up the stairs into the street. She will climb into the waiting car and we will drive off over a bridge or through a tunnel forever. The next day she will have brunette hair, cut short, and different clothing, and we will be in San Francisco or London or back in New York with different names and ages and accents.

I have tried to explain to her why this is not a reasonable course of action. I have tried to explain everything to her, tried to give her a rational account of my whole situation—with what success, it is hard to say.

"Nick, explain to me once more your theory of what happened to your body." The expression on her face is one of smiling innocence or perhaps of mockery—I am never quite sure, but I am always dazzled. "Tell me again what a *quark* is."

"It's perfectly simple, really. It's one of the basic building blocks of matter. What the whole world is composed of. Although really, I suppose, it's more a mathematical abstraction . . . in a manner of speaking."

"So that the world would be composed of mathematical abstractions? You know, I think I prefer my own manner of speaking. I think you've misunderstood everything that's happened. You're a ghost after all. You died in that accident, and you've been sent back to accomplish certain very important things."

"What sorts of things?"

"Doing the right thing by me, to begin with. I think I'd like a church wedding."

"I don't see how that's possible, practically. Or even theologically, given your theory that I'm a ghost."

"It's your job to figure it all out. You promised you'd do whatever I wanted."

Time is running out and I can't stay here much longer. But it seems to me that in the end I'm going to try to do what Alice wants. I don't know. It is preposterous, but what's the point of it all otherwise? Anyway, as long as we keep moving, we should be all right.

H. F. Saint lives in New York City.
This is his first novel.

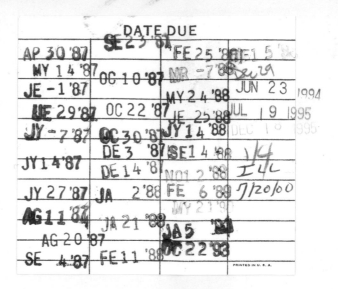

DATE DUE

AP 30 '87	SE 23 '87	FE 25 '88	FE 15
MY 14 '87	OC 10 '87	MR -7 '88	DE 29
JE -1 '87		MY 24 '88	JUN 23 1994
JE 29 '87	OC 22 '87	JE 25 '88	JUL 19 1995
JY -7 '87	OC 30 '87	JY 14 '88	DEC 1 0 1995
JY 14 '87	DE 3 '87	SE 14 '88	1/4
	DE 14 '87	NO 2 '88	ILL
JY 27 '87	JA 2 '88	FE 6 '89	7/20/00
AG 11 '87	JA 21 '88	MY 27 '9	
AG 20 '87		JA 5 '9	
SE 4 '87	FE 11 '88	OC 22 '93	

PRINTED IN U.S.A.

Saint, H.
  Memoirs of an invisible man

DOVER PUBLIC LIBRARY
DOVER. N.H.